Sign up for our newsletter to hear
about new and upcoming releases.

www.ylva-publishing.com

THE Lily & THE CROWN

ROSLYN SINCLAIR

ACKNOWLEDGMENTS

I would like to thank the brave souls who helped me whip this story into shape: my fabulous content editor, Lee Winter, who got this started and then kept me going, and my copy editor, Amanda Jean, who stopped my commas in their tracks. And, last but not least, Charlotte. She knows why.

CHAPTER 1

Ariana Geiker was delighted with how *Barmensis nobu* was coming along. Her petals were brilliant, lustrous, and evenly shaped; her leaves a full, flourishing, healthy green. She'd come a long way from being the skinny, scraggly, little thing she'd been when Ari had acquired her.

Should Ari put her away? No. No, she'd leave her on the table. Doctor Phylyxas was bound to see her when he arrived to inspect Ari's collection, and while *Barmensis* might just be a simple little plant, Ari was proud of her.

Dr. Phylyxas's latest book had said that oftentimes the simplest victories were the most rewarding, at least on an everyday basis. Sure, it was immensely satisfying to keep up an enormous garden, discover new plant species, all that, but what did you wind up seeing the most, day in and day out? The flower on your kitchen table. So, you might as well do a good job tending to it. Ari hoped Dr. Phylyxas would notice *Barmensis* and would realize she'd taken his lessons to heart. Coming face-to-face with her idol was more nerve-racking than she'd ever thought it would be.

It really was very kind of him to come—the Senior Royal Botanist. Ari's father might be the most important official in this sector, but surely Dr. Phylyxas had many urgent demands on his time. They were opening a whole new wing of the Imperial Arboretum on Homeworld in less than a month. It was to be the most impressive wing yet. Ari thought it might be nice to see it someday.

Not, she had to admit dolefully, that this seemed likely in the immediate future, with all the pirates marauding around. It had been a huge relief to learn that Dr. Phylyxas's ship had landed safely in the space station's hangar bay a few minutes ago.

She looked again at *Barmensis.* Yes, that was good, but something was missing. She'd meant to put out something else. What had it been—oh! Thank goodness she'd remembered it just in time.

Ari hurried out of her kitchen and back into her living room. Maybe calling it a "living room" was pushing it—as the stationmaster's only daughter, she had been given quarters with more room than one person could possibly need. She'd been delighted anyway, because surely it was a sign that her father must care for her, if he'd arranged for her to have rooms that accommodated her...unusual requirements. Specifically, her requirement to maintain an enormous, flourishing garden, including trees, in the dead of space. He'd never told her how he'd managed it, but then, he never told her a lot of things.

Anyway, she'd have to remember not to call it her "living room" when Dr. Phylyxas finally arrived. Although, he might think it was an endearing quirk; if anybody could understand how she did, in fact, *live* with her plants, it must be the Senior Royal Botanist.

Ari rushed through her garden toward her goal, brushing aside various leaves and branches as she went. On fleet feet, she reached her shelves and peered at her dozens of specimen jars. "A woman does not live by plants alone," she muttered. Then she smiled to herself. Maybe that'd be an okay joke to trot out for Dr. Phylyxas?

Yeah, maybe. She had to pick a specimen first, to show him that she was about more than flowers and shrubs. Yes, Cranli might do. The praying mantis waved his front legs as she took down the jar, no doubt eager to get back to his favorite plant. Well, he and *Mustopher illis* would have to endure their separation for a few hours longer.

"I'm just going to show you to a very important gentleman," Ari said soothingly to him. "You're such a pretty little guy. And you do such incredible work in the garden." Cranli did not look appeased. Then again, Ari supposed it was hard to tell with a praying mantis.

Maybe she should take a few deep breaths. It was obvious that her nerves were making her act even weirder than usual. *Come on. Get out of your shell for once in your life. When is this going to happen again?*

Okay, that thought wasn't very soothing. Deep breaths were a better idea.

Just then, she heard the bleep that announced someone requesting entry to her quarters. Without further ado, the door to her suite hissed open. Ari gasped and almost fumbled the jar. He was here already? That was fast. Too fast. Was she really prepared for this?

Then she heard the voice of a sentry saying—jeeringly!—"All right, you. In you go. Enjoy yourself."

Ari's jaw dropped. Was that any way to talk to the Senior Royal Botanist? Gripping her jar, she hurried back through the trees, vowing to have a very stern word with the sentry. But then the door hissed shut again, and Ari realized she was too late. She winced and emerged past the last tall bush that separated her from her kitchen and living area.

Then she blinked in surprise. Apparently, someone had...misinformed her about Dr. Phylyxas.

For one thing, he was a she. For another, she looked nothing like Ari had always imagined a Senior Royal Botanist would look. Not that she'd ever really thought about it. If she had, she guessed she would have imagined a portly, balding man with holo-spectacles, wearing tweedy robes.

But apparently Dr. Phylyxas was a tall, regal-looking female, her short black hair going silver at the temples, matched by a silver forelock. She appeared to be about Ari's own height, though her bare arms were far more muscled.

She was looking around Ari's quarters with an expression that was two parts wary and one part disgusted. She was no doubt horrified by the sentry's behavior in welcoming her.

"Oh, gosh," Ari said, and Dr. Phylyxas nearly jumped as she turned to regard Ari with wide eyes. "I am so sorry," Ari added, clutching Cranli's jar to her chest.

The woman looked at it briefly before her gaze flickered back to Ari's face. Her own sharp-featured face was closed, cold, reserved. The look in her eyes made Ari quake in her shoes.

Ari's feeling had to be fear, right? Intimidation? How odd—it didn't seem like any fear Ari had ever experienced before. More like an electric shock that was making her fingers and her toes tingle.

This wasn't the time to figure it out. "I-I'll speak to that sentry," Ari said. "I can't believe he was so rude to you."

Now Dr. Phylyxas looked surprised. "You can't?"

Ari frowned. Had their outpost gotten a bad reputation for hospitality somewhere? She hoped not. It would be dreadful if Dr. Phylyxas had come all the way here expecting to be treated that way.

"Um," she said hesitantly, "w-won't you sit down?" She gestured toward the kitchen table. The sight of *Barmensis nobu* quickly revived her, and she beamed at Dr. Phylyxas. "I hope you'll like it." She pointed at the plant. "It took me a long time to perk her up, but I've been working hard at it."

Dr. Phylyxas looked at her, and then at the plant, with an utterly blank expression on her face.

Ari gulped and then gasped. Bad hospitality, indeed. She set down Cranli's jar on the kitchen table. Dr. Phylyxas looked at that, too.

"I'm so sorry," she repeated. "I... Do you want something to drink? I've got coffee. And tea."

"Do I..." Dr. Phylyxas shook her head quickly. It really was an elegant head. She was, in fact, an exceedingly elegant woman, even though she was dressed a little...simply...for a royal official, in a plain white tunic that looked remarkably like what servants and slaves wore. Then again, it wasn't at all practical for a botanist to wear fine clothing—you spent so much time mucking around in the dirt and getting scratched by branches and thorns.

Maybe Dr. Phylyxas had come to Ari's quarters in readiness to do actual work. The thought made Ari's breath catch in anticipation.

"Coffee," Dr. Phylyxas said, seating herself at Ari's kitchen table and giving Ari another, even warier look.

Well, that was sort of weird. "I-I grow and roast the beans myself," Ari offered. "The coffee beans. And the tea." She smiled again. "It's much better than what you'd get in the mess hall. I mean, if I do say so myself."

"Oh." Dr. Phylyxas looked back and forth between Ari and *Barmensis* as if she had no idea where she was. "Well. That's..." She looked Ari up and down, taking in Ari's dress which, Ari was only now realizing, was covered in dirt.

She felt her face turning its most brilliant red and gave a feeble laugh as she brushed down her skirt with one hand. "I guess I don't look very formal right now," she said. "I mean...not that I ever do, really..."

"I'm getting that impression," Dr. Phylyxas said.

"Well," Ari said helplessly, "I've been so excited about your visit, so I've been working all morning, trying to get everything—"

"My visit?" Dr. Phylyxas looked astonished.

Ari stared at her. Then Dr. Phylyxas added, "I think you've mistaken me for somebody else."

"Huh? You..." Ari blinked. "You're not Dr. Phylyxas?"

"I'm afraid not," not-Dr.-Phylyxas said, resting her elbows on the table and crossing her ankles, looking almost amused.

"Oh, no." Ari gasped, knowing that she was even redder now. "I'm so—you must have thought... I'll go get your coffee." Face burning, she plunged back into her garden, cutting branches from *Coffea maliksika* with a trembling hand. Then, when she had the red beans in her hand, something occurred to her.

She poked her head back into the kitchen, where not-Dr.-Phylyxas was still sitting at the table, ankles still crossed, but looking positively boggled now.

"Excuse me," Ari said, "but who are you, then?"

The woman began to say something, but just then the door chime beeped again. The woman darted a swift, wary glance at the door. Ari had just enough time to see her posture grow stiff before it opened.

This time, a portly, well-dressed man entered, followed by a sentry. The portly man looked exactly as Ari had expected him to look, right down to the holo-spectacles. He blinked at the sight of Ari standing in the middle of her kitchen with a coffee branch in her hand, and then looked down at the woman seated at the table.

"My goodness, Your Ladyship," he said to the woman at the table. "It's a pleasure to meet you. Ah, please don't get up."

"All right," the woman said, and indeed made no move to do so.

"Um," Ari said.

"I have to admit, I thought you were younger," Dr. Phylyxas added.

"My God," the woman said. "It's like watching a farce."

"I beg your pardon?" Dr. Phylyxas said.

"Excuse me," Ari blurted, "but I'm Lady Ariana. Not her."

"I should say not," snapped the sentry, and both Ari and Dr. Phylyxas startled. He was scowling at the woman at the table. "Get on your feet in front of your mistress or we'll whip your back to ribbons and be happy to do it."

"I wondered when we'd get to that," the woman said and rose gracefully.

"I don't..." Ari looked back and forth between all of them. What had happened to the quiet, scholarly morning she'd hoped for? "I'm sorry, but what...who's..."

The sentry gestured in disgust at the woman. "She's Your Ladyship's new slave."

Ari stared at him. "My what?"

Now the sentry looked surprised, too. "Did Your Ladyship not receive the message your father sent this morning?"

Ari's gaze immediately went to the intercom panel by the door. Sure enough, a red light was blinking, signaling that someone had tried to contact her. As usual, she'd been off doing something else, either inspecting the garden or perhaps getting dressed before going out and messing up her clothes again. She hadn't heard the beep of the intercom—it was a lot quieter than the door chime.

And it had been her father. Her face heated. She'd missed a message from her father, and he didn't try to contact her often.

Focus. She dragged her mind back to the present. "No, I didn't get the message."

6

"She was captured off a pirate rig last night," the sentry explained. "Tiny little scouter. All killed but her—their serving-woman. And now she's your serving-woman, courtesy of your father." He glared at the woman. "Too stupid to know she's a lot better off now, if you ask me."

Ari looked at the woman whom the sentry had just called stupid. That assessment seemed a little off, to say the least. *Impassive* would have been a better word. Maybe even a little bored, as if she couldn't believe she was wasting her time like this. She certainly didn't seem to care about the sentry's poor opinion of her.

But Ari did. Ari cared about this whole situation a lot. "I don't want a slave!" she said, horrified. "I mean...I don't need—"

"Well, they can come in handy," Dr. Phylyxas said. Ari turned to look at him in astonishment. He nodded toward the slave woman and shrugged, like this was no big deal to him. "Fetching and carrying and whatnot. I have four to help me maintain my personal garden alone. You'll be amazed how much easier everything is."

That seemed doubtful. Ari was used to doing just fine all on her own. She looked helplessly at the woman. "Um. Which pirates?"

"Had the sign of the lily on the side of the scouter," the sentry said, sounding downright gleeful. "Mir's own private fleet."

Dr. Phylyxas raised his eyebrows, finally seeming impressed by something. "You don't say?"

Ari couldn't be nearly so cool about it. She almost dropped the coffee plant. "Mir?"

"Yes, Your Ladyship. Only a scouter, mind you. Seems like it had gotten into some trouble—it was sending out a distress signal on a frequency only the pirates are supposed to know. But your lord father's on top of things, isn't he?" The sentry glared at the woman. "Bet your former mistress won't be happy about that."

"I should say not," the woman replied.

"Oh, my goodness," Ari said weakly. The idea made her shudder, that a ship, even a tiny scouting vessel, from Mir's fleet had come that close to their station. Everyone knew the queen of all the pirates had no mercy and no shame.

7

"It's all right, Your Ladyship." Dr. Phylyxas laid a comforting hand on her shoulder. "I'm sure you have nothing to worry about. This place seems quite well-fortified."

"Nobody's getting in here, Your Ladyship." The sentry glared at the woman. "As your former masters have discovered."

"To their cost," the woman said, her voice mild, but with something much harder to decipher in her eyes.

"Well." Ari laughed awkwardly. "Let's not... I mean—"

"Indeed, indeed," Dr. Phylyxas said heartily. "Let's not trouble our heads about all that now. I've come here to see your garden."

"Oh!" Ari had nearly forgotten in all the excitement. "Yes! Thanks," she added to the sentry. "That'll be all. Oh, wait." She frowned at him. "Were you the one who showed her in here?" She tilted her head toward the woman.

"Yes, Your Ladyship."

"Then I think you ought to apologize," Ari said.

All three of them stared at her.

Ari squirmed under the scrutiny. This was important, though. "If she's a slave you rescued from a pirate ship, then she's obviously had a very hard time of it. There was no need for you to be so rude." She raised her hand to wag her finger for emphasis and realized she was still holding a coffee branch with it.

Both the sentry and the woman looked at Ari as if she'd grown another head, but the sentry turned to the woman anyway. "I'm so very sorry," he said, dragging out each syllable for the maximum possible sarcasm. *"My lady."*

A smile played around the woman's lips. "Apology accepted," she said sweetly.

The sentry scowled at her and left.

Dr. Phylyxas clapped his hands and rubbed them together. "Well! An interesting start to our visit, wasn't it?"

"Oh, yes." Ari smiled weakly. "Talk about strange."

She looked hesitantly at the woman, who raised her eyebrows. "Indeed," she said. "I've never been through quite so many cases of mistaken identity in a single day."

"Well...um..."

"My lady," Dr. Phylyxas said to Ari, "I am most anxious to begin our tour."

"Of course!" Ari looked down at her coffee branch and then at the woman. "Oh, goodness. I'm sorry. We'll sort all this out later, I promise. Until then, would you, um, mind waiting for your coffee?"

The woman opened her mouth, closed it, and then spread her hands in a gesture that said, *why not?*

"Great," Ari said, relieved. "Help yourself to anything you can find in the kitchen if you're hungry. The bathroom's over there." She pointed it out. Then she beamed up at Dr. Phylyxas, vowing not to let anything else ruin her morning. "Shall we begin? Oh!" She snatched up Cranli's jar from the kitchen table and led the way back into her garden. "I thought you might be interested in this..."

~ ~ ~

Four hours later, Dr. Phylyxas had concluded his inspection of Ari's garden. He'd apparently enjoyed himself and had many nice things to say about Ari's work, plus several suggestions that Ari vowed fervently she would take to heart. He also seemed to enjoy patting Ari on the shoulder a great deal, or putting his hand on her back. Well, maybe that was how they did things on Homeworld—people must be a great deal more urbane and sophisticated there. Ari certainly wouldn't know.

When he left, Ari offered him the plant on the kitchen table. The woman wasn't sitting there anymore, and Ari wondered where she'd gone. Maybe she was in the bathroom. Or had gone outside to stretch her legs.

Hopefully she'd reappear soon. Ari had a lot of questions for her, and it might be easier to talk to a perfect stranger about this situation than it would be to talk to her father.

Dr. Phylyxas took *Barmensis nobu* with a polite smile and told Ari to look him up if she ever made it to Homeworld. "Always a pleasure to meet a fellow enthusiast," he proclaimed as he left.

His visit had gone so well. Better than she could have hoped for. Ari glowed.

Her glow lasted for about ten minutes, when her door hissed open again and the slave woman stumbled inside, shoved by the sentry.

"Get in there, you ungrateful bitch." He winced when he saw Ari. "Begging Your Ladyship's pardon for my language."

Ari stared in horror at the woman, who had a livid bruise forming on her right cheek. "What happened?"

"Trying to run, wasn't she?" the sentry said, glaring at the woman. "Without so much as a by-your-leave. We all thought you'd sent her on an errand until we saw her heading for the hangar bay."

"Why did you hit her?" Ari demanded. "I'm sure she didn't mean any harm. Did you?"

"Oh, no," the woman said, giving Ari another one of those inscrutable looks. "Perish the thought."

"There," Ari snapped at the sentry, "you see? You can go now." Her own tone of voice shocked her. How often did she snap at anybody?

This is important, the little voice in the back of her head reminded her, though she was still trying to figure out how important. And why it felt that way. There were slaves all over the station. It wasn't anything Ari had ever agreed with, but she couldn't do anything about it, and she was used to it. So why were her hackles raised now?

The door shut behind the indignant-looking sentry, who no doubt wondered why Ari didn't share his barbarous outlook on life. The unfamiliar voice in her head growled, *Too bad.*

Gosh.

"You sit down." Ari nodded at the kitchen table. She winced at the woman's bruise. "Oh dear, that looks bad. Hold on, I've got some slave. Salve!" she corrected with a little gasp when the woman raised an eyebrow. "Uh, I'll be right back. I make it myself. I mean the salve," she added over her shoulder as she rushed back into the garden.

She re-emerged a few minutes later holding a tiny pot. She unscrewed the lid and dipped her fingers into the salve before reaching out to the woman's face. The woman looked back at her with such a stony expression that Ari gulped and offered her the pot. "Uh, m-maybe you'd rather do it yourself." She wiped her sticky fingers on her skirt.

"Thank you," the woman said neutrally and took the pot. She dabbed the ointment over the bruise on her face like a pro.

She probably was. Ari swallowed hard when she thought of what this woman must have endured at the hands of the sort of people who worked for Mír. No wonder she was so untrusting. She'd undoubtedly been traumatized.

"It's not so bad here," Ari blurted.

The woman looked at her and said nothing.

Perhaps more was called for. "It won't be like what you're used to. I won't let anybody hurt you." The bruise made Ari wince again. "I mean, I won't let it happen again. I promise."

"Oh," the woman said. "Good." She dropped the pot of salve on the table, where it landed with a *clunk*. "I'm sure it will be most pleasant, being your slave."

Ari gasped. "I didn't mean it like that. Please don't think of it that way." She clasped her hands. "Really, I wouldn't..." She frowned. "I'm sorry. What's your name?"

"Slave."

"Oh, come on. Please. Really. What is it?"

"What else could it be? That is what the pirates do. Their slaves have no name but 'Slave.'"

Well, *that* sure sounded horrible. "I'm not a pirate," Ari snapped. "Nobody here is. We're not like that."

The woman snorted derisively. "Aren't you? You will have a hard time convincing me of that."

"I won't have to," Ari said stubbornly. "You'll see it for yourself." If her father wanted Ari to have a slave, well, then she didn't have much choice. She didn't really have any. But at least she'd be better to this woman than Mír's marauders had been, surely.

"If you say so."

11

"But what's your name?" Ari pressed. Then a horrible thought occurred to her. "You do have one, don't you?"

"No."

"Oh, my goodness." Righteous indignation swelled inside Ari. "That's terrible!"

"Is it?"

"Of course it is! Everybody's got the right to have a name!" Ari thumped her hand on the table. "We'll just have to give you one." She glanced at the spot on the kitchen table where the flower had been resting. "Barmensis!" she said. "That's the flower I had sitting here. She was really pretty."

As soon as she said it, her face flamed again. *Pretty?* She hadn't meant anything by that, but once the word was out of her mouth, somehow it sounded inappropriate. This woman wasn't pretty. She was...compelling. Arresting. Dominant. Nothing like what you'd expect a slave to be, and Ari couldn't say any of that. Ari added quickly, "Would you like that name?"

The woman looked utterly appalled. "You are not," she said, "calling me 'Barmensis.'"

"Oh." Ari bit her lip. "Sorry. I should let you pick it, shouldn't I?" How thoughtless could she get? You didn't name people like they were pets. No wonder the woman expected no better out of life, if that was how she'd been treated. "I'm sorry," she said again. "I'm, I'm not around slaves too much." She wasn't around a lot of people. What was it going to be like, having another person always here, in her space, in her home?

"I would never have guessed," the woman said.

"I don't want a slave, either," Ari added. "I think it's awful." She wrung her hands together before she could stop herself. "You...you don't have to stay with me, if you don't want to."

The woman glared at her. "And where else would I go? If not you, they'll pack me off to somebody else. I belong to your father, not to you."

"Oh," Ari said, blushing. That was true. They'd barely spoken for two minutes, but the woman already had good reason to think she was an idiot. How could this ever work? "I guess that's right."

12

"I have no name here. I want none."

"Well, I am not calling you 'Slave,'" Ari said, trying to sound firm. Somehow it was a lot harder to do that with this woman than it had been with the sentry. "So...um...how about..." Her face lit up. "Assistant!"

The woman blinked. "Assistant?"

"Sure," Ari said, suddenly excited. "Dr. Phylyxas was right. You can help me in the garden." She clasped her hands together. Maybe there was a way for this not to be a total disaster. She had to think of something, anyway. "Oh, I'd really appreciate that. I mean, since you have to be here, and if you wouldn't mind. I'm working on this big new project, and it would be really nice to have another set of hands."

The woman looked down at her own hands. Ari could see they were slender and elegant, like all the rest of her, but also roughened from work—in a few places, anyway, like she was used to holding one thing in particular all the time. Like Ari was, with trowels.

"I'm working on developing a cross-strain between two different pea plants," Ari added. "Dr. Phylyxas said it sounded really interesting. It's never been done before, either. I'm hoping to come up with a totally different kind of pea."

"Really."

"Yes. Hardier than the other two. If it can thrive in harsher climates, then maybe people in rougher environments can have a new crop to..." Ari's voice trailed off, and she flushed. "And you don't care." Like everybody else, except Dr. Phylyxas. "Right. I didn't mean to rattle on. Sorry." She took a deep breath and tried to smile. There were probably a lot more fake smiles in her future from now on. Just the thought was exhausting, but she certainly couldn't let the woman know how uncomfortable her presence here was, especially when neither of them could do anything about it.

The woman kept looking at her, her own face expressionless.

"So," Ari managed, "if you don't want a name...is 'Assistant' okay with you?"

13

"I don't see why not," the woman—Assistant—said dryly.

"Good." Ari gulped. "I guess—oh. Did you want your coffee? And oh, gosh. Did you get anything to eat?" When the woman shook her head, Ari added, "Then let's do that right away." She stood quickly and then swayed as the room spun around her.

"Are you all right?" Assistant asked, although she made no move to help.

"Oh, yeah." Ari waved her hand. "I guess I'm hungry, too. I forgot to eat this morning." She raised her eyebrows as she remembered something. "And this afternoon. And last night, too, I think. I was really busy. Sometimes I don't even think about stuff like that when I'm into a project." She gave Assistant a quick look. "But you won't let me forget, will you? I mean, if you get hungry, don't hesitate to say something. I've probably just forgotten all about it."

"I see," Assistant said. "Don't worry. I will not forget to remind you if my stomach is on the line."

"Oh, good." Ari gestured at the kitchen cabinets. "I think I've got some ration bars in there."

Assistant's eyes widened. "Ration bars?" she said. "Aren't you the stationmaster's daughter?"

"Yes," Ari said, nonplussed.

"And you're eating ration bars?"

"They're fast," Ari protested. "I told you, I'm in the middle of something important."

"You don't cook?"

"No," Ari said. "I mean, I try sometimes, but I'm no good at it." She tended to get distracted when she had a project on her mind, and her food burned to a crisp if it didn't catch fire outright. "Um...we can call for something from the mess, if you prefer."

"I prefer," Assistant said flatly.

"Oh," Ari said, feeling very foolish.

"That's the intercom?" Assistant rose to her feet and headed for the box on the wall. The red light from Ari's father's message was still blinking.

14

"Yes," Ari said. "You—uh—why don't you call for two plates? I don't know what they're making today."

"I'll take my chances, if the alternative is ration bars," Assistant said.

"Okay." Ari looked longingly back at her garden, where the plants never tried to talk down to her, or made her feel dumb like people did. "I'll...I'll just be working back there. I can show you everything later, after you've—we've had something to eat. Oh," she added quickly, "I don't think you should try to leave again. The sentries aren't very nice, and they might be looking for you."

"I've worked that out for myself," Assistant said. Her eyes were flat and cold.

Ari shivered.

Assistant glanced back at the intercom box. "Looks like you've got a message. Do you have a passcode?"

Ari blinked as Assistant's fingertip hovered over the intercom's touchpad. "Well, yes, obviously."

"What is it?" Assistant asked, sounding remarkably patient this time. When Ari bit her lip, she said, "Don't tell me that slaves don't listen to messages around here."

"Right, right," Ari mumbled. That sounded okay. Her father's personal slaves did that. He had a reputation for being a good master, so it must be all right. "It's 0243545AG." Assistant stared at her. "What? It's easy to remember. It's—"

"Your birthday and your initials," Assistant said. When Ari gaped, she added, "Wild guess."

Ari raised her chin. There was being nice, and then there was accepting open ridicule, and she'd grown tired of the second long ago. Keeping to herself was one way of dealing with it, but since that wasn't an option anymore...

She said, "It's no big deal. It's not like I have access to anything classified or important." Just because she was the stationmaster's daughter didn't mean she was trusted with state secrets. She crossed her arms. "And you don't have to ferry messages for me, or do anything else. I was getting by just fine without having anybody here."

Instead of replying, Assistant sighed and keyed in Ari's code. When she'd pushed the last key, Ari's father's voice spoke, a little flat from the recording.

"Ariana, this is your father. I suppose you're off gardening somewhere."

Was that an affectionate note in his voice? Ari wanted so much to believe.

"I don't have long to speak, but I wanted to alert you that you're getting a present."

A present? Ari couldn't look Assistant in the eye.

"We've captured a slave from a pirate scouter. I'm sending her to you as a helper. She seems physically capable and reasonably well-spoken, if a little…standoffish."

Now Ari couldn't even look anywhere in Assistant's general vicinity. She gulped and studied the wall instead.

"But that might suit you, since you're accustomed to solitude."

Her father's bland tone gave no indication of whether he thought this was a good thing or not.

"I'm sure you'll find a use for her in your garden. If she doesn't please you, let me know, but give her a chance first. Let's say a week-long trial period before you insist yet again that your plants are all you need. That is"—and her father's voice grew firmer—*"unless she proves dangerous or disobedient. Then I'll find another use for her immediately. Geiker out."*

The intercom grew silent. Ari's father could only have embarrassed her more if he'd decided to talk about the time she'd fallen on her face while accepting an award for scholastic excellence during her final year at school. Why not just come right out and say, "I'm forcing someone to live with you so you'll have to talk to another human being"?

Like other human beings had ever done a lot for Ari.

"Another use for me," Assistant mused, making Ari glance at her with a nervous twitch. She was still facing the intercom box. "What do you think? Sewage duty? Or just throwing me on a shuttle and sending me planetside to work in the ore mines?"

"Neither!" Ari shifted from foot to foot. The truth was, her father would probably do exactly that. "Sorry. I don't think you were supposed to hear that. But you don't have to worry about it." She assayed another smile. Maybe it'd get easier with lots of practice. "I'm sure we'll get along fine. And it's not like you're dangerous, are you?" She wasn't going near the *disobedient* part.

"Me, dangerous?" Assistant looked away from the intercom and back at Ari, who nearly jumped. "What would ever make you think a thing like that?"

Her blue eyes seemed to skewer Ari, but somehow, this time Ari couldn't look away. They were really blue eyes. And Assistant's bearing was so grand, so proud—no wonder Dr. Phylyxas had mistaken her for the lady of the house.

Ari's father had said *dangerous.* What a ridiculous idea. Ari would be kind to Assistant and would treat her as an equal. Assistant plainly wasn't stupid, and even if she wasn't very friendly, either, she'd know better than to try to harm the stationmaster's daughter.

Ari wasn't in danger from anything at all. And yet, somehow her knees felt shaky as she mumbled, "Anyway, you can go ahead and get some food, just call me when it's here." She ducked back into the refuge of her garden.

No. This day had not turned out at all like she'd expected it would.

CHAPTER 2

It was not until four days later that Ari found the courage to ask Assistant a question.

They were hard at work in the garden. The past four days hadn't been that bad, really—strange, yes, but not bad. It was odd, but kind of nice to have someone else to help. It turned out that Assistant was a natural at taking charge of things, and everything went much more quickly and smoothly with her there.

It felt less lonely, too, to have another person around. That had been really unexpected. Ari spent so much time in her quarters that sometimes it was easy to forget that anything existed beyond them. Not that she really needed anything out there. Her rooms were enough for her. The kitchen area was right by the door, and her bedroom and en suite bathroom lay at the end of a tile path, one of the few reminders of what her rooms had looked like before her plants had invaded.

Now she lived in a forest out of a fairy tale—a weird one, where the adventure started in a kitchen and then led down a magical path into trees and ferns and flowers. Behind the trees lay a cleared patch of earth for the peas, and the walls were lined with shelves and her specimen jars, but other than that, the illusion was convincing. In fact, Ari was sure she'd caught Assistant looking around a few times with an expression that was almost like wonder.

Who could blame her? When you lived with space pirates, you probably didn't see a lot of gardens.

For her part, Ari didn't see much of anything else. Her experience of Nahtal Station was fairly limited. She'd never explored much—even though a population of four thousand people wasn't much compared to other stations, much less planetside cities, she felt crowded when she ventured into the corridors or the mess hall. She didn't like the attention she got as the stationmaster's daughter, either, especially since they all probably laughed at her awkwardness when her back was turned. Much better to stay with her plants. And with her new slave.

It had been such an awful prospect at first, having somebody *there* all the time. But Assistant's presence was nowhere near as intrusive as Ari would have imagined, if she'd ever imagined such a thing, which she hadn't. She had feared the invasion of her space, the creeping awareness that someone was always looking over her shoulder, but Assistant seemed to have no interest in doing that. Sometimes she didn't seem to have much interest in Ari at all.

Ari was eating more now, though. Neither was Assistant shy about saying when it was time to give up work and get some rest. She didn't eat or sleep until Ari did, so Ari was trying very hard to be more thoughtful about such things, but it was nice to be reminded. Assistant slept on a small bed in an alcove away from the garden. Ari had her own bed, of course, a bigger one, but more often than not she slept on a cot near her beloved plants. They were her home, her dearest friends. Why shouldn't she be near them?

Assistant didn't get Ari's love for her plants. Well, nobody did. But she worked without protest, although Ari could tell that she wasn't really content. Restless, that was the word. Like she was waiting for something. Wanting something.

Whenever the thought of what Assistant wanted crossed Ari's mind, it made her shiver, for some strange reason. Not in a bad way, either. Beyond just having company around, a pair of helping hands, there was something kind of exciting about Assistant in a way Ari couldn't quite pinpoint. Four days after Assistant had arrived, the sight of her black hair and sharp blue eyes every morning was starting to make Ari's heart beat just a little bit faster.

Maybe there was more than one kind of danger.

19

Mercifully, Assistant never seemed to guess at Ari's thoughts. Thank goodness for that. No doubt she'd find them ridiculous. But she didn't seem to resent Ari; in fact, she seemed more bewildered by her than anything else. Sometimes even amused. Ari got the feeling not a lot of things amused Assistant, so she wondered if it might not be a kind of compliment.

Therefore, on the fourth day, Ari felt marginally confident enough to ask, "Assistant? What was it like? Living with pirates, I mean."

Assistant gave her a sharp look. The bruise on her cheek had nearly faded completely. "What do you mean?"

"I mean, what are pirates like? What do they do all day? When they're not..." Ari gestured vaguely with her trowel and threw dirt on her own chin. "You know. Marauding and stuff." She wiped her chin.

"Chiefly they're going between places where they maraud," Assistant said. "I understand there is also drinking and whoring involved. For some of them." She dug her own trowel forcefully into the dirt. "Not the ones I lived with, however."

"Whor..." Ari gulped and blushed. She wasn't used to that kind of language, but even more than that, it sounded strange coming from Assistant's usually refined mou...vocabulary. The base of her spine tingled. Grasping frantically for a different subject, she said, "Did you ever see *her?*"

"Her?"

"You know. Mír." Ari kept her voice low, out of reflex. It was silly, but for two decades Mír had been used as a story to frighten children. Be good, or the ruthless pirate queen will snatch you away in the dead of night. Ari herself had gotten various versions of the tale when she'd been young.

"What about her?" Assistant inquired, lifting an eyebrow.

"Did you ever see her?" Ari repeated. "They say nobody has. No free person. She's never on the holos. Nobody even has a voice recording."

"Yes," Assistant said. "From what I understand, she takes great care that this should be the case."

"Well, some people even say she's not real. Because nobody's seen her, you see. They say she's just a story to frighten children and somebody else is in charge of the pirates. Or several somebodies. Pirates-by-committee," she added, inspired.

"Oh, she's real enough," Assistant said, turning back to the dirt.

"So, you have seen her?" Ari gasped. What would she do with this information if Assistant had? Would she be obliged to tell her father about it?

"No," Assistant said, rendering the possibility moot.

"Oh." Ari deflated. "Then how do you know she's real?"

"I know. You pick things up out there."

"Is she as bad as people say?" That didn't even seem possible. How could one person be as vicious as all those stories painted her? And even though she was a grown woman now, memories of those stories from her childhood suddenly sent a chill through her. "They say she never lets anyone go."

"True enough." Assistant looked Ari dead in the eye. "She wouldn't spare your pretty face, I'll tell you that."

"Oh," Ari squeaked.

Assistant stabbed her trowel into the ground as she dug. "So you should be very, very glad that you are in such a sheltered"—stab—"protected"—stab—"*well-guarded* place."

"Hey, be careful." Ari reached out to still her hand. "You'll damage the bulbs." Then she realized that Assistant had gone stiff beneath her touch and pulled her hand away.

They worked in silence for a few moments. Then: "You think I'm pretty?" Ari said timidly.

"Oh, for God's sake."

"Sorry." Ari looked into the nearest packet of seeds, her face burning. "I, um, is it time for lunch?"

"Past time." Assistant stood and stomped toward the intercom, trailing sods as she went.

~ ~ ~

Assistant seemed rather miffed after that. Her replies to Ari's instructions were clipped and short. But she did as good a job as she always did, and they had all the bulbs planted.

"I think they look good," Ari said happily and glanced over at Assistant, who was looking right back at her instead of the plants. "Don't you? I, I think we did a good job."

Assistant only looked back at her stonily.

"Look, I'm sorry," Ari said. "About asking you yesterday. About the pirates. I know you probably don't want to remember it." She glanced away. Obviously, she still had a lot of work to do when it came to making a stranger feel welcome.

"Why do you never leave your quarters?"

Ari looked up at her, startled. "Huh?" she said. "I mean, I do, sometimes."

"I've been here nearly a week. Not once have you left these rooms."

Ari blinked. "Well, I get busy," she said. Hadn't Assistant noticed? "I've always got something going on in here. Oh." Her eyes widened. "You've been going stir-crazy, haven't you?"

Assistant raised a sardonic eyebrow. "Just a bit."

"Oh!" Yes, Ari needed serious improvement here. "I didn't realize. Come on, let's get out of here. Let's go for a walk. I know! The Observatory." She brushed down her dirty apron. Assistant had been making her put on aprons instead of crawling around the garden in her clothes. "We've got some great telescopes. I like astronomy, you know, when I'm not working with the plants."

"Head in the stars, hmm?" Assistant asked, with a gleam of actual amusement in her eyes.

Ari smiled. "I guess so. Do you like stars?"

"Love them," Assistant said, and for once she sounded sincere. "Especially star charts."

"Oh." Ari blinked. "Really?"

"Really," Assistant said firmly. "Are there any in the Observatory?"

"Of course!" Ari was delighted to stumble on something Assistant enjoyed. She'd started to wonder if that would ever happen. "Dozens of them. I'll show you."

"How kind of you," Assistant said.

Ari looked away again so Assistant wouldn't see her blush. "I should have thought of it before," she murmured. "That you'd want to get out, I mean. Let me just change my clothes."

She brushed down her apron again and glanced back over at Assistant, who was watching her with one side of her mouth quirked up. It was as close as Ari had ever seen her come to a smile. Ari's heart stuttered, nearly stopped, and she no longer knew what to do with her hands.

"I'll be right back," she mumbled, and for some reason, now she was really worried about what she should wear.

~ ~ ~

She went with red. A dark, rich red that was more like ruby. Growing up, she'd been told that it flattered her pale skin tone and the long chestnut hair she usually kept pulled back in a ponytail. Though why wearing a "flattering" color should matter when she was just walking to the Observatory with Assistant, she had no idea. But it did matter, so she put on her red dress with its long flowing skirt, brushed her hair, made sure her fingernails were free of dirt, and even added a bracelet.

Her surge of pleasure when Assistant laid eyes on her was almost embarrassing. Assistant's eyes widened for just a moment, and—had her breath caught? That couldn't be right.

All Assistant said was, "That's...quite a difference. And to think I believed I'd show you up in all this magnificence." She touched the skirt of her plain slave's tunic.

"You probably will," Ari heard herself say, like an idiot. It was true, though. Assistant didn't need nice clothes to look like a queen.

Wouldn't she look amazing in them, though? In a red dress like Ari's? No—a blue one. Blue would complement her black hair and bring out her eyes. She shouldn't wear sleeves, though, not with those muscled arms. A necklace could grace her long, elegant neck.

They'd been staring at each other without saying a word for several seconds. Ari didn't figure this out until Assistant suddenly cleared her throat and looked at the door. "Shall we, *mistress?*"

"Don't call me that," Ari whispered, "please."

"As you wish." Without looking back, Assistant marched to the door and keyed it open.

It took a little longer for Ari to find her own footing, even after Assistant's incredible eyes were no longer trained on her. Was the ground buckling? No, that wasn't possible. Ari's knees were shaking. Thank goodness for her long skirt.

Dangerous, the little voice said in the back of Ari's head, and she shushed it at once.

~ ~ ~

On the rare occasions when Ari left her rooms, it was always a little shocking to see how expansive the space station was, even after she'd been here for three years.

In fact, all things considered, the station's size was unexpected. On her second day here, Assistant had referred to the Nahtal Sector as "a grubby little imperial outpost." True, it was on the outskirts of the Empire, and Ari's father was of a high enough rank that it seemed strange for him to be stationed somewhere so remote. But he had requested the position himself, claiming he could be "of more use" all the way out here instead of at a more prestigious station, guarding a more prestigious planet that was much closer to Homeworld and the seat of power.

Before his arrival, he'd commissioned extensive additions and modifications to Nahtal Station, insisting on more docking room to accommodate space-faring ships instead of the usual shuttles that went to and from the planet below. There were also more barracks for an increased number of troops, and he'd upgraded all the weapons systems. Ari didn't know much about the specifics—he'd never volunteered the information, and it wasn't exactly her area of expertise—but based on what little gossip she'd overheard, the station had undergone quite a change before he'd shown up to take command of it officially. By then, everyone had already known he was a man not to be crossed. Ari had been so proud of him.

It might be wishful thinking on Ari's part, but Assistant seemed a little impressed, too, as they headed down the corridors together, taking elevators up multiple levels to the station's top floor, where the Observatory provided a magnificent view. One side looked over the planet below, orange with the rich minerals mined from it, and the other looked out into the endless expanse of stars. These days, you saw a lot more ships coming and going, too, blinking out of hyperspace as they headed for the station's docks.

During their journey, Ari and Assistant passed by many of the station's inhabitants: mostly workers, troops, and slaves, but some families, too, spouses and children of imperial personnel. Ari's father wasn't thrilled about having them here. He said the outpost was no place for "a village in space." He'd even been reluctant to let Ari come with him at first. However, very few stations could justify having no civilian quarters, and Nahtal was one of them.

So, Ari tried to smile and make eye contact with civilians when their paths crossed. Like it or not, she was Lady Ariana, even if she'd never felt like a noblewoman in her life. She was the only daughter of the stationmaster and ought to do her father proud. At least the civilians didn't have to salute her like military personnel did. They usually bobbed their heads respectfully if they recognized her, though.

The deference didn't seem to bother Assistant. She looked at everyone with a cool eye, whether they were her fellow slaves or ranking officers. Once, when an ensign saluted Ari, Ari could have sworn Assistant nodded as if in approval. Could pirates really have the same kind of discipline as imperial soldiers?

Ari timidly broached the question when they reached the top floor. She hadn't dared to speak until now, because something hot had been clogging up her throat, even hotter than the ball of warmth in her lower belly that had begun from the moment Assistant had seen her in the red dress.

Assistant replied, "Mír's fleet is run with as much structure and discipline as any imperial force. More, from what I've seen."

Though Assistant's voice was cool, Ari could have sworn she detected a trace of pride in it. How strange, to be *proud* of people who had captured and enslaved you. There was something even stranger about that statement, too. "Have you seen a lot of imperial forces? I guess you must have, if you can make the comparison."

Assistant blinked, as if the question surprised her. She sounded a little evasive when she replied, "Here and there." When Ari opened her mouth to follow up, her shoulders stiffened. The clearest way possible to say, *Don't push it.*

Ari wouldn't push it, then. She tried to take a deep breath without it being noticeable. As she did, in the confines of the lift, she caught a whiff of Assistant's scent: earth from the garden, a trace of sweat, and something else Ari couldn't identify. Her hair, maybe? Hair always seemed to have its own smell, different from person to person. What did Assistant's hair smell like?

Ari looked away before Assistant could catch her staring.

They arrived in the Observatory. Thankfully, it wasn't very crowded, with just a few people sitting on the couches in the middle of the lounge, or studying at the carrels that lined one side of the room. Nothing impeded Ari's view of the stars, which always took her breath away. It was so different from her garden, where every few feet the view was blocked by a tree or bush. Space stretched out into an infinity of loneliness without even plants to keep you company. "Living among the stars" sounded poetic, but it never came close to capturing the immensity of floating in orbit.

Assistant didn't seem to notice that any more than she'd noticed Ari staring at her. The look she turned on the stars seemed more analytical than awed. Her gaze skimmed across both windows as her brow furrowed. Then she walked to the window that looked over the planet below, a tiny sphere that hadn't even merited a proper name—its imperial designation was XR-43. Everyone on the station called it "Exer."

Exer provided invaluable ore to the Empire, ore that could be used in fuel and construction, but no question that it wasn't the prettiest planet. No blue oceans or great landmasses crossed it like they did Homeworld. It had no sparkling rings of asteroids, no glowing moons.

When Ari joined Assistant—standing so close that their shoulders were just a few inches apart—Assistant said, "I remember when the mineral deposits on this planet were discovered."

Ari blinked. "Really?" That had happened before she was born. How long ago was it, exactly? "That must have been..."

"Forty years ago, or thereabouts. Back when your Empire knew how to move fast. They had an operating mine out here within ten years." Assistant glanced at Ari, and if she was surprised at how close together they were standing, she didn't protest. "I was a child then."

It would be rude to do the math with Assistant standing right in front of her, so Ari simply tacked on "less than fifty years old" to the tiny list of things she knew about her gardening partner. "Oh."

"It's an invaluable resource." Assistant looked down at Exer again, and for a second, something like hunger flashed across her face. How long ago had lunch been? They'd have to order dinner as soon as they returned to Ari's quarters. Or maybe they could even eat in the mess hall, if Assistant wanted to keep going with their...their night on the town, or whatever this was.

Ari fidgeted. "I'm sure it is."

Suddenly, Assistant shook her head and blinked, as if coming out of a reverie. She gave Ari a quick look. Was that caution in her gaze? But why?

"So," she said, "the star charts?"

"Oh!" Ari twitched, yanked from a reverie of her own, a brief fantasy of staring into Assistant's blue eyes for a long, long time and not having to be embarrassed about it. "Right. They're by this wall over here. Just tell me which ones you want me to pull for you."

Assistant definitely liked the star charts. Sitting next to her on one of the couches, Ari watched how she flipped through them, missing no detail. She realized for the first time just how smart Assistant really was. Oh, she'd never thought she was dumb: she was much too well-spoken. Sharp-tongued, even. But this woman bent over the star charts obviously had a keen and fine mind.

"We can come back here again," Ari offered. "As often as you like."

Assistant gave her a long, considering look. "Thank you," she said neutrally. Then she added, "You are very generous in how you treat a slave."

Ari squirmed. Why did Assistant keep reminding her of that? It wasn't like Ari wanted things to be this way. "Really," she said, "don't say things like that."

"But you are," Assistant persisted. She tapped a star chart with her finger, though her gaze never left Ari's face. "You are far kinder to me than Mír would have been to you. For example."

"Well." Ari laughed awkwardly, "I'm not exactly a pirate queen." She looked down and fiddled with her sleeve. "I mean, why shouldn't I be nice to you?"

"Why not, indeed." Ari looked up and saw that Assistant was smiling. A real smile. It seemed to change her whole face, softening its hawkish lines, bringing light to those blue eyes. Ari's heart nearly stopped at the sight of it, and she almost didn't hear Assistant add, "I'm trying to imagine the sort of pirate queen you'd make."

"A lousy one," Ari said at once. "Just awful."

Assistant chuckled.

That was even better—no, worse—no, *more* than the smile. Her head spinning, Ari kept talking, willing to follow this conversation as far as it could go just to keep that look on Assistant's face. "I don't think pirate queens get much chance to grow plants or do experiments. And they probably have to be, you know." She swallowed. "Harsh."

"That they do," Assistant acknowledged. Then, to Ari's surprise, she added, "But not always." She tilted her head to the side. "Even Mír can be gentle, or so I've heard. When she wishes."

"Well, of course." Ari tucked a strand of hair behind one ear. "Everybody can. That is, I hope everybody can. Nobody can be horrible all the time."

"As you say." Assistant looked back down at the star chart.

Ari glanced at a clock on the wall and gasped. "Oh, no!" It was nearly time to— "We've got to go turn the lamps on, or the *dellinses* won't bloom!"

How could she have forgotten? Her plants had never slipped her mind before. There was certainly no time to go to the mess hall. Making a mental promise to take Assistant there another time, she snatched the book of star charts from Assistant's hands and closed it with a thump.

"But—" Assistant began.

"No time! Come on! We'll come back later, I promise!" Ari grabbed Assistant's arm and hauled her to her feet, hurrying toward the door. Now Assistant wasn't smiling. She had the same look on her face that she often got when dealing with Ari: plain and simple bafflement.

Ari had no idea why. It wasn't like she was that complicated.

CHAPTER 3

Two nights later, Ari was obliged to leave her quarters again. She wasn't nearly as excited about it this time. Assistant had to accompany her. Ari got the feeling she wasn't happy, either.

It was a banquet, of the kind her father occasionally threw for visiting dignitaries. Ari hated them. She had to get all dressed up and be awkward in front of dozens of people and try to remember which spoon to use. And when she tried to explain this to Assistant, it didn't go over very well.

"Surely you were taught basic etiquette," Assistant said in obvious disbelief, her voice carrying through the bedroom door as Ari struggled with her dress—a much more formal gown than the one she'd put on to go to the Observatory.

"Not really," Ari called back. "My mother died almost thirteen years ago, and ever since then my father hasn't had much to do with me." She swallowed hard. "Which is fine. I keep really busy, as you can see."

"Yes, I see," Assistant said.

Assistant probably did. She saw everything. Ari ran her palms over the skirt of her dress as she looked in the mirror. Maybe Assistant would like this outfit, too—not that she'd say so. She'd never mentioned the red dress again. Why would there be a reason to?

Tonight's dress was a pale green, like leaves in spring on Homeworld, which was why Ari had chosen it even though the shop assistant had warned the color washed her out. It was covered in lace the same color as the silk blend beneath. She'd had it fitted, but she'd lost weight since then while being isolated and forgetting to take regular meals, so it was a little baggy in places. And it covered her up from throat to toe, with long sleeves, a high collar, and a skirt that touched the tops of her shoes.

When Ari emerged from her room, her hopes of Assistant being impressed by her attire were dashed. Assistant's eyes went wide, like they had for the red dress, but this time she said, "Is it the latest imperial trend to look three times your age?"

Ari's cheeks flamed. "Hey. It's my only formal dress." Wonderful. Assistant thought she looked awful—though why that should hurt so much was a mystery—and now Ari was already off-balance for the rest of the evening. She needed more confidence than this to deal with all the important people her father was hosting tonight. She couldn't make him look bad.

"Then you must wear it, I'm sure." Assistant looked over at the clock on the wall. If they didn't leave now, they'd be late.

And yet Ari blurted, "Well, do *you* have any ideas?"

Then she shuffled her feet. What a silly question. Assistant wore a slave's tunic, day in and day out. Not that it made a difference; here Ari was, the stationmaster's daughter, practically unable to dress herself. And Assistant looked like an empress from the moment she got out of bed to the moment she retired back to it at night, no matter how much dirt she'd knelt in. She wasn't exactly in a position to be a fashion maven, and she didn't need to be.

To Ari's surprise, though, Assistant said, "Let me in your closet."

When Assistant talked like that, there was no choice but to obey, so Ari sat in befuddlement on the side of her bed while Assistant strode into her walk-in closet, looked around, and sighed heavily.

Maybe this was a chance to learn more about her. Ari cleared her throat. "Did you, um, work for a woman before, too?" she tried. "Helping her get dressed and stuff?"

Assistant snorted. "Was I a maid to some pirate's spoiled mistress? I think not." She pulled open a chest of drawers and peeped inside. "Hmm."

So, pirates had mistresses. Maybe they had families, too. People they cared about. That didn't make any sense in Ari's head, not with the way her father talked about pirates as little better than animals. But just two nights ago, Assistant had told Ari that even Mír could be… What word had she used? *Gentle.* Pirates were human beings, too.

Assistant whipped out a silk sash from the chest of drawers. "Stand up. And straighten your shoulders."

More instructions followed, and Ari stood, turned, held out her arms, and straightened up some more until Assistant was satisfied. By the time she was done, Ari had a white silk sash tied around her middle. Assistant had told her to put on a gold pendant—one of the few pieces of jewelry she had, something that had belonged to her mother. She didn't have pierced ears, so no earrings, but Assistant scavenged her jewelry box and found the bracelet Ari had worn when they'd gone to the Observatory.

"Gosh," Ari said, looking at herself in the mirror with wonder. What a huge improvement. She had a waist and everything. "You're good at this."

"You sound so surprised."

Ari met Assistant's gaze in the mirror and fought not to blush. How was it that Assistant seemed to be able to read her every feeling? "I guess I shouldn't be. You're good at everything. Even fashion." She gave a halting laugh.

"You'd be amazed at how important it is to have style, Ariana. That sets the example, the standard. No matter what you do."

There was something a little off in that remark—since when did slaves set standards?—but that wasn't what grabbed the bulk of Ari's attention. Assistant had never said her name before. But then slaves never addressed anyone that way except for other slaves.

Ari wasn't about to object. Not when her name in Assistant's mouth sounded like *that*—so elegant, almost musical.

"S-so I look okay now?" she managed, looking at her reflection in the mirror and not really able to take it in.

"You have leaves in your hair," Assistant said.

Well, that was just typical. Of course, Ari hadn't noticed and Assistant had. She sighed and headed into her bathroom, picking samples of *Barbissa noctes* out of her hair. "I wish I didn't have to go to this stupid thing."

"I admit I'm having a hard time seeing you chatting with ambassadors' wives."

"Oh, I never talk," Ari said quickly. "I mean, unless somebody tries to talk to me. And then they never want to hear what I have to say, since I don't want to talk about politics or anything, so it doesn't last too long. Thank goodness."

"Really?" Assistant seemed truly surprised. "You're quite the little chatterbox in here."

Ari saw herself blush in the mirror as she reached for her comb. "I don't mind talking to you," she said earnestly, dragging a comb through her de-leafed hair as she exited the bathroom. "I hope you don't mind it, either. You don't make me feel like I'm stupid. Much," she added, in the interests of honesty.

Assistant looked even more surprised. "You're not stupid." She gestured at the little forest in Ari's quarters. "Just look what you've done here."

Ari shrugged. "Nobody cares about what I do in here. Maybe they will, though, when I finish work on that new pea. It might be of use to somebody." Which was all she wanted, really—to be of use. Not just to be the weird girl who played with plants all the time.

"Perhaps it will," Assistant said, her voice unusually kind. But when Ari gave her a quick glance, her face was as blank as ever.

~ ~ ~

It only took a few minutes for Ari to remember why she hated these dinners so much. For one thing, everything was much too noisy and out-of-order. For another, all the slaves had to kneel by their masters' sides, which Ari had always thought was really stupid and embarrassing, only now it was even worse because she had one of her own. So, Assistant knelt by the side of her chair, and Ari could practically feel the rage emanating from her.

"We'll leave early," she promised. "I'll say I have a headache. I can get away with that sometimes, if I don't do it too often." And she hadn't done it the last time.

Assistant did not reply. Ari did what she usually did at these events: she kept her head down and listened to people talking around her, hoping nobody tried to talk *to* her.

There was no shortage of luminaries, anyway. A delegation from Homeworld was doing a perimeter tour under heavy security, and Nahtal Station was their last stop before they returned to the capital. Ari's father wasn't usually one for pomp and circumstance, but a quick glance around the room showed that he'd gone to unusual effort tonight. The station's banquet hall, formerly utilitarian and plain, had been painted months ago with murals of scenes of great imperial victories over the centuries. The center table was hand-carved from the magnificent darkwoods that the planet Illiard was known for, and it was covered with candles, fine china, and savory dishes of all kinds.

And spoons and forks. Lots of them. Ari looked dolefully at the selection and tried to keep an eye out for what the other guests were doing as they ate.

A low voice came from her right side: Assistant whispered, sounding as though she was talking through her teeth, "Outside in."

When Ari glanced quickly down at her, trying to be unobtrusive (slaves got in huge trouble if they spoke unbidden at dinner), Assistant gave the cutlery a pointed look. Ari looked at her salad and then placed an uncertain hand on the fork that was farthest to the left of her plate.

Assistant nodded, barely perceptibly.

Ari tried not to let her hand shake with relief as she picked up the fork and saw that the other guests were doing the same.

Assistant knew about clothes and etiquette. No matter what she said, surely, she must have been in some grand places. Did pirates even have grand places? Had Assistant known another life before being enslaved by them?

34

Given the tenor of her thoughts, perhaps it was no surprise that when someone across the table said, "Well, I'm just so grateful we haven't needed all that extra security against pirates," Ari snapped to attention.

"All that expensive security," the ambassador agreed from where he sat to the right of Ari's father at the head of the table. "And with the budget under such strain. Still, better safe than sorry, I suppose. Lord Geiker, what do you think is going on?"

Ari's father frowned. He didn't look well tonight—pale and kind of tired. Now that Ari looked closely at him, he seemed to have lost weight. His thick blond hair appeared grayer at the temples, and his usual upright military posture looked more relaxed. Not in a good way, though. More like he was slumping. But his dress uniform was as crisp and pressed as ever, and his hazel eyes as sharp. The tall, male slave next to him was well-groomed and attentive. Lord Geiker was the very picture of the imperial discipline Assistant had said was so sorely lacking.

"Mír's ships have not been spotted in days." His deep voice commanded the attention of everyone in the room. Including Assistant. From the corner of her eye, Ari saw her glance up to the head of the table. That was something else slaves weren't supposed to do. "Anywhere. The latest scuttlebutt is that her fleet must have hidden itself in some out-of-the-way, abandoned station, though nobody knows why."

The ambassador hadn't said Mír's name. That didn't matter. When it came to the pirates, one was known above all others. Everyone else at the table was nodding.

"It's not as if she suffered a big loss recently," the ambassador's wife said, sipping her wine. "At least, not that I've heard about."

"I don't like it when she's this quiet," Ari's father said. "I know her patterns by now. She's planning something."

"Do you think so, Lord Geiker?" asked a man to Ari's left. He'd introduced himself to her, but she'd been so nervous that she'd already forgotten his name.

"Of course she is." Her father looked surprised that anyone had needed to ask. "That's what she does. That's who she is. Vicious animals don't suddenly become tame."

"I hear your people captured a scouter of hers," another woman said, and the excited murmurs rose all around the table.

Ari immediately bit her lip and darted a glance at Assistant, who was holding herself as still as stone. Sure enough—

"Yes, but there was only one survivor," Ari's father said. He pointed at Assistant. "My daughter's new slave, right there."

Ari winced as everyone turned to look at Assistant. But Assistant did not cringe from their stares; she met them with her own, cold and unafraid.

"Did she have anything to say?" said the ambassador's wife, excitement in her voice. "Was she able to give you any useful information?"

"Unfortunately not." Ari's father shook his head. "She was a slave on their ship. We questioned her, but she said she knew nothing. And you know our lie detectors are never wrong."

"Oh, the poor thing," another woman said, looking sympathetically at Assistant. But it didn't quite seem like real sympathy. It didn't seem like what Ari felt when she thought about what Assistant must have endured—a feeling that was both sweet and painful.

Assistant's own expression did not change one jot.

The woman looked less sympathetic then and glanced at Ari as she said, "I hope she realizes how lucky she is." Then she turned back to talk to the woman seated next to her, and thankfully, everybody's attention was off Ari.

Well...almost everybody's. "Do you keep her busy?" inquired the man on Ari's left, pointing at Assistant as though Ari might think he was talking about somebody else.

Thinking wistfully of excuses about headaches, Ari managed, "She...she helps me in my garden. She's really good at it."

Of course, the man didn't ask her about her garden. He just wanted to know about her slave. Typical. "I've always felt that a woman of rank

36

should have at least one house slave," he said. He glanced down at Assistant again. "Not bad. How old is she? She looks healthy enough."

"More than enough," Assistant said softly.

The man raised his eyebrows and looked displeased at this insolence. "Well, she's in need of discipline."

"Oh, um," Ari said. Thank goodness her father was far enough down the table that he couldn't hear this, especially since he was already talking to the ambassador again.

"How often does she need whipping?" the man asked, in the same tone as if he'd asked what Ari's favorite food was.

"I don't whip her!" Ari's skin crawled at the thought. "I'd never do that!"

He raised his eyebrows. "Your prerogative. But she'd obviously benefit from it." He glared down at Assistant. "I know her sort. She takes advantage of any kindness you show to her. I hope she won't make you regret it."

He reached out to touch Assistant—take her by the chin, pet her hair, something like that. Ari saw Assistant take a deep breath, saw her bare her teeth—

"No!" Ari blurted, and raised her own hand, ready to slap the man's hand away from Assistant. Then she realized what a diplomatically awful idea that was, and she turned the motion into a weak finger-wagging. "I mean, I'm sure I won't regret it. I mean, please don't touch her."

The man stared at her in astonishment.

Ari stood, attracting the attention of everyone around her. "Um. I'm sorry. I have a headache. Please excuse us both."

Then she fled her seat, hearing Assistant rising to her feet behind her. She hurried up to the head of the table as her father glanced up at her.

"Sorry, Father." She bent to give him a gentle kiss on his cheek. "I'm not feeling very well tonight."

He raised an eyebrow. "Again?" he asked, his voice soft enough that only she could hear. Ari gave him a guilty smile. He glanced to where

Assistant was making her way to his seat, watching them both. "How does your slave suit you?"

"Oh, she's..." Ari's voice trailed off. This didn't seem like the moment to ask him why he'd given her a slave. "She's fine."

"Tell the kitchen slaves to send some of the feast to your room," her father said, and patted her hand. "No need to go hungry tonight."

Ari smiled at Assistant, who'd drawn up within hearing range. "Oh, she never lets me go hungry."

Assistant only raised her eyebrows and did not look the slightest bit deferential in the presence of the stationmaster.

"Good," her father said. He added to Assistant, "Don't let her run herself into the ground."

Assistant did not reply. Ari patted his arm awkwardly, wishing she could say as much to the slaves who cared for him. Maybe he didn't talk to Ari or see her all that much, but he was her father. It was reassuring to know that he was out there doing his work, taking care of things like he always had. Hopefully he'd feel better soon. He worked so hard.

Ari and Assistant left the room, and Ari managed not to make eye contact with anyone, especially the man who'd tried to touch Assistant. Neither she nor Assistant spoke until they reached their quarters. Then, when the door shut behind them, Assistant exhaled a long, hissing breath.

Ari saw that she was shaking with the fury she had been containing for the past hour. Her fists were clenched and her jaw was tightly set. Worse than any of that, though, was the fire in her eyes. Just the sight of it made Ari's stomach roll over with what little food it had inside.

"I-I'm sorry," she stammered. "I'm sorry about—"

Assistant turned her look on Ari, then, and it was impossible not to cower a little bit at the sight. "Do you remember what you told me?" Assistant said softly. "That nobody here was like those horrible, nasty pirates? That you would never treat your slaves like that?"

"I..."

"How often do I need whipping, anyway?" Assistant said. "Tell me that. I'm interested to hear your opinion."

"No!" Ari said, appalled. "You know I'd never do that. Don't you?" she added hesitantly.

"Not you, perhaps," Assistant said, and began to prowl the room. "You're unusual. I'll give you that." She glanced at Ari. "Why?"

"What?"

"Do you know how I felt, when they told me I was a gift for the stationmaster's only daughter?" Assistant said. "What I envisioned you to be?"

"No," Ari said in a small voice.

"A pampered brat. Rolling around in wealth and luxury, never having known a hard day's work, utterly ignorant of the realities of life—" She paused and looked Ari up and down. "Well. One out of three isn't bad, I suppose." Before Ari could offer any kind of protest, she continued, "But you are not. You're... I don't know what you are. I've never seen anything like you."

Ari hoped that was meant in a nice way.

"How is it," Assistant added, "how is it even possible that a girl like you has grown up in a world like your father's...and you have no idea how to treat a slave? That you react with such surprise when a fool tells you to beat me?"

"Well, you know I don't go out much," Ari offered feebly. It took all of one second to see that Assistant would not be satisfied with that. So, Ari swallowed hard and continued, "My mother died when I was about seven years old. And my father never had much to do with me. Like I said."

Assistant nodded.

"So, I was raised by, you know, servants. And slaves. They took care of me. I was used to doing what they said."

"Not to ordering them around," Assistant said, her eyes going wider with sudden understanding.

"Right, exactly," Ari said, relieved that she'd caught on. "I mean, I never thought of them as, as *slaves*. They were the people who helped me grow up and told me what to do. And—it never seemed right."

Suddenly, it was hard to meet Assistant's gaze. She looked longingly toward the shelter of her trees. "I don't know much about politics, but when I was learning about history as a kid, I kept asking questions about why we had slaves at all. If the Empire's so rich, why can't we pay them, or let them come and go when they want to? I guess I asked too many times, because later Father sat me down and told me to stop. When he found out I'd been speaking to our own slaves about it, that's..."

She shivered. "It's the only time I can remember him getting angry at me. He said it was dangerous to talk that way. I'd already started getting attention, so he pulled me out of school and put me with tutors, and I liked that better anyway." No bullies. No laughter.

"You, a rabble-rouser? Somehow I can't picture it."

Assistant's voice wasn't scornful or cruel—it held that slight edge of amusement that Ari had come to recognize as something both rare and precious. That made it a little easier to say, "I wasn't trying to cause trouble. I was little. I didn't understand."

"Stop using the past tense. You still don't understand. As you ably demonstrated tonight."

Wherever Assistant had learned about table manners, she'd learned about sarcasm, too. But this particular topic was one where Ari wasn't ashamed of her ignorance. It wasn't a bad thing that she didn't "know enough" to treat a slave—a person—cruelly. She sidestepped that and said, "We moved around a lot, and we never took anyone with us. So, when I was fifteen I told my father I didn't want any more slaves or servants. I figured I was old enough. I just wanted to be left alone and tend my garden."

"Which you've done," Assistant said. "You're not like your father. I knew that right away, when I saw him."

"My father doesn't beat his slaves, either," Ari offered.

"Oh," Assistant said. "Well, good for him."

Ari gulped and wished she could think of something helpful to say.

"Your Empire," Assistant said suddenly, "is the most useless power structure in all of creation."

Ari stared at her. "What?" Where in the stars had that come from?

"You heard me." Assistant clasped her hands behind her back. "Perhaps it was great once. Generations ago. But what has your Emperor achieved lately, hmm? You tell me. Why has he left the defense of the Empire to the outposts—to men like your father?"

"Nothing's wrong with my father!" Ari said at once. "Everyone respects him. He's here because he told the Emperor he wanted the post!"

Assistant rolled her eyes. "Oh, yes. Believe me, I've heard all about the great Lord Geiker. I meant, why is the Emperor so disengaged, so uninterested, when it's getting easier and easier for pirates to breach your defenses out here? Why did your father have to *request* that a capable commander protect a valuable planet? The Empire is only as strong as its weakest point. Any half-decent strategist knows that from birth."

"Well...I guess." That made sense, even to a non-half-decent strategist.

"And it's rotting from the inside out. Do you think pirates are the only threat?" Assistant continued. "Or the threat of the Kazir, only a system away... Have they told you those are only children's stories, too? Like the wicked pirate queen?"

Ari blinked. "The Kazir? But they're not a threat. They haven't made an attack in ages. Everybody says so. The holos—"

"The holos." Assistant snorted. "There is one military force out there that is capable of withstanding an attack from beyond the Empire's perimeter. And that is the pirate fleet. The rest of you are sitting ducks."

"But they've been quiet lately. The pirates, I mean. Like everybody was saying at dinner."

A muscle jumped in Assistant's cheek. "Yes."

"So maybe there's nothing to worry about." Ari hesitated. "Why are you so upset?"

Assistant stiffened.

Ari added, "It's because of what that man said at dinner, isn't it? I'm sorry. He was a creep."

Assistant's shoulders remained rigid for a moment—then they relaxed, and she gave a rueful chuckle. "On that we agree."

"We don't have to go to another banquet for a while," Ari said. "Maybe next time you can pretend to be sick and I can leave you here."

"Maybe so," Assistant said. Then she frowned at the door. "Wasn't someone meant to be bringing us dinner?"

"Oh!" Ari smacked herself on the forehead. "I forgot to stop and send someone to the kitchen—"

Assistant glared at her and stalked to the intercom. "You don't need a slave," she said. "You need a keeper."

"You're doing a good job of that," Ari said, suddenly shy. "I mean, I really appreciate... Not that you have a choice, and you haven't been here that long, but..."

Assistant looked at her with that flat, guarded expression.

"I can't even remember what it was like without you," Ari finished in a rush. "That's all I wanted to... Sorry. Thank you."

"You're welcome, I'm sure," Assistant said. Her voice was as dry as ever, but there was something Ari couldn't read in her eyes.

CHAPTER 4

The chime went off at the fourth hour. Time to monitor *Cambrensium*. Ari pried her eyes open with a groan. She loved her work, she really did, but every once in a while it was tempting to sleep through an alarm.

Not this time, though. *Cambrensium* deserved just as much attention as everyone else, and if he didn't get his nutrient infusion, his grafts weren't going to come out well next week. Too bad Ari couldn't do this herself. This was an ambitious project that she'd only undertaken now that she had a second pair of hands. And she hated to wake Assistant up in the middle of the night, but it couldn't be helped. Oh well. It was just this once, and they could sleep in later.

She rose from her cot and stumbled sleepily over to Assistant's alcove. Assistant was wrapped up in her bedcovers, her brow puckered fiercely. She was mumbling a little. Evidently her dreams were not pleasant tonight. Well, maybe she wouldn't mind getting up after all.

Ari reached out and then hesitated. She didn't, as a rule, touch Assistant. Not deliberately. Oh, sometimes when she was passing her a tool, or that one time she'd grabbed her in the Observatory, but that was rare. There was something about Assistant that said, "Hands off," and Ari tried to respect it.

Even if sometimes she maybe kind of wanted to touch Assistant. For reasons she didn't really understand. Assistant probably wouldn't like it, and the idea made Ari's skin prickle with heat, which must be a sign that it was a bad idea.

Well, that was all the more reason to say "Assistant?" in a soft voice instead. But Assistant didn't wake up. "Assistant," Ari said more loudly, feeling very foolish. Also as a rule, she didn't call Assistant "Assistant" very much, because it sounded silly. But what else was she supposed to call her? Assistant didn't have a name. And Assistant still wasn't waking up.

No help for it, then. Ari sighed, reached out, and shook Assistant by the shoulder. "Assist—"

Then she was on her back, the breath driving out of her lungs as Assistant flew out of the bed like a thing possessed and shoved her to the ground.

"Wha—" Ari began, but couldn't manage anything else because Assistant's left hand was around her throat while the right had clenched into a fist and was swinging toward Ari's face. It stopped about an inch from Ari's nose and froze. Ari, who had stopped breathing entirely, stared in pure shock into Assistant's wide, wild eyes.

"Urk," she managed.

Assistant let go of her at once and sat back on her heels, breathing quickly. Her eyes glittered and color sat high on her cheeks.

"What," Ari wheezed. "What was—"

"Don't wake me up. Don't do that."

Ari raised one shaking hand to touch her throat. "You...I..."

"I could have hurt you," Assistant said, her eyes no less wild, although she was wide awake now. "I could ha... Do not do that again, do you understand?"

"I," Ari managed, "I didn't, at first. I tried to call you, but you wouldn't..."

"Do. Not. Do. That. Again."

"I'm sorry," Ari whispered. She was. And scared. She'd had no idea that Assistant was so strong. Or so fast. Or, apparently, so lethal.

But that was obviously what you had to be, to survive among pirates. What must Assistant's life have been like, if those were the reflexes she'd developed—if her response to being woken up was to attack somebody?

"What did you want?" The wild look had left her eyes, and her face was already reassuming its usual guarded placidity.

"W-what did I what?"

"You woke me for something, didn't you?"

She had, hadn't she? Ari tried very hard to remember. Her head was spinning and her throat hurt. "*Cambrensium*," she managed. "Infusion. Nutrient infusion. It's...it's almost past the hour—"

"Oh," Assistant said, and stood. "I...you mentioned that last evening. I'd forgotten." She glanced down at Ari. "Shall we, then?" she added, as if they were going for a stroll, and turned as if to go into the garden. Then she paused and looked back down at Ari, who still lay in the dirt.

"Y-yeah." Ari sat up carefully. No pain, nothing was broken, she'd just had the wind knocked out of her. Well, that was a relief. She prepared to get to her feet.

Before she could, two strong hands took hold of her beneath her biceps and hauled her upward, so fast that she stumbled and almost fell right back down again. But instead of falling, she bumped into Assistant, who took a very quick step back and kept her hands on Ari's arms while she looked her up and down.

"Well," she said briskly. She did not meet Ari's eyes. "You seem to be in one piece."

Ari's arms were burning where Assistant touched her. "Uh-huh," she croaked.

"Glad to see it." Assistant let go of Ari, whose arms suddenly felt chilled, and turned to walk into the garden.

It took a few more seconds before Ari was able to follow.

So that was what it felt like to touch Assistant. Maybe she'd been better off not knowing. Who knew when it would happen again?

It wasn't until Assistant was perched gracefully on a high limb pruning off a branch for a sample, while Ari took the readings at the roots that Ari felt comfortable enough to say, "So...it looked like you were, uh...having a bad dream. Maybe?" She looked up and realized that from here she could almost see up the skirt of Assistant's night tunic, which was nearly identical to her day tunic—just a little shorter.

Ari couldn't see much under there, nothing too, nothing too, but anyway she could see her calves, both slender and muscular, and the paleness of one thigh.

"I was," Assistant said in a clipped tone that recaptured Ari's attention immediately.

"Do you, um." Ari licked her lips. "Do you want to tal—"

"How are the readings coming along?"

"Oh." Ari kept her gaze very, very carefully on the monitor. "They're fine."

~ ~ ~

They never referred to the incident again, but Ari made very sure never to wake Assistant up personally. She got Assistant her own alarm chime for when they had work to do in the middle of the night. And if something unexpected ever came up, then…well, Ari didn't have a contingency plan in place for that, because really, nothing unexpected ever did come up in her life. Except for Assistant.

Ari gave her a wary look as she potted a bulb and decided, in that unlikely event, she'd just chuck a pine cone at her head or something. From a safe distance.

In the meantime, though, Ari had noticed something rather disturbing. Something else involving safe distances, and keeping them from Assistant. And how maybe she possibly didn't want to.

Assistant might not be "pretty," as Ari had known all along, but she *was* beautiful. Really beautiful. Okay, so she had a big nose and was kind of a lot older than Ari. (Ari still had not dared to ask her how much older.) And even besides the nose, her features were…sharp. But she never made a move that wasn't graceful, and she looked more naturally regal than any of the women who'd ever attended Ari's father's banquets. Once or twice she'd even smiled, and Ari had seen her perfect teeth.

And her eyes were so very blue. Mostly they were cold and watchful, but every once in a while, they could light up with warmth, however fleeting. Like when Ari had realized that the cross-strain of the new pea was working, and, about to pop with excitement, had hurried to tell Assistant, who was re-potting a *freniumis*. She'd babbled on for whole minutes without stopping, occasionally even hopping up and down, until Assistant had risen to her feet, gently taken away the trowel Ari had been waving wildly, and told her to take a deep breath and wash her face before they had dinner. Which, far from being a let-down, had made Ari feel bubbly inside because of the warmth, yes, the real warmth she had seen in Assistant's blue eyes.

She had lovely arms and shoulders. And, from what Ari could tell, shapely legs. Those thoughts made Ari's face burn, though, and the rest of her skin, too, and sometimes her hands shook and she almost dropped things. But really, it wasn't Ari's fault that no matter how old she was, Assistant looked good enough to—

"Eat," Assistant commanded, tapping Ari firmly on the shoulder.

Ari gasped and looked up at Assistant before she could stop herself, even though she knew her own face was red. Could Assistant, *did* Assistant know what Ari often thought about? She seemed to have the uncanny gift of reading minds. But, as always, her face gave nothing away.

"I let you skip breakfast," Assistant said, and Ari realized she hadn't even noticed that she'd been working straight through morning. "But I called for lunch. It's on the table. Come along."

"Oh. Thanks." Ari rose shakily to her feet, following Assistant out of the garden.

"Wash first," Assistant ordered.

Ari twitched guiltily. She had learned very quickly that Assistant tolerated dirt and slovenliness in the garden just fine, but that beyond the garden, people were meant to both presentable and hygienic. She hurried to the bathroom.

They ate in silence for a few moments. Then Assistant said, "Why does no one ever come here?"

Ari swallowed—Assistant also hated it when she talked with her mouth full—and said, eloquently, "Huh?"

"I have never seen a soul in these quarters other than the two of us. Except for the day I arrived, when you were talking to that fat botanist."

Assistant tilted her head. "Not that I'm pining for visitors, but it strikes me as odd."

Ari looked down into her food. "Odd?" she said, trying to keep her voice light. "Why should it be odd?"

"You're a young woman," Assistant said. "Your father is the stationmaster. There are nearly four thousand occupants of this station. Why am I the only person you speak to, day in and day out?"

"I…"

"What society did you have before I arrived?"

"I just don't talk to people much," Ari mumbled, still staring down at her plate.

"You handle yourself fine when we go for walks," Assistant pointed out. "You seem a little shy, but that's all. And you've got curiosity about the universe to spare. It can't be simple agoraphobia."

"I'm not agoraphobic!" Finally, Ari looked up to glare at Assistant, who, cool as a cucumber, looked right back. She tried not think about how *curiosity to spare* sounded a bit like a compliment. "I just like it in here with my plants."

"As opposed to?"

Ari tilted her head toward the door. "Out there with them."

"Why?" Assistant, persistent and merciless, leaned forward over the table. "Why are there no friends who come to visit, no young men knocking down your door? How isolated can one person possibly—"

"Shut up!"

Assistant's mouth snapped shut, and she stared at Ari in obvious surprise. Frankly, Ari was surprised herself. She never spoke to anybody that rudely. But what did Assistant expect, implying that Ari was some kind of, of… "Nothing's wrong with me!"

"I didn't say there was," Assistant said, sounding cautious now.

Ari looked back down at her food. "My father and I moved around a lot, okay?" she said. "I told you that. Almost every year he gets a new posting. Always a promotion," she added quickly.

Assistant nodded, her expression never changing.

"I-I mean, he's really good at what he does—but every time I made a friend...and, you know, I didn't make many." Ari swallowed hard and shrugged. "I never cared about what other kids cared about. I don't care about clothes, or music, or boys, or how I look. And I'm not very good at sports or games. I just like science. I like my plants." She stabbed her fork into a piece of celery. "My plants like me. They don't talk about me behind my back, or tell me to stop asking questions, or make me feel stupid and ugly."

"You are neither," Assistant said quietly.

"That's very nice of you." Ari stood, her lunch not even half-eaten. "I need to get back to work."

"But surely you—"

"You take as long as you want to eat." Ari hurried back into the garden, glad to disappear behind the leaves.

~ ~ ~

Later that afternoon, as Ari tapped the sap of *Quercus alba*, she said, "You know, if...if you're lonely here...I, maybe I could—" Could what? The sentries would never let Assistant walk around by herself after what had happened when she arrived.

"I was thinking of you," Assistant said. "It isn't good for a person to be so much alone."

"I'm not, though." Ari kept her gaze firmly fixed on the sap. "I mean...plants can't leave. I had to leave people all the time, so I found plants. They work really well."

"Plants," Assistant said, "are no substitute for people."

"That's a strange thing for you to say," Ari observed.

Assistant blinked. "What do you mean?"

"I mean, your experiences with people don't seem to have been the best." Ari fought not to look away as Assistant's eyes grew cool, which they did whenever Ari brought up her past. "I might have had some bullies at school, and people might have laughed at me, but you must have seen so much wor—"

"Don't presume to know what I've been through," Assistant didn't look angry, exactly, but the tone should have been enough to stop Ari in her tracks.

It wasn't. If Assistant wanted to make Ari self-conscious, then she should be ready to have that turned back on her. Besides, more than ever now, there was something Ari just had to make her understand.

She looked her in the eye. "I know I can't presume," she said. "I'm not saying I have a right to know. But what *you* need to know is that nothing like that's ever going to happen to you again. Nothing—" Were those actual tears gathering in her eyes? While Assistant gave her that closed, hooded look? Shoot, shoot, shoot! Ari focused on the sap again. "Look, even if I'm not the most exciting company, I'll never let you get hurt. That's all I mean."

Assistant was silent.

Ari couldn't look up. Her heart was racing.

"You'd take on the pirates for me, would you?" There was no mockery in Assistant's voice. There wasn't much of anything, it was the neutral tone she often used, but there might have been the slightest— *slightest*—tinge of respect.

Well, that would be something. Ari still didn't look up, because maybe she was misconstruing that and there would be laughter in Assistant's gaze after all. That would be unbearable. Instead, she just shrugged. "Well, it's not like I'll ever have to, but...I mean..."

She knew what she meant, but how could she say it? How could she tell Assistant what it felt like to have somebody—a person—to look out for, to care for, for the first time in Ari's life? Assistant might be the one who arranged for the food and told Ari to wash her hands, but Ari's responsibilities to her were so much greater.

That was a terrifying idea. Terrifying, and wonderful, and it threatened to overturn everything she knew about herself and everything she'd thought she'd wanted. All this because she'd been given a slave she didn't want, and whose servitude Ari found horrible to begin with.

She managed, "Anyway, it's not like I *never* talk to people. You're here now."

"So I am," Assistant said, and the conversation was over. Ari tried not to sag against the tree in relief.

They spent two whole hours in the Observatory that evening, and Ari made a point of complimenting the superintendent on how much he'd grown the library since her father's arrival. "There's a lot of great...things," she said, looking at the datapads and antique books that filled the shelves next to the study carrels, where Assistant sat looking over the star charts again.

"Thank you, Your Ladyship," the superintendent replied, obviously surprised at speaking with the stationmaster's notoriously reclusive daughter. It was enough to make Ari's stomach writhe with discomfort. She glanced over to see Assistant looking at her, instead of at the charts, and she felt like she might explode from either embarrassment that Assistant could see her ineptitude firsthand, or hope that Assistant might see that at least she was trying.

Either way, Assistant said nothing about it when they returned to their quarters. But when they retired for the night, she told Ari, "Sleep well, Ariana."

Ari didn't sleep well. She couldn't stop thinking about what Assistant had said earlier, when Ari had said she was here now. *"So I am."*

Sure, Assistant was here. She didn't have much of a choice. And she might not be nice, not exactly, but she was good to Ari and deserved a better shake out of life than she'd gotten. From being a slave to pirates to being a slave on a space station where people talked about whipping her—of course she didn't have to worry about that anymore, or about anything else. But, well, it wasn't exactly anybody's ideal life, was it?

Ari's hands fisted in the blankets she'd pulled up to her chin. The low hum of the air recycler was the only sound in the room.

She had responsibilities, both to Assistant and to her own conscience. There was only one way to satisfy them both. It didn't matter what Assistant thought about human nature. Sometimes people could do the right thing. And soon, Ari would prove it to her.

CHAPTER 5

It was one thing to make a noble, selfless decision and quite another to carry it out.

The first part had felt almost good. The second part was far more painful than Ari could ever have guessed. Two days after the banquet, and after a great deal of careful (and painful) consideration, Ari made a rare journey beyond her quarters by herself.

She told a curious Assistant that she'd heard a new shipment of plants had come in and was sitting in a cargo bay. "I just want to see them," she said, heading quickly for the door. "You stay in here. Just, um, relax." She herself didn't manage to relax until the door shut behind her and she could no longer see the questions in Assistant's blue eyes. After all, it would be best not to think about Assistant's eyes so much now.

Ari didn't go to any cargo bays. Instead, she went to her father's rooms, about a ten-minute walk away, following an elevator ride up two floors. Yet again, she crossed paths with several people, many of whom seemed to recognize her. She could seldom return the favor.

There was one person she knew, however. When she got closer to her father's quarters, the station's top medical physician met her in the hall.

Dr. Eylen was a petite woman with dark skin and short-cropped, curly black hair. She was also military personnel, and she greeted Ari with a short bow. "Your Ladyship."

"H-hi," Ari said. She wasn't often approached, and apparently the superintendent of the Observatory hadn't been sufficient practice for her. Hopefully, small talk wasn't in her future. "I mean, hello, Doctor." She glanced down the hallway that led toward her father's quarters. A sudden pang of unease struck her. "Um, you've just been to see my father?"

"Yes, Your Ladyship." Dr. Eylen's face grew more cautious. "Just a routine visit, nothing more."

Since when did Ari's father require routine visits? He'd never mentioned anything like that. "Oh. That's good." She shifted from foot to foot. Eye contact—maintain eye contact. It was what Assistant would do. "I guess that means the fever isn't back or anything."

"If the fever was back, he'd be quarantined, Your Ladyship. I assume you're on your way to visit him?"

Of course he would have been quarantined. What a dumb question. "Yes. I didn't call ahead, though. He's usually taking a break this time of day." It was nearly time for lunch. Maybe they could eat together. "He's well enough to see me?"

Did Dr. Eylen hesitate? It was hard to tell, for then she said, "I should think so. I'm sure he'd like to see you. It's not often that you're out and abou—" She stopped and cleared her throat.

Ari's face scalded. "No. I'm very busy. I'm working on a big new project in my garden. Maybe you heard about it?" Maybe from her father? Surely when he met with a doctor or someone, that someone would politely ask after his daughter. And surely he'd say something about the work that consumed Ari's life.

"No, I haven't," Dr. Eylen said with a smile and raised eyebrows, the kind that meant fake interest. "If I weren't heading back to sickbay, I'd love to know all about it. You'll have to stop by and tell me sometime."

"Right," Ari said, her mouth going dry. Well, her father was a busy man. When he met with doctors, then the conversation was undoubtedly limited to medical issues and nothing more. "That's nice of you. Thanks."

Dr. Eylen gave Ari another short bow before leaving. Ari waited until she was out of hearing distance to heave a deep sigh and then continued on her way.

Dr. Eylen's assurances that Ari's father was fine didn't seem to hold up at first. When Ari arrived at her father's quarters a few minutes later, he was resting and looked paler than he had the night of the banquet. Today, his smile was tired.

"Good morning, Ariana," he said, and turned his head so she could give him the usual, oddly formal peck on the cheek.

"Good morning, Father. I saw Dr. Eylen leaving your quarters." Ari couldn't help fidgeting as she straightened up. "Is everything okay?"

Her father's expression never changed from the slightly bland smile. "It's just my usual check-up. I'm sure it's time for yours, by the way, isn't it?"

"She didn't say anything about it." Hopefully Ari hadn't sounded too evasive. When had her last check-up been, anyway? Last year? "I feel fine. Great."

"I'm very glad to hear it. What brings you here today?"

Ari wondered if other parents and children needed excuses to see each other. But all she said was, "Father, I've come here about Assistant. My, um. My slave." She swallowed. "You remember? You met her at the banquet."

"Yes. The one we captured from the pirate vessel." He smiled grimly. "I remember quite well."

"Oh," Ari said. "Well...yeah, her."

"Is there a problem?" Her father's gaze sharpened. "Is she disobedient?"

"Oh, no," Ari said quickly. It was the truth. It was hard to be disobedient if nobody ever gave you orders. "I like her. A lot." She tried not to blush. "She's great."

"Then what is it?"

"I was wondering if..." Ari wrung her hands and looked at her feet. Why was this so difficult, when it was obviously the right thing to do? "Would you set her free?"

"Free?" Her father sounded incredulous.

"It doesn't feel right." Ari took a deep breath at her father's surprised expression. "She's not a piece of property. She's a person. I don't like thinking of her as my slave."

She remembered her father's disapproving face after she'd questioned the practice of slavery as a child. He'd warned her not to speak of it again. It was hard not to retreat and apologize just from the memory.

"But a slave she is," her father said and added very firmly, "and a slave she will remain."

"What? Why?" There were so many slaves on the station already. One more or less couldn't possibly make any difference. And here was Ari, making a proper, daughterly request and everything.

"I wished for you to have a companion," her father said. "And I saw at the banquet that you were happy with her."

What, that again? First Assistant, then Dr. Eylen, and now her own father—apparently everybody thought she was a pathetic hermit. Ari heard a surprisingly sharp note in her own voice when she said, "I am. But I wish you'd set her free."

"I don't want you to be alone," her father said flatly. "You have been, for far too long, and now I'm..." His voice trailed off, and he repeated, "I want you to have a companion. If not her, then I will find another. And this one seems to suit you well."

"She does!" Ari said, wringing her hands again. "But, I mean...if you set her free..." She looked down at her feet. "Maybe she might stay anyway."

Yes, maybe Assistant would stay. The station wasn't so bad, obviously, and Ari would hold firm to her promise to provide for and protect her. Besides, where else did she have to go?

There was a long moment of silence. Then her father said, kindly but with no yield in his voice, "I will not set her free. That is my final word on the subject."

But it made no sense! Ari opened her mouth to say so, and her father said, "Now, I need to rest. I have a great deal of work to do this afternoon. Give me a kiss, and don't worry so much."

So much for having lunch. He tilted his head again and Ari, defeated, kissed his cheek. It was clean-shaven, per the military guidelines Lord Geiker followed as closely as the lowest private, but pale from serving aboard ships and space stations with no source of natural sunlight. Was he spending enough time beneath the heat lamps? Ari often hadn't herself, but that was another detail Assistant had started insisting on.

Dismissed, she drifted along the corridors back to her own room. It took longer this time, because she was lost in thought. Not just over her father's odd behavior, but over her own reactions to it.

Sure, she was confused. And sorry that she'd failed Assistant. But other than that, buried deeply in a tiny little part of her that she still found shameful, she was relieved. She'd tried to free Assistant. It hadn't succeeded, though, and Assistant wasn't going anywhere. Wasn't leaving Ari. Like everybody else always did.

As Ari had said, Assistant might have chosen to stay anyway; after all, she had no money of her own, and once she was allowed freedom of movement, no doubt she'd have found plenty to entertain her on the station other than the Observatory and Ari's garden. But—well, now they'd never know. Assistant was staying. With Ari. Who'd done what she could, who'd tried, who couldn't be blamed.

When Ari returned to their quarters, Assistant gave her a long, cautious look. "You weren't gone long," she said. Ari glanced at a clock. Sure enough, only ninety minutes had passed. "I thought that an entire shipment of plants would keep you absorbed until dinner, at least."

"A shipment?" Ari said, wondering eagerly if such a shipment had indeed arrived. Then she remembered her lie and felt like a complete idiot. Had she really been so distracted? "I mean, yes. It wasn't...there was hardly anything there. Just a few ferns, practically." She laughed shakily.

"Where were you?" Assistant said. "Really."

Ari straightened her shoulders and tried to sound very firm as she said, "None of your business." Except that it was probably more Assistant's business than anybody else's. So,, when Assistant gave her an extremely pointed glare, Ari sighed, bit her lip, and mumbled, "I went to see my father."

"Oh," Assistant said after a moment. "Is he unwell?"

"No! He's fine. I mean, he doesn't look very good, but I'm sure after some rest, he'll..." Ari stopped, took a deep breath, and said all in a rush, "I asked him to set you free."

Assistant's eyes went wide. She looked positively stunned.

"But he wouldn't," Ari added, realizing she might have given Assistant false hope. Judging by the shadow that passed over Assistant's face, she had. "I'm so sorry," Ari said, and this time she meant it. "He wouldn't listen to me. I don't know why."

A faint, bitter smile tugged at Assistant's lips. "I do," she said. "Your father will never let me go. I am too dearly bought and paid for."

Ari blinked. "Huh?"

"Do you remember that I was the only survivor aboard the pirate ship?"

"Yes."

"There were not many of your father's soldiers left, either," Assistant said quietly. "The pirates were vastly outnumbered. But I assure you they did not go down without a fight."

"Oh," Ari said, feeling something cold settle in her stomach and chest.

"And there was nothing worth keeping on the pirate vessel," Assistant continued. "All the information had been destroyed in the databanks. There wasn't even any loot." She smiled again, and again it was bitter. "I understand they'd heard that someone important was on the ship. But again, they came up empty-handed."

"Oh," Ari said again. "Um. H-how many people died? From the station?"

"Thirty-two, so I hear," Assistant said. Ari gasped. "Felled by only nine of Mír's people. And I was the only thing they got out of it. No. Your father will not be in a hurry to let me go."

Ari bowed her head. "I'm sorry," she said again. "I just thought I'd try."

"Don't think I don't appreciate it." Assistant's look was inscrutable.

What was going on in that blade-like mind of hers? Maybe someday Ari would be able to tell. It looked like they were going to be together for a while after all. "But you're... I know you don't like it. Being a slave. Who would?"

"You know very little of how I feel," Assistant said in her sharpest voice.

Ari flinched.

"But," Assistant continued more gently, "I am fully aware that I could be much worse off. Much, much worse."

"I guess." Wasn't that what she'd told herself a thousand times already? But somehow it was different when Assistant admitted it out loud. It made her feel a little better.

"I'll try to be less boring," she blurted.

Assistant looked stunned again. Well, she often looked stunned around Ari, so that was nothing new. But then she actually chuckled. "In order to be boring," she said, "you must first stop surprising me. You haven't done that yet."

Huh? That was a weird thing to say. Ari and Assistant did the same thing, day in and day out: working in the garden, sometimes going to look at the stars. There was probably nobody in the whole Empire more predictable than Ari. "Okay," she said doubtfully.

Perhaps Assistant was just being polite. There was a first time for everything.

~ ~ ~

Two days later, Ari made a decision. It was much harder and more painful than she'd thought it would be. But it was for the best. It *was*, she told herself.

At the fourth hour, Ari looked at Assistant, who was cutting samples from a young sapling, and said, "Hey, you know what? Why don't we get cleaned up?"

Something in her voice must have alerted Assistant, because she instantly looked suspicious. "Why?"

"Oh. No reason. I mean, I thought we might go to the Observatory," Ari said. "I'm getting kind of restless."

"You have been jumpy," Assistant acknowledged. "Very well."

With relief, Ari said, "You go first." They had to take turns using the only bathroom. "I'll just finish up here. I won't be long."

As usual, Assistant was in and out of the bathroom in about five minutes, wearing her clean dress (she had two dresses, and rotated them in the laundry daily). She looked as immaculate as ever. But Ari couldn't quite resist reaching up and pushing her silver forelock out of the way, so she could see Assistant's eyes better.

Assistant looked startled. "What are you doing?"

"Nothing," Ari said quickly. "I just thought, you know, your hair... It'd be pretty if you did it like..."

"Pretty?"

"Yes," Ari said, and tried not to blush. She failed. "You have, you know, blue nice eyes. I mean nice blue eyes."

Assistant's cheeks went distinctly pink.

Oh wow. Really? Ari's heart jumped into her throat. Maybe she should find the courage to compliment Assistant more often. She added, "It's good when people can see them."

"People?" The pink in Assistant's cheeks vanished as if it had never been. She narrowed her nice blue eyes. "What exactly is—"

The door chime rang. Ari jumped. Assistant twitched.

"Oh!" Ari said. "It's still early!"

"Early? Early for what?"

Ari hurried for the door, narrowly evading the grab Assistant made for her arm, and pressed the 'Enter' key.

The door hissed open to reveal a tall, well-built man, about Assistant's age, wearing the white tunic and black leggings of a male slave. He took in Ari's tousled hair and dirty apron with wide eyes, but only said, "I'm Orin, Lady Ariana. I'm reporting for the work order you called in this morning."

"Great! Great," Ari said, and clasped her hands together, hoping her terror didn't show on her face. She turned to look at Assistant, who was staring at both of them as if they'd grown wings. "Orin, this is Assistant. She, um, doesn't have another name."

Orin raised his eyebrows.

Assistant kept staring.

"Assistant, you're, um, you're going to go help Orin with the cooling unit," Ari said. "You know, we haven't been getting water flow in here for the garden like we should, and I thought, who better to fix it than..."

She glanced back at Orin, who was regarding Assistant with no small degree of interest. Ari told herself that this was absolutely fine. Then she looked back at Assistant and saw comprehension dawning in her eyes. Along with something that looked very much like horror.

"A-anyway, we don't have any more work to do tonight," Ari babbled, looking back and forth between the two of them and trying not to make any eye contact. "So, you know, whenever you're done, you don't have to come back right away."

"What?" Assistant said.

"She, uh, worked on a small pirate rig," Ari said to Orin. "I'm sure you two will have a lot to talk about."

"Talk?" Assistant said.

"We'll get the job done, Your Ladyship," Orin said. "Never fear." His eyes wandered back to Assistant again, and they gleamed.

"Well," Ari said, trying very hard for "chipper" and fairly sure she only managed "deranged." "You, um, off you go!"

Orin inclined his head politely at Assistant and stood to the side of the door, holding out his arm for her to precede him.

Ari was sure Assistant was looking at her as she walked through the door, but she couldn't be certain because she kept her gaze on her feet. The door closed behind them, and Ari felt like her knees were going to turn completely into jelly. But they didn't, and she returned to her garden with an oddly heavy heart.

It was the right thing to do. Certainly, it was the right thing for Assistant. She must be bored out of her mind, stuck here with only Ari for company. And Ari only talked about dull things, so that just made it worse. Walks to the Observatory couldn't possibly be enough to entertain someone as smart and interesting as Assistant. Not every day. She'd need more than that.

And she was such a beautiful woman. She deserved to be with a man, to have that kind of pleasure in her life. Judging by the way Orin looked at her, it wouldn't be too difficult to accomplish that.

Ari gulped around the rock-hard lump in her throat and told herself to stop being so selfish. To be happy for Assistant, who would no doubt enjoy herself more tonight than usual. Ari had just given her the entire evening off, after all, and surely it didn't take very long to fix a cooling unit, did it?

Two hours later, Assistant still had not returned. Maybe it took longer to fix a cooling unit than Ari had thought.

Three hours. Maybe it took a *lot* longer.

Three and a half. Ari finally admitted that Assistant and Orin were almost certainly not fixing any cooling units now and curled up on her cot, needing the comfort of all her plants around her.

For the best. Really. It was.

CHAPTER 6

Ari woke up to someone shaking her fiercely and also the drip of water on her forehead.

When she opened her eyes, Assistant was looming over her, face twisted in rage, as she shook Ari back and forth like a rag doll.

"Wake up," she snarled. "Wake up!"

Dizzy, confused, Ari thought that perhaps Assistant's evening might not have gone well, and became sure of it when she saw that Assistant was dripping wet and covered in mud. "Oh!" she gasped, and scrambled to sit up, which was difficult, because Assistant was still grabbing on to her shoulders. "Oh, my gosh! Are you okay? What happened?"

"Cleaning the cooling unit," Assistant said. "Have you ever, in your life, cleaned a cooling unit?"

"Uh...no?"

"It took five hours," Assistant roared, and finally let go of Ari, who fell backward off the cot and landed in the dirt with a yelp.

"I—" she began, but Assistant charged on.

"Five hours! Five hours of mucking around in water that was alternately freezing and boiling...with that disgusting oaf trying to feel me up every chance he got—"

Ari whimpered and tried to scoot backwards on her behind, but Assistant reached down, hauled her to her feet, and shook her again. "What? What could you possibly have been thinking?"

"You didn't like him?" Ari said weakly.

"No," Assistant whispered, her voice as low and deadly as Ari had ever heard it. Their noses were about one inch apart. "No, I did not like him at all. And now he knows it."

"H-he does?"

"Don't worry. I'm sure he'll tell his master that he got his black eye and lost all those teeth doing something very manly."

"Oh—"

"And he didn't even know how to do it. I practically had to do the whole goddamned job by myself—"

"I'm sorry!" Ari wailed. "I didn't know—I-I thought you'd have fun—"

"Fun?" Assistant let go of Ari again, and Ari crashed to the ground again, because for some reason her knees wouldn't support her.

She looked pleadingly up at Assistant. "You...when you asked me all those questions about why we never see anybody... I mean, aren't you lonely? Aren't you bored?" She gulped. "I just wanted to give you a chance to..." Then she hung her head, feeling like the most idiotic creature in the universe. "I'm sorry," she mumbled again. "I didn't know it'd be awful." She kept looking at the ground.

After a moment, Assistant sighed heavily. "I am getting a shower," she said.

"Okay," Ari whispered.

"And I am sleeping in tomorrow. As late as I want to."

"I'm sorry," Ari said yet again. Then she looked up and blurted, "I'll do better next time. I'll find a job that won't be terrible and someone who won't—"

It must have been difficult to look utterly, completely terrifying when you were soaked through with water and mud, but Assistant managed it quite well. "Look at me," she said softly, as though Ari could look anywhere else. "There will be no next time. Period. That's all."

"Oh," Ari said, feeling about two inches tall.

"Go back to sleep," Assistant snapped, whirled on her heel, and stalked away, still dripping.

Ari fled the cot and retreated to the safety of her bedroom, where she huddled under the blankets and squeezed her eyes shut. But sleep, as she'd expected, eluded her completely.

~ ~ ~

The next day, Ari apologized with practically every motion that she made. She knew Assistant didn't have much patience with people who repeated themselves all the time, so instead she worked penitently in the deepest silence until Assistant woke up, asked her with the greatest meekness to do easy and non-dirty tasks, called for breakfast and lunch herself, and made sure that the mess hall sent up Assistant's favorite kind of tea. And she made very, very sure never to meet Assistant's eyes, although she constantly checked on Assistant when she wasn't looking back.

Assistant did not speak to her. Not one single word.

But then, before dinner, Ari looked up, and saw Assistant looking back. Ari bit her lip and managed a tremulous smile.

Assistant sighed, closed her eyes, and rubbed her hands over them. "It's like kicking a puppy," she muttered.

"Um. What is?"

"Being angry. Being angry at *you*." Assistant glared at her fiercely. "I have very little difficulty being angry with most people, for the record."

"So, you're not angry anymore?" Ari asked hopefully.

"I am no longer enraged," Assistant said. "You may consider me downgraded to 'peeved.'"

"Oh," Ari said in enormous relief, because "peeved" was very near to "normal," for Assistant. "Good. I really am sor—"

"Don't say it. Do not say it."

"Oh. Okay. Sor—okay."

"And get those leaves out of your hair."

~ ~ ~

The next day, Ari emerged from behind a bush and caught Assistant looking at the jars on the shelves. Specifically, she was looking at Cranli's jar, where he rested on some leaves. And she was lightly tapping the glass and smiling at him.

Ari cleared her throat. Assistant twitched and turned around. It was the first time, Ari realized, that she'd ever snuck up on her. While she was awake, anyway. Ari grinned and nodded at the jar. "You like Cranli too, huh? He's my favorite."

"He's just a bug," Assistant sniffed, her cheeks going the tiniest bit red.

"Okay," Ari said, still grinning.

"He reminds me a little of you," Assistant said. "Hopelessly friendly and trusting, once he gets to know you." She peered thoughtfully back at the jar.

Ari blushed with pleasure. "Do you want to put him on *Mustopher illis*?" she asked. "He likes her the best. But he always comes back to his jar at night."

"Believe me. I don't care about a bug," Assistant said, but she opened the jar anyway.

"Sure you don't." Ari laughed as Cranli hopped out and buzzed away.

"I really don't."

"You do. You like a bug. Who's your second favorite? I like Beliss. She's that pretty iridescent cricket. Very sociable. You two would get along great."

"Don't we have work to do? As in, immediately?"

"If you want," Ari said, and laughed again at the almost sheepish expression on Assistant's face.

CHAPTER 7

Ari's fingertip scrolled down her datapad screen. The latest quarterly issue of *Botany Today* was due for release on the booknets, and she'd already checked twice. Thankfully, right after the breakfast she'd been too excited to eat, it was ready.

"No digging around today?" Assistant said. "My fingernails might die without their daily helping of filth."

"Today is for theoretical stuff," Ari said firmly. She didn't know what Assistant was complaining about, anyway. At her own insistence, they'd both started wearing gardening gloves. Ari glanced at Assistant and added, "Do you want me to read it out loud, so you can hear it too?"

A shudder ran through Assistant's whole frame. That had probably been too much to hope for.

"What do you want instead?" Ari asked. Slaves weren't allowed to access reading materials on their own, so Ari downloaded anything Assistant wanted.

"Newsfeeds will be fine," Assistant said. "I do like to keep up with things."

"Oh! Sure." Ari typed in her code for three of the major newsfeeds. "You know, if you remind me, I can get these for you every day. I just forget about stuff like that."

"Thank you," Assistant said, sounding surprised. "I will."

"Uh-huh." Ari absently handed her a datapad and settled down to read, already forgetting all about newscasts and whatever else. "Oh!" she said, as she skimmed the table of contents. "Dr. Phylyxas has a big article!"

"How exciting." Assistant headed rather quickly out of the kitchen. "I'll be reading in my alcove."

"Okay." Ari decided to save Dr. Phylyxas's article for last, as a way of prolonging her enjoyment.

The Letters to the Editor section was always fun. Ari had even had a letter published there, two issues ago. That was how she'd caught Dr. Phylyxas's attention, and why he'd offered to come visit her. After the Letters section, she read the News In Brief, and then an article about the very same conference Dr. Phylyxas had attended before visiting Ari. It sounded very exciting, Ari thought wistfully.

Maybe she'd go to the next one. Well...why shouldn't she? It wasn't nearly as dangerous to travel now, what with the pirates being so quiet. And Assistant was right—it was ridiculous to stay holed up in here all the time. Nothing said she couldn't get out of the station for her own reasons, instead of just trailing around the Empire with her father.

Maybe Assistant could even go with her. She'd probably jump at the chance, even if botany didn't exactly thrill her. That could be fun. A real adventure. Already tingling from the possibility, Ari turned happily to Dr. Phylyxas's article.

And read. And read.

And read some more, sure that she had to be mistaken in what she was reading.

At some point, Assistant returned to the kitchen, still holding her datapad. "This newsfeed is run by idiots," she said irritably. "Do we have any of that tea left?" Then she looked up and saw Ari sitting very still at the kitchen table. "What's wrong?" she asked.

"Wrong?" Ari said, unable to take her eyes off the datapad.

Assistant reached down and took the datapad from her. Ari felt too stunned to protest. Assistant glanced over Dr. Phylyxas's article, brow furrowed in the same expression of blank incomprehension she always wore whenever Ari talked about botany. But then, as Ari watched, her eyes widened.

"*Pisum sativum*," she said. "Isn't that—in fact, isn't all of this—"

"It's a pea," Ari said, staring at the space on the table where the dapatad had been. She bit her lip. "My pea."

"I thought it looked familiar," Assistant said quietly.

Ari gulped. "I didn't finish reading the article. He, um... I don't think he mentions me, though."

"Did you tell him about this when he came here?"

"Of course I did!" Ari said. "It's—it was my big project. And he's the Senior Royal—" She gulped. "I wanted to impress him."

"It looks like you did." Assistant's face was, as always, impossible to read, but her eyes were dark. With what emotion?

"Why did he do that?" Ari asked. "He's a brilliant botanist. He has so much he can do—he's so important—why did he steal my ideas?" Because that's what he'd done. He'd stolen them. *Stolen* them.

"I daresay you are not the first person he's stolen from," Assistant said, speaking in a gentle tone she rarely used. "People who get to the top are often gifted at that sort of thing." Then, suddenly, her voice got sharp. "Ariana."

Ari blinked. Why did Assistant sound so angry all of a sudden? Nobody had stolen *her* life's work.

"People will use you," Assistant continued. "Do you understand? That is what people do." She waved the datapad in Ari's face. Her inscrutable expression was sliding into something that looked almost upset. "This man, this fat, brilliant botanist, is a thief. And he is no better or worse than anyone else."

"What?" Ari gasped. She stood. "That's not true!"

"Isn't it?"

"I-I..." Ari shook her head. "No. That's awful. That's a terrible thing to say. I don't think people are like that."

"How would you know?"

Ari stared at her, wounded. Like Ari didn't already feel bad enough, now suddenly Assistant wanted to jeer at her? "I—"

"Get used to it," Assistant said flatly, and thrust the datapad back into her hands.

"I'm not going to get used to that!" Ari drew her shoulders up straight. "I'm going to write a letter."

Assistant looked like she wanted to laugh in Ari's face. "A letter?"

"Yes!" Ari said, her face burning with humiliation and anger. "To the magazine. I'm going to tell them exactly what Dr. Phylyxas did. He shouldn't be allowed to get away with that."

"Well," Assistant said. "Do your worst."

"I will!" Ari's hands curled into fists. Suddenly, the metaphor about people having "boiling blood" when they were mad no longer seemed like a metaphor. She had fire in her veins. "And there's no need for you to be so—so *mean* about it."

Assistant blinked.

"Why do you care, anyway? You don't even like botany!"

"No," Assistant said. "I don't."

"So why don't you go back to your alcove," Ari said, "and not-like botany over there. I'll be in my room." Writing her letter.

She stormed off and didn't let the tears fall until the door was safely closed behind her. She even locked it.

She wrote her letter and then wrote it again about five times. Wished she could ask for Assistant's advice on it. But she wasn't going to do that. Go meekly to the woman who thought this whole idea was stupid and ask her what she thought? Forget it.

Ari wasn't feeling all that meek anyway right now. She might lose her temper and make things worse. Talk about "surprising" Assistant, and not in a good way.

After the sixth attempt, Ari tossed the datapad on her mattress and flopped back down on her bed, rubbing her forehead in an effort to hold off the headache she knew was coming.

Someone knocked on the door.

"What?" Ari called.

"I've called for dinner," Assistant said through the door.

"I'm not hungry."

"Stop sulking."

"I'm not—I'm not sulking! I'm *upset.* I'm allowed to be upset," Ari snapped.

"Have you finished your letter?"

"Yes," Ari lied, after a pause that went on for just a moment too long.

"Let me in."

Ari didn't want to, but there was something about Assistant: something that meant, when she gave you an order in a certain tone of voice, you obeyed her. Ari had pressed the 'Enter' button by the side of her bed before she'd even realized it. Assistant glided in, regal as always—and then, to Ari's surprise, sat down at the foot of the bed.

"Do you want me to read your letter?" she said.

"I don't think so. No."

"Are you planning to send it?"

Ari shrugged miserably.

Assistant sighed. Then, to Ari's astonishment, she reached out and patted Ari's shin.

Ari forgot about Dr. Phylyxas, and thievery, and even botany for a few seconds, because Assistant was touching her, for no obvious reason, and it felt marvelous—even if it was through Ari's skirt, and was only comforting, and wasn't meant to be...intimate. Her hand was warm, and her touch was light, and it made Ari blush so hard that it felt as if her whole face was going to melt off.

And Assistant noticed. Of course she did. She never missed anything, not a single detail. Her eyes went wide, and her hand stiffened on Ari's leg. Then she slowly, cautiously pulled it away.

Ari had never been so horrified in her life. Dr. Phylyxas's theft was nothing to this. She had a sudden vision of herself burrowing into the roots of a tree, hiding herself beneath wood and sod and other living things that knew better than to have feelings, to care. That had to be an improvement over looking into Assistant's beautiful, shocked blue eyes.

But then the door chimed, signaling that dinner had arrived from the mess hall, and digging herself into a hole abruptly seemed like an impractical idea.

Assistant gave Ari one more long look. Ari stared back at her, stricken, feeling as if she should apologize for something she hadn't said or done, only felt.

But all Assistant said was, "Come along."

Now she looked...not warm. Not quite. But she didn't look angry, upset, or mocking, either. Ari didn't know what that look was.

"I'm really not hungry," Ari croaked, deciding that she would stay in her bedroom for the rest of her life.

"Are you sure about that?" Assistant said, raising an eyebrow before she left Ari's room.

Ari tried not to whimper out loud.

~ ~ ~

After dinner, they went to the Observatory, where Ari spent the whole time peering into telescopes or looking out the window or paging through star charts or doing anything but looking at Assistant. And any time Assistant came within two feet of her, Ari started chattering about anything astronomy-related that came into her head, shuffling away as she talked until the two feet had grown back to a comfortable three or four or even five.

But Assistant didn't seem to get Ari's hints and kept trailing Ari around the Observatory like the most obedient, attentive slave who'd ever lived, which she'd never done before, and what was she up to? Was she still mad at Ari about the cooling unit thing? Why else would she be doing her best to make Ari want to sink through the floor?

She might stop if she knew about the other feeling, the one that stirred in Ari's heart and stomach and brain all at once whenever Assistant got close enough to touch but never did. There was no other way to describe it than the *hot* feeling. So hot that Ari almost wondered if every single cooling unit in the station needed replacing immediately.

When they returned, Ari knew she should look in on *Paxium nollinium*, but she decided he would just have to fend for himself tonight. She'd get up really early the next day and check on him. Before

Assistant woke up. In the meantime, she mumbled, "I'm really tired, I'm turning in early," and fled into her bedroom before Assistant could reply.

Only, she couldn't sleep. After two hours of lying awake in the darkness, she gave up and turned on her lamp. It would be better to read than just toss and turn. She might go out and make some tea in a few more minutes—at this hour, Assistant was sure to be asleep—but not just yet. Better to make sure.

But Ari hadn't been reading for more than five minutes when her door hissed open. Assistant stood in the doorway, clad in her night tunic, her feet bare. Ari looked her up and down before she could help it, even though Assistant looked like she always did whenever they worked at night. How strange, though, that the shorter skirt on Assistant's night tunic made Ari feel a little dizzy in a way it hadn't before.

Ari fumbled her datapad. "What...why—"

"Your light was on," Assistant said blandly. "I wondered if you were all right."

"I'm fine!" Ari spluttered. "What are you even doing in here?"

"You didn't lock your door."

"So?" Ari said. "That doesn't mean you can just walk in on people!" She was astonished, really. Assistant, though she could be very rude in some ways, observed all the proprieties in others.

"I'm sorry," Assistant said, a small smile playing around her lips. "Did I interrupt something?"

Ari blinked, not sure what to make of the almost...purring...tone in Assistant's voice, except that something began to stir on the very edge of her awareness. Something too much like the hot feeling for comfort.

"I was just reading," she said.

"Oh," Assistant said, and came into the room. She pressed the button on the wall and the door shut behind her. "Well, then."

"Um, I'm fine," Ari said hastily. "As you can see. I'm sorry if I, uh, worri...disturbed you. You can go back to sleep now."

"Do you know," Assistant said, sitting at the foot of Ari's bed again, "I'm having the most difficult time nodding off myself."

"Oh." Ari tensed up, wondering if she should scramble out of bed. "D-do you want me to make us both some tea?"

"No," Assistant said. "I have a better idea." She slid up the bed until she was sitting next to Ari, looking down at her.

And for all the heat that had been lurking inside her blood all night, Ari felt frozen solid, clutching her datapad like a shield to her chest. She couldn't move, couldn't think, couldn't breathe. What...surely—

Assistant was so close. Her body was so warm. Her eyes were so blue.

"I'll tell you a story," Assistant said. "Perhaps that will help you sleep."

"Oh!" Ari's breath left her in one huge rush that sounded so ridiculous she nearly cringed. What had that been? A gasp of relief, or what? What was there to be relieved about?

Or disappointed about?

Of course, Assistant hadn't meant anything wrong. She might have been teasing Ari like she did sometimes, but that was all. This was obviously benign, even if the offer of story time was still kind of weird. Ari wasn't a child who needed nursery rhymes to get through the night. But if Assistant wanted... "Okay. I mean, if you like. What kind of story?"

"A pirate story," Assistant said. "What else?"

Ari's eyes widened with both surprise and interest. "I thought you didn't like to talk about that."

"Well, you wanted to know what it was like to live among pirates," Assistant said. "Didn't you? What it was like to keep company with the dangerous pirate queen?"

"You said you never saw her," Ari reminded her.

"I heard the stories. Everyone did. Everyone in the fleet." She smiled. It was a little scary. "Though the stories rarely made their way to outsiders."

"Oh." Ari curled up on her side, looking up at Assistant. "Okay. That sounds interesting." Thank goodness, her tone hadn't sounded too eager. Assistant had already known Ari was wildly curious about this, but it wouldn't do to sound... Oh, what was the right word, voyeuristic? Like Ari regarded stories of pirate culture as pure entertainment, and not something that happened to real people. People like Assistant.

Still, though, it would be neat to be privy to something that so few outsiders knew.

"Once, nearly ten years ago," Assistant said, "Mír's fleet advanced upon a little armpit outpost in the Leinea sector. It wasn't an official outpost. It didn't even have a name. What it did have was a rogue, roving band of shabby little mercenaries who had been attacking small trading ships. Small, but sometimes loaded with very lucrative cargo."

Ari nodded. "And they refused to pay tribute."

"Tribute?"

"Oh, yes. What do you suppose it means to be a queen? You take tribute. Or taxes. However you want to put it."

"My father says Mír gets a cut of everything," Ari said, remembering.

Assistant's lip curled. "Or getting a cut. Fine. It means the same thing."

"Okay," Ari prompted. "So, they wouldn't pay her?"

"Indeed, they would not. They thought they were dealing with one small ship from Mír's fleet and prepared to engage them. I'm sure they thought they could win, run, and hide. They did not know that Mír's own flagship was in the same sector, cloaked, biding time between much larger targets."

"The flagship?" Ari said eagerly. Rumors abounded about that ship, each one more unlikely than the last. "You mean the *Crown Lily*? Did you ever see it? What's it like?"

"I've seen it. Schematics of it," Assistant amended. "Nothing like a lily. It's black. And large. As large as the biggest Imperial vessel." She reached down and combed her fingers through Ari's hair. "More than a match for anything within the Empire or beyond it."

Ari went still. Assistant had never touched her like…this…before. But her fingers were very gentle in Ari's hair. Almost soothing. And her voice was low, hypnotic, mesmerizing. Yet again, Ari felt like she couldn't move, couldn't do anything but listen as Assistant continued.

"And those little swamp rats tried to withhold their tribute from Mír. To deny her something she had demanded." Assistant's knuckles brushed lightly over Ari's forehead. "That never ends well."

Ari swallowed, and Assistant smiled almost gently.

"There are some people who always get what they want, and she is one of them," Assistant continued. "Do you know what it is like, to be a person like that?"

Ari shook her head.

"No. Of course you don't." Assistant shook her own head. "Anyway. To return to my tale.

"The mercenaries engaged the small ship of the fleet. Mír's people held their own, but Mír heard of it while it was happening and became upset. Most upset. It was an insult, you see, and if there is one thing pirates do not tolerate, it is insult. The *Crown Lily* arrived quickly, uncloaked, and demanded the mercenaries' immediate surrender and payment of tribute. She promised them mercy. They agreed."

"I bet," Ari whispered, her eyes wide. "So, what happened? They joined her crew?"

"She killed them," Assistant said, looking Ari dead in the eye. "Every single one."

Everyone knew that pirates were awful, so Ari had no idea why Assistant's words hit her like a stone to the head. Maybe it was the realization—again—that the woman next to her, the closest thing she had to a friend, had lived in such a way that such an atrocity was business as usual. Ari gasped again, and this time, there was no pretending it was anything but horror.

She curled up harder in the bed until her knees were almost at her chest. "That's terrible." Her voice cracked.

Assistant's fingers paused in her hair. "Is it?"

"Of course it is!" Why did Assistant even have to ask? Was she that brainwashed? "Mír said she'd be merciful. She lied."

"Did she?"

"Well, yes! She, she—"

"From what I understand, the mercenaries were quickly and cleanly killed. That is mercy, in the world of pirates." Assistant dragged her knuckles down Ari's cheek before returning to her hair. The gesture could have been innocent, even tender, but the look in Assistant's eyes made it something else. "They chose that life. They chose that fate. Just as you've chosen to wall yourself off in this little jungle of yours."

"But what's wrong with that?" Ari asked. "So what if I do? I'm not hurting anybody else. I'm not killing anybody, or stealing... I'm not as bad as a pirate or even Dr. Phylyxas!"

To her surprise, Assistant's nostrils flared, and she almost looked upset. "If I were you," she said, "I would not compare Mír to the Senior Royal Botanist."

"Why not?" Ari demanded. "They both steal stuff. At least Dr. Phylyxas doesn't kill people."

Assistant yanked her fingers out of Ari's hair.

"Ouch! Well, it's true."

Assistant scowled at her. Ari scowled back.

Then Ari rolled over and looked at the wall. "I didn't like that story," she said, her voice shakier than she would have liked. "And it's not going to help me sleep, thanks."

Then she felt Assistant's fingertips again. They were warm. They were stroking lightly over the nape of her neck.

Ari froze again. Then she began to shake like a leaf of *Quercus alba* in a stiff wind as Assistant leaned down, her breath soft and warm on the side of Ari's face.

"You didn't like that story?" Assistant murmured in her ear. "Not even a little?"

Ari swallowed, tried to say something, but she couldn't make a sound. Assistant's mouth was nearly touching her ear, and only her ear, but for some reason the hot feeling was back, blooming through her whole body.

"It did not excite you?" Assistant added.

"It wasn't exciting," Ari whispered, making her voice work at last. "I told you, it was terrible—What are you doing?"

"You know nothing of the world." Assistant's voice was soft as the fuzz on a baby leaf. She smelled wonderful. Intoxicating, like the one time Ari had tried wine. She had beautiful arms and legs. And her voice still wove around Ari like a spell.

Ari felt the lightest, barest brush of Assistant's lips on her shoulder, against her throat; heard Assistant inhale; realized that Assistant was smelling her, too. Her fingertips dragged slowly up and down Ari's arm, making goosebumps rise everywhere.

"But tell me," she breathed in Ari's ear, curling up behind her until their bodies touched from back to front and Ari thought she might faint from the heat. "What do you know about this? Anything at all?"

And then her lips stroked down the side of Ari's throat.

Assistant's lips were soft, and between them hid the hot tip of her tongue. Her breath was a warm puff of air. The three elements combined into one experience, the experience of a kiss such as Ari had never known, touching only her neck, but somehow making her scalp tingle and her toes curl. She tried to say something, but all that came out was a sob. Her body felt very strange—she couldn't breathe normally, couldn't keep her eyes open, couldn't stop shaking—and she hurt, her breasts hurt and ached, her nipples were drawing up tiny and tight—

Assistant let go of her with one hand. Ari gasped, but Assistant only reached over her and turned off the bedside lamp, drowning them in darkness.

Then Assistant was on her. She rolled Ari over, pinned her beneath her own impossibly warm body, and she kissed Ari, kissed her until she couldn't breathe.

Ari had been kissed on the mouth once before, when she was sixteen, by a boy who hadn't really liked her. She didn't know if

Assistant liked her, either. But she didn't kiss like the boy had. She kissed Ari with her mouth open, with her tongue, never letting up, never letting Ari breathe or protest—not that Ari wanted to protest.

Maybe Ari *should* protest, but no possibility had ever been less appealing in the history of the galaxy.

When Assistant lifted her mouth, Ari tried to say something to her. But all that came out was "*Oh*," a whimpering moan. She'd never made a noise like that before.

Assistant hissed and kissed her again, and then began touching her nipples through the thin cotton of her nightgown.

Ari arched up into her pinching, twisting fingers with a strangled gasp and grabbed Assistant by the shoulders, unable to do anything but hold on while Assistant coaxed reactions from her that surely science could never explain. She wriggled and writhed and tried to talk, to beg, but she didn't know what to beg for and her voice wasn't working anyway.

Assistant's hands slid down from her breasts to her hips, where they seized the skirt of Ari's nightgown and pushed it up around her waist. She caressed Ari's skin beneath and passed one palm over her navel.

"Oh!" Ari gasped, shivering and shocked. Had her abdomen always been this sensitive? Assistant dipped one thumb into her navel, massaged it a little, and Ari throbbed between her legs. Assistant's palms and fingertips felt cool against Ari's fevered skin, and dry, too, while Ari was sweating through her nightgown. Was Assistant totally unmoved by this? How could anyone be—

When Assistant's hands swept down Ari's hips and then down to her thighs, her breath caught, and she froze.

Why? She wasn't going to *stop*, was she? Ari croaked, "What's— what's wr—"

"No underwear?" Assistant whispered, which had to be a rhetorical question under the circumstances.

"N-no. I don't usually wear—not to bed—"

"All those nights I've been plodding around in the dirt out there, and you've been—" Instead of finishing, Assistant slid her thigh, still covered by her night tunic, between Ari's. She parted Ari's legs and pressed down against Ari. Now it was between Ari's legs, and Ari was arching up against it, rubbing against it frantically because she couldn't help herself. She felt as if she'd lost all control over her own body, which did whatever Assistant told it to do with her mouth and hands. And her words.

"So responsive," she purred in Ari's ear, "yes, yes, do that..."

Ari arched up against her, moving her hips faster than ever, realizing that she was getting wet and rubbing it all against Assistant's tunic and making an awful mess.

"Doesn't it feel so good?" Assistant asked.

"Uh...I...uh..." Even if she could talk, Ari would have had no idea how to answer that. Did it feel good?

No. "Good" wasn't good enough. She just knew this was turning her into somebody she didn't recognize and had no control over, and she'd never realized it was somebody she wanted to be. Someone who could be hot, and hungry, and *ready* but not ready at all—

"Please," she cried, not sure what she was asking for. Maybe it was everything, every touch and feeling she'd ever been denied, or had denied herself. Maybe it was what had always been waiting beneath all the thoughts she'd had of protecting Assistant, staying by her side, looking into her eyes and at her beautiful body that suddenly seemed made to press against Ari's own.

"Please," she said again, whimpering it. Maybe Assistant would know what she meant.

Assistant let go of her breasts, reached down, and cupped Ari's rear firmly with her astonishingly strong hands. Then she pushed Ari harder against her thigh, moving Ari faster and rougher, bending down to suck and lick at Ari's throat.

Ari began to pant harder, feeling like she was one step away from hysteria as she shuddered her way closer and closer to something but close to what, to what?

"Come now," Assistant said harshly against her throat. "Come now, for me—"

Ari had no idea what Assistant was talking about, or how she was supposed to come or go anywhere, but then Assistant pushed Ari up, pressed her thigh down, and began squeezing Ari's bottom rhythmically. And Ari tossed her head back and wailed as something convulsed inside her, hard and fast, releasing all the trembling and the tension in her body while she writhed and sobbed in orgasm.

It was better than anything Ari had ever felt in her life. Sort of like the end result of the timid explorations she'd done with her fingers as a teenager, but that were never quite satisfying enough, certainly not enough to distract her from her work or her thoughts.

This was not that. This was pure ecstasy, a throb that went from between her legs all the way up to her head and all the way down to the tips of her toes. If she could have done that with her fingers, she'd never have stopped, and now she never wanted *this* to stop, either. This mind-blowing feeling that Assistant was taking such delight in giving her.

Assistant kept whispering, kept saying, "Yes, like that, exactly like that, yes," and kept Ari moving against her leg until, incredibly, the ecstasy began to fade.

Ari simply couldn't take it anymore and began pressing against Assistant's shoulders because the convulsions were slowing down, lessening, and the joyful throb beginning to turn into discomfort. Nothing had ever seemed more unfair. Why did it have to end?

"There," Assistant said. "There now." She rubbed her thumb against Ari's hip. "Very good. Very good indeed." She kissed Ari's forehead softly. "Lovely."

"Oh." Ari gulped and then whimpered, "Wow."

Assistant chuckled. "Quite." She kissed Ari's forehead again. "Shush, now."

Now wasn't the moment to shush, was it? Ari had no idea what to say, but she wanted to say something—ask what on earth Assistant had meant by starting this, or say how amazing it had felt and ask if they could do it again really soon, or say something sweet or funny or clever.

"I messed up your tunic," she blurted.

Then she winced. Shushing would have been a better idea.

Assistant hummed, stroked her cheek, and rolled off Ari. Without her heat and energy, or that astonishing power, the recycled air of the station suddenly seemed cold. Maybe some of that was the sweat cooling on Ari's sticky skin. Should she take a shower? The idea of getting out of this bed seemed as unthinkable as going for a stroll through the Exer gas clouds without a protective suit.

Without meaning to, she made a soft, bereft noise. And Assistant, to her surprise, settled in next to her side and took her in her arms once more.

"Utterly lovely," she repeated, sounding very satisfied indeed.

Lovely? Really? Assistant thought Ari was lovely?

Ari blinked slowly. It wasn't getting any easier to think. Now that the excitement was over, her body was growing soft and heavy, begging for rest. She should ask something, though. "Why did you do that?"

Assistant tensed for a moment. "Did I hurt you?" she inquired, threading her fingers through Ari's hair again.

"No!" Ari said quickly. That was the last idea she wanted Assistant to get.

The tension dissipated from Assistant's frame. She sounded almost teasing when she asked, "Did you dislike it?"

"No." Now Ari couldn't stop herself from giving Assistant an incredulous look, even though Assistant couldn't see it in the dark. "Did it seem like I did?"

"The 'pleases' didn't seem to suggest that, no."

It could have been embarrassing, but the drawl in Assistant's voice proved that she hadn't minded it a bit. Ari felt her lips spread out in a smile that probably looked dopey but that she couldn't help at all.

"I liked it," she managed.

"Well, then." Assistant petted her on the shoulder. "We'll just have to do it again sometime, won't we?"

Nothing had sounded better, ever. But even though her body felt great, and exhausted, a few of Ari's brain cells were starting to wake up. They were clearing their throats and suggesting that maybe Ari and Assistant should talk about this a little more, think it through, and establish what it meant.

"Oh," Ari said. "I don't...I don't know..." She tried to sound assured. "I don't know if we should." She added hastily, before Assistant could get the wrong idea, "That is, until we—"

"There is no 'should,'" Assistant said softly. "Not when it comes to this. Forget 'should.'" She stroked Ari's back, and Ari shivered. "Trust me," she murmured. "Trust me."

"I do," Ari whispered, because she did. However sharp-tongued she could be, Assistant had never lied to Ari. She looked out for her. She *liked* her. And if they were going to start doing this, then Ari could be willing to trust her just that much more.

Especially if it felt that good all the time.

Assistant touched her chin, and tilted Ari's face so that she could kiss her mouth. It was much softer now, much gentler. She didn't use her tongue. "It will be so good," she said. "You don't even know the half of what can be done. Of how I can make you feel." She kissed Ari again. "There will be no pain. Only pleasure. Trust me," she repeated.

Ari's eyelids were already drooping as she was lulled to sleep by Assistant's soft words, strong body, and her own exhaustion. She tried to say "Okay" but didn't quite manage it before she conked out.

~ ~ ~

Ari woke an indeterminate time later to a loud, intrusive noise. She gasped, stiffened, and opened her eyes, in that order. Someone's arms clung to her waist, someone was spooned up snugly behind her back. Someone was snoring right in her ear.

Assistant. Ari gasped and blushed as she remembered what they'd done only—um—she squinted at the clock by the bed. Only three hours ago. But she was having a hard time thinking about that, because

Assistant was snoring loudly enough to wake a hibernating Theriun bear. Ari hadn't noticed she'd done that in her alcove. Maybe she was just really tired tonight.

But it was dangerous to wake Assistant. Ari shivered at the memory. Then again, Assistant's arms were wrapped securely around her—awfully securely, as if Assistant was making sure Ari wasn't going anywhere. So she wouldn't be able to wake up swinging. Still, better safe than sorry. Ari wriggled against her and cleared her throat loudly.

It worked. Assistant snorted, twitched, and said, "Wha?"

"You're snoring," Ari said.

"What?" Assistant sounded blank and sleepy. Then, "I am not."

"You were too. Right in my ear. You woke me up."

"I don't snore," Assistant said, still sounding out of it. "Go back to sleep."

"I can't sleep when you snore!" Ari protested. "Here. Let me get up." She had some ointment that cleared up your sinuses when you smeared it below your nose. Sometimes it helped snoring, too. Or at the very least, she could make it to her cot and sleep there in peace and quiet.

"No," Assistant said, and without further ado, tightened her grip, hooked one leg over Ari, and went right back to sleep.

Ari fought the urge to laugh hysterically. Assistant held her more tightly than any vine wrapped around a tree. Nope, Ari definitely wasn't going anywhere. And she probably wasn't getting any more sleep, either.

But perhaps Assistant had taken Ari's words to heart after all, because she didn't snore after that. She just breathed, deeply and regularly, on the back of Ari's neck, sending tingles down Ari's spine. Ari, who wanted nothing more than to go back to sleep and stop thinking, couldn't help remembering Assistant's breath on her cheek and throat, her throaty voice whispering in Ari's ear. Her offer of future pleasures that Ari was going to have a hard time refusing.

Only...why should she refuse? It had been Assistant's idea. And Assistant had promised not to hurt her. Something about it still felt wrong, though, in a way that had nothing to do with how she felt about Assistant, or even how Assistant might possibly feel about her.

Talk about questions that would have to wait until morning. In the absence of Assistant's snoring, and with the memory of pleasure still aching between her thighs, Ari fell into a very deep sleep indeed.

CHAPTER 8

In the morning, Assistant was no longer in Ari's bed, although the spot where she'd lain was still warm. Ari heard her moving around in the kitchen. No doubt she'd already called for breakfast.

Abruptly, Ari remembered *Paxium nollinium* and cried out, "Oh!" Then she flew out of bed, straightening her nightgown around her as she bolted into the garden, the cool dirt pressing into her bare feet. She'd neglected him for hours. The stars only knew what...

Whew. He was okay, though obviously drooping. Ari reached for the nearest watering can with shaking hands. If she'd been just another hour later—really, how careless of her. If anything had happened to *Paxium nollinium*, she never would have forgiven herself. Or any of her plants. They depended on her for their food and water, their proper upkeep—their lives. She was responsible for them. They were more of a family to her than her father was. Or anybody else, except maybe Assistant, and Ari wasn't so sure about that, either.

She didn't know what Assistant was to her now. A companion, someone to help around the garden, make Ari eat, talk with her—and, apparently, surprise her with brain-melting sex in the middle of the night.

Last night, all Ari had been able to think about was that she desperately wanted to do that again. Now, in the garden and without Assistant's arms around her, matters didn't seem that simple. They weren't simple at all. Had last night been a mistake? Would it ruin whatever it was she and Assistant already had?

Right before she'd gone back to sleep, when Assistant had stopped snoring, she'd felt in the pit of her stomach that something about this was not okay. It wasn't about how good anything felt; it was about something Ari couldn't name but absolutely had to figure out.

"What's wrong?" Assistant demanded behind her.

Ari jumped about a foot in the air, sloshing water everywhere. It spattered on her feet and ankles. She whirled around to see Assistant, fully dressed and looking like she always did, frowning at her.

"I heard you cry out," Assistant said.

"Oh." Ari grabbed the watering can tighter. "I realized, when I woke up..." She nodded toward *Paxium nollinium*. "I almost forgot about him. He wasn't looking so good." Quickly, she turned her back to Assistant and poured the water into *Paxium*'s pot, her hands still unsteady.

"I almost forgot him," she repeated.

"Well, you didn't."

Although Ari didn't look at her, she figured that Assistant probably understood what Ari was thinking about. She usually seemed to. Would Ari ever be able to return the favor?

"Come and have breakfast."

Assistant said it as if this was any normal day. Like Ari was just supposed to sit down, eat breakfast, and talk about the garden or whatever the newsfeeds said, instead of thinking about Assistant's hands on her skin. She looked around frantically until her gaze lighted on a tiny *billinallis* seedling. "No, I need to take care of this, too. I've got too much to do. I'll eat later. I'll—"

Assistant's hand was cool and firm as it closed around Ari's elbow and spun her around. Her grip was strong as she tugged Ari into her arms, bent down, and kissed her.

After one dizzy second, Ari couldn't think about anything but her mouth, and the way Assistant's own mouth felt against it—firm and hot. Assistant cradled her chin in one hand, tilting Ari's head to exactly where she wanted it to be.

Then she pulled away and nipped softly at Ari's bottom lip. Ari squeaked and felt Assistant's smile against her own lips. "You're delicious," she said.

Delicious. Lovely. Since when did Assistant call Ari these things? Maybe it was just the sort of thing everyone said in passionate moments. The sort of thing you had to say.

Had to. Ari froze against Assistant as she finally figured out what that *wrong* feeling was.

When Assistant bent down for another kiss, Ari turned her face to the side, and gasped, "No!" with enough conviction that it stopped Assistant, who looked astonished. That seemed fair enough, given how Ari was practically melting against her.

"No?" Assistant repeated, her eyebrows drawing together.

"You're—you're a slave," Ari said softly, looking at Assistant's chin instead of her eyes. That was good enough for her to see Assistant's jaw tense. Ari tried not to shove her away as she spoke the words she'd never wanted to say, that it hurt to admit. They were the truth, and this was a moment for truth.

"And?" Assistant said tightly.

Ari, who should be stepping backward and keeping a cool head, curled her fingers into the fabric of Assistant's tunic. Assistant, who seemed so cautious, tightened her grip around Ari's waist.

"Am I so lowly?" Assistant asked. "Unworthy to touch the great Lord Geiker's daughter?"

Ari looked up at her in horror. Assistant stared back, the ice in her blue eyes again, even though she didn't loosen her arms.

"No!" Ari said. "Are you serious?" Assistant couldn't really believe that. "That's not what I meant."

"Then what?"

With Assistant's grip on her so strong, with her eyes so forceful, it seemed absurd for Ari to say, "I'm supposed to protect you." She said it anyway.

Assistant's eyes widened. The icy look vanished at once. And though Ari had surprised Assistant many times by now, the expression that took over her face went beyond that—it seemed to be true shock.

"Well, it's true," Ari mumbled. "I told you before."

Assistant said slowly, "Let me see if I understand this. You are protecting me from having sex with you."

Put like that, it sounded ridiculous, but that wasn't what was really at stake. Ari lifted her chin and tried not to look at Assistant's mouth. It might weaken her resolve. Surely any second she'd be able to wiggle out of Assistant's grip, too, away from her body. She licked her dry lips.

Assistant saw it, and her nostrils flared.

Ari said, "It's a power thing, isn't it? I'm taking advantage of you. It'd be wrong. What if you ever felt like you couldn't say no?"

Assistant stared at her.

"I mean, you could." A breathless, nervous giggle escaped Ari before she could stop it. "You probably know you could. But that doesn't mean..."

Assistant finally let go of Ari. She let go of her so she could start laughing so hard she had to bend over and put her hands on her knees.

Ari looked up at the leaves over her head and fought back a sudden surge of fury. Assistant was laughing at her about something so important? She didn't take this seriously at all, when what had happened last night meant *everything* to Ari?

"Cut it out!"

"I just need a moment," Assistant wheezed. She waved her hand and straightened back up, her pale skin flushed with amusement. Her eyes sparkled.

Ari had never seen her laugh before. Why did it have to be under these circumstances?

"Ariana," Assistant said, "the day you can force me into your bed is the day—" She paused and shook her head. "I honestly can't think of anything. It's not going to happen."

She spoke with as much certainty as if she'd been describing the orbit of the space station around Exer. Just a fact, nothing more.

"You're here because you're forced to be here." The words created a chill deep in Ari's chest. "I know that."

Assistant blinked. Her amusement disappeared at once. They looked at each other, and Ari shifted miserably from foot to foot. Maybe she'd just cut herself off from those wonderful feelings she'd known last night, but she had to do it, just as she'd had to go to her father and ask for Assistant's freedom.

Why was doing the right thing so painful? Shouldn't she feel virtuous and secure in her decisions?

Then, to her surprise, Assistant reached out and gently brushed away a stray lock of hair from Ari's face.

Ari's breath caught.

"You are very kind." Assistant's voice had softened, as if in wonder. "And you feel things so deeply. Most of the time it seems like a stiff breeze might knock you over, but then—" She shook her head again and drew her knuckles down Ari's cheek. She'd done that last night, but today it felt different, and it made Ari feel different, too: flush with a new kind of heat, something deeper that went all the way to her heart. "Then you surprise me."

Ari's hands were trembling. So were her knees. If Assistant took her in her arms again, she'd be a lot less likely to collapse. "You surprise me, too," she whispered.

"I'm sure." Assistant's lips quirked. "You're not forcing me into this. Or into anything else." Assistant stepped in closer.

Ari's peripheral vision began to blur.

"Would you like me to prove it?" Assistant asked.

Not a trace of the ice in her eyes remained. Now there was only fire, burning even hotter than it had last night, as if what Ari had said only aroused her more. When Assistant had that look on her face, it didn't matter what she'd asked, because the blood was buzzing too loudly in Ari's ears for her to hear. Her fingers and toes were tingling, and the hot ache between her legs had returned. There was only one answer.

"Yes," she breathed.

"Wonderful." Assistant put her arms around Ari again and slid her fingertips up and down Ari's spine, burning Ari's skin even through the cotton of her nightgown. "Truly wonderful." Her eyes gleamed. "You said there was a lot to do today."

"Uh…" Had Ari said that? The last few minutes were already kind of fuzzy.

"You were right. There is a great deal still to do." She brushed her lips lightly over Ari's cheek. "It will take me a very long time to get to all of it." She kissed Ari's shoulder. "Because I will do a very, very thorough job."

"Oh." Ari's knees did, in fact, buckle.

It didn't faze Assistant in the slightest. She just tightened her arms around Ari's waist and chuckled. "Well, now is as good a time as any to begin."

Ari sure wasn't objecting. When Assistant touched her like this, *any* time would be a good time.

Still, while Assistant was obviously great at this, Ari still had no idea what to do. At least Assistant already knew that and wouldn't expect her to be an expert. She raised her face and pressed her lips to Assistant's.

Assistant inhaled sharply and showed no hesitation at all when she kissed Ari back. Ari gasped, too. Assistant's mouth seemed to take possession of hers, hungry and made of desire. She slid one hand up from Ari's back and into Ari's hair, taking hold of it and keeping Ari in place as if to make sure she couldn't run away.

Why would anyone want to run away from this? One kiss and Ari was already panting, her nipples as hard as they'd been last night, the sweet pulsing between her legs stronger than ever.

"Oh yes." Assistant kissed her again. "Now."

"Now," Ari said vaguely, just because it was a word that she remembered and could say.

"How about here?" Assistant pressed Ari against a tree trunk. "Up against your favorite oak?" She licked at the side of Ari's neck. "Or down in the dirt with your favorite little seedlings?" Her hand wandered up and down Ari's side while Ari trembled and gasped. "It doesn't matter. I will have you in both places. I'll have you everywhere in these rooms." She licked again and sounded almost playful as she whispered, "Because it is my will. And I shall have my will."

That seemed like an odd thing to say in a moment like this, although it was also oddly appealing. *I shall have my will.* A note in Assistant's voice made that sound so inevitable, and like something Ari didn't want to resist.

"I'd like that," she murmured, feeling more daring than she ever had before.

Assistant went still against her for just a moment. Then, next thing Ari knew, the clasp that held straps of her nightgown popped open beneath Assistant's nimble fingers. The straps went slack, and the nightgown fell open to reveal Ari's breasts to Assistant's hungry gaze.

Ari gasped and fought a sudden urge to pull away. Her pale skin was flushed, her nipples were tight, and this was different from last night, when they'd been in the dark and no clothes had come off. Now Assistant could see her. How could Ari have known what it would feel like to be so exposed? What if Assistant thought her body was ugly or something? She was so perfect herself that—

Assistant bent and put her mouth on Ari's breast.

Ari arched up, expanding and rising even as she grabbed Assistant's hair and clutched her tight, to hold her there because she couldn't *ever* stop doing this. For once, Assistant allowed the touch. In fact, she gave a pleased hum that vibrated against Ari's flesh and somehow made everything *more*. More intense, more powerful, when that should have been impossible. Every kiss and lick made Ari's breasts ache as they'd done last night when Assistant had teased them through her nightgown.

"That's so good," Ari heard her own voice saying—panting, really. "It's so good."

Assistant pulled away just long enough to chuckle, her breath a hot rush against Ari's wet flesh. "Ariana...I'm just getting started."

She meant it. Assistant's tongue on her nipples was alternately soft and rough, and her perfect teeth nipped and bit and tugged until Ari was practically crying. She'd never known that pleasure could make you cry.

Assistant switched back and forth between her breasts, her hot breath on Ari's skin. Sweat beaded on her temples, and her hair grew damp beneath Ari's hands. Her fingertips dug into Ari's back as she held her close.

When Ari's knees gave up completely, Assistant bore her down to the ground and, true to her word, had her among the seedlings. She covered Ari's body with her own, cupped and squeezed her wet, aching breasts, kissed her mouth. "Beautiful," she panted. "So ready for this. I knew you would be, I knew—"

"You kn-knew—" Ari arched her head back again as Assistant bit down on her collarbone.

"The moment I saw you in that red dress." Assistant laughed softly. "And I was right." Once again, she slid her thigh in between Ari's. "Wasn't I?" Once again, she raised Ari's hips to meet her. *"Now."*

Just like last time, it worked, and Ari obeyed Assistant, quaking and gasping her way through a feeling that was as much relief as it was pleasure when the wave finally broke. By the time she was done, she was too breathless even to moan.

She had to hold on to Assistant while she got her breath back, craving that comfort from the same woman who had just driven her half-crazy. Assistant's muscles were firm beneath her hands, more than strong enough to hold Ari together as she collected herself. Maybe it really was laughable to say Assistant needed protection.

She held Ari for a few moments, nuzzling contentedly at her hair and temple. Then she said, "Breakfast, I think."

"Oh," Ari whispered. "Okay." Then she remembered something Assistant had said a few minutes before, something that had nearly escaped her notice in the haze of passion. "This isn't my favorite oak tree."

Assistant stopped nuzzling and pulled back, looking at Ari with a frown. "I beg your pardon?"

"I said, he's not my favorite oak tree." Ari pointed at another tree ten feet away. "She is." Then she reached out and apologetically patted the trunk. "Sorry," she murmured.

Assistant stared at her. "What difference does it make?"

Ari stared right back. "What difference...?" Then she realized she was half-naked, and struggled to sit up, covering her breasts again. "Yes, it makes a difference! You know that." If Assistant didn't understand that, after all this time, then...then who would, besides Ari?

Assistant rolled her eyes as she rose to her feet. "I do apologize for forgetting your favorite tree." She reached down and pulled Ari up with one hand. Then she smiled slyly and leaned in again.

"No," Ari said, before she could change her mind, and turned her face away. "I'm getting a shower."

"What?"

"I feel dirty," Ari said, and brushed herself down. "And I'm not supposed to eat while I'm dirty. That's your rule."

"'Dirty'?" Assistant looked outraged. "You crawl around on the ground every day, and you're saying—"

"I'm getting a shower," Ari repeated, and headed for the bathroom, feeling sort of cross and upset, even though her body was incredibly happy.

How could another person cause you to feel like this? Physically sated, but emotionally off-kilter? Sure, it wasn't a big deal that Assistant had forgotten which tree was Ari's favorite, but to say *what difference does it make*, like all plants were the same, like it was ridiculous to get attached to them...

And to say it right after she and Ari had gotten as close as it was possible to get. The contrast was too jarring for Ari's peace of mind. She was glad when Assistant did not try to detain her again.

Her shower didn't do much to soothe her, and when she returned to the garden, she saw only one set of plates on the table and realized Assistant had eaten breakfast by herself.

~ ~ ~

Assistant left her alone for the rest of the day. They worked together in silence that, only twenty-four hours ago, would have been companionable. And it wasn't angry today, not exactly, just sort of tense. Tense certainly on Ari's part. More than once, she heard utter silence coming from Assistant's part of the garden, instead of the steady thump or motion of tools and earth. And she realized that Assistant was not working because she was watching Ari.

She also realized that they weren't going to talk about whatever was happening between them unless she brought it up first, and growing coffee beans from her own hair seemed like an easier proposition.

They ate lunch in silence and returned to work. Dinner was a quiet affair as well. It was completely ridiculous, and Ari realized that she was going to start screaming if she didn't get out of these rooms. So she gave Assistant a hopeful smile and said, "Want to go to the Observatory?"

Assistant looked at her through hooded eyes. It was an expression Ari had never seen on her face before. Not the usual closed watchfulness, nor the predatory gleam of earlier. But all she said was, "No. I'd like to stay here and read. But you should go."

At her words, Ari had to fight the most childish urge to stamp her foot and say that Assistant had no business telling her what to do or where to go. But if that was how just a few words made her feel, then going to the Observatory by herself might be a better idea. Maybe it would even be easier to wrap her head around this if she wasn't distracted by Assistant's presence.

So she nodded hard and said, "Yeah. You, you stay here and rest. We've had a busy—" She almost choked. "I'll, um, download—"

"Newsfeeds," Assistant said, "please."

The trip to the Observatory seemed shorter than usual—or perhaps Ari had just been too lost in her thoughts. The place seemed more crowded, too, which was just what she didn't need tonight. There were families here, parents with children, off-duty soldiers come to enjoy the view.

People who probably had sex all the time and might be able to look at Ari and see the confusion radiating from her face. Best to avoid eye contact.

Ari didn't quite know what to do in the Observatory without Assistant there. The superintendent was surprised to see her alone, she could tell. But she peered through the telescopes at the same old stars, gazed at the same old star charts, and thought of a million things she could have asked Assistant—who really did know a lot about stars— except Assistant was reading back in their rooms and wasn't with Ari. And, somehow, she managed to pass two and a half hours in the Observatory without observing much at all.

She returned to their quarters. It was late—Assistant was probably asleep. Sure enough, when the door slid open, everything was dark. Even the little light in the kitchen, which they usually left on, was out. If she turned it on, she'd probably wake Assistant.

Fantastic. Ari hoped she didn't break any toes while she tried to navigate her silent way to her bedroom. Where she might lock the door, because whatever happened next, she wanted Assistant to knock first. Really, it was just rude to pounce on people in the middle of the night, no matter how thrilling it fe—

Two hot hands snatched her, pressing her tight against an even hotter human body. A mouth like a burning coal pressed hard against her own.

"Oh!" Ari cried, seized with terror, before Assistant's familiar scent and muscled arms told her this was no intruder.

"You certainly took your time." Assistant began to kiss Ari beneath her ear.

"You startled me," Ari said, trembling against her. Grabbing her in the dark was a few degrees beyond what had happened in her room last night. It was *extra* rude, and yet Ari's knees were knocking together in the good way again, and the familiar heat was spreading through her body. "Don't...do that." She was almost positive she meant it.

"If you wish," Assistant said after a slight pause, and resumed nibbling.

"I can't see you. I didn't hear you—"

"I heard you." Ari felt her lips curve in a smile. Felt the edge of her teeth. "Your steps. Your movements." Assistant dropped one hand from Ari's waist to take hold of her arm, and pressed her thumb against the pulse at Ari's wrist. "And your heartbeat is very loud." Then her arms slid around Ari's waist and pressed her in very tight. "I'm sorry if I frightened you."

The words knocked Ari out of her sensual daze for a second. Assistant never apologized. "You are?"

Assistant did not reply, but trailed her warm, dry lips gently up Ari's jaw, her cheek, all the way to her forehead. "I have been very patient," she said. "All day. Don't you think?"

She kissed Ari's mouth again, and Ari's insides filled with heat. She'd never, ever felt anything like what she felt when Assistant touched her. And before she knew it, she'd melted against Assistant, kissing and being kissed, and not thinking about anything at all, for once.

"I couldn't tell," she whispered when they came up for air. "I didn't know what you were thinking."

Assistant kissed her again. "How could you? You spent the whole day avoiding me."

"That isn't tr..." It somehow seemed impossible to lie in the dark. Besides, a note in Assistant's voice had caught Ari's attention. "Did it bother you?"

Assistant didn't say anything for so long that Ari wondered if she should repeat herself. She must have sounded breathless. But then Assistant said gruffly, "I assure you, I can survive for a few hours without constant updates on *Paxium*-whatever-he-is."

"*Nollinium.*" Ari pressed closer to Assistant. "I didn't mean to be rude." Was that huffing noise from Assistant a laugh? "I just wasn't sure what to think about what's happening. I don't—" She couldn't help hesitating. "I don't even know what is happening."

"What's happening is that you're about to have a very good time." Now Assistant brushed a kiss across her temple. It was light and would have been tender if Ari hadn't felt the edge of her teeth again. "It's time for you to stop thinking, for once."

When Assistant's hands went from around Ari's waist to stroke and cup her bottom, Ari couldn't help but agree wholeheartedly.

They ended up in the bedroom again, and this time, when Assistant shoved Ari's skirt up her hips, she found underwear beneath. "Cotton," she murmured. "The stationmaster's daughter in cotton."

"It's comfortable," was all Ari could manage to say while Assistant's fingertips were stroking the hollows by her hipbones.

Assistant didn't seem to hear her. "You should be in Auroran silk." She traced over the rise of Ari's thigh. "I'd like to see that very much."

As her prefrontal cortex gave its final gasp, Ari vowed to order some Auroran silk panties with her next personal expense allowance. Then thought became impossible.

Assistant slid the underwear over Ari's hips, down her thighs, with maddening slowness while Ari tried not to squirm impatiently. The experience was strangely sensual—cotton easing down over her skin, pulled by the warm fingers of someone who wanted her, until she was fully exposed below the waist for the first time.

Assistant's gaze fell on the neat, dark thatch of hair between Ari's legs. Her lips curled up like she was two seconds away from licking them.

Ari gulped. This morning, she'd been so self-conscious when Assistant had looked at her breasts. Now she knew Assistant found her beautiful, and she *wanted* Assistant to look, wanted her to see what she was touching.

"Well, well, well," Assistant breathed, combing her fingertips through Ari's curls.

Ari's hips twitched again, and she gasped when Assistant's fingers slipped down between her lips, where she was slick even though all they'd done was kiss and take off some cotton underwear. Every nerve ending in her body felt alive, and when Assistant traced one finger over her opening, she groaned.

Assistant's cheeks were flushed as she watched her own hand moving between Ari's legs. "Have you ever done this to yourself?"

"Some. N-not much." Ari felt her legs spreading wider apart without any input from her brain. "Not in a long time. It wasn't...I mean..."

Assistant drew circles around Ari's entrance, then pressed down a little—not enough to go inside, but enough to make Ari throb. "It wasn't what?"

"Good enough," Ari choked. She lifted her hips again. "It wasn't like this."

"What a pity." The hoarse note in Assistant's voice gave the lie to the coolness of her words. "You're so ready for this. You should have spent years with your hands between your legs, making yourself come, enjoying your beautiful body."

I didn't know it was beautiful. "Uh, sorry," was all Ari could think to say. When in the stars was Assistant going to *do* something about all these sensations she was stirring up?

"And now it's my turn." Assistant bent down to kiss her mouth. As she did, she pushed forward with her hand and slid one finger inside Ari, who stiffened and squeaked. Assistant paused and pulled out of the kiss to say, "Does that hurt?"

Ari squirmed experimentally. "No," she decided. "It's just different. A little weird."

"Nothing's ever been in here?" Assistant sounded incredulous, even though Ari had just finished telling her she didn't have a long history of masturbating.

"No!" Ari focused again on the finger inside her, wishing the fog of desire would envelop her again, instead of beginning to evaporate. "And I guess I wasn't missing much, because it doesn't feel—"

Assistant slid her finger almost all the way out, and just as Ari was about to apologize for criticizing her, she pushed back inside and curled her fingertip up. She pressed with surprising firmness against a spot that felt different somehow, eager and responsive to the extra pressure. And then she began to rub it.

Ari's breath rushed out of her in an "Oh."

"Doesn't feel what, Ariana?" Assistant asked sweetly.

"I-I..." Ari walked back every doubt she'd had. "It's amazing," she choked when Assistant slid a second finger inside her while nuzzling her collarbone. "*Oh!* You're...you're amazing..."

Amazing didn't even cover it. Couldn't Ari do better than that? Why didn't she read more poetry when she was growing up, listen to more music, something that would let her know what to say in a time like this?

"I've hardly begun," Assistant purred against her skin, rubbing against that sensitive spot again with her fingertips. "Do you know how tempting it is to introduce you to everything at once?"

"Uh..." That did sound tempting. Ari rested her shaking hands on Assistant's shoulders while she writhed against the fingers inside her. She could only say, "That's...that would be..." *Fine. Great. Perfect. Oh, please.*

Assistant sighed as she began to kiss her way downward, pushing the top of Ari's dress out of the way so she could nibble at the rise of her right breast. "You have no idea how good it can feel. I'm going to show you." She moved to Ari's left breast.

"Now?" Now seemed fine.

Assistant chuckled, though it sounded a little strained, and she was breathing more quickly than usual. "So eager." She licked the very tip of Ari's nipple, which began to ache—an ache that once again seemed directly connected to the one between Ari's legs, where Assistant continued to tease her.

Really, really tease her. Just when Ari was on the verge of orgasm yet again, she stopped pressing against that wonderful spot and drew her fingers out.

"Hey!" Ari gasped, grabbing her elbow. "Wait—I was—"

"You were what?" Assistant danced her fingertips over the inside of Ari's thigh, so lightly it was almost like a tickle. But Assistant surely didn't tickle people.

"I was about to...um..." Saying "have an orgasm" seemed like the least sexy thing possible. "You know!"

"You were about to come. Say that for me." Assistant kissed Ari's hip. "Say you *want* to come."

"Of course I—Can't you tell?" Ari tugged on Assistant's elbow again. "You made it so wonderful last time." She tilted her head back and looked up at the ceiling as she struggled for breath. "I want to feel like that again. Please."

After a pause, Assistant said with a hitch in her voice, "Close enough."

She pressed her fingers back inside, stroked that sensitive spot, and to top it off, she swirled her thumb around Ari's clitoris. Again and again, and Ari's hands grabbed at the sheets as if that was supposed to keep her from falling into pieces. It was better than last night, even better than this morning, because Assistant's other hand went to her breast again, stroking and pinching her nipple, so sensitive now that pain mixed in with pleasure and somehow made it feel even *better*. "Oh," she cried, "oh."

"Say it," Assistant urged. She kissed Ari's stomach and flicked her tongue in Ari's navel.

Ari was too far gone to protest anything now. "I want...I want," she whimpered, "I want to come...please—"

"Soon," Assistant promised. She slowed her caresses. "Soon. It will feel so much better if you wait."

She couldn't be serious. "*What?* No, please—"

"Wait." Assistant kissed her. "Trust me to bring you pleasure. Oh, Ariana, if you could see yourself. You're made for this." She nibbled Ari's earlobe and whispered, "Made for fucking."

Ari gasped and turned her head, nearly whacking Assistant's temple with her nose. Assistant pulled back in surprise.

"Don't say that." In spite of her own need, Ari grabbed at Assistant's wrist to stop her moving her hand. "Oh, please don't call it that. That's a horrible word."

And it was. Not just because it was obscene, but because it sounded wrong, somehow, sounded like something rude and base and meaningless. This wasn't any of those things.

"No? Then what should I call it?" Assistant asked, her voice light.

Ari wished she could see her face better. "I don't know," she croaked, because the words "making love" wouldn't come to her mouth. She had a feeling they wouldn't go over too well.

Not yet, whispered that little voice inside her, and she silenced it.

"Then let's not call it anything at all," Assistant said softly, and slid one more long, slender finger inside Ari. That made three, and Ari felt so full, so deliciously full. It might have hurt if Assistant hadn't taken such care, and if Ari weren't so wet she could hear the soft, slick noises accompanying the movements of Assistant's fingers.

"Ahh," she moaned. "Oh, it's so..." She spread her legs wider. Assistant hissed in a sharp breath. "It's *so* good. Please—"

"Yes," Assistant said hoarsely.

Assistant thrust her fingers slowly in and out until Ari forgot about words and language and anything but how Assistant made her feel. It wasn't like last night or this morning, when Assistant had brought her to the peak as fast as possible. Tonight, she drew it out, and it felt like the pleasure had lain in wait until finally—finally—

Ecstasy bloomed inside Ari, sweeter and hotter than she could have imagined. Assistant had been telling the truth. Waiting had only made it better, and after all the teasing, it was arriving tenfold. Ari arched up, clenched around Assistant's fingers, and writhed on them while Assistant rubbed against the spot inside her that drew the ecstasy on and on.

"Yes," she heard herself gasp. "Yes—more—" Though how could she ask for that? How could you survive more than this? She'd thought she'd be ready for it by now. She wasn't. She'd never known it was possible to feel this way.

Assistant slowed her caresses and nibbled the side of Ari's neck, making Ari's whole body twitch in the aftermath. It was almost too much. "There will be more. So much more."

"Oh," Ari whispered as she sank, trembling, back against the mattress. She wanted to describe how she felt, but only one metaphor came to mind, and it wasn't very poetic. "Bees and pollen and...and stuff..."

"And stuff," Assistant agreed, kissing her yet again. She was panting too, and her skin was even hotter than before.

"Is—" Ari laid a hesitant hand on Assistant's leg. "It's your turn now. Right?"

Assistant hesitated. Then, to Ari's surprise, she took Ari's hand and gently pushed it away. "No."

"What?" Ari said. "Why not?" Then she figured it out, and flinched. "Well, I know I don't know how to do it."

"That's not—"

"But I learn fast. You know I do. And I want to." She'd seen Assistant's shapely legs (or parts of them), had felt Assistant's breasts and thighs against her. Was it so wrong that she wanted to touch and taste them as well? Wasn't that fair? Part of the deal?

"No," Assistant said, firmly now. She pressed Ari's hand down on the mattress. "Perhaps later. But not now."

"Oh." Maybe that made sense. Assistant had said they weren't going to do everything all at once. Perhaps Assistant was just trying to get Ari used to this whole thing and show her what to do before she let Ari fumble around with her own body. In fact, maybe Assistant was showing Ari what she liked herself. The thought made Ari flush all over again.

In any case, Assistant had said "later," and that was that. How could Ari think about pushing the boundaries when she'd spoken of not forcing Assistant into anything? She could be patient. Instead of pressing the issue, she sighed again and consciously relaxed the tension that had started to gather between her shoulder blades. When she relaxed, so did Assistant, who settled down next to her.

"This is nice," Ari murmured.

"There will be more."

It sounded like a promise, which was great, but... "I just meant this." Ari rested her head against Assistant's shoulder. Then she added, "Unless you start snoring."

"I don't snore," Assistant said flatly.

"Maybe not usually, but you did last night."

"Nobody has ever accused me of snoring before."

"Well, I heard it. Anyway, if you start, I'll just go sleep on my cot."

But like last night, Assistant hooked her arms and leg around Ari just at the suggestion. "You'll grow fur and live on Theti Six first," she said.

"That's not fair," Ari protested. Then she added, "You know, I've got some stuff you can put on your nose—"

"Go to sleep," Assistant growled. That tone of voice meant business. And since Assistant's arms felt so very nice around her, Ari decided she might as well obey.

CHAPTER 9

Seven days felt like seven dreams.

Nice dreams, Ari guessed. Well, maybe not "nice." Sometimes she felt bubbly and fuzzy and downright romantic. This was usually when she was by herself and thinking about Assistant, however. When she was *with* Assistant, nothing seemed romantic at all. Then it seemed scary and thrilling and not at all safe, no matter what Assistant had said before.

Assistant had developed the habit of grabbing Ari and making free with her whenever she felt like it. Although after the first time she'd surprised Ari with a trowel in her hand, and had nearly received a black eye as a result, she chose her times more cautiously, no matter how much Ari had apologized. And the things she did…Ari would never have imagined, never at all. And until Assistant did them, Ari was fairly sure she'd never have given her permission because some of them, on paper, seemed shocking.

But in actual practice…

It was like getting down in the earth and planting flowers, and getting the thrill of watching them flourish, compared to sitting down and reading about botany in a textbook. It wasn't the same at all.

Nothing could have prepared Ari for Assistant's hands and mouth on her, all over her, in broad daylight next to a *malinusis* shrub, or in Ari's bedroom at night, where somehow the utter darkness brought out darker impulses, where Assistant did things she didn't do in daylight, things that made Ari howl like an animal. Fitting, since sometimes Assistant had her get on all fours.

That should have felt humiliating, wrong, but it brought such pleasure that Ari did her best to maintain the position as long as possible. It let Assistant stroke that little spot inside her more firmly while she rubbed her thumb against Ari's perineum, and the combination never failed to turn Ari's arms and legs to soup. Then she inevitably came, collapsed, and Assistant purred wonderful things in her ear about how delectable she was.

On the third night, Assistant put her mouth between Ari's legs. At first, Ari cried out and tried half-heartedly to wriggle away because... Well, she didn't know why, exactly, just that it was more intimate than she'd thought anything could ever be. More than fingers, more than rubbing against someone's thigh. And it didn't seem possible that Assistant could enjoy it all that much—surely it didn't taste good?

But Assistant seemed to like it just fine. She laid one strong arm over Ari's belly and held her down, kissing and licking until Ari wasn't protesting, wasn't doing anything but sobbing and staring up into the darkness and whispering the occasional "Oh please, oh gosh, oh please."

It was incredible. Sometimes Assistant was gentle, kissing as softly and as tenderly as she kissed Ari's mouth after sex. Sometimes she pointed her tongue and used it like a whip. By the time she was done, Ari's lungs were aching from her cries. It felt marvelous.

Afterward, Assistant kissed her. Without washing her face or mouth or anything. She kissed Ari, and Ari tasted the sticky fluid on Assistant's mouth and cheeks, fluid that had come from *her*.

So that was another thing that should have been repellant, but wasn't. Not at all.

The next night, Assistant told Ari to get on all fours and licked her again, only from behind. This meant she worked at a new angle and could get at new bits of Ari, tease her in different ways, which felt amazing. And then—oh, then—she moved her tongue up until it was doing something that had to be unclean, licking at Ari's anus, painting patterns like a five-point star until Ari could feel herself twitching back there. She couldn't believe something like this was making her so wet, but it was.

Assistant kept her tongue moving, but she reached down and slid one, two, and then three fingers inside Ari, pumping them in and out—it stretched and burned, and she was still licking and nuzzling—

Ari grabbed on to a pillow for comfort as she buried her face in it and screamed and screamed while she came. When she opened her eyes again, Assistant was soothingly rubbing her back and whispering praise into her ear. She didn't try to kiss Ari this time, and for that, Ari was profoundly grateful. Getting down and dirty was turning out to be lots of fun, but it had its limits.

But sometimes Assistant suggested stuff that was weird. Not shocking or wrong, necessarily, but just plain weird.

"Tie me up?" Ari asked over the dinner table. Assistant liked to bring these things up while they were eating, as calmly and casually as if they were discussing a new shipment of seeds, while Ari trembled and blushed. But tonight, Ari wasn't sure what in all the stars she was talking about, so there was no blushing at all. "Why would we do that?"

Assistant blinked. Evidently, she had expected the usual response, and Ari felt foolish, sure that she'd missed something. And Assistant's retort—"Why not?"—was a little weaker than her usual.

"But...I mean, okay, I guess," Ari said, and shrugged as she took a sip of tea, deciding to be accommodating. No doubt Assistant would find a way to make it as pleasurable as everything else, even if Ari couldn't currently see the appeal. "If that's what you want."

"I'm overwhelmed by your enthusiasm," Assistant said, starting to look a little put out.

"Well, why do you want to do it?"

"Don't you like the idea?" Assistant persisted. She smiled wickedly. "Lying still and helpless while I do whatever I wish to you?"

"But we do that now," Ari said blankly. "Every day."

This was obviously not going as Assistant had planned. "But you would not be able to respond," she said. "To touch me. You would—"

Ari looked down at her plate. "I can't anyway," she mumbled. "You won't let me." She couldn't quite keep the wistfulness out of her voice.

106

Or the disappointment. Almost a week, and Assistant still said, "No, not yet," when Ari tried to touch her. Every single night.

There was a long moment while Ari waited hopefully for Assistant to relent. To say—

"Well then," Assistant said, and Ari knew that, yet again, she would not be touching Assistant tonight.

To her surprise, Assistant didn't tie her up, either. Instead she handled Ari roughly, biting her and gripping her until it hurt more than it felt good and Ari begged her to stop.

Assistant stopped. For the first time in a week, they stopped without finishing. Instead, Assistant kissed Ari more gently than she ever had before and stroked her arm and side. It seemed like her version of remorse. She was careful when she curled her body around Ari's before they went to sleep.

That was something they did, every night: sleeping together. And Ari really did like that, now that she'd gotten used to it—just like she'd started to love having Assistant around after her initial reluctance. It was very easy to believe that no harm in the universe could touch her when Assistant held her so close. Not that harm ever had touched her, not that she'd ever felt unsafe, even with pirates swarming around. It was just...

It was just that her life was so different now. Ari had always thought she was happy with her plants. Sure, she'd gotten a little lonely from time to time, but then she'd get wrapped up in another experiment and it hadn't gotten her down for long. Only now she had a helper, who not only did magnificent things to her body, but who also toiled next to her in the garden and shared her table at mealtimes and, shoot, made sure there were mealtimes.

Ari had said before that she couldn't remember what life had been like before Assistant came. That was still true, only now she wondered how she'd managed to live at all. Compared to this—to an existence that was tranquil one moment and thrilling the next—her old life seemed so hollow, so empty. Maybe that had been contentment, but this, this was happiness. She couldn't imagine living without Assistant now.

And no matter how shameful it was to admit, she was glad she didn't have to find out.

~ ~ ~

"Oh my God. Has this been here the entire time?"

Ari put the last bowl in the dishwasher and shut the door. Assistant's voice had come from Ari's bedroom, where she'd gone to have a post-morning-sex, pre-gardening shower. Ari wiped her hands on a dishtowel and called, "Has what been where?"

A few moments later, Assistant emerged with a wooden box in her hands. "It was under your sink, of all places."

"Oh, the Q'heri board." Ari dropped the towel on the counter. "I must have stowed it under there when I moved in. What were you doing under my sink?"

"Because I was excited to discover whether you'd run out of lotion." Assistant set the box on the counter. "You have."

"Oops. I'll order some later tonight."

"Promises, promises." Assistant opened the box and peered inside at the Q'heri set. "It's very old-fashioned. No holos, just wood." She sounded approving.

"It was my mother's. She liked antiques." Ari leaned over the box as Assistant pulled out the cloth bag that held all the pieces and then pushed the latches that let the box itself unfold into a Q'heri board. "Do you know how to play?"

Assistant did not look up as she straightened the board. "I learned many things during my time with pirates."

Of all the things Ari had heard that pirates did, teaching slaves to play complex strategy games hadn't been one of them. "Really?"

"Really." Assistant opened the tie on the cloth bag. Then she paused. "Do *you* know how to play, or is this merely a keepsake?"

A pang hurt Ari's chest. "I haven't played since I was very young." Her father had taught her. It had been a brief, brilliant period, perhaps a year after her mother's death, when he had tried to take an interest in her. He'd taught her to play Q'heri and taken her to the great gardens in the Capital on Homeworld. His attention hadn't lasted, and neither had the Q'heri, but the plants had stuck with her.

Assistant reached into the open bag and withdrew the pieces one by one, half of the little figures carved from mahogany and the other from pale oak. The overlapping circles on the board were ordered the same way. The board was dusty from disuse, and Ari rubbed her skirt over it, earning a glare from Assistant. She just shrugged in response. At some point, Assistant would have to accept that Ari would never be a hygiene freak.

"I expect it won't take you long to pick it up again," Assistant said. There was a lot more enthusiasm in her voice than there had ever been for gardening. It was different from her enthusiasm for sex, too.

Ari didn't have much interest in playing Q'heri, but she had a lot of interest in that enthusiasm. Besides, the morning had featured tedious repairs to a heat lamp, and a broken hose that had sprayed all over both their tunics, followed by a slip in the mud that had occasioned Assistant's shower. She was due for some relief. Ari tried to sound suitably peppy when she said, "We'll have to see!"

She made coffee, and when all was prepared, she and Assistant sat on either side of the kitchen table, leaning over the board. "Right," Assistant said. "Time for a brief refresher."

Ari listened attentively while Assistant explained the name and function of each piece, as well as how it was allowed to move across the board. She was surprised by how much she remembered. Nearly everything, in fact, and by the time they were ready to start, she was feeling enthusiastic herself.

No doubt she was about to get defeated seven ways from Celandor, but she wasn't really competitive. It would be nearly as fascinating to watch Assistant maneuver around the board, to examine the way she thought, as it would be to win.

When Assistant finished explaining the rules, she said, "Well, why don't you start?"

Surprised, Ari said, "Okay." She chose a soldier piece at random and moved it forward.

Assistant's eyes gleamed, as if this first move was somehow significant, and the game was on.

As Ari would have predicted, she was on the defensive right away. A few moves in, she realized she'd started without any kind of strategy or idea of what would happen after she'd moved that piece. Assistant clearly didn't play that way. She was striking out, arranging her pieces in accordance with some larger design Ari couldn't see. Some she sacrificed, and others she marshalled as if they were real troops, hemming Ari in until defeat was assured.

When she captured Ari's emperor piece, her glee would have been visible from Exer's surface if the windows hadn't been hidden behind trees and bushes. Ari couldn't muster any ire. It was nice to see Assistant so happy, and besides, Ari had been right—she'd had a chance to watch Assistant think. When Assistant thought, she furrowed her brow, pursed her lips, and seemed to go deeper inside herself, almost as if she'd forgotten Ari was right there in front of her. She was totally absorbed in winning the game.

The game that, now Ari had had a chance to get reacquainted with, didn't seem all that hard. Not if you had a good plan. Assistant obviously had several, probably a whole storehouse of them that she'd used before, but you only needed one—if it was the right one.

"Not bad," Assistant said as she began to rearrange the pieces.

"It was pretty bad," Ari pointed out.

"It was pretty bad," Assistant agreed. "But you were working at it. I could tell."

She could? So much for Assistant being wholly focused on the game. "I was. Want to play again?"

Assistant's mouth twitched. "Certainly."

Ari lost the second match too, but she put up a much better fight this time, and at the end of it, Assistant's compliment seemed sincere. Ari's chest warmed.

Right. Maybe the third time would be the charm.

It was Ari's turn to lead again. She moved the same piece she had the first time. Assistant appeared surprised, but said nothing as she moved her own piece—the same one as before, too.

Ari bit her lip to conceal a smile. Yes, it was good to have a plan. If Assistant took it for granted that she would do the same thing she'd done before, but do no better, then she would be easier to surprise.

In fact...what if...

Ari pointed to the dark circle on the top right corner of the board. "If I took that one, I'd get double points, right?" she asked innocently.

"Only if you had three soldiers lined up in the dark circles next to it."

"Uh-huh. So *theoretically* I could still win just on points alone, even if my emperor fell again."

There was no mistaking the nigh-diabolical gleam in Assistant's eye as she assessed the current state of the board and prepared herself for yet another victory. Ari wasn't in a good position to take that circle. "Theoretically."

"Oh, that's good to know."

"I've never liked the points aspect of the game. The idea that you can win even if your emperor is taken..." Assistant shook her head. "There's no game that requires a better head for strategy, but I'd prefer to play without points entirely. Sometimes I do. It's more realistic."

"Maybe, but it takes a whole dimension out of the game," Ari reminded her. "I like that there's different ways you can win. It makes you think harder."

She brazenly moved a soldier toward the circle in the top right corner, just like someone who wasn't thinking at all.

Assistant's lips twitched, and she moved her second commander to capture the soldier at once.

"Oh, darn." Ari rapped her knuckles against the edge of the table and didn't look at Assistant's face.

"You're bound to make mistakes." It figured she'd be gracious while she was getting ready to slaughter her opponent. "You did much better last time."

"Yeah, well, I'm going to get you on this points thing. I bet that's even harder to win that way than if I just took your emperor." The capture of the emperor earned the captor fifty points, and was also the end of the game, something to be avoided if your opponent was ahead by *more* than fifty points. In the second game, Assistant had gotten exactly fifty-one points ahead before putting Ari in a position where she'd had no choice but to take Assistant's emperor, and had therefore lost the match. Assistant might not like the points system, but she didn't seem to mind using it to her advantage.

"We shall see." Assistant didn't bother hiding the smug menace in her voice, her surety that Ari was on the path to a third defeat.

Ari said nothing. She watched every move Assistant made, all the time maneuvering around the board, ostensibly grabbing up points. Meanwhile, Assistant plunged farther down the board in search of Ari's emperor.

Then, just as she was about to move a lord one circle to the left, she glanced down at Ari's high priest and froze, holding the lord in the air.

Ari bit back a smile.

Assistant said nothing. Her eyes narrowed as they searched over the board. Her body grew completely still. She didn't even seem to breathe as she concentrated, weighing her options.

There weren't many. Ari had tied her up but good.

"Well, well, well," Assistant said after a few moments. She placed her lord back down in its former place.

"There's a couple of things you could do," Ari said helpfully. She pointed at the center circle. "You have a way clear to that. It's ten points."

"And then I give *you* a clear way to my emperor. I've only got thirteen points. I'd lose."

"Well, you could block my high priest by moving that soldier." Ari propped her chin in her hand and grinned.

"For exactly one move before you captured him."

"And then jumped two circles forward," Ari agreed. "And took your starship, too."

Assistant sat back and put her hands in her lap. She surveyed the board again and stuck her tongue in her cheek.

Then she threw Ari a sharp glance. "What if I moved that starship?"

It took Ari one startled moment to realize Assistant wasn't asking for advice. She was posing a test. "You can't, not this move."

"And by the time I could, next move?"

"I'll either have taken your lord or sacrificed my soldier right there." Ari patted the soldier's little wooden head. "Sorry," she told him.

"How long do you think it will take you to win this match?"

Ari pursed her lips and looked over the board. "Depending on what you do...four or five moves? I think?"

"Four, if you sacrifice that soldier."

"Oh, then I can wait for five. I'd feel bad for him."

Assistant rolled her eyes. "He's made of wood."

Ari held back another smile and crossed her arms. "So are my trees."

That made Assistant snort. "Point." She looked over the board again and sighed. "Very, very clever. I'm almost sorry to do this."

"Huh?"

Assistant picked up her emperor and moved him three circles to the left, then diagonally two circles to the right, knocking down a soldier in the process. She hopped straight over Ari's high priest and left the emperor right in front of Ari's; the intricately carved faces seemed to be looking each other right in the eye.

"What?" Ari gasped. "You can't..." Her voice trailed off as she looked over the board. Then her mouth parted slightly as she took in the formation of Assistant's pieces, a formation that had seemed almost random moments before, but that were now perfectly poised to execute the rarest maneuver in the game: one emperor directly capturing the other.

"Evidently, I can."

"But the emperor never moves around the board. It's too risky. My father told me that first thing."

"Just because he rarely moves doesn't mean he can't move. Most players are just afraid to take a risk with him."

Ari frowned while the two emperors stared impassively at each other. "It's not about being scared. It's more prudent for the emperor to stay secure. Same as in real life."

After a pause, Assistant leaned back in her chair and crossed her arms. "Really," she said, tilting her head as if asking Ari to continue.

So, Ari did. "The real Emperor never leaves Homeworld. He's the most powerful person in the realm. He needs to be kept safe."

"Mull that one over for a second," Assistant said. "The most powerful person needs safekeeping? You've just made your Emperor sound completely helpless."

Well, when you put it that way... "I didn't mean it like that. But you don't think the Emperor ought to be in a secure location? It'd be crazy if he didn't have protection."

"I never said he shouldn't have protection. But he and his ancestors have languished on Homeworld for generations now, completely out of touch with the Empire and its needs. A leader should go out among her people. Show them a good example."

It made sense. Ari's father had done a lot of that wherever he was stationed—at least, when he was feeling well. Ari looked all over the Q'heri board. "Well, if he did, he'd surprise a lot of people. That would be a good thing, wouldn't it?"

"Yes. Yes, it would."

"You sure surprised me," Ari said cheerfully.

Assistant raised her eyebrows. "That's gracious. You really aren't competitive, are you?"

"Me? No, not me. So, you'll take my emperor next move?"

"Obviously."

"Obviously. So that's sixty-three points for you..."

She moved her little soldier on to the center circle, gaining ten more points.

Assistant's eyes widened again.

"And sixty-four for me," Ari concluded. "Gosh, that was an exciting game."

Assistant stared at her, and Ari added "thunderstruck" to her mental inventory of Assistant's facial expressions. She had a feeling she wouldn't be seeing this one often.

"I told you I wanted to win on points," she reminded Assistant.

Assistant shook her head, and the stunned look vanished. "That wasn't what you were really trying to do. I saw through that immediately. Why do you think I—" She gestured at the audacious arrangement of her troops.

"I was hoping to get to your emperor," Ari admitted. "Looks like I can't, but I still won."

Assistant's mouth slowly opened. Then she closed it again without saying anything.

"I can see why you don't like having points," Ari added. "I mean, if it was just about the maneuvers—honestly, that was amazing." It was her turn to wave at the board. It might not be a flower or a tree, but the endgame was beautiful.

"So are you."

Ari raised her head at once to see Assistant watching her with a steady, even gaze. She barely stifled another gasp. "I am?"

"Right at this moment? I'd venture to say so. Nobody's made me sweat that much at Q'heri in years, even before your little surprise." She tapped her emperor. "I enjoyed it."

"Even though you lost?" Ari hadn't meant to sound so breathless.

Assistant rolled her eyes again. "Well, not *that* part." She tilted her head. "But I will admit to being...impressed."

Ari felt her shoulders drawing up nearly to her ears before she could stop them, while a shy smile formed on her face. She straightened up immediately and cleared her throat. "Well, so am I. You're really good."

Assistant's lips twitched, but the assessing look remained on her face for a moment longer, as if she was recalculating what she knew about Ari all over again. Moving the pieces around into something that fit.

Then again, Assistant already knew Ari better than anyone else in the universe, including Ari's own father. Not so long ago, the thought would have stung; here and now, it made Ari's heart flutter.

"You're good at a lot of things," she added, and smiled hopefully.

Assistant sat back in her chair. "Are you seducing me, Your Ladyship?"

Ari nodded hard.

Chuckling, Assistant rose to her feet. "Good news. You win this one, too."

~ ~ ~

Afterward, they lay in Ari's bed. They were still sweaty, but neither of them was particularly sleepy yet. And to Ari, it seemed the Q'heri match had opened a door of some kind—a door to her own past, at least.

"Maybe I could show you something," Ari said shyly, and when Assistant had nodded, she brought out the holo-chip she kept in the top drawer of the nightstand.

She pressed the button, and the pictures leapt to life. Ari quickly skimmed through them until she found the one she wanted. It didn't take long—there weren't many. She and Assistant looked silently for a moment at the dark-haired woman who floated before them in pixels and lights.

"That's my mother," Ari said. "Lady Fara."

"I'd have guessed it," Assistant said. "You look remarkably like her."

"Oh, no," Ari said. "She was so much more beautiful. Everybody said so." She chuckled a little painfully. "When I was a kid, sometimes I overheard people saying that it was a shame that someone like my mother had given birth to someone who looked like me—you know, gangly and plain and all that."

"Mmm." Assistant trailed her hand up and down Ari's bare stomach and thigh. "I do not appreciate someone disagreeing with my own assessment."

Ari blushed. "Well." She cleared her throat. "Anyway. She was so pretty, and she loved parties and music and all that. But she was a good mother, too—I don't remember much, but I know that. I have memories of her holding me and smiling."

Assistant nodded.

Ari took a deep breath. She was getting to the painful part. "But when I was seven, she came down with Etelian Fever."

"Oh," Assistant said. "Yes. I remember there was an outbreak about thirteen years ago."

"My father got it, too. He lived, but sometimes he still has relapses. The fever comes back sometimes, but not as badly. I never caught it because I was so young."

Assistant nodded again.

"So...that was my mother." Ari kept looking at the beautiful woman with the dark hair and warm smile. Life would have been so different if...

"You and your father do not speak much," Assistant said, sounding almost cautious.

Ari bit her lip. "Well, everybody's always told me how crazy he was about my mother. After she died, maybe I reminded him too much of her."

"You were his responsibility," Assistant said. "Grief or not, he had no right to abandon you."

"He didn't!" Ari protested. "I told you, he always made sure I was taken care of. He has more to worry about than I can even imagine. Or you, for that matter." That wasn't meant to be condescending—just honest. Assistant was immensely smart and capable, but she was a slave, not a stationmaster. How could she know what it was like to have Ari's father's responsibilities?

"No indeed. How could I imagine such a thing?"

Ari wouldn't give Assistant the satisfaction of engaging with her sarcasm. "And he's always been really good about letting me look after my plants. Wherever we moved, he made sure I could transport my whole garden with me, and that I'd get quarters that could hold it all."

"Yours are rather vast," Assistant conceded. She glanced through Ari's open bedroom door into the foliage. "Although it's hard to tell sometimes because it seems a little crowded out there."

"So, you see?" Ari persisted. It seemed important for Assistant to understand. "He loves me."

Assistant took the holo-chip gently and turned off the projection. "Yes."

"Well...he does." There hadn't been doubt in Assistant's voice, but you could never be sure with her. "What about your parents? I still don't know anything about..." *You.* "How you grew up."

"My parents were killed by pirates when I was very young," Assistant said, her voice as bland as ever. "But they kept me. I must have been three or four. So, I grew up among the pirates. I remember no other life."

This time, Ari understood her inflection—the *I'm-done-talking-about-this* tone. "Oh," she said in a small voice. Then she dared to squeeze Assistant's hand with her own.

"Yes." Assistant pulled her hand free. But her voice was kind when she leaned over Ari, put the chip on the table, turned off the lamp, and said "Get some sleep. We have a busy day tomorrow, don't we?"

"The saplings!" Ari said, and quivered happily.

"Indeed," Assistant said, and stroked her cheek.

CHAPTER 10

"Don't touch that!"

At Ari's call, Assistant's hand paused over the intercom button. She frowned. "Is it malfunctioning? It was fine at lunch."

"It's working as far as I know." Ari hurried out of the garden into the kitchen, pausing to untie her apron and hang it up on the rack by her shelves. "I just thought, it's time for me to honor my promise."

"Your promise?" Assistant didn't sound terribly focused as she looked Ari up and down. She usually did that when Ari's apron came off at the end of the day, and more often than not it led to very enjoyable shenanigans.

Ari wasn't about to let herself get distracted, though. "Remember? The first time we went to the Observatory, I said we could go to the mess hall, too. I never followed through. I thought..." She put her hands behind her back, lifted her chin, and let a teasing note enter her voice. "Tonight could be the night."

Her cheeks warmed. It was becoming easier to get a little suggestive, even to express a bit of open affection from time to time. Mainly she followed Assistant's lead, which didn't exactly go anywhere demonstrative, but she'd also covertly been searching for tips over the Infonets with her datapad. She'd even found a couple of romantic poems that would have seemed ridiculously sentimental once, or at least alien to her own experience, but that now made a lot more sense.

To her delight, Assistant responded. She didn't always, but tonight she folded her arms, cocked her head to the side, raised an eyebrow, and said, "The mess hall, hmm? Be careful, Ariana. I might swoon."

Ari grinned. "I've got half a bucket full of water left over from *Cambrensium*. I'd revive you." She looked down at her grubby skirt.

"Let's get cleaned up and go. What do you think I should wear, the red dress?"

When Assistant did not reply, Ari looked up and was surprised to see a touch of darkness in her gaze.

"No, I don't think the red dress," Assistant said, her voice a little rough.

"I thought you liked that dress." Ari blushed at the memory of how, exactly, Assistant had told her she liked the dress. "Wouldn't it be nice for me to bring it out again for you?"

"For me, yes." Assistant stepped forward. No, not "stepped"—more like "prowled."

Ari's heart began to beat faster.

"But you're talking about everyone else," Assistant continued. "Did you even notice how people's eyes followed you when you wore it that night?"

Ari tried to laugh it off, but it sounded much too breathless to be casual. "Oh, come on. Nobody did that. And if they did, it's because I'm the stationmaster's daughter and I'm hardly ever outdoors."

"And what a waste that is." Assistant was close enough to trace a fingertip over Ari's cheek.

Ari's eyes fluttered shut for a moment as the touch made her tingle.

"Not that I've seen a great sampling of this station's population," Assistant added, "but I'm having a hard time imagining that a single woman here is more luscious than you."

Ari looked away from her eyes even as her mouth widened in an unstoppable smile. "That's—that's sweet of you."

"I'm not sweet." Assistant's arms slid around Ari's waist.

Instead of looking up, Ari rested her head on Assistant's shoulder and breathed in her scent, felt the strength of her.

"So why shouldn't I wear the dress if I look nice in it? I'd like to look good for you." That had sounded as teasing as it should have—it had come out much too sincerely for Ari's peace of mind. She didn't want to sound as sappy as those poets. "So people see you out and about with someone who doesn't look like a complete disaster."

"'Out and about?'"

Ari heard the frown in Assistant's voice and stiffened. When Assistant put it like that, suddenly the phrase sounded a lot more suggestive than she'd meant it to. "Well—yeah. We'll be out of my quarters. Going...about. Right?"

"Ariana." Assistant pulled back, holding her at arm's length, to Ari's dismay. The darkness had vanished from her gaze, and now she only looked serious.

"I am delighted to get a better look at this station—believe me—but if you don't want attention, then don't treat your slave as your equal in public. Or, worse, as a friend."

Or a lover went unsaid. Ari's face flamed.

Before she could object, Assistant shook her head. "I know what you're going to say. What *I* am saying is a reality that we must both accept outside these rooms."

We. Both. There was no way Assistant had meant for Ari's mind to grab onto those particular words, but Ari couldn't help the glow they created in her belly. The stupid, irrational glow. Put like that, it almost seemed like Assistant was upset about it too.

"What does that mean?" she asked. "I'm not even supposed to talk to you? People talk to sl—"

She nearly gasped. What had she been about to imply? That slaves weren't people? Assistant's lifted eyebrow proved that she'd caught what Ari was now desperately trying to cover. "Owners...masters..." Ari was, technically, neither of those things to Assistant. Her father was. "You know what I mean. Slaves are talked to. What else should I do?"

Assistant's face had already relapsed into its most neutral, inscrutable look. "The normal thing would be for you to talk to other *people*, Ariana. Friends or acquaintances whom you see in the mess hall."

The warm glow in Ari's belly had entirely vanished, replaced with a much less pleasant kind of heat: anger. The odds of her encountering an acquaintance in the mess hall were miniscule, much less of her encountering a *friend*. All her friends were within the walls of her quarters. Assistant knew that perfectly well. "Well, I guess I'm not exactly normal, then. Look, do you want to go or not?"

Assistant looked up at the ceiling and sighed. "Yes, you little cricket, I want to go."

"Well then, let's... Did you call me a cricket?" Maybe Ari hadn't heard that correctly.

"I did." Assistant did not look either embarrassed or malicious, just exasperated. "Chirp, chirp, chirp, all day long."

It probably wasn't a nickname, but it sure sounded like one. For the moment, Ari decided to pretend it'd stick. She'd never had a nickname before. To hide her sudden rush of pleasure, she turned around and headed for her bedroom. She called back, "I'm wearing that dress, and you can't stop me!" Then, unable to prevent herself, she looked back over her shoulder, smiling.

Assistant stuck her tongue in her cheek, folded her arms, and said, "I do appear to be rather helpless. Go on with you, then."

Still grinning, Ari rushed into her bedroom, listening to Assistant's tread as she went to her alcove.

~ ~ ~

Assistant had obviously been imagining things. Ari checked subtly to see whether people looked at her differently in her red dress, but she noticed nothing other than the usual deferential nods or salutes. Certainly, nobody looked at her like Assistant did.

"See?" she asked Assistant in a low voice. "Nobody cares about what I have on."

A pause ensued, during which Ari thought Assistant had decided not to reply. Then she heard a murmur that thrilled her from her head to her toes: "I do."

She was still blushing as they reached the Officers' Mess, reserved for ranking officers and their families. The food there was better, the furnishings more refined, and more importantly, it held fewer people.

Unfortunately, Ari had forgotten that officers were more likely to approach her than enlisted troops. Many of them knew her father personally and wanted to convey their greetings while she fought to keep smiling. Her face didn't want to smile, especially because she'd also forgotten that slaves weren't allowed to sit with their masters in the Officers' Mess. It wasn't such a big deal in the regular mess hall, because so few enlisted troops had slaves, and sometimes soldiers and slaves even befriended each other, although it was technically frowned upon.

Lady Ariana Geiker had no such allowance, and when she saw the slaves standing obediently to the side while their masters ate, she almost turned right around and dragged Assistant out of there.

But Assistant placed a hand on her elbow and then withdrew it before anybody noticed. "No," she said softly. "We'll stay."

"But I forgot you can't even sit down." Ari's elbow tingled, the only pleasant sensation she could feel while her face burned with embarrassment. Assistant had hated kneeling next to her at the banquet. At least here she didn't have to do that, but still, they'd be able to talk even less than they would have in the regular mess.

"Trust me." Assistant ever-so-slightly nudged her farther into the mess. "Sit down, eat, and pay attention to what's going on around you."

A private wearing a dress uniform ushered both Ari and Assistant to a small table by a window with a lovely view of the stars. Even though there were two seats, Assistant couldn't sit down, which so ridiculous. Why were people treated like this? Why couldn't a human being, tired from a long day in the garden, sit down in a chair nobody else was using?

In her memory, her father's voice said firmly, *Don't ask questions, Ariana.* For the first time ever, she imagined herself telling him that he was wrong and she'd ask as many questions as she wanted about this barbarous practice.

The idea was so shocking that when a waiter appeared with a menu and a slight bow, she nearly jumped in her chair. Assistant, standing to her left by the window, didn't quite manage to stifle a sigh.

The waiter frowned at her. "Would Your Ladyship like to begin with something to drink?"

Ari almost asked for water, but then she caught sight of the Blue Bubbly, a fizzy drink in a shade of bright teal that had just a touch of alcohol. She couldn't remember the last time she'd drunk anything alcoholic—she hadn't touched her wine at her father's banquet.

And right now, she felt like she could use it. So, she ordered one, along with a glass of water to be prudent, and quickly tacked on an order for the first item she saw on the menu so she could eat and get out of here as fast as possible.

The waiter left. Ari fought not to fidget. She and Assistant had eaten in silence multiple times, though not as much lately. It was usually a comfortable silence, bought at the end of a long day while Ari thought about her experiments or what she'd do first thing in the morning, or anticipated what would happen in bed when the lights went out.

Silences, it turned out, came in different guises, and this one was awful. Ari couldn't even see Assistant, just feel the warmth of her body that stood at too far a remove.

"Pay attention," Assistant repeated, so softly Ari barely heard it. Ari had no clue why—pay attention to what?—until she realized someone was heading to her table. A colonel, judging by the insignia on his shoulders, though she didn't recognize him.

He saluted when he stood before her. Other people in the Officers' Mess were taking notice. A dim memory of etiquette scrambled through Ari's mind, and she made ready to stand up, already bunching her skirt in her sweating hands. This didn't have to be hard.

The colonel held out a restraining hand as she prepared to rise. He was a man of middle age with salt-and-pepper hair and a strong jaw. "Oh no, Your Ladyship, please. I just wanted to convey my greetings. It's not often we see you here."

Why did everybody point that out? Just because it was true didn't mean you had to make a big deal of it. Ari managed a smile. "Oh, well, thank you. It's—nice to be here." He seemed to be waiting for more. Uh-oh.

What would Assistant say if she were in Ari's place? Stupid question. If Assistant were in Ari's place, this colonel would have been too intimidated to say hello. Ari would just have to do the best with what she had. She held out a hand and fought to keep it steady. "I don't believe we've met."

He cleared his throat as he took her hand and gave a slight bow. "Actually, we have, Your Ladyship. Just very briefly, when you and your father were taking a tour of the station upon your arrival. But you met so many people, and it was quite a while ago." He smiled at her. "I wouldn't remember me, either."

That touch of humor was all that kept Ari from wanting to melt into the floor. "I'm sorry," she said. "It was a little overwhelming. It's nice to meet you...um, again...Colonel?"

"Colonel Haktari, at your service, Your Ladyship. Please don't let me bother you further. I had just finished my dinner and wanted to say hello, and hope you'll convey my respects to your lord father."

"I sure will," Ari lied. Then she remembered what Assistant had said twice now: *Pay attention.*

People usually didn't pay attention to Ari, and she didn't usually pay attention to them. But if Assistant had to stand back there with nobody to talk to and nothing to do but watch Ari eat, then the least Ari could do was provide her with some other stimulus. Besides—it really wouldn't hurt to learn to be more sociable. At the very least, she would have something else to talk about over dinner with Assistant when they could sit at the same table.

"What division do you work in, Colonel?" she asked, making sure the smile was still on her face.

Haktari was evidently well-mannered enough not to let his surprise show for very long. He probably hadn't expected much more than a greeting from the stationmaster's shy daughter. "Security and defense, Your Ladyship. The station's shields are undergoing a complete redesign, as I'm sure you know."

Ari knew nothing about it. "That, ah, sounds like a lot of work. Big project."

"It is. Lord Geiker has entrusted me with a first-rate team, however." His smile was a little warmer now, his respect for Ari's father obvious. "I obviously can't go into any details, but we hope to have the work completed by the end of next cycle."

Ari nodded. It would be nice if this sort of thing interested her as much as plants did, if this subject matter wasn't already making her whole brain glaze over in boredom.

"There will be a ceremony when the work is done," Haktari added. "I hope we'll see you there."

There would be no way around it. Maybe it was something Ari should make an effort to go to anyway. "You will," she said resolutely. "I'll be happy to tell my father you said hello." A memory stirred of something she'd heard her father say to his troops countless times. "Thank you for your service to the Empire."

Haktari straightened his shoulders, saluted again, and returned to his table, where two other men in uniform were glancing back and forth between him and Ari, curiosity evident on their faces.

From behind, Assistant murmured, "You handled that perfectly."

Ari bit her lip to repress a smile. "I tried."

"There will be more visitors. Just do that every time, and you'll be fine."

More visitors? That was the last thing Ari wanted. Thankfully, that was the moment the server arrived with Ari's food and a glass of Blue Bubbly far taller than she'd anticipated. When she sipped from it, she realized it also contained more alcohol than she'd remembered. Wasn't it supposed to be basically water, fruity syrup, and a touch of Mangerian rum?

"Better go slow," she mumbled just loudly enough for Assistant to hear.

"If I had any money," Assistant replied in the same way, "I'd give it all to watch you get drunk."

Ari had never been drunk. "Is it fun?" she whispered.

"Under these circumstances, no."

That was for sure. If Ari ever got tipsy, she wanted it to be with Assistant in the privacy of her quarters, not in front of her father's troops in the Officers' Mess. Nevertheless, she had to admit that a few sips of the Bubbly, taken slowly as she ate, helped her relax a little.

This proved to be an undeniable benefit, for Assistant was right as always. Colonel Haktari was not the only one to stop by and pay his respects. Ari wasn't exactly besieged by visitors—and it was probably her time with Assistant that made her cynically think of them as suck-ups—but four people stopped by her table, apologized for interrupting her meal, and then kept on interrupting it while her food grew cold.

She followed Assistant's instructions and just repeated what she'd said to Haktari. A polite greeting, an inquiry into their work, a word of thanks for their service. And Assistant had been right—it worked every time. By the end of the meal, Ari had learned about overhauled shields, the arrival of four top-of-the-line fighters next quarter, a series of upcoming drills, and an addition to the library that would make room for more children's books, along with creating a new area for them to play.

"Well, that's great," Ari told Lieutenant Arnistad. By now, her cheeks were starting to ache and her smile felt fixed on her face. It probably wasn't the best time to mention that her father didn't like having children on the station at all. "Kids are...great. Thanks for your service!"

Arnistad saluted and returned to her table. Ari looked back down at her plate of cold food and sighed.

Time to make an executive decision. She'd done her image rehabilitation for nearly an hour, she was still hungry, and Assistant had to be both hungry and bored out of her mind. Ari signaled the server and gave him her credit chip.

"Was the food not to Her Ladyship's liking?" the server asked, giving her plate a concerned look as he swiped the chip on his data reader.

"Oh, it was, it was," Ari said quickly. "In fact, could you have two plates sent to my quarters? I...didn't really get much of a chance to eat."

His lip quirked. He'd understood what she meant, and he sympathized.

127

Ari couldn't help smiling at him. How strange that such a small gesture of fellow-feeling should mean so much. Maybe she really should get out more.

"I'll alert the kitchen staff, Your Ladyship."

"Thank you." A flight of fancy prompted Ari to add, "And two glasses of Blue Bubbly as well, please."

~ ~ ~

On the way back to her quarters, she realized she might have drunk more water and Blue Bubbly than she'd thought, because she urgently needed to pee. Suddenly, the return walk seemed very long.

She spied a door to a restroom along the corridor and said to Assistant, "Um, I'm just going to duck in here for a second. Of course, if you need..."

Assistant nodded silently at the words "No Slaves" inscribed in small red letters beneath the restroom sign—something else pointless and demeaning.

Was it a useful protest not to use a restroom when nobody was paying attention? Ari's bladder informed her that no, indeed it was not. "I'll be right out," she sighed.

She used the facilities and washed her hands. A quick glance in the mirror showed her that she looked a little flustered—pink-cheeked, and her hair could use a comb. Had dinner really worn her out that much?

Maybe the red dress was bringing out the color in her cheeks. It was pretty, but Ari had no idea why Assistant had made a big deal out of it. It didn't look much different from what the other civilian women in the mess had been wearing. She patted down her hair and left the restroom.

Assistant wasn't in the corridor. Ari blinked as she looked to the left and right. In fact, nobody was in the corridor.

There must be a slave restroom somewhere nearby. Trouble was, Ari had no idea where. Might as well wait here for Assistant to come back instead of wandering around. She sighed, leaned back against the wall, and waited.

And waited. And waited. Waited while she grew increasingly nervous, not of the passing people, but why it was taking Assistant so long. If she had indeed gone to the bathroom, then she must be sick. Or something else could have befallen her, but what? How much trouble could somebody get into during a three-minute wait in a corridor?

She rounded the corner and walked until she saw the nearest data terminal. Feeling shaky in a way that had nothing to do with the Blue Bubbly she'd drunk, she touched the "Search ID" button and entered in Assistant's identification number. In some remote outposts where ancient traditions held true, slaves still got tattoos on their arms; here, they were given microchips just beneath their skin. It was something else Ari found barbaric, no matter what technology you used. People should have the right to come and go as they pleased.

But here she was, using the system to her advantage to find Assistant. She sighed. Principles were easy to compromise when you were worried—you could find all kinds of excuses as to why, this one time, it was okay to...

That was bizarre. What was Assistant doing outside a control room?

Nothing good. Ari's instincts were already propelling her down the corridor in the direction of the room. It was one of the station's data retrieval centers. Not Central Control where the classified stuff went in and out, but it was still barred to slaves.

As Ari left the mess hall area, the corridor grew less crowded, and when she rounded the corner and ducked into the side corridor leading to the control room, there was nobody there except for her and two other people: Assistant, and a guard who'd handcuffed her to a rail while she struggled and snarled, and who was currently pulling out a shock rod.

The guard pressed the button with his thumb, and the rod glowed red. Assistant stopped struggling. Mute with horror, Ari saw her place her feet apart and brace herself, squaring her shoulders for something she had obviously endured before.

Ari's tongue was frozen in her mouth, but her legs were working just fine, because—as if somebody else was controlling her body—she picked up her skirts and flew down the hallway toward Assistant and the guard. She wasn't thinking. She *couldn't* think, unless you counted the little voice in the back of her head that was shrieking, *No, no, no!* She only found her voice when she was nearly upon Assistant and the guard, just as he was raising the shock rod in one arm that didn't look very strong, not really, not strong like Assistant, who held Ari so close every night—

She wanted to scream, but she only managed to gasp out, "Stop!" as she reached out to grab his forearm before he could swing.

It all happened very fast, then. The guard and Assistant both turned at the same time, and Assistant's blue eyes widened even as the guard instinctively brought his arm down to fend off an attacker.

In fact, he brought it down so fast he whacked Ari with the shock rod on her left side with all the force that otherwise would have been brought to bear on a disobedient slave.

All Ari knew was pain. It drove out her breath so hard she couldn't even scream. Her legs buckled and she fell while the left side of her body caught fire. An electric shock rattled all her bones and made lights flash behind her eyelids. For a second, she wondered if she had been stabbed instead of struck because the pain radiated so viciously from the rod's point of contact.

Then it was over, leaving her gasping on the floor—sort of whimpering, really. The stabbing pain was gone, but every muscle in her body still ached, every nerve still moaned in protest.

"My God," somebody gasped.

Ari opened her eyes to find that a fuzzy world awaited her, and a fuzzy guard was bending down, reaching toward her.

"Your Ladyship. Oh God. I'm—"

Ari's tongue was thick, and somebody had sewn shut her throat. She still managed to croak, "D-d-don't touch me."

"My lady—I'm so sorry, but you require—"

Ari managed to turn her head, though that made everything ache again, to see Assistant still handcuffed to the rail. As Ari's eyes finally began to focus, she saw that Assistant was paler than usual, her jaw slack, looking as dazed as if the guard had struck her, too. Which had been his plan all along. To strike Assistant with that rod, and probably with far more blows than he'd just doled out to Ari.

"Don't touch me," Ari repeated, cringing from the hands stretched out to her, the hands that had been ready to beat her only friend. "Release her. Right now."

"Your Ladyship, I can't... She said she was going to the restroom, but I'm sure I saw her venturing down this corridor, and slaves have no business—"

Well, Ari thought vaguely, that answered the question of what Assistant had been up to. She'd become lost on the way to the bathroom. "Release her."

The guard continued, eyes wide with panic, as if he hadn't heard her. "And then she was insolent, Your Ladyship. Looked me right in the eye, used language no lady's slave should even know!" He no longer attempted to touch her, but crouched over her while he babbled his explanations.

Behind him, the shock was draining from Assistant's face. Her lips were pulling back over her teeth like a snarling wolf's, and red spots were appearing on her pale cheeks. Her eyes grew wild. She began yanking on her cuffs, slamming the metal links against the rail as if trying to break them with her strength alone. Even over the roar in her own ears, Ari could hear her panting with effort.

The guard turned around, saw Assistant's expression, and actually raised his arm, as if to ward off a blow himself. He'd deserve it. Nobody deserved it, but he'd deserve it.

Ari shook her head with a groan. The pain had obviously scrambled her wits as well as her insides. The ache was beginning to shrink, to localize around her left ribs where the shock rod had made contact.

She had to think. She had to think fast, because this was very, very bad. The stationmaster's daughter had just been assaulted by a guard, because the stationmaster's daughter's slave was accused of being in a restricted location. And, to top it all off, the slave was not, in fact, the stationmaster's daughter's. She belonged to Lord Geiker, and if word of this incident reached him, Assistant would be sent down to the mines in a trice, no matter how Ari pleaded with him, told him that the guard had lied and Assistant had just been on her way to the bathroom. Her father would send Assistant away and get Ari another slave as if one person could replace another, no trouble.

Ari licked her dry lips. Assistant was still making a racket, yanking and rattling her handcuffs against the metal rail. Someone would hear her soon. Once there were witnesses, there would be no fixing this.

"Assistant, calm down," she said, giving Assistant a direct order for the first time she could remember. "You have...*ow*...you have to be quiet. And you..." She turned her gaze on the guard. "L-leave me the key to the cuffs. Then get out of here and do...whatever it is you do. I don't know who you are. We'll pretend this never happened."

The guard just stared at her. Assistant, as if to prove miracles were possible, went still. The murderous look never left her eyes.

"This didn't happen." Ari wondered if her words were coming out all jumbled or something and that was why he had such a stupid look on his face. Why didn't he move? "Nobody gets in trouble. Nobody says anything. You just...just..."

She couldn't keep lying here on the floor. She sat up on her elbows, and when that didn't make her collapse, she pushed a little harder, whimpering again as the pain elbowed her in the ribs. Then she sat all the way up. Another sound wanted to escape her mouth, something super undignified that the guard had no business hearing. A squeak, probably.

"You just be on your way. Leave the key," Ari repeated. One glance at Assistant's face made her add, "And don't look back, okay? Just leave the key and go."

"But—"

Officers had been saluting her all night. Her father was the stationmaster and one of the most respected men in the Empire. She was supposed to be suitably forceful, too, similarly able to think on her feet and play the part she'd been born into.

Ari set her jaw against the lingering pain and made her voice as hard as it had ever been. "Soldier, I might not be your commanding officer, but you know who I am. You want to do what I tell you. Right now."

She rubbed a hand over her forehead and closed her eyes. Before she could open them again, she heard the thump of something hitting the floor next to her, and then the sound of rapidly retreating footsteps. When she looked up, she and Assistant were alone in the corridor.

They might not be for long. She had to hurry, especially since the guard might change his mind, turn himself in, and ruin everything. If only hurrying didn't seem so difficult.

Ari could only do her best. She took the abandoned key and struggled to her knees.

"Slowly." Assistant's voice was soft, nearly breathless, as she watched Ari from where she was bound to the rail. "You might be dizzy."

"I am definitely dizzy," Ari groaned. That didn't mean she got to laze around. She picked up her skirts so she wouldn't trip and clambered to her feet. For a second, she had to steady herself against the nearest wall and nearly dropped the key.

Assistant never stopped watching her. The red spots had vanished from her cheeks. She looked almost back to normal, unless you counted the wild look in her eyes that had yet to fade.

"Right," Ari muttered. She painstakingly made her way to the rail. She couldn't believe how much one single blow from a shock rod had hurt. How many times had that guard meant to beat Assistant with it? How many times could you *survive* a feeling like that? "Okay—let me see the cuffs."

Before she saw the keyhole, though, she saw the blood. The metal of the cuffs had abraded Assistant's skin during her struggle to get free, and now there were cuts and slices on her wrists, as well as reddened patches of flesh that would probably bruise.

"Are you all right?" Assistant asked tightly.

"Oh, peachy," Ari snapped. She couldn't help it—pain wasn't conducive to a sunny disposition. "Just like you. Why did you do that?"

"I told him I was looking for the slave's restroom." Assistant kept her gaze focused on Ari's fumbling efforts to fit the key into the keyhole. Her hand-eye coordination wasn't the best right now. "I'm not very familiar with the station's layout."

If her eyeballs hadn't hurt, too, Ari would have rolled them. "I didn't mean that. I heard him say that. I meant why did you cut up your wrists so much? That didn't do any good."

"Why did I...?" Assistant trailed off and looked at her wrists.

Ari glanced over in time to see her eyes widen, as if she hadn't even noticed her injuries until now.

"Oh."

Finally, Ari got the key into the keyhole, turned it, and popped open the cuffs. "Now we're both hurt. I didn't want to see you get hurt—that was the whole point!" She took off the cuffs. "Or didn't you notice?"

"What I noticed was you charging at someone who had a deadly weapon without even announcing yourself," Assistant hissed. Anger burned in her eyes again. "You're the stationmaster's daughter, which you should have remembered before you got yourself knocked to the ground. He'd have stopped, and you wouldn't be..."

She took Ari by the shoulders and looked her up and down. "He hit you." Her nostrils flared. "He *hit* you."

Ari pulled away, stumbled, and would have fallen if Assistant hadn't caught her again. Her cheeks burned. How dare Assistant be angry at her now? "Yeah, and we don't have time for this. We need to go before somebody shows up and sees us this way."

"Why?" Assistant asked. She let Ari go. Her eyes were still burning. "Why did you step in? And why in God's name did you send him away? He deserves to be punished."

"Are you crazy? You know what would have happened. I wasn't there when he met you. It would have been his word against yours about what you were doing, and my father would have believed him. He would have dismissed you." Ari looked into Assistant's eyes. Didn't she understand? "I'm supposed to let you get sent to the mines because you had to go to the bathroom? I mean, what would you even want with a data control center?"

"I..." Assistant pressed her lips together. She brushed a tendril of hair away from Ari's face. "I wouldn't. He was a small man who needed to feel big. That's all." She inhaled, then exhaled a deep breath. "Back to your quarters. I'll take a good look at you and decide if you need to go to sickbay."

"I'm fine. I'm getting better every second." Ari looked around for somewhere to dispose of the handcuffs and key. There were no trash receptacles or garbage slots, so she dropped them in one of her skirt's pockets and felt the weight of the cuffs strain the delicate fabric. "You just watch, I'll be dancing by the time we get back."

She wasn't dancing, or even close to it, by the time they returned to her quarters. Her head had cleared completely, but her side still ached, as if she'd taken a very hard fall. She was fairly sure nothing was broken; shock rods in and of themselves weren't terribly heavy or dense. That was why it was so easy to beat people with them.

Ari keyed in her entry code. As soon as the door had shut behind them both, she staggered toward a kitchen chair with a groan.

"No," Assistant said. "To your bedroom. I need a good look at you. Lean against me."

Ari longed to protest, but by now leaning on Assistant sounded like a very fine idea. "I feel pathetic," she grunted as she put an arm around Assistant's shoulders. "He only hit me once."

"You're not used to physical pain." Assistant helped her to the bedroom. "It comes as a shock to people who are so unprepared."

"Pun intended?" Maybe a joke would help.

Assistant glared. Maybe it wouldn't. Ari sat down on the edge of the bed.

"Let me see your torso," Assistant ordered.

I'm not the one bleeding. We should do your wrists first. You could get infected."

"Ariana." The tight note was back in Assistant's voice. *"Let me see."*

All the authority Ari had mustered with the guard was draining out of her along with her energy. She reached for the zipper on the back of her dress, but Assistant beat her to it, sliding it down and then pushing Ari's dress off her shoulders, down to her waist. The red fabric puddled in her lap. The handcuffs still weighed heavy and hard against her thigh.

Assistant lifted Ari's left arm as she inspected her skin. Ari looked down, too. There would be a bruise—a big one that would turn ugly shades of purple and green. It was already forming. Assistant touched the edges of it. "Tender?"

"Yeah."

"Hmm." Assistant's touch wandered up and down her side, but not like it did during sex, when she was driving Ari to distraction. Now she was careful, clinical, almost as impersonal as a physician—except for the dark look that was back in her eyes. She pressed gently at a couple of different spots.

"You were able to walk relatively well, and you're not screaming or pushing me away, so I'm guessing you haven't broken any ribs. Look into my eyes." Now she took Ari by the chin and squinted at her. "Your pupils aren't enlarged." Took her by the wrist. "Pulse is steady. I would have checked on this before, if you hadn't been in such a damned hurry."

"We had to get out of there," Ari reminded her. "I'm fine. Really. Now can we please take care of your wrists? And, um...anything else. Did he do anything else?"

Assistant straightened up and stuck her tongue in her cheek. "He didn't do anything to me at all, unless you count pointing his gun at me so I'd permit him to put me in handcuffs."

Assistant could have fought off the guard once he'd gotten close enough, whether he had a gun or not. Ari had no doubts in her mind about that—she'd never forget how quickly Assistant had thrown her to the ground on the night Ari had awakened her. But what would have been the point? Slaves had no right to defend themselves from guards. She'd only have made things worse.

Ari swallowed hard. "Would you please bring the salve from my shelves? Then go and wash off the wounds, and I'll put it on you."

"I can put it on myse..." Assistant trailed off. Then she sighed and left the bedroom, heading back out into the garden toward the shelves. When she returned, she tossed the pot onto the bed next to Ari before detouring to clean her wrists.

Ari opened the pot and sniffed its contents. Still fresh.

When Assistant came back, she also brought the standard first-aid kit that sat beneath the sink. All the private quarters had them. Assistant opened the kit, and Ari winced to see that she'd already used up nearly all the bandages and gauze inside. "I should have ordered a replacement by now."

"It'll do. You put it on my face when that sentry struck me, didn't you? Remember?"

How could Ari ever forget anything about the day Assistant had come into her life? "Yeah."

Assistant smoothed the salve over Ari's bruised skin, and now her touch was less clinical than before. It wasn't arousing, either, though. It was tender. Even kind. Assistant had never touched her quite like this before. What did it mean? Did it mean anything at all?

When she'd finished, Assistant extended her left wrist to Ari. Not only was Assistant's wonderful skin damaged, this was the only opportunity so far Ari had really had to touch it. She'd wanted to touch it for so long. Why did it have to happen like this?

"Shh," she said, though Assistant had said nothing. Ari gently daubed the salve over the wounds, trying to replicate the way Assistant had touched her. They weren't as bad as they had looked at first, now that Assistant had washed the dried blood away. She hadn't had a chance to struggle for long.

"You weren't going to break those chains," she said, not looking up from her task. "You know that, right?"

"I wasn't thinking clearly. Some reactions are instinctive."

But Assistant hadn't been struggling when Ari had first seen her chained to the rail. She'd been braced for impact. She kept her eyes on Assistant's wrist when she asked, "Reactions to what?"

Assistant said nothing.

After a few more seconds, Ari sighed, "Okay. Doesn't look like you need stitches."

"No. Just pass me the—" Assistant paused. "I assume you know how to apply bandages."

"Yep." Ari still wasn't looking at her. She didn't know why she couldn't. Just that her throat was thick, her lips were trembling, and her eyes were burning. Would she cry? Why? They were both safe now. Maybe it was a delayed reaction to the shock rod.

At least her hands were steady. She wrapped Assistant's right wrist, and then her left. "Do you know how long these will take to heal? We might need to get you a long-sleeved tunic or something for when we go…" Go out? Ari couldn't think of anything she wanted to do less than leave the safety of her quarters again.

"A week, perhaps more." Assistant's hand cupped Ari's face. Her thumb brushed back and forth over Ari's cheek. It was more important than ever before to hold back tears. "Ariana—"

The door buzzer rang. Assistant dropped her hand at once, and Ari gasped. Oh, no. What if the guard had turned himself in and somebody had arrived to investigate?

"Wait here," she said. She stood with a groan and straightened her shoulders. Assistant zipped her dress back up. The fabric stuck a little to the salve, but there was no help for it. "Right. Do I look okay?"

Assistant's mouth had gone tight. She reached into Ari's pocket and took out the handcuffs and key. "You look fine. Might I urge you not to do anything else incredibly stupid in my defense?"

"You can urge all you want. Just wait here. If they ask for you, I'll…" She rubbed a hand over her forehead. "I'll say I sent you on an errand. You're not here."

"Then they'll check the databanks and track me. They'll see I'm still here. That will only make things worse." Assistant put a hand on Ari's shoulder. "Tell the truth: I am an exceptionally well-behaved slave. The guard is poorly trained and lacks control. You were hurt, though not badly, by him. I think you'll find you've got the upper hand here. Just remember that."

That made a lot more sense. "Okay. Wait here," Ari repeated, and headed for the front door as the buzzer rang again.

Instead of opening it, she pressed the intercom button. *"Yes?"*

A woman's voice answered.

"Lady Ariana? I'm here from the kitchen with the food and drink you ordered."

Ari's mouth opened. Then she leaned forward and pressed her forehead against the wall. She laughed, unable to help it. *"Oh, that's wonderful. That's great. Come on in.* Assistant?" she called over her shoulder. "Dinner's here!"

By the time they'd set the table and laid out the food, even Assistant was smiling.

"What a relief, huh?" Ari asked.

Assistant shook her head as she opened the chilled bottle of Blue Bubbly and picked up their glasses. "It would have worked out. But I admit, I'm looking forward to a drink."

"Me too," Ari said feelingly. She took a big gulp before she touched her food and coughed. Was there even more alcohol in it this time?

Assistant sipped hers and made a face.

"What's wrong?" Ari asked.

"It's...sweet."

"Duh. That's why I like it. I'm not much for wine or beer or..." What did her father call liquor? "The hard stuff."

At that, Assistant laughed out loud. Ari beamed. Relief was more intoxicating than any drink could possibly be, and the sound of Assistant's laughter only made her feel even more lightheaded.

"Pirates drink something called grog," Assistant said. Her mouth still had a merry twist to it.

Assistant was volunteering information? This seemed a lot more benign than the story about slaughter. Ari sipped her drink more carefully and tried not to seem too interested in case Assistant clammed up again. She asked, "Have you ever tried it? What's it taste like?"

"It's hard to describe. Imagine a combination of rum, bitters, blood, and piss, and you might come close."

Ari shuddered. "Ew! Why would anybody drink that?" With all the raiding pirates did, surely they could steal better alcohol.

"It's something of a rite of passage. Once you can drink a whole pint without gagging, you can..." Assistant frowned. Then she shrugged. "Get drunk on grog, I suppose. I've never known that it made anyone a better soldier, though there's something to be said for a touch of liquid courage. Just a touch, mind you."

"A better soldier? Don't you mean a better pirate?" Ari couldn't imagine the eyebrow her father would raise at someone calling pirates "soldiers." It would rival Assistant's best efforts.

Assistant narrowed her eyes. "I told you, I lived among Mir's crew. They are different. There's no need to say anything else about it."

"But...there might be." An idea occurred to Ari then, maybe knocked loose out of her brain by the relief and the Bubbly. "Hey! Why don't you tell my father about them?"

Assistant froze. "Why don't I what?"

Ari leaned forward, and then regretted it as her side ached. "Tell my father about what you know. There has to be something good. Right?"

"No." Assistant pursed her lips. "Didn't you hear at the banquet? I was thoroughly interrogated when I was brought on board. I knew nothing useful to them. Do you think they would have sent me to you if I hadn't been vetted?"

"Whoa. Calm down." Ari held up her hands. "I was just thinking it might—you know—" She swallowed hard. "Well, they might free you, if you knew something good enough. Maybe it's something you haven't thought of before."

"Believe me, I have nothing to say to your lord father about Mir's fleet."

The lighthearted mood had vanished. Ari sighed. She should have just kept her mouth shut. "I vote that next time we wait to use the bathroom until we get home."

Assistant's mouth quirked. It wasn't the real smile she'd given before, but it was an improvement over the pursed lips. "Or perhaps I just should study the station maps and directories more closely."

"Or that," Ari agreed. It was silly that Assistant had been here for so long and knew so little about her environment, all thanks to Ari's own reclusiveness. "I'll download a couple for you."

"I'd appreciate it." Assistant took a bite, then dangled her fork over her plate. "You were very foolish. But also very brave."

Ari almost choked on her mouthful of Wistel fowl. Her face flamed again, and she managed to swallow it down. "I wasn't brave. I wasn't thinking at all."

"Now you know how I felt when—" Assistant stopped. Her cheeks pinked a little, too, and she took a bite of rice. "Well, never mind that. Maybe this sugar water 'drink' will have improved now that I've got some food in my stomach."

Now you know how I felt. Assistant could only be talking about one thing. She'd said she wasn't thinking when she'd tried so hard to free herself from the cuffs. All she'd wanted was to get to Ari.

What did that mean? Didn't it have to mean *something*?

Assistant sipped her drink. She grimaced. "No. Still dreadful."

"If I'm all that brave, maybe we ought to order some grog," Ari suggested. She ventured a smile.

At that, a gleam appeared in Assistant's eye. Her lips turned up in a smile that looked almost mischievous, but not quite. Mysterious—that was better. Ari wondered if she should just start keeping notes on the mental catalogue she was making of Assistant's facial expressions.

"Maybe we should, Lady Ariana," Assistant said. "Maybe we ought to see how well pirate life would suit you."

Ari snorted. "Or maybe I'll just stick with my sugar water." Her eyes widened as inspiration hit her, unpredictable as a lightning bolt. "Oh my gosh. You know what I just thought?"

"Is it about..." Assistant's brow puckered. Then she shook her head. "I don't have the least idea, do I?"

"Hummingbirds!" Ari slapped her hand against the table as her heart began to race. "Maybe we could get a couple in here. They're so pretty, and I've been thinking about moving more into flowers anyway." It wasn't like her pea project had led her into anything but trouble. "Wouldn't that be exciting?"

"I hope I'll be able to sleep." Assistant took a really long swig of her Blue Bubbly.

"Oh, you'll love them. We both will. They'll add a nice touch—of course, we'll have to clear out some stuff. I'll start making up a plan. Do you have any favorite flowers? I'll see if I can get some of those in, depending on how well I can regulate the temperature conditions..."

She trailed off. Assistant was looking at her with a resigned, but undeniably affectionate smile as she said, "Keep on chirping, if you must."

Ari's chest warmed. She lifted her chin. "At least hummingbirds are quiet. You'll like that."

"Indeed, I will." Assistant raised her glass. "To hummingbirds, cricket."

Ari didn't even bother trying to repress her grin. She clinked her glass with Assistant's. "To hummingbirds."

CHAPTER 11

As it turned out, it would take a while to get in some hummingbirds. They weren't exactly native to a mining planet, and they would need to be shipped from halfway across the system on the next carrier that could support animal life. Then they'd have to sit in quarantine for a month before they were allowed inside the station.

"How long do hummingbirds even live?" Assistant asked when Ari told her the news.

Ari bit her lip as she re-read the datapedia entry. "A few years in captivity if they're properly cared for. More in the wild. I only want two to start with." Better to start small. She could just imagine a score of dead hummingbirds lying all over the place because she hadn't known what she was doing.

Assistant peered over her shoulder. "Sounds like we better not get too attached to them."

"I'm trying it anyway." Ari slid her finger over the touchpad, taking in the pictures of all the lovely birds. "I'll do my best. And even if they don't, um, do well..." A snippet of something flashed into her mind and she quoted it.

The experience is better lived than not / better the bones than the untilled grave.

No response. Ari glanced up to see Assistant staring down at her. "Well. That was suitably grim," Assistant said.

Ari blushed and looked back down at the datapad. "It's part of a, uh, poem I know." It had been one of the famous ones she'd downloaded.

No wonder Assistant hadn't heard of it, even if it was well-known. Pirates weren't known for being poetry lovers. "I guess it sounded kind of morbid, but that's not what the whole poem's about. It's about—um—"

It was about love. About how it was better to know love, and lose it, than never to have known it at all. Even if the loss was painful. It was the sort of thought Ari would never have agreed with before, but now that Assistant was in her life, she couldn't imagine not having known her—even if she was freed someday. Even if she left.

"Poetry, hmm." Assistant backed away from Ari's chair as if it had caught fire. "Can't say I know much about that. I'm going to go check on those cuttings."

Ari couldn't help a chuckle. It figured. Even if Assistant did know about poetry somehow, it probably wouldn't be her favorite thing, especially sappy love poetry. It hadn't been Ari's thing before, either. "Sure."

She didn't stop smiling even after Assistant had fled from poetry into the thick of the garden. Assistant had changed everything. Ari hadn't wanted her here, but now her life before seemed sterile and lonely. She didn't ever want to go back to that.

It was true that Ari didn't know much about the world, as Assistant had said over and over again. But she did know that having Assistant around made her happy—happier than anything else ever had. Happy enough that she wouldn't trade anything for the experience.

A feeling like that had a name.

And it only seemed right to let Assistant know, to tell her how much Ari valued—treasured—her companionship. Pirate slaves probably weren't told that kind of thing very often. Assistant had lost her parents when she was very small and didn't remember much about them. Maybe nobody had ever told her that she was valued and treasured.

Or loved.

Ari could relate. She couldn't remember the last time anybody had told her that, either, certainly not since her mother had died. Her father showed he cared through actions, not words; he didn't even sign birthday or holiday messages with "Love"—just his name. It would have meant the galaxy to her as a young girl to hear her father say, "I love you." How much more would it mean to someone raised among murderers, whose instincts were to kill at the first sign of a threat?

Maybe Assistant didn't love her back. Not yet, anyway. But she must care, at least. Otherwise why would she still have those bruises on her wrist that hadn't faded after three days? The evening afterward had been so pleasant, too. They'd teased each other, and though Ari hadn't been up for sex, Assistant had allowed Ari to hold her hand when they went to sleep, the better not to hurt her side with the usual embrace.

I'll tell her. Ari swallowed hard as she looked back at the datapad, not focusing on hummingbirds, or on anything but this idea that refused to let go of her. *She doesn't have to say it back. I just want her to know. She needs to know.*

So, that night, after Assistant had given her the usual tender, sticky kiss, Ari struggled to get her breath back. Then she said, "You remember that poem from earlier today?"

Assistant rolled off her with a faint groan. Yet again, she had refused Ari's touch, but maybe that would change now. "How could I forget bird bones?"

"It wasn't about birds, and it wasn't about bones." Ari hadn't meant for her voice to sound so tight or so nervous. She was usually relaxed and happy when Assistant had driven her out of her mind before holding her close. At least her quarters were completely dark tonight, so Assistant wouldn't be able to see how nervous she probably looked. "Those were metaphors."

"Metaphors. My favorite. For what?"

Ari swallowed. "Well, taken in context, you see, the bones symbolize death."

"You don't say?"

Ari elbowed her. Did she get to make this declaration or not? "And *loss*. The poem means that it's better to—" *To love. Say it.* "To...have something meaningful and lose it, instead of never having anything meaningful at all."

"'Better the bones'," Assistant mused. "So, you'd prefer to have dead hummingbirds than none? That doesn't sound like y—"

"I'd rather have you," Ari said.

Silence. Maybe the absolute darkness wasn't such a good thing after all. What did Assistant's face look like? Ari couldn't quite get up the nerve to roll over and turn on the lamp.

"*Have* me," Assistant said.

"Well, yeah—I mean, no!" Shoot. "Not like that. Not like *own* you, I meant I'd rather have you here with me. Because I..." *Say it, say it.* She could hardly bear to voice the thought. It had seemed easier in her head. "I love you, you see."

Assistant's body went very still. Tense. Ari did, too; she couldn't help herself. She'd been right about one thing, though, she certainly hadn't sounded like a poet. But she had gotten to the point, which Assistant should appreciate.

Oh gosh, and she'd forgotten to add something absolutely essential. "Of course—"

"I doubt it," Assistant said.

"Huh?" What was that supposed to mean?

"People often say things like that post coitum." Assistant stroked Ari's hair. "Think nothing of it."

Oh. Assistant thought it had just slipped out of her because she felt so good. That seemed like an easy fix. "No, no," Ari said quickly. "I've been thinking about it for days. I really do." She considered. "What if I tell you again tomorrow morning?"

"No," Assistant said, her voice surprisingly sharp. "I suggest that you don't."

"Oh." Ari's heart was turning into a cold lump. So much for this going over well. She really had to say the second thing. "Listen, I don't expect you to—"

"You have no idea what love is," Assistant said, and Ari's eyes went wide in the darkness. "You don't know."

"What?" Ari tried to sit up, but Assistant's arms, as strong as ever, continued to hold her down. "What do you mean? Why shouldn't I know?"

"How could you? I'm the only person you see. Of course you're attached to me. This is an infatuation."

Infatuation? Ari cringed.

"No doubt it feels real enough to you," Assistant added. "But don't get too carried away."

"Carried..." Ari hadn't felt this hurt since Assistant had accused her of being a recluse. "H-how do you know how I feel? You aren't me." She heard Assistant take a breath, ready to say something, and added, "That's an awful thing to say to somebody."

"You don't—"

"And if you just listened for a second, I'd tell you that I don't expect you to love me back." Was Ari going to cry? Oh no. That would only make things worse. She sounded too strangled for her peace of mind when she added, "I don't expect anything. I just wanted you to know, I wanted you to hear me say it. That's all, just *hear* me."

Assistant sounded wary. "Ariana—"

"What's wrong with being told that you're loved? I'd think it would feel good!"

In the darkness, Assistant took in a sharp breath. Then she said slowly, "You'd think?"

Ari froze against her. She'd said more than she'd meant to, and Assistant never missed anything. "I meant—that was rhetorical."

"No, it wasn't. You think it would feel good, but you don't know. Is it what you want to hear from me now?"

This time, when Ari struggled away from Assistant, she meant it. She shoved with all her strength, and Assistant let go with a surprised-sounding *oof.* "I don't expect anything. I never have. I just wanted to tell you—that's all. It doesn't have to change anything."

"You don't even know me. You know nothing about me. You have no idea—"

"Just because you won't tell me! But what do you mean, I don't know anything about you?" Ari sat up and fisted the sheets in her hands. "I might not know everything, but I know some things. I know you like praying mantises, and having sex with me, and Q'heri, and you're funny sometimes, and..."

"That is hardly a basis for—"

"And I know sometimes you can be horrible! Like right now!"

Then Ari put her hand over her mouth. She certainly hadn't planned to say anything like that tonight. How had it all gone so wrong, so fast?

"You know I'm horrible, do you?" Assistant asked, a definite edge to her voice. Ari heard her sitting up too.

This was ridiculous. She turned around and fumbled in the darkness until she found the lamp by her bed. When the room filled with soft light, she turned back to scowl at Assistant, only to find Assistant giving her a cold look that Ari hadn't seen on her face in a long time.

If she is dangerous, Ari's father had warned, what seemed like an eternity ago. Ari should have listened. Yes, Assistant was dangerous, in a way he could never have anticipated. This woman with the cold eyes could break Ari's heart into pieces if she wanted.

"Not always horrible," Ari managed, trying to keep a lid on her temper. They both needed to be reasonable about this before Ari's heart did, in fact, break. Why had it gotten so complicated? Why couldn't anything ever be simple and straightforward where Assistant was concerned? "I mean, most of the time you're really ni—" *Nice* was not correct. "You're only horrible sometimes, and everybody is sometimes."

Judging by Assistant's expression, that hadn't been the right thing to say, either.

"Oh, shoot. I'm sure I am, too—"

Assistant ground her jaw and looked away. "I'm going to my alcove."

"What? No!" Ari said. "What's going on? Why are you upset? How many times do I have to tell you, I don't need you to say it, too."

"Good." Assistant rose from the bed. Her face was flushed, though whether that was from anger or sex, Ari couldn't tell. Her silver forelock dangled over her brow, a stark contrast to the black hair Ari loved running her fingers through. It was one of the few parts of Assistant she'd ever been allowed to touch. Assistant had her arms down by her sides, but she'd curled her hands into fists.

"Because I'm not going to," Assistant continued.

Ari's heart fell. She hadn't realized until now how much she'd sort of been hoping that Assistant would after all.

"Because I don't," Assistant said. "Because love is not what I know. In the world of pirates, loves makes you stupid. Love makes you *weak.*"

"But you aren't with the pirates anymore!" Ari leaned forward, clasping her hands. She was stark naked, and Assistant's slave tunic somehow seemed more impenetrable than armor. "You're with me!"

For some reason, Assistant's lips pulled back over her teeth for a second, just as they had when she was furious at the guard. Only a second. Then she said, her voice hoarse and brimful of rage, "*I know!*" She whirled on her feet and stalked to the door, her hands still clenched into fists. The door hissed open.

It had taken Ari far too long to get enough breath to speak. She managed to croak "Wait," but Assistant was already gone without another word as the door closed behind her.

Ari didn't move. Everything in Assistant's face and body had warned her not to follow. Ari had never seen her so angry. She'd never seen anybody so angry. *Why?*

She flopped back down on the bed while her heart hammered in her chest. Why so angry, indeed? Ari could only think of one thing— Assistant might be tired of Ari's constant reminders that she was safe here, that she never had to go back to Mír's crew. Maybe it sounded like Ari was trying to lord it over her instead of being a friend and protector. It was just so hard to figure her out, and Ari didn't have the best insight into the subtleties of social cues.

Assistant usually knew what Ari meant, even if she expressed it clumsily, but she seemed to have missed the mark tonight. By a lot.

Realizing she was trembling, Ari slid beneath her blanket, alone for the first time in eleven nights. Only eleven nights after twenty years of solitude, and sleeping alone already felt unnatural.

So much for love.

~ ~ ~

The next day, they didn't say anything about it. They ate both breakfast and lunch separately. Assistant didn't make advances to Ari in the garden, or the kitchen, or the bathroom, or anywhere else.

This might or might not have been a good thing. On the one hand, Ari was still working through the bizarre fight they'd had the night before, and she wasn't sure she even wanted advances; on the other hand, everything felt wrong today. She and Assistant should either be working in companionable silence, or talking about gardening, or Assistant should be listening patiently while Ari chirped at her, watching her with that odd affection.

Or pouncing lustfully on her. Either one.

Assistant always did the pouncing. She didn't want to be touched, so Ari was sure she didn't want to be pounced on, either—especially given her usual reaction to being surprised.

She'd sure seemed surprised last night, though. Assistant hadn't thrown a punch, but Ari had felt winded all the same. Now, after hours of the silent treatment, her anger and confusion were beating a retreat, and she was left only with the urge to apologize to Assistant. That was unthinkable, though. Why apologize for loving somebody? How was Ari supposed to see the most wonderful thing that had ever happened to her as something she ought to be sorry for?

But they couldn't go on like this, either. One of them had to say something. Assistant never would. Surely, she'd said her piece last night by insisting that Ari didn't truly love her and that she didn't know anything about love herself. The second thing explained the first, since

Assistant obviously wouldn't recognize love if it bit her on the ankle, but there didn't seem to be anything else for her to say on the subject.

Ari should have predicted that Assistant might not say anything, but she would most certainly *do* something.

They did eat dinner together because Ari couldn't stand another silent second. She wouldn't take back her confession of love, but she could apologize to Assistant for making her uncomfortable with it. Say she hadn't meant to. Maybe that would be enough and they could go back to normal.

She didn't get a chance. The words kept sticking in her throat. Then, in the middle of dinner, Assistant threw down her spoon, stood, and pulled Ari out of her chair. Ari gasped, but Assistant silenced that with a hard kiss. Then another.

Ari wrapped her arms around the woman she loved and kissed back with her whole heart. Kisses seemed to solve everything.

She'd never known that before.

When they stopped for breath, she gasped, "Um...I—"

"Hush," Assistant said roughly, and dragged Ari to her alcove without another word.

They hadn't done it there yet. They had a tacit understanding that the alcove was Assistant's space alone. But this evening Assistant pressed Ari down on the narrow bed, muttered, "Here—yes—in here," and did her very best to devour Ari whole.

And tonight, Assistant—who was usually very quiet, compared to Ari—moaned while Ari writhed beneath her, growled when she had her hand between Ari's legs, hissed and sighed as she took Ari's nipples in her mouth. She made Ari come again and again, melted her right into the thin mattress that felt as heavenly as a cloud.

And when Ari was whimpering with exhaustion and sensory overload, when she just couldn't take any more, Assistant kissed her and whispered, "We do not need love, you and I. Do you see?" She kissed Ari's throat as hungrily as if they hadn't been going at it for over an hour. "Don't you understand?"

"No," Ari whispered. But then, before Assistant could get any ideas, she grabbed her arm and said, "That's okay, though. I mean, I, I don't mind."

She did mind. But what could she say? She couldn't make Assistant love her. She could only make Assistant not want to leave their bed in the middle of the night. And Assistant liked her, anyway, which was better than nothing.

Anything was better than nothing. That was practically a scientific truth, wasn't it? And she'd had nothing before, so anything was better now. It was perfectly simple.

"Good." Assistant finally gave her the usual gentle kiss. "Good," she repeated softly, and stroked Ari's hair.

Ari tried to be as happy as she'd been twenty-four hours ago. Her love confession hadn't exactly gone as she'd planned, but now she could see that things could have been a lot worse.

Then Assistant said, out of the blue, "Did you ever send your letter to that botany magazine?"

"Huh? I mean, no," Ari said, nonplussed. "I got a little, er, distracted." She paused. "By you."

Assistant chuckled. "Do you still have the draft?"

Ten minutes later, they were curled up on Ari's bed, Ari resting her head on Assistant's shoulder while Assistant made suggestions on how to write an extremely nasty letter. Ari refused to follow all of them—she especially thought the insinuations about Dr. Phylyxas's parentage were inappropriate—but by the time they were done, they had a letter that she never would have written by herself, but which she had to admit was both accurate and cutting. As it happened, Assistant had quite a lot to say on the subject of "pillaging," as she called it.

"Am I really going to send it?" Ari asked breathlessly, her fingertip hovering over the 'Send' key.

"If you're not, I am," Assistant said. She took Ari's hand in her own and bore gently down on it until Ari, laughing, hit the key and watched their letter go flying off into the Infonets, toward a junior editor at *Botany Today.*

"Oh, wow," she said.

"I couldn't have put it better myself," Assistant replied.

~ ~ ~

They were at opposite ends of the garden three days later. Assistant was bedding down some *Filas mnthali* while Ari checked on *cambrensium*. His weekly nutrient infusions were going well, and his grafts were taking excellently. She remembered the first time Assistant had helped her with the infusions—she always did, whenever she worked with *cambrensium*—and blushed yet again, thinking of Assistant's legs. She hadn't realized what she was feeling, not exactly, not then. But in hindsight it seemed so obvious. And just thinking about it now, she got the usual little tingle between her thighs; the little shiver up and down her spine.

"Are your grafts coming along?" Assistant called, and Ari almost jumped.

She thought about saying that the grafts were fine and maybe they could have sex now. Assistant might not like being pounced on, but she loved it when Ari made the occasional suggestion or overture. But for some reason Ari didn't reply today. She wasn't sure why she was being so quiet, or why her heart had suddenly started thumping pleasantly.

"Ariana?" Now Ari could hear the frown in Assistant's voice. "Where are you?" She sounded puzzled, and maybe even a little concerned.

Ari got a warm glow that had nothing to do with sex. Maybe it had a little to do with love.

She heard a faint rustle. Assistant standing up.

"If you're passed out from fertilizer fumes, so help me," she grumbled, and Ari felt a pang of remorse for worrying her needlessly. "Ouch!" she added, and Ari realized she'd stubbed her toe for the second time on a pesky outgrown root.

Assistant wasn't the kind of person who stubbed her toes, and the thought (plus the look that was probably on her face) made Ari giggle. She quickly covered her mouth with her hand, but it was too late.

Then everything went still and silent. "Ariana?" This time Assistant's voice drawled with possibilities. "What are you up to?"

Ari grinned so hard her face hurt, and bit her bottom lip. She gathered up her skirts and crept, almost crawling, to a new hiding place behind *malinusis*. Then she reached down, picked up a micropine cone, and tossed it to her right so that it would make a noise.

"Hide and seek?" Ari shivered at the soft menace in Assistant's voice. She was reasonably sure it was a pleasant shiver. "At your age?" A pause. "Very well. Just so long as you understand what I win at the end."

This time Ari's shiver was definitely pleasant. She huddled up into a smaller ball, her heart pounding.

But then there was nothing but silence. No more taunts from Assistant, no sounds of moving in the undergrowth, of seeking. Ari suddenly remembered how Assistant had leaped on her in the darkness on their second night together. But she hadn't been expecting it then, hadn't been listening for it, and now she was. And she still couldn't hear anything.

Her excitement suddenly blended with fear. Which was so strange— Assistant had said she'd never hurt Ari, and she hadn't except for that once when she'd been too rough in bed. Even then she'd stopped as soon as she'd realized what she was doing, as soon as Ari asked her to. So there was no reason to feel apprehension, instead of the giddy glee of a few seconds before.

Just...it'd be nice if maybe Assistant could make a little noise.

Or maybe she was just standing still. Trying to freak Ari out. Which was working beautifully, and Ari was ridiculous for falling for it so easily. Assistant was obviously trying to lure Ari out of hiding by confusing her. Maybe she was even standing very close by. As quietly as she could, moving as little as possible, Ari peeked around the shrub.

Nothing. Just leaves and ferns and soil and seedlings. Paranoid now, Ari looked over her shoulder. Nothing behind her, either. Or to either side. As far as she could tell, she was the only person in the whole garden. Except the front door hadn't open or shut, and Ari knew Assistant was out there—in here—somewhere.

Her heart was pounding harder than ever, and she was sweating and trembling a little. Adrenaline rushed through her until she couldn't tell if it was fear or excitement or what, only that it made her feel completely and totally alive. This had never happened before Assistant. Never. She almost wanted to call out, to end the game and tell Assistant where she was, but she didn't—she—

A cool fingertip tapped her on the shoulder.

Ari gasped and looked up, just in time to be shoved back down in the dirt by Assistant, who hadn't been standing there only five seconds ago, or anywhere in sight. Ari had no chance to respond before Assistant covered her body with her own, grabbed Ari's face in her hands, and kissed her so greedily that Ari wondered if she'd ever breathe again. Without preamble, Assistant reached down and cupped Ari between her legs, through her dress, squeezing and rubbing, and Ari came with a wheezing cry.

Adrenaline, plus the lack of oxygen, made it feel like she came all the way from the crown of her head to the tips of her toes in one exquisite spasm of sensation. When she was done, the room was spinning in and out of focus while she struggled for air.

"I win," Assistant said.

Ari gulped, wheezed again, and managed, "Me, too."

Assistant laughed. Ari blinked. It was a real laugh, such a wonderful sound. If only Ari could hear it every day. Now she laughed breathlessly, too, until Assistant kissed her again, still laughing and making no move to get up from the ground.

"We do not need love."

Assistant had said that. But maybe she hadn't meant it. Not completely. Maybe she loved Ari just a little bit, and felt like she couldn't say it. It was possible, right? Anything was possible in a universe as vast as the one that lay beyond the station.

Ari wrapped her arms around Assistant while Assistant nuzzled at her neck and decided that a little would be good enough, if she could get it.

CHAPTER 12

Lord Geiker died forty-eight hours later. Ari never saw it coming.

The day had begun as usual. Assistant had graciously permitted her to finish tending their saplings before pressing her against an oak tree—her favorite this time—and sliding her fingertips up the inside of Ari's thigh.

"Why don't you just go naked all day?" she suggested. "I'd enjoy that very much." She squeezed Ari's thigh. "Seeing this at every turn."

"Oh, no," Ari said, firmly prepared to refuse if Assistant pressed the issue. "I'd get scratches everywhere."

"True," Assistant acknowledged. She patted Ari's thigh. "I don't want this damaged." She leaned in, bit Ari's earlobe, and whispered. "It pleases me exactly as it is. Your skin."

"Oh." Ari shivered. Assistant's skin pleased her, too—at least, what she'd seen of it. Should she say so? She arched up as Assistant's hand crept higher. "I...you know, I also like—"

The door buzzed. Ari jumped and gasped, and Assistant pulled away in surprise. Ari quickly straightened her dress, wishing hard for her underwear, while Assistant smirked at her and headed to answer the door.

An official stood there, dressed in deep blue. The color of mourning. And he regarded Ari with solemn, sad eyes.

Ari, who'd just arrived in the kitchen, knew immediately what had happened. Judging by Assistant's stiff posture and closed expression, she had figured it out, too.

"Your Ladyship," the official said quietly, "it is my sad duty to inform you that your father passed away two hours ago this morning. In his sleep."

"Oh," Ari said. She couldn't think what ought to come next. She just looked at the man, completely bewildered, while he expectantly awaited her response.

"What happened?" Assistant asked, taking up the slack.

The official frowned at being addressed by a slave, but he looked again at Ari and apparently decided to overlook it. "His heart," he said. "He has not been well for a long time, Your Ladyship. You know, the fever, all those years ago...and he works—worked—so hard. It seems the strain finally got to him. Though nobody could have seen it coming," he added quickly.

"No," Ari said faintly. "No. He saw it coming." Because suddenly she saw her father's pale face in her mind, telling her that he would not free Assistant, that he wanted Ari to have a companion, *"Because I'm..."*

He'd known. He'd *known*. Why hadn't he told her? Why hadn't he allowed her to help care for him, or at least to say good-bye?

"Your Ladyship?" the official said.

"Are you sure?" Ari whispered, wringing her hands. Perhaps the guard was wrong. Perhaps they were all wrong. "You said he was asleep. Maybe...maybe..." She began to tremble. "Maybe you just haven't tried hard enough to wake him up."

The official opened his mouth, closed it, and then said, "I'm afraid it is certain that he is gone, Lady Ariana. I am so very, very sorry." He swallowed hard. "He was a good man. A fine stationmaster."

"Oh." Ari trembled harder.

Assistant noticed. She said quickly, "Are there death rites? Funeral arrangements?"

This time, the official turned to her with relief. "Naturally. But the Lady Ariana need not trouble herself about that. All will be arranged. He wanted nothing grand, nothing ceremonial that people would have to come from all corners of the Empire to attend. Something simple. He left very specific instructions." He smiled sadly. "He was always a thorough man."

Ari couldn't bear any more. She turned around and plunged back into the foliage, hearing the official exclaim something. But then she made it through the garden to the foot of her favorite oak, where she sat down very hard and leaned against the trunk until she felt the bark pressing into her cheek. She couldn't hear anything but the chirp of the occasional cricket and her own rasping breath.

Thorough. He was a thorough man. Except when it came to his own daughter…somehow neglecting to inform her that he was about to die.

She would have done anything for him, anything to see to his comfort before they said good-bye. She would have told him how proud of his life's work she was. She would have made sure the doctors gave him everything he needed. She would have held his hand.

Maybe he would even have lived longer. Wasn't there evidence for that? That when sick people were surrounded by love and support, they sometimes made surprising recoveries? Her father might not have known. A doctor should have told him. Perhaps he would have wanted Ari then.

After some length of time, she heard footsteps.

Assistant usually didn't make any noise, so she was probably trying to let Ari know she was coming. Sure enough, after a moment, she appeared from behind a shrub, her lips held in a thin line.

"I'm sorry," she said.

Ari looked up at her. She had no response to that. No words. It would be nice if Assistant sat down next to her on the ground, put an arm around her or something. Then Ari wouldn't have to talk; they'd just sit there until, perhaps, Ari started to cry, or do something else to prove she wasn't numb inside.

Assistant didn't sit down. "You need to get up," she said, her voice soft but firm. "There is work to be done. You will need to attend to your father's affairs."

Ari kept looking at her. Assistant was getting blurry. "I want to see him," she said, her voice thick.

"Are you certain?"

"Yes." Ari had seen precious little of her father in life. The least she could do was grab the last chance she'd ever have.

"All right." Assistant gave Ari her hand, pulling her gently to her feet. "Shower and dress. Then we will go to his quarters. I understand he is still laid out there."

"Why didn't he tell me?"

"I don't know." Assistant pushed Ari's hair out of her face, looking seriously into her eyes. "Come along now. Attend to your duties—do what you can for him, even though he's gone."

Ari wasn't sure what happened next, except that she thought Assistant was probably right—she usually was—and so eventually she found herself showered and dressed and walking down corridors with Assistant to her father's quarters. She forgot where it was a couple of times, but Assistant seemed to know. She'd probably already memorized all the maps Ari had downloaded for her.

Why didn't he tell me? An awful little voice in the back of her head was already answering the question. She didn't want to listen, but she couldn't silence it. Maybe it would never be silent again.

He didn't tell me because he didn't want me there. He never wanted me at all. He wanted to die without ever seeing me again.

Assistant allowed Ari to walk very closely beside her, and even to hold her hand once or twice.

When they had almost arrived, a solemn voice on the loudspeaker announced to the whole station that Ari's father was dead. The people in the corridor stopped and stared at Ari as she walked by with Assistant, and before Ari's eyes, their faces filled with pity. She didn't want to see it. She couldn't bear to look at them. Why should today be any different? So she kept her gaze on the floor, and let Assistant guide them the rest of the way to her father's rooms, and press the door chime for entrance.

Lord Geiker was laid out on his bed, already magnificent. The sheets were fresh beneath him, and he was in his dress uniform with the insignia of the Imperial Order of the Falcon shining on his breast. He'd always been proud of it. One of Ari's earliest memories, from before her mother's death, was of him polishing it with loving care. She'd even been allowed to hold it once or twice. It had felt so heavy in her little palm.

Dr. Eylen stood at the foot of the bed and bowed her head to Ari in greeting. Then she took her hand. The official who'd broken the news was not there, but a sentry, wearing a blue armband, tipped his head respectfully as well.

The doctor did not let go of Ari's hand immediately. Ari had preferred Assistant's grasp. But Assistant stood three paces behind her now.

"My condolences, Your Ladyship," Dr. Eylen said.

"Thank you," Ari heard herself reply.

"Funeral rites will begin in two days. That will give enough time for emissaries to arrive. Here. You may see him."

Ari couldn't say a word this time. She stood at her father's deathbed and stared down at him. They'd closed his mouth and his eyes. He really did look like he was sleeping. But his chest did not move, and breath didn't whistle out of his nose. Ari touched one of the hands folded on his breast. It was cold. She shuddered and pulled her hand away.

"You have never seen death before."

Assistant's voice. Ari started, and turned to see that they were alone in the room. Apparently, the doctor and the sentry had departed to give them some privacy.

"You've never seen it," Assistant repeated, and there was a look in her eyes that Ari had never seen there; it was a look of almost childlike wonder. "You don't remember your mother's death, do you?"

Ari shook her head.

"Did you even see her body?"

"M-my father wouldn't let me." Just like he hadn't permitted her to know of his own failing health. Or know anything else about him.

Assistant reached her hand up and traced her fingertips over Ari's cheek. Ari's dry cheek. She still wasn't crying. Why wasn't she crying? Nothing around her seemed real.

"I don't know what to do," she said. "What happens now?"

"The funeral is in two days," Assistant said. "And then you attend to your father's affairs. You might well be his sole inheritor."

"He might have left stuff to the Empire," Ari whispered. "He...sometimes they do, soldiers... He, he was very devoted..." She choked.

"Shush now." Assistant took Ari's hand. "We'll find out soon enough."

"He didn't tell me," Ari said. "He didn't tell me."

"I know," Assistant replied, and squeezed her hand.

"He didn't want me," Ari said, before she could stop herself.

Assistant's mouth parted a little, but she said nothing. In an ordinary time, Ari would have enjoyed seeing her lost for words.

"He never wanted me at all." Ari looked back at her father's corpse. "Why not? Is it because I look like my mother? I really don't think I do. He made a mistake." Her eyes grew hot. A lump built in her throat. "I feel like I could shake his shoulder, wake him up, and tell him he—he made a mistake—"

"Ariana..."

"But there's no more time. I thought maybe someday—but there's no more time, and he's never going to want me." The lump in her throat grew bigger. Her stomach writhed. Maybe she was about to vomit.

"Ariana." Assistant let go of her hand, took her by the shoulders, and tugged until Ari wasn't looking at her father anymore. Instead, she stared into Assistant's eyes, blue and troubled. "This isn't the place. Let's go back to our—your quarters. You don't want to go to pieces here." She squeezed hard enough to jolt Ari out of her daze. "Come along now. Come along."

Ari came along. There didn't seem to be anything else to do. As they left, she saw that more people were gathering outside her father's door, many of them already clad in blue. Ari wasn't wearing blue. She hadn't thought to put it on. Would she look like a bad daughter? Like she didn't care?

161

Guess it runs in the family, that horrible little voice said. Luckily, the bitter laugh that burst out of her mouth could have passed for a sob.

At that, Assistant put her arm around Ari's shoulders, as if she didn't care at all about the people who were looking. "Come along," she repeated. "Quickly."

Ari didn't know about "quickly," but at some point she found herself standing in her kitchen while the door shut behind Assistant. Her garden lay ahead of her, the same as it had been this morning at the hour her father had passed away and she'd known nothing about it.

Her eyes weren't hot anymore. No lump in her throat, either. Just the numbness, back again and without ceremony.

"I can't feel anything," she said to the nearest bush.

Assistant answered for the bush. "You can, and you will. But you're in shock now." Her hand touched Ari's shoulder again, much more gently now. "That's all. You need to rest. There's nothing to be done."

There was undoubtedly a lot to do—by people other than Ari. People who were following her father's orders for how he wanted his funeral, people in charge of distributing his estate, people who would contact the Emperor and let him know Nahtal Station needed a new Lord Commander. But nobody needed Ari to do anything.

"Yeah," she said thickly.

That night, for only the second time, Ari and Assistant lay in Ari's bed without having sex. Ari kept her face tucked into Assistant's shoulder. Assistant rubbed her back until she fell asleep.

She didn't dream.

CHAPTER 13

Ari wore a blue cloak to her father's funeral. Its deep hood covered her face from the curious stares she knew she was getting. She had to sit on the front row between two important officials whose names she didn't know or care about. Assistant stood with the other personal slaves at the back of the auditorium. Her father had kept four house slaves. Two wept at his loss as if their hearts were breaking. They'd obviously known him better than Ari ever had.

So had everybody else. Two days after Ari's father had died, little, insignificant Nahtal Station was full of dignitaries, ambassadors, and a personal representative from the Emperor himself. Many of them spoke about Lord Geiker's illustrious career as a soldier and diplomat. A couple of them mentioned his "humility" and even the "noble sacrifice" he'd made by volunteering to come all the way out to the Rim instead of taking a more prestigious posting. It didn't seem as if he'd lacked prestige, though. Everyone spoke of him with the greatest respect.

When the fifth person rose to speak, Ari tuned out and stared at her father's body instead, laid in state at the front of the room, maybe ten feet away from her. He was dressed and posed just as he had been the last time she saw him. Now, though, she couldn't imagine that he was only sleeping. She'd spent most of yesterday staring off into the distance, or looking at the few holo-chips of them together, and wondering if he truly ever had been alive when she was in his presence.

She got her answer when she waited in the endless receiving line after the rites were over. When the guests had ceremonially bowed to her father's body, they shook her hand before proceeding on to other important station officials. She hadn't been introduced during the service because nobody had spoken about her father's family. Most of the people here seemed either to have known or guessed who she was, but more than one guest blurted out, "Oh, I wasn't aware he had a family. My apologies."

Every time, all Ari could manage to say was "Thank you for coming" before shaking their hands in her own cold, clammy fingers. Was she as cold as her father now? Sometimes breathing felt difficult.

After an eternity, the last guest had shaken her hand and departed for a reception that Ari could not, could *not* make herself attend. She could skip it. The funeral director could say (if anybody cared) that Lord Geiker's daughter was overcome with grief and had needed some time to herself.

Or maybe that she had a headache. The thought almost started another bitter, horrible laugh out of her, but she stifled it in time.

Last to leave were the slaves. Her father's slaves were still sniffling as they knelt before his body instead of bowing to it.

Assistant did not kneel. When it was her turn, she stood before the corpse for far longer than Ari would have expected her to, regarding it silently. Then she inhaled, pressed her hand over her heart in a salute, and inclined her head. There was nothing in it that suggested groveling, affection, or even obedience—anything a slave was supposed to show. Assistant's gesture was one of genuine respect. For some reason, that made Ari's heart seize up in a way that no weeping or kneeling could do.

She looked mutely at Assistant as she came to Ari's side. They were alone but for the two soldiers covering her father's body with a sheet emblazoned with the Imperial sigil: a flame motif around a circle, signaling the burning loyalty citizens were supposed to feel for Homeworld, the Empire's origin.

"From what I heard, Mír's fleet saw your father as a worthy foe," Assistant said quietly. "There are few like him left."

For a second, Ari thought Assistant would touch her: stroke her cheek or push back a tendril of her hair from where it had fallen over her eye. Ari's own hands seemed too heavy to be up to the job. But two soldiers stood right beside them, and that would have been a terrible idea.

Just then, one of the soldiers spoke, plainly unaware that the former stationmaster's daughter and her slave were standing a few feet away, partly hidden behind a pillar. Or maybe he just didn't care, now that Ari was the *former* stationmaster's daughter. She probably wasn't going to get more salutes or visits at the Officers' Mess.

"Did you see His Lordship's slaves? Putting on that display," he said in disgust.

"Crying because their next master won't be so kind, most likely," the other soldier replied.

She sighed as she folded the final pleat on the corner of the bier.

"What a ridiculous display," he continued. "You know they don't feel things like ordinary people."

Ari's breath caught. Assistant's hand briefly touched her elbow in caution, but it was too late. She had to say something. Slaves *were* ordinary people. They came from everywhere—children whose parents sold them out of poverty, people captured during war or raids, people who had gone too deeply into debt and had only themselves left to sell for repayment.

"Why shouldn't they have cared about my father?" she demanded, her voice high-pitched and too obviously distressed. "He was good to them. Slaves feel things. Of course they can love people!"

The soldiers whirled around, eyes widening with embarrassment as they realized they'd been overheard, and by the dead man's daughter, no less. They bowed, but before they could stutter out apologies, Ari turned on her heel and fled the auditorium. Assistant followed.

They didn't get far before a woman in a blue robe, wearing a deep green dress beneath, approached Ari. Her fine, black hair was pulled up in a professional-looking bun, and she had a no-nonsense look about her.

"Lady Ariana, please accept my condolences," she said briskly. "I'm glad I found you. I am your father's solicitor. I understand now might not be the best time, but if you are not going to the reception, then there are some matters we should clear up right away, including his will and legacy. It's far better if you don't put them off."

"Um," Ari said. Nothing seemed less possible than doing such a thing right now.

"My lady," Assistant murmured behind her, "you should go."

The solicitor raised an eyebrow at this impertinence, but said only, "Wise advice from a slave."

"Thank you, Your Solicitorship," Assistant said. "Oh, I ask pardon. I was never taught how to speak to lawyers."

The solicitor turned back to Ari. "My secretary will also be there. The office is a little small for four."

"Go on back to our quarters," Ari told Assistant. Her shoulders slumped. How had her energy drained from her so entirely? She certainly didn't have enough to protect Assistant from her own sharp tongue. "I'll see you when I get back."

Assistant acquiesced. Without bowing either to Ari or the lawyer, she proceeded down the corridor by herself.

The solicitor watched her go, then turned back to Ari with her eyebrows raised and her mouth open.

Ari held up her hand. "Forget it. Let's go." She hadn't known she could sound so much like her father. That was his voice inside hers, for the first time she could ever remember. Maybe he'd left her something after all.

As Ari found out when she sat down with the solicitor and her secretary, he'd left her a lot. It seemed he had not, in fact, forgotten she existed. In simple terms, she'd inherited almost everything except for a bequest her father had set aside for the Empire—funds to build a library in one of the minor Rim stations. He'd always been a big believer in education. But the rest was Ari's.

It turned out that her father had been an extremely wealthy man. Ari supposed that, on some level, she'd always known as much. She'd never worn fancy clothes or jewels, but how else could her father have afforded to transport a miniature forest between space stations? How else had it been possible for her to acquire some of the rarest specimens in the system? She'd just never known how wealthy "wealthy" was. As the solicitor kindly informed her, Ari was now one of the richest women in the whole sector.

It was something else she couldn't bring herself to care about. She hadn't felt anything since she'd reprimanded the soldiers.

That night, Ari returned to her quarters still feeling as if everything was some kind of awful, bizarre dream. Assistant was waiting for her back at her rooms.

Tonight, Ari didn't want to go to sleep chastely. Tonight, she flung herself into Assistant's arms, seeking her mouth. Assistant gave it to her.

That, and so much more. Assistant kissed her, touched her, as if she was in a fever too, as if she, too, needed something to hold onto tonight, even if she hadn't lost what Ari had. Ari knew that in the morning she would have bruises from where Assistant grabbed and kissed her with such desperation. That was fine with Ari. Now, at last, she felt something other than blank disbelief, than shock.

When Ari had come, Assistant waited all of ten seconds before starting again, licking her way down Ari's body while Ari trembled and cried out.

"Soft," she muttered. "Sweet. *Ariana.*" It was the first time she'd said Ari's name while they were in bed, and Ari moaned. "So perfect," Assistant whispered.

Ari had never felt perfect, or anything like it. But tonight, of all nights, when Assistant said it with such fervent conviction, Ari allowed herself to believe that at least someone else thought it was true.

~ ~ ~

Ari stared into her porridge at breakfast the next morning. "They're packing up my father's things today," she said. "So the new stationmaster can have his old quarters. I have to go through it. To decide what to keep."

She gulped as she realized she didn't even know what her father had. His shiny medal had been shot out into space along with his body. The rest was a mystery. "It's...I can't believe all that stuff is...I mean, it's his. It's not mine. I feel like I shouldn't be allowed to look at it."

"But it *is* yours," Assistant said. "Everything is."

"I guess," Ari whispered, and picked at her food, even though Assistant hated it when she did that.

She heard Assistant take a deep breath and prepared herself for a lecture on table manners. But instead Assistant said: "Including his slaves."

Ari blinked and looked up. Assistant hadn't touched her own porridge. She was regarding Ari with unwavering, almost deadly intensity.

"Yes," Ari said. "The solicitor said—"

Then the force of what Assistant meant struck her. She nearly gasped. Assistant was her slave now, in both name and deed.

"Right." Ari blinked again. The feeling of unreality, of numbness, was settling back around her. "That's right. I just—I've never thought of you as—"

"I know. You care about me," Assistant said. She reached across the table and took Ari's hand. "Don't you?"

"Of course I do!" Ari said, her eyes widening. *I love you.* "You know that!"

"Then set me free."

Ari froze. Assistant's grip on her hand became very, very firm. Almost painful.

"I-I..."

"Set me free," Assistant repeated. "You asked it of your father, once. Now it is in your hands, and yours alone."

Assistant was right. She always was. "Yes," Ari whispered. "Of course I will. When? Oh. Right now. Sure, right now."

Assistant's grip relaxed on her hand a little, though she never stopped staring right into Ari's eyes.

"Then," Ari said, swallowing hard, "once I take care of that...it won't take more than a few..." It was a surprisingly simple matter to free a slave, if you were the owner. "Oh, I need to get my father's codes and—"

Assistant reached down into her lap and pulled out a datachip. "I retrieved it this morning," she said. "Before you woke up. From that stack of your father's documents you left by the bed." She placed it on the table between them.

"Oh," Ari said. She was having a hard time breathing. "Um. But a-after that...I mean, would you be willing to... I'm sure you've got lots of stuff you'd rather do, but would..." She shook her head. Get it together. "I mean, maybe you could help me with my father's..."

"There is a small freighter bound for Carellian One in two hours," Assistant said. "I would like very much to be on it."

"Oh," Ari said yet again. "I...yes..." She took a deep breath. "Are you going to visit somebody?" Did Assistant have somebodies? How many times had Ari wondered, told herself that Assistant would stay with her because she didn't have anywhere else to go? Also, the word *visit* was very important here, because—

"Will you come back?" Ari managed.

Assistant pursed her lips. She looked over to the side. For the first time since they'd met, she couldn't seem to look Ari in the eye.

"Oh." Ari began to shake.

Assistant looked at her again. "I cannot stay here," she said, her voice as low and hypnotic as the first time she'd pinned Ari down in the dark. "I want to leave."

Ari nodded wordlessly, hardly aware of what she was doing.

"Let me go."

"Maybe," Ari said, feeling like she couldn't breathe at all, "if, if you waited a couple of days while I sort things out. Maybe I could c-come with you. I wouldn't—" Wouldn't what? Get in the way? Be a bother? Ari didn't even know what Assistant was off to do.

"I don't think that's a good idea," Assistant said.

"Oh," Ari said, "right," and she stood so fast she banged her knee on the table. Assistant looked at her with some alarm, but Ari just said, "I'm fine. I'm just going to go, and I'll take care of everything." She reached down and grabbed the datachip. "You...you can stay right here. Just—just stay—"

She was out the door before Assistant could say another word.

She didn't precisely sprint down the corridors, but she moved at a fast clip. Not fast enough to outrun her thoughts, though, which chiefly consisted of one phrase.

"I want to leave."

Assistant wanted to leave. Assistant, who had said Ari was perfect, delicious, and so many other things. Assistant, who had kissed her, who'd started kissing her, it hadn't been Ari's idea—surely Assistant cared about her a little bit? Just a little? Surely?

But there had been no caring, no passion, in the eyes of the woman who had looked at Ari across the breakfast table. Just cold, hard intent. *"I want to leave."* She'd practically broken Ari's hand from grabbing it, she was that desperate. And she hadn't wanted Ari to tag along, either.

Why had she done all that, then? Why had she kissed Ari, why had she slept at her side every night? Why, if she didn't care?

Ari looked up, and realized her steps had led her to the Observatory. Well, this place would do as well as any other. It had a data console. She inserted the datachip and logged in. All her father's passwords had been converted to her own.

There were five slaves listed in the chip. All but one of them had a name.

SLAVE:ASSISTANT;HOUSE
>CAPTURE/SPL-OF-WAR

Then, just staring at the words, Ari realized it. *Capture. Spoil of war.* She remembered the cold, proud woman sitting at her kitchen table that first day, who'd tried to escape and had been bruised for her troubles. Assistant had never been happy here. Assistant had always wanted to get out.

So she had made Ari love her.

She'd said they didn't need love. But, but…but she'd also kissed Ari, told her wonderful things, made her feel special, like nobody ever had before—like she *knew* nobody ever had before—so that Ari would love her. So that Ari would deny her nothing, when the time came. So that Ari would set her free.

"You didn't have to do that," Ari told the console.

She pressed keys and buttons and then waited for the command to go through.

"You didn't have to," Ari said. "I would have done it anyway."

SLAVE:ASSISTANT;FREE
>BY: ARIANA GEIKER;OWNER
THIS COMMAND IS FINAL AND CANNOT BE REVERSED. PROCEED, Y/N?

"I always would have done it," Ari said, and pressed *Y*. "I'd, I'd have done anything for you."

SLAVE: ASSISTANT NOW FREED: AWAIT NEW CHIP

A new chip popped out, next to the one Ari had slipped in. Ari removed both of them from the console and kept staring at the monitor. She wondered if she could stare at it indefinitely. Until she could forget that the only real friend she'd ever had in her life had only stayed with her because Ari's father had forced her to, and was getting away as fast as she could at the first available opportunity.

Assistant wanted to get to Carellian. Carellian wasn't anywhere special—a station orbiting an uninhabitable planet, mainly known for being a conveniently placed port of call between larger stations. The only reason Ari could see for Assistant wanting to go there was that it was the next flight out of Nahtal. She probably hadn't even cared where she was going. Just that she wanted to be gone.

But she didn't have any money. She couldn't afford passage on a ship.

Ari logged in again and put Assistant's new chip back into the console. Then Ari looked at how much money she had. Assistant was going to need some to get around. *(To get away.)* To go places. *(To go away.)* She did not want to stay. She wanted to leave. She'd need money. Ari punched in a random number, and then just started pressing the zero key until the computer told her she'd overdrawn her account. So she deleted several zeroes and then it told her it was okay and she put the money on Assistant's chip.

Ari put the chip in a small bag she had hanging at her waist. It had a few seeds in it. She saw a young slave boy lingering by a window in the Observatory. He glanced at her, and she waved him over. Then she gave him the bag.

"Go to my quarters, please," she said. "Give this to Assis—to my sl— the woman in there. It's, it's seeds," she added, and she saw the boy's eyes glaze over in instant boredom. It was for the best. Sometimes you just couldn't trust people. "Hurry. Go straight there."

"Yes, Your Ladyship." He left the Observatory.

While she was at it, Ari freed her father's four slaves. Including the two who had been crying, although now that she thought about it, maybe, no, *probably* they hadn't cared that much about her father after all.

Then she checked the flight schedules. One small freighter, CR-921, was slated to fly out to Carellian forty-five minutes from now. Ari hadn't realized how much time had passed. Assistant was probably on board right now, or at least getting ready to board. Assuming the little boy had delivered the bag. Otherwise they wouldn't let her on.

Ari looked at the passenger logs. "Assistant" had checked in on the vessel, along with ten other people whose names Ari didn't recognize.

Assistant would get a name now. She'd have to. Ari wondered what she would choose.

She left the Observatory, but instead of going to her rooms, she headed for another observation deck. From there, you could see the ships flying in and out of the main hangar bay. And soon enough, a small freighter labeled CR-921 flew out of the bay. Ari watched it go farther and farther away until it reached the hyperspace jump-off and vanished into a small, bright point of light.

Maybe Assistant had changed her mind, Ari thought suddenly. Maybe she'd changed her mind at the very last minute, had disembarked after checking in, and hadn't left the station. Maybe she was back in their rooms right now, getting ready to order dinner and wondering where Ari was.

By the time the doors to her quarters had closed behind Ari, her hands were clenched. When she called out "Assistant?" and received no answer, they were trembling. As she wandered through the garden, checking around every tree, under every leaf, she started having trouble breathing again. By the time Ari reached Assistant's empty alcove, with its small bed neatly made, tears were running freely down her face.

Then she noticed the little slip of paper on Assistant's pillow. A note? Ari swooped down on it like a Fetalyn hawk, unfolding it with shaking hands. Maybe Assistant would say something about coming back, or how much she'd grown to care for Ari during their time together.

There were only two sentences.

Thank you for your kindness to me. I will not forget it.

Ari sat down hard on the thin mattress, her breath coming out of her in a painful wheeze. Well. Wasn't that nice? Assistant appreciated Ari's kindness and wouldn't forget it; she hadn't said that she wouldn't forget Ari herself. What a difference that one word would have made. *I will not forget you.*

Yeah, right. Ari's own father had forgotten her for over a decade. A slave who'd been longing for escape would forget her in a day.

173

The intercom buzzed. Ari gasped. After a moment of crackling silence, a man's voice said, *"Lady Ariana? Are you there?"*

"Yes," Ari croaked.

"Your Ladyship, we understood that you would be coming to your father's quarters today," the voice said respectfully. *"To take care of his possessions."*

"Take care of them yourself," Ari said. *"Throw them out. Give them away. Keep them. I don't care."*

"But Your Ladyship!" Now the voice sounded shocked.

"I said I don't care," Ari repeated, and then cried out, *"Go away! Leave me alone! Just go away!"*

"...Yes, ma'am," the voice said after a few silent moments, and the crackle and static faded out.

"Just go away," Ari said to nobody at all and sat down once again at the foot of her oak.

What did she care about her father's things? They weren't him. They wouldn't bring him back. They couldn't bring anybody back.

She sat there for hours, staring at nothing. Eventually she got up and went to bed and stared at the ceiling, which made for a change of scene. Assistant's arms did not wind around her and hold her close.

~ ~ ~

The next day, Ari discovered that the voice on the intercom had not taken her at her word. Slaves arrived carrying boxes of her father's possessions, which they stacked in the kitchen, in Assistant's alcove, in clear spaces in the garden—everywhere. Ari would be lucky if she didn't trip over them at every turn. The slaves glared at her resentfully as they left, except for one, who lingered.

"You freed your father's slaves," she said. "They found work. One with a family in the station, and three somewhere else."

"Oh," Ari said. Then she said, "Did they love him?"

The slave stared at her. "How should I know?" She paused. "Your Ladyship."

"I just wondered," Ari said.

The slave gave her a long look and departed with the rest.

~ ~ ~

"Maybe she will come back," Ari said to her second-favorite oak tree.

The oak tree didn't say anything. Cranli hopped down on her shoulder, rubbed his front legs together consolingly, and hopped away again.

"Maybe she will," Ari repeated as she packed fertilizer around some tulip bulbs. "Maybe she'll get bored out there, once she's seen…" Everything else in the universe. "She might want to come home."

The bulbs didn't answer, either.

"It might take a little while," Ari acknowledged, dropped her trowel, and started to cry.

CHAPTER 14

"You gave away nearly two-thirds of your cash holdings," the solicitor said.

"Oh," Ari said. "Did I?"

"Two days ago. To your slave."

"She's not my slave."

"Whyever did you do such a—Well. You still have your father's various properties. And his things... I understand he had some valuable personal assets. Have you looked?"

"No. They're still in boxes."

"Might I suggest you look?"

"Is the new stationmaster going to let me stay here? I don't know what to do with my plants, otherwise."

"He says you can stay," the solicitor said, and sighed.

~ ~ ~

Ari decided that she couldn't slip up when it came to the plants. They were her family. Her children. When you got right down to it, they were always the ones who didn't leave. She owed it to them to care for them. To repay their trust. She'd always known that. She'd just forgotten for a little while.

"We'll get by just fine," she said to Cranli, as she let him out of his jar. She swallowed hard. "Or...I mean, we'll get by." She closed her eyes. "Just like before. It won't take long. You'll see."

She remembered a line from the poem she'd told Assistant about: *Better the bones than the empty grave.* Better to have had something wonderful in your life, and lose it, than never to know anything wonderful at all. It had made perfect sense at the time, before she'd lost anything.

It was nonsense now, of course.

That night, she went for a walk. She didn't go to the Observatory. That didn't seem like a good idea. Instead she went to the same observation deck where she'd watched Assistant's ship take off four days ago. Her heart had taken off with it. When the phrasing occurred to her, she wondered if any poets would approve.

No ships were going in or out tonight. She'd heard some mention, in passing, about being more careful because pirates had started to prowl around again after months of silence. Maybe that was because her father was gone. As Assistant had said, even Mír had respected him— and now he was no longer here.

It still seemed unreal, though, that pirates would ever come to this lonely little outpost, no matter how much her father had insisted they would. It also seemed impossible to care. Space was so vast, and Ari was so very small and alone—what were pirates to her?

After she went for her walk, she ordered dinner to be sent from the mess hall and ate it by herself. She used her very best table manners.

She tended her plants until the twelfth hour chimed, and then she went to bed. It was important to get on a good schedule and keep to it.

That night, she dreamed that Assistant was with her again. Then she dreamed that Assistant left her again. She woke up gasping, rolled over, and realized that she was alone in the bed, and that there was no warm spot next to her because nobody had been lying there. She immediately grabbed the second pillow and held it tight to her body, burying her face in it, mumbling a prayer that she would never dare say in daylight.

Please come back. Please, please come back.

~ ~ ~

The next day, Ari decided to return to the Observatory after all. No sense doing otherwise. Her life wasn't over just because her father was dead, just because Assistant had left to start her own life afresh. There was no reason why she shouldn't keep doing the things she always did. The sooner she got back to normal, the better, really.

The superintendent came forward to see Ari the moment she entered the room. "My earnest sympathies, My Lady," he said quietly, and at his kindness, Ari almost burst into tears again. "I am so sorry for your losses."

"Thank you," Ari said. And then she added, "Losses?" Plural?

"Your father and your slave," he said. "You were always in here with her. I saw that you were fond of her."

Ari immediately decided to return to her quarters. "Yeah," she said. "We were...um. Thank y—"

"These are dangerous times," the superintendent said, shaking his head and looking angry. "To think of our brief respite—and now this. It's sheer brutality and barbarism, is what it is."

"Brutality and—" Ari blinked.

"That little freighter never stood a chance," the superintendent said, shaking his head again. "Not against a pirate vessel that size."

Ari just stood there and stared at him. And stared, and stared some more, wondering when he was going to laugh at his own joke, because Ari sure wasn't going to laugh at it for him.

He looked right back, his eyes widened, and he looked horrified. "You didn't know."

"Know."

"About the—but it happened three days ago," he said helplessly. "I thought everyone knew."

"Knew."

"That freighter going to Carellian," he said. "The CR carryall. They captured it the moment it exited hyperspace in the Carel sector, as if they were waiting for it."

"Captured," Ari said. Her body was going numb. It was a very strange feeling.

"And...and left behind." Ari kept looking at him, until he finally said softly, "A wreck. They left no survivors. It was all over the newsfeeds, Your Ladyship."

"Assistant's the one who reads the newsfeeds." Then she said, "Thank you for telling me," and walked away very quickly.

He did not try to stop her.

On the way, she stopped at a public access console and surfed to a newsfeed. There was nothing about a destroyed freighter today. Maybe the superintendent had been wrong. Then she remembered he'd said it had happened three days ago. She searched the archives of the last week's news.

And there it was. CR-192. A picture of it, just as it had appeared when she'd seen it leaving the station. With the caption, "WRECK AND RUIN: The freighter from Nahtal Station found ravaged by pirates."

Below the caption was a picture of a gutted husk—the remains of the freighter. An expert said that it was the work of Mír's pirates—that she had reappeared after months in hiding, and was already up to her old tricks. "This kind of efficient savagery," the expert said, "can be the work of nobody else."

Ari tried to read the whole article, but the only phrase that mattered was, *"No survivors found."*

"The mercenaries were quickly and cleanly killed," Assistant had told her. "That is mercy, in the world of pirates."

The corridor swayed a little as Ari returned to their rooms. *Her* rooms. She thought maybe people were looking at her funny as she passed by, but that didn't matter.

Then she was standing in her kitchen and walking toward her garden. The kitchen floor stopped, the soft dirt started, Ari felt something hot gathering in her throat and behind her eyes, and then everything went all weird for a little while.

When she opened her eyes again, her whole body hurt. She was curled up in the dirt and panting for air. She raised her head painfully and saw that somebody had torn down her shelves from the wall and that all her precious jars had crashed to the floor.

She sat up and her elbow slid back into something sharp. Ari looked down, then blinked, trying to understand what she was seeing. Cranli's jar lay smashed under the edge of a fallen shelf. Amid the dirt and glass, she could see him, still lying beneath his branch, pulped. Ari had wood splinters in her hands. She moaned and swayed where she sat, but she didn't pass out, even though her head hurt something fierce. But that didn't matter, either.

Assistant wasn't coming back. Assistant was dead. Assistant was dead, Ari's father was dead, Cranli was dead, and nobody was coming back, ever.

"You're just a bunch of stupid plants," Ari said to her garden. The garden didn't reply. "I wish you were dead." She dug her fingernails into her scalp. "I wish you were all dead and they'd come back."

If she hadn't let Assistant go right away. If she'd detained her for another day. Or even another few hours. If Assistant hadn't been aboard that freighter. If Ari had acted differently.

But she hadn't, and she couldn't change any of it. She didn't get to make those kinds of decisions. She didn't get to decide anything at all. She never had, she'd never been used to making decisions, and the one time she'd decided, when she'd let Assistant go, she'd done it wrong. She'd made the wrong decision, and now everyone was gone.

Ari stared down at the dirt and figured that if she just sat here and didn't move, she wouldn't have to decide anything else for a while.

CHAPTER 15

That night, Ari finally got up from the ground and started cleaning up the mess she'd made, trying to avoid the broken glass and mostly succeeding. She worked all night long.

The next day she checked meticulously on all the saplings. Every single one. Every single leaf. And after that, funnily enough, she sort of lost track of the days. She forgot to wash and eat, because nobody was there to remind her, or make her. She slept wherever she lay down. And after a few days (who knew how many?), when she opened her eyes from sleep, she couldn't get up again. She couldn't move. Oh. Maybe she should try again later. She closed her eyes once more.

When she opened them again, everything was bright white and her arm hurt.

"She's awake," a voice said.

A woman leaned over her. Dr. Eylen: the physician who'd attended her father's deathbed and who'd told Ari earlier that everything was fine. Ari wondered if Dr. Eylen was dead, too, then realized that didn't make much sense. But what did?

"Lady Ariana," Dr. Eylen said in obvious relief. "Welcome back."

Back? Ari tried to say, but her mouth was too dry. She licked her lips. The doctor waved her hand, and a nurse pressed a cup of water to Ari's lips. Ari sipped. It tasted wonderful.

"You have been unconscious for two days, maybe more," Dr. Eylen said. "The new stationmaster arrived two days ago and expressed a wish to see you. You didn't respond to intercom calls, and eventually we got worried enough to check on you." She took a deep breath, and let it go. "Lucky thing, too."

The new stationmaster. Oh, that was right. Ari's father was dead, and so was Assistant. Ari opened her mouth, tried to say something, but all that came out was a very strange noise, a low, animal moan.

Dr. Eylen put a hand on her shoulder. "I know you grieve your father," she said. "And your slave, too, or so I hear. But shutting yourself up to starve to death is not the answer to that."

Ari wanted to say that she hadn't meant to do any such thing; it was only that nobody had reminded her to eat. But that would probably sound stupid to a doctor.

"We've got you on a nutrient drip," Dr. Eylen continued. "When you're well enough, you can go back to your quarters, as long as you understand that we'll be checking on you."

Ari nodded.

"But for now, you stay here. Stay and just rest." The doctor patted her arm. "Just rest, that's all."

"I killed Cranli," Ari said. "My praying mantis." She shut her eyes, wondering if she could keep them closed forever.

"Did you?"

"It was an accident. But it was my fault. He was her favorite, too."

"I'm sorry. It's all right. Rest," Dr. Eylen said again, and her voice was kinder than it had been in the corridor, when Ari's father had still been alive.

"I killed both of them."

"You killed no one." Now Dr. Eylen's voice was much firmer, though not sharp at all. "The pirates killed your slave. Not you. You must understand this."

"She wasn't my slave. She belonged to my father."

"Shh, Your Ladyship." Dr. Eylen reached up and touched a button. "I'm sending a sedative down your nutrient tube. Now—rest."

"It won't make me dream, will it?" Ari said, but then she fell asleep before the doctor could reply.

~ ~ ~

Ari spent a week in sickbay. She had a room to herself, a small one, like a pod—it was like being a seed, perhaps. But she never felt shut in, and she was free to come and go as she pleased so long as a nurse or orderly accompanied her. That meant she didn't really go anywhere, since she felt bad about depriving the medical unit of on-call personnel, who probably had more important things to do than walk aimlessly around corridors with her.

She was made to talk to the station's only counselor, who was overworked and underpaid, and who asked her a series of questions that basically amounted to, "Are you going to try and airlock yourself into space?" Ari was not, and she had no desire to "talk through her feelings," even though everyone strongly encouraged her to do so.

"Maybe later," she kept saying, and they had to be content with that.

She figured by the third day that she was well enough to get around on her own, but the medical staff kept an eye on her anyway. It was all right. Although she didn't leave sickbay, the same two nurses tended to her on rotation, and sometimes Dr. Eylen, so she didn't feel too overwhelmed by lots of new people. And the nurses were nice—caring, compassionate, and they never took no for an answer. They didn't condescend to her or treat her like a freak. They made her talk, even if it was just about silly stuff—her plants (which they assured her were being cared for), goings-on at the station, trends that were finally making it all the way out here from Homeworld, whatever.

Often Ari just listened uncomprehendingly to their chatter—she couldn't remember the last time she'd read a society newsfeed—but it was better than the aching, endless silence that enveloped her at night. She still needed sedatives to sleep.

She liked the sedatives. She even came to like the nurses' chatter. She liked anything that wouldn't let her think.

But on the fifth day, Rellin, the younger nurse, hurried into Ari's room, looking both agitated and excited. "Did you see the newsholos?" he asked, sounding breathless.

Ari and Dr. Eylen both looked up in surprise. "Rellin, I'm in the middle of checking Her Ladyship's blood pressure," Dr. Eylen said sternly. "You know not to get her excited."

"Carellian fell!" he said. "It surrendered!"

Dr. Eylen sat up very straight, giving Ari an apprehensive glance. So she must know something Ari didn't.

"Surrendered?" Ari said. "To what?"

"To Mír's fleet," he said. At Dr. Eylen's glare, he said, "She would've found out soon enough."

"Mír's fleet?" Ari said, thinking of the Carel sector, where Assistant had died, where they said it had been the work of Mír because nobody else was that awful. "I didn't know—"

Dr. Eylen was still glaring at Rellin. "We've heard rumors of pirates out there," she said. "I'm sorry to upset you, Your Ladyship."

"No. I want to know," Ari whispered, wondering how many thousands dead there were.

"Rest their souls," Dr. Eylen said, obviously thinking the same thing.

"No, no," Rellin said quickly. "That's just it. They surrendered to Mír. They didn't even put up a fight."

"When has that ever stopped her?" Dr. Eylen said.

"They didn't just surrender to her," Rellin said. "They joined her."

There was a very, very long period of silence. Then Ari summed the whole thing up by saying, "What?"

~ ~ ~

If Ari had expected Imperial forces to rally quickly, to defend or take back Carellian, she was mistaken. If anything, the Parliament seemed intent on dithering endlessly about what should be done, and for two days nothing was done at all. The Emperor made no statements, although a few images of him found their way into the newsfeeds— chiefly looking anxious and sweaty.

In the end, three days after Mír's forces had taken over Carellian, the Empire sent a diplomatic vessel to meet with Mír. The vessel was destroyed within an hour of its arrival in the sector without meeting with anyone.

Mír's ships had not destroyed it. Carellian's crew had. The crew who had surrendered to Mír had joined her as if they had only been waiting for the opportunity. Perhaps they had. The newsfeeds and holos immediately branded them traitors to the Empire, and who could disagree?

Reports made their way back to Homeworld: reports of the strength of Mír's fleet, her apparently limitless reserves of wealth and firepower, the fanatical devotion of her crew. There were even whispers that the Empire wasn't immediately moving to stop her because, quite simply, it couldn't.

The pirate queen now had an entire Imperial outpost for her playground. Nobody could predict what she would do next, once she was settled. Nobody had ever been able to.

The Empire held its breath.

CHAPTER 16

"Transmission for Your Ladyship," a slave boy said at the door of Ari's quarters.

Ari had come home yesterday, after a week in sickbay, with the understanding that Dr. Eylen would stop by to check on her tomorrow morning and make sure that all was well. Ari could already tell that her plants had received substandard care in her absence; the seedlings alone would need careful attention if they were to recover.

Ari tried to tell herself that she cared about this.

"Thank you," she said to the boy, and took the chip to insert it into her datapad. Because of the trouble with the pirates, private transmissions were now screened. Some people in the station were getting political about it, saying it was an invasion of privacy or violation of rights or something, but Ari found she couldn't care less. Why would anybody write to her about anything important?

The transmission was a reply from *Botany Today.* Only two weeks ago, with Assistant at her side, Ari would have been in a frenzy to read it. Today, she skimmed over the words.

```
Not the first to come forward with allegations… if
you can offer proof… would welcome more information…
anxiously awaiting your reply.
```

They'd have a long wait. Ari tossed the datachip down the garbage chute and sat quietly at her kitchen table for a while.

~ ~ ~

A month after her "episode," as the nurses called it, Rellin and Dr. Eylen were still regularly stopping by Ari's quarters to say hello. They appeared to have grown fond of her, for some reason.

She was fond of them, too, she supposed. They were nice. They didn't really stand to gain anything from being nice, either. She wasn't the stationmaster's daughter anymore, and she couldn't do much for them one way or the other. So maybe it was okay when they smiled at her, or stopped by for a friendly word. Rellin even taught her how to play a card game called Catch.

Because he meant well, Ari tried to enjoy herself instead of thinking about playing Q'heri with Assistant. Sometimes she thought about throwing away the wooden box beneath her bathroom sink but couldn't bring herself to do it yet.

Rellin seemed surprised at how quickly she picked it up and then began beating him. "You really are smart," he said. Then he added quickly, "I didn't mean it like that, Your Ladyship. Obviously, you're very accomplished." He glanced toward the garden. Ari had offered him the most cursory of tours on his first visit, more to be polite than anything else. "Just look at that. I only meant..."

"That I'm good at more than gardens." For the first time since Assistant had left, Ari felt her mouth stretch out into a smile—just a very small one, but it seemed to startle Rellin. "I did well in school. But nothing ever really grabbed me like botany does."

"No other sciences?" Rellin tilted his head to the side, giving Ari a better glimpse of the tattoo on his neck: a star with a flower around it. "You never thought about medicine? Or engineering? Astronomy?"

Astronomy always made her think of the Observatory, and the Observatory made her think of Assistant. Ari looked down at her hand of cards and swallowed. "No. I don't think I could do medicine. And all the other science, physics and engineering and... It's dead science to me, just wires and motors and particle waves. My plants are alive." Again, for the first time in far too long, Ari felt a revival of interest in her life's work. A surge, almost, of affection. "They need me. Say, what does your tattoo mean?"

He grinned. He had a nice smile—it never seemed forced or fake. "It means I got drunk one night six years ago and made an error in judgment."

"Why not have it removed?"

Rellin shrugged. "The design means something to me. It reminds me of my home and my family. And I don't get to go home often. I decided I might as well keep it. To remember."

To remember. Ari thought about that long after Rellin had left with his usual respectful bow. All she'd been wanting to do was forget, but since she couldn't manage to do that, maybe allowing herself to remember was a better idea.

Remembering her father and Assistant was the closest thing to having them alive and with her. Even if it was painful, it would be better not to forget them.

That wasn't as easy as it sounded, though, as Ari learned when Dr. Eylen stopped by for a chat a couple of days later. "I only saw your slave at your father's funeral," Dr. Eylen said over a cup of herbal tea. "Your...Assistant, you called her?"

"She didn't want a name." Ari looked down into her cup. "And she wasn't mine, she—"

"Was your father's. I remember now." Dr. Eylen sat in Assistant's chair, the chair where Assistant had asked her why she was so alone all the time, or talked about things she wanted to do to Ari in bed.

"I asked her if she wanted a name," Ari said. "But she didn't."

"I know you miss her, but she seemed like a proud one," Dr. Eylen said. "I could tell just from looking at her. The way she held herself. Nose in the air. Too good for everyone, I'm sure she felt."

"That's not true," Ari said, still looking into her tea. "She was just unhappy. She hated it here. That's all it was."

"Well, I'm sure I don't know why." Dr. Eylen added more gently, "But I am sorry about what happened to her."

"I..." A month later, and Ari still felt like she was going to die every time she thought about Assistant's face, about her voice. She still lay awake most of the night, still had nightmares, still needed sedatives every few days just to get some rest. But she didn't want to go back to sickbay, no matter how kind everybody was. So she didn't say anything but, "Yeah."

"It was odd, though," Dr. Eylen added, "that little freighter. I wonder what they wanted it for? Why did they attack it before going for the main station?" She shook her head. "And they've been too quiet since then. I don't like it. That sector turning traitor was a shock." She gave Ari a hesitant glance. "Your father would have known what to do better than this new man, this Lord Koll."

Oddly, it didn't hurt quite as much to think about her father's death as it did Assistant's. Maybe because, in the grand scheme of things, it somehow seemed less senseless. He'd been sick. He'd worked too hard during his illness. And he'd been a great man who had accomplished many things—more than most people would in four lifetimes. But Assistant had been cut down in her prime with no warning, right as she was about to start a new life.

That said...it still hurt.

"Yeah," Ari repeated. Dr. Eylen had a point. Ari's father had always been one of the best in the business when it came to thwarting pirates and keeping his own people safe. And apparently the "new man" wasn't coming up to scratch.

For the first time since Assistant's death, anger stirred in Ari's breast. Her father had literally given his life to keep the Empire safe. Was his work supposed to be for nothing, now that somebody else was in charge? He would never have wanted that. He'd have been working ceaselessly to stop Mír in her tracks however he could, even from a remote outpost like Nahtal.

But apparently everybody else was happy enough just to sit back and let events unfold as they would, even as the Empire was overrun by murderers. How could Lord Koll, and others like him, face themselves in the mirror every day? Even Ari would try harder than this, for crying out loud.

"But thank goodness it's out of our hands, eh?" Dr. Eylen added. "I wouldn't want to be in Lord Koll's place."

"I guess not," Ari said, and deliberately did not look toward the alcove where Assistant wasn't, and never would be again.

~ ~ ~

That night, Ari dreamed yet again of Assistant. She often did— vague, fleeting, nightmarish impressions that never added up to much, except that she woke up crying every time.

But tonight, she dreamed of Assistant in her white dress, walking away from her toward a door. "Come back," Ari implored. "Please, please come back."

Assistant did not turn around, or even act as if she'd heard Ari.

Ari, who longed to run to her, to stop her, couldn't move. "They're going to kill you!" she cried. "Don't get on the ship! Can't you hear me? Please come back!"

Assistant kept walking. And before Ari's eyes, the doorway vanished, and she realized that Assistant was walking into a sun: something so bright and terrible it hurt Ari to look at it. But she never wavered, and Ari could only watch helplessly as she strode confidently into the heart of the star, until she became nothing but light and flame.

~ ~ ~

The next day, the Thellian sector, adjacent to Carel, announced its allegiance to Mír.

It had not been attacked. It had not been under siege. It had not even been under the threat of siege. And it welcomed the peaceful arrival of Mír's flagship, the *Crown Lily*, with open arms. Within days, the flag of the Empire had vanished, and Mír's colors ran high in its place.

Four days later, Ankar, next to Thell, announced its decision, not to surrender, but to "ally itself to the rebel cause against a corrupt and decadent Empire." Which was when everybody else finally figured it out.

Mír was no longer looting and pillaging. Mír was quickly and methodically making her way around the Empire's periphery, offering better deals to neglected, out-of-the-way stations than the Empire did. Offering protection, manpower, and wealth. Offering a change. Offering a "cause."

She was not leading a band of ruffians. She was leading a revolution.

~ ~ ~

"But the Empire can't just do nothing!" Ari said. She, Dr. Eylen, Rellin, and another physician named Dr. Ishti were sitting in the main mess hall over cups of coffee. Ari was glad not to go back to the Officers' Mess, even if the food was better. "They're supposed to protect us—they can't just let this, this monster—"

"Protect us from what?" Dr. Ishti said. "All three of the sectors have either surrendered peacefully or actively offered their allegiance. They want Mír there. For whatever reason."

"Why would anybody want her?" Ari asked, appalled. "Doesn't everybody know what she *is*?"

"Compared to the Emperor?" Rellin said. "Maybe she's not so bad." The three women stared at him. He squirmed, but added defiantly, "She's doing things. Taking care of things. Everybody knows the Kazir are out there, and the Empire won't admit it—but her fleet can hold them off. And it's getting bigger every day." This was true. Ships from all the sectors were flocking to Carel, Thell, and Ankar to join Mír's growing group, while the Empire still trembled with indecision. "What has the Empire ever done, except tax us for services they don't even provide?"

"The Empire never killed any of us, either," Ari didn't think she'd ever spoken with that much venom in her life before. "They never blew up our ships and slaughtered a bunch of innocent people." The other three looked at her in surprise.

"I mean, I'm not saying she's a nice person," Rellin said awkwardly.

"I want her to die," Ari said. They stared some more.

"The good news is, she will," Dr. Eylen gave Ari's arm a gentle pat. "That's the only sure outcome for all of us, isn't it?"

In Ari's memory, Assistant said sardonically, *That was suitably grim.* " Ari couldn't meet Dr. Eylen's eyes, and instead let her gaze drift over to the other side of the mess, where she surprised someone looking back at her.

She blinked. It was the guard from the corridor—the one who'd handcuffed Assistant and then struck Ari with the shock rod. As their eyes met, he went pale, turned away, and abandoned his food on the table as he headed for the doors in a big hurry.

Ari's stomach lurched. Her companions appeared not to notice as they chatted amongst themselves.

She was pulled under by a wave of shame and regret. If the guard had reported what had happened, Assistant would have been sent to the mines, but she wouldn't have been sent to her death. When Ari's father died, Ari could have freed Assistant and brought her back, and even if Assistant left right after that, she wouldn't have flown out on the doomed carrier. She would have lived, at least.

If Dr. Eylen could hear Ari's thoughts, she would tell her firmly not to blame herself or make up impossible stories that could only upset her more. Dwelling on what-ifs would never bring anyone back. It was too late.

Silently, Ari watched her man-shaped guilty conscience flee the mess hall.

~ ~ ~

What killed Ari—well, what nearly killed her, anyway—was the money. The money she'd given to Assistant. She didn't want it for herself; she didn't particularly need it, although she was starting to realize how expensive it was to keep up a large garden, and feared she'd have to cut corners soon. No, what enraged her was this.

She'd given Assistant lots of money, in the full knowledge that Assistant was going away and might never return. She'd given it with a breaking, but full heart—with all the love Assistant had claimed Ari "knew nothing about." She had hoped Assistant would be able to start a new life for herself, in fine style, no less—to find somewhere she could be truly happy and free.

All that money was in the hands of the pirates now. Filling the coffers of Assistant's killers. Helping to fuel Mír's rebellion instead of giving Assistant everything she'd ever wanted. It wasn't just unfair. It was hideous, horrible—no, it was *evil*; that was the only word for it. Every time Ari thought about it, which was often, her throat filled up and she wanted to scream. Sometimes, when she was alone in the night, she did.

She wished she knew what Mír looked like. She wished she had a face to pin her fury and misery on. It wasn't difficult to hate someone without a face, but it was frustrating and unsatisfying.

However, a week after Thell announced its allegiance to Mír's rebellion, Ari got part of her wish. For the first time in her storied career, Mír began to appear in holos and clips. Never her face, and always from a distance: a body clad in black armor and helm, covered from head to toe, gun on one hip and sword on the other. She never spoke. Even from far away, she looked nothing like the shabby little mercenaries Ari's father had captured from time to time, and even Ari could admit that it would be easy enough to follow someone with that sort of presence, that air of command.

If that someone hadn't killed your favorite person in the universe, anyway. Which was a big deal-breaker.

Mir probably would be a better leader then the Emperor. She probably would provide a better defense against the Kazir. She could probably do a lot of things. But Ari didn't care if Mír could bring a millennium of peace and prosperity to the system, and then the galaxy, and then the universe; nothing she ever did could make up for killing Assistant. Nothing.

Worse—nothing Ari could ever do would make any difference to someone like Mír. Any difference at all.

CHAPTER 17

The same day that Mír appeared in holos (that quickly found their way all over the system), Ari finally finished going through all her father's things.

Much of it she'd given away: clothes, shoes, any personal things that might be useful to charities and such. Some of it she'd tossed out. A few things she'd keep in storage. What puzzled her were the boxes and boxes of holochips. Hundreds of pictures. Thousands. Of places her father had been, people he'd known—a whole life he had apparently lived in the public eye and without Ari's knowledge. While she'd been puttering around in her garden, or suffering through school, he'd been having lunch with an ambassador from Ceta Five or going to a ball on Homeworld with glittering, shining people.

Of course, Ari had never wanted to do any of that with him. Banquets were bad enough. But...but it might have been nice if he'd asked. Just once.

And then there were the pictures of her mother. There was, in fact, a whole box devoted to datachips of pictures of her mother, apparently chronicling her life from birth to death—pictures of her as a child, as an awkward teenager (who really did look remarkably like Ari had at that age), as an astonishingly beautiful young woman (who surely didn't look like Ari at all). There were pictures of her parents' wedding, of them on various trips and vacations, of Ari's own birth.

In all of them, Ari's father was radiantly happy. He wore a smile that Ari had never seen, or could never remember seeing. Just being near Ari's mother, near his wife, appeared to be a source of limitless energy and pleasure for him.

There were pictures of Ari, too, but they were a lot fewer after Ari hit seven years old. After her mother died. She'd always known her father had sort of lost interest in her, but it was stunning, and hurtful, to see that in empirical proof by all the pictures that suddenly weren't there. In the pictures that showed them as a family, Ari's mother always held her close, always smiled at her, laughed over her, kissed her and cuddled her; Ari's father looked at Ari's mother with love in his eyes, and rarely at Ari herself. Without her mother in the frame, Ari supposed there hadn't been much reason to take pictures of her anymore.

They'd been married ten years by the time Ari's mother had died. Would he have felt the same if he'd known her for as short a span of time as Ari had known Assistant? Would his grief have poisoned his life a little less? Or—on the flipside—if Ari had known and loved Assistant for ten years, if they'd had that decade together, would her own pain be even worse? She didn't like to imagine what that would be like.

"You were his responsibility," Assistant had said. "Grief or not, he had no right to abandon you."

Ari bowed her head and wondered if maybe she was more like her father than she cared to admit. After Assistant's death, nothing seemed as important as it had before. In fact, Ari often selfishly wished her father alive again—not for his own sake, but because while he'd lived, Assistant had been with Ari. Had been alive. Without her, Ari had stopped caring about eating, sleeping, hygiene—and about her plants. Her own children. Her own responsibilities that she had no right to abandon. Assistant would never have approved of that.

So that was no good. Responsibility. Caring for her garden. She had to do that. Maybe soon she'd even enjoy doing that once more.

Once, she'd thought of planting flowers, of having hummingbirds. Obviously, that was never going to happen now. Instead, she'd started making some medicines for sickbay at Dr. Eylen's request. They weren't exactly standardized medications—home remedies, at best—and Ari often wondered if the doctor didn't just order them to make Ari feel useful and then throw them away. But she never asked. She didn't want to know. It was another responsibility. And even if it felt like it was going to crush her eventually, it was probably good for her, too.

Speaking of which, the seedlings needed watering now. Ari sighed and tossed the datachips back in the box. She'd figure out what to do with them later.

That night Ari dreamed yet again that Assistant was walking toward the doorway. She had this dream nearly every night now, and always woke up straining for air. Yet again, the doorway turned into a sun; yet again, Assistant ignored Ari's pleas; yet again Ari watched her vanish into the fire and brilliance.

But tonight was different. Tonight, even in her dream, Ari knew she couldn't bear it anymore; knew she couldn't bear waking up without Assistant there, working in the garden and eating without her, talking to other people, and thinking about her the whole time, going through every hour of every day knowing she would never see Assistant again and that people expected her to get over it eventually. And worst of all, that maybe she *would*, she'd just go back to being the weird girl who played with plants, and she'd forget how much she had loved another human being. *Better the bones.*

So tonight, Ari ran after Assistant, ran toward the star, which got bigger and hotter as she approached. She couldn't see Assistant. As the star's light brightened, she couldn't see anything. She cried out "Where are you?", but nobody replied, and Ari kept stumbling forward, feeling her dress catch fire, wondering if she would find Assistant before she—they—roasted to death. She had to try. Even if she failed, even if she burned, it was better than…better than…

Ari woke up, trembling and gasping as always. And this time, stronger than grief, she felt the sting of failure. She hadn't been fast enough, hadn't tried hard enough, hadn't been in time, had lost Assistant in the star.

She should probably want to get over this. She didn't. And she couldn't.

~ ~ ~

"There has to be something we can do," Ari pleaded, twisting her hands.

The new stationmaster, Lord Koll, regarded her with patience. He was a tall, thin stick of a man with a long, lean face and deep green eyes that didn't really seem to see her. "I understand you are grieving, Lady Ariana," he said. "But surely you know there is nothing to be done."

Ari stared at him in frustration. It was two weeks since Thell had defected, and Mir's fleet was swelling. Surely it was only a matter of time until she made another move. "But don't you want to help?" Ari said. "I mean—Your Lordship, the stations near Thell and Carel—they're sitting ducks. I bet, I bet if they had a little more support, more soldiers, more—"

"I can on no account spare any of our soldiers," Koll said firmly. "And unless Homeworld Command itself tells me to do so, they will stay right here."

"But the pirate fleet isn't even near here," Ari said. "They're half the system away. They're going station by station. You could help stop them long before they arrived!"

"Lady Ariana, I understand you are an expert botanist," Koll said, a smile on his lips and a sneer in his eyes, "but you are, with respect, no tactician."

Ari imagined herself bent over a Q'heri board, working through a dozen scenarios in her head as she fought to win. True, it wasn't like marshalling real troops and ships, but at least it proved she could see farther than the tip of her own nose. Her temper flared. "My father never would have stood by like this."

Koll's eyes went cold. "Thank you for your visit," he said. "And please do call ahead next time. I'm afraid my schedule might not be as flexible as it was today."

Ari ground her teeth all the way back to her quarters. This was ridiculous. Surely somebody, somewhere in the Empire, was planning to do something about the fact that a murdering pirate was set to take over everything? Surely nobody was going to sit and do *nothing* while it happened?

Perhaps Assistant had been right. She'd always been right. She'd said the Empire had been useless, relied too much on insufficiently protected perimeters while the center grew weak and decadent, like a rotting tooth. Maybe that was true. Once Mír gained enough of a foothold on the rim, nothing would stop her from advancing inward until she had control of Homeworld itself, if she wanted.

Feeling helpless, that was the worst. If there was only a war effort Ari could contribute to—a fund, supplies, heck, even making medicines from her plants—something she could do...but there was nothing. And it looked like nobody would be interested if she tried to organize something all by herself. Not that she knew how to do such a thing.

Ari's door hissed shut behind her, and she stood in her kitchen, staring at her hands, trying to imagine them tearing through a suit of black armor like paper.

~ ~ ~

Two nights later, at the hour when most people were asleep, the station's security tower went dark and silent. All power except for emergency life support failed. The force fields went down. In the space of a few seconds, the entire space station was as vulnerable as a naked child in a desert.

There was a shiver of space, a flicker of light, outside the station windows. And then, in the blink of an eye, what appeared to be a hundred ships uncloaked, surrounded the whole station with cannons mounted and trained on every hangar bay. And in the middle of all of them, an enormous, black-hulled ship, grotesque in its power and menace, stared down the security tower itself.

It didn't take long for the panicked graveyard shift to put the entire station on red alert. As the alert spread, so did the news that a silver lily shimmered on the side of the enormous black ship.

In less than an hour, four thousand people, sitting ducks all, knew that Mír had come.

CHAPTER 18

Huddled beneath her favorite tree, Ari wondered how it had happened so quickly. Her father had labored long on improving the station's defenses—hadn't that colonel in the Officers' Mess said as much? But those defenses had been bypassed as if they were nothing. As if the pirates had known every weak point, had known how to override every failsafe. Not a single shot had been fired in the station's defense. With the shields down and enemy ships surrounding it like a sea, to fight back would be suicide.

Ari remembered Assistant's fate, remembered that a quick death was mercy in the world of pirates, and thought that maybe suicide wasn't such a bad idea—that was, to go down fighting instead of hoping for clemency that would never come. She hugged her knees to her chest and leaned against the tree trunk, just as she had done when her father had died, and countless times since then, always looking for comfort that remained just as elusive.

And it wasn't just that it had happened so fast—Ari couldn't figure out why it had happened at all. Their station wasn't anywhere close to Thell, Ankar, or Carel. They hadn't made any overtures of peace or friendship to Mír—thank goodness, Ari couldn't have endured the shame—and it must have taken enormous effort to get here, and to bring such a large fleet, when there were smaller and more eager targets nearby. Why had Mír come here, of all places?

Just then, the station-wide intercom crackled to life. Ari jumped as a trying-to-be-calm voice made the announcement.

All crew and family members to remain in quarters. Do not go outside. Do not try to override the lockdown on your quarters. Pirates have boarded the station.

Ari hid her face in her knees. So, this was it. This was how it happened—just waiting for the end, instead of doing something. She felt like she'd been waiting all her life, though she'd never known for what until Assistant had come, and now she was going to die waiting, too.

She remembered the last time she and Assistant had been together—the frenzy of it, the desperation—like Ari was trying to fight off death itself and forget what had happened to her father. It sure would be nice if Assistant was here now. Maybe they could have passed their final hours that way, instead of dying too far apart. It would be nice to have that one last thing, for one last hour.

The time seemed to crawl. Ari had deliberately placed herself where she could see the clock from beneath the tree, curious to see how many minutes it would take before her life was over. She was surprised at how scared she wasn't. Then again, none of this felt real—more like a child's game, like Lord Koll would get on the intercom any second and say, "Just kidding!"

Then, even as she thought about it, the intercom crackled again. It was, in fact, Lord Koll. But it wasn't a station-wide announcement; instead, Koll said in a hesitant voice, *"Lady Ariana? Are you there?"*

For a moment, Ari couldn't respond. This was too unexpected. It seemed highly unlikely that Koll was calling to apologize for their earlier conversation and to concede that she'd been right all along about the pirate threat.

Then she rallied and rose to her feet. Her knees shook as she approached the intercom and mashed the button. *"Um...yes?"*

"Are you all right?"

What? *"I—yes,"* Ari said. *"I mean, I guess?"*

"Thank goodness." Koll sounded relieved. *Really* relieved. *"I need you to come to my office right away."*

"Me?" Maybe she'd fallen asleep against the tree and this was all a dream. She pinched her arm and winced at the sting. Nope. *"What for? Isn't the whole place on lockdown?"*

"We can, er, unlock your door remotely," Koll said. *"So, if you could just—"*

"But the pirates!" Ari rubbed a hand over her forehead. *"What's happening? Aren't they here?"*

"Yes, Your Ladyship." Koll's voice was strained now. *"They are here. In my office, actually. In fact, the pirates have demanded you come,"* he finished heavily. Then, *"Ah! Very well. Excuse me. The* rebels *have demanded you come."*

"What?" Ari's eyes widened. *"Why?"*

"Their lieutenant has declined to answer," Koll said, *"and yet, looking at him right now, I believe he is a man unaccustomed to refusal. Lady Ariana, please come right away."*

What was this? What could a bunch of pirates possibly want with Ari? They probably didn't need her advice on planting seeds. The only possible reason was...

She'd been Lord Geiker's daughter. And her father had always been a dangerous foe to pirates. Even Assistant, a slave to Mir's fleet, had known that. Was this revenge on a dead man? Something to send a message to the rest of the Empire? Were these bullying cowards out to kill Ari just like they'd killed Assistant—another woman who'd never done anybody any harm, just one unarmed person up against a whole pack of bloodthirsty mercenaries?

Ari saw red. She began to shake with anger.

"Lady Ariana?" Koll prompted, sounding extremely nervous now.

"Forget it," Ari heard herself say. *"I'm not coming."*

"You're what?" Koll obviously couldn't believe his ears. *"My lady, the station is surrounded by pirates on all sides. This is the only demand they have made of us thus far—"*

"Oh, is it?" Ari curled her hands into fists. *"Is it? Well, if it's so important, then...then they can come and get me!"* Before Koll could object, she mashed her thumb against the intercom's power button and turned it off, which was quite against station regulations.

Then she stood in her kitchen, trembling at what she'd just done. She'd just invited a bunch of murdering pirates to attack her in her own quarters. She'd probably made them angrier. They might even want to take it out on her plants. Stricken at the thought, Ari flew back into the foliage and wrapped her arms around her second-favorite tree. Only half aware of what she was saying, she stammered, *"I-I'm sorry, I won't let them, I'll protect you,"* just as she'd told Assistant once upon a time.

It hadn't been true then, either.

What could she do? Nothing, really. Now that she'd taunted the pirates, she could count on rougher treatment. It would probably be easier if she just behaved meekly when they came to get her. The thought galled her to the core. But what else was there to do? She didn't have a gun or a shock rod, and even if she did, she'd certainly have no idea how to use either of them.

Maybe she could attack them with a pair of pruning shears. Or the edge of her trowel. She laughed before she could help it, high and hysterical, and then chewed on her knuckle in agitation and tried to think.

Well, that'd be better than nothing. Hadn't Ari thought of going down fighting? Assistant certainly wouldn't sit back and cower by a tree—not the woman who defended herself even when she was asleep. Ari should take a page from her datapad. Heck, she should have asked Assistant to show her some self-defense moves. Why had that never occurred to her?

She could only work with what she had. Pruning shears it was. She'd left them on a self at the other side of the room, but if she hurried—

Footsteps sounded outside her door. Loud, heavy-booted footsteps. Several of them.

No time to grab the shears. Ari's mouth went dry. Sweat pooled in the small of her back and made her nightgown tacky against her skin. Her heart pounded so hard she could hardly breathe. Before she could think about it, she darted away from her tree, back into a farther corner of the garden, where she hid behind an enormous leaf of *Filathen merins.*

The door opened, and the heavy footsteps tramped inside. Ari was shaking so hard it felt like the whole garden trembled with her. She told herself, *Stay calm. Be brave. Can't you be brave?*

A man's voice, loud and harsh, said, "Ariana? Daughter of Geiker?"

Ari gulped and realized she didn't have the breath to respond. She'd been so wrong. This wasn't like a child's game at all, and she didn't want to die—even if life was painful, it was still *life*. And even if she had still been in the terrible darkness that had taken her after Assistant's death, she wouldn't have wanted to be tortured and murdered by pirates. Was there anything she could do? She couldn't bring herself to plead for her life, although that would be the sensible thing. Even death would be preferable to debasing herself that way. Still, fighting off pirates with her bare hands seemed like the most ludicrous idea she'd ever—

Then she saw it: a medium-sized shovel propped up against a wall.

"Do we have the right room?" a woman's voice said.

"Do you think there's more than one suite on this station with a jungle in it?" the man snapped.

"Lady Ariana," a third voice, another man, called out. "We know you're in here. We heard you talking to Lord Koll." Ari gripped the shovel in her hands and hefted it, quivering all over. "Show yourself. I promise you will not come to harm."

Oh, sure. Ari wondered if they'd said that before boarding Assistant's freighter and killing everyone on board. And now it really hit her—these were Mír's people. They might even have been the exact same pirates who'd killed Assistant. Who was to say otherwise? And even if they weren't, they might know the pirates who did; they were all part of the same crew, the same evil, murderous—

"Fan out," the second man sighed, and Ari heard footsteps moving into her garden. "Lady Ariana," he continued, his voice heading to the other side of her quarters, "I repeat: we mean you no harm. Our orders have only been to bring you to the *Crown Lily* in safety."

What? That didn't make any sense. Unless for some symbolic reason they'd decided to kill her on Mír's ship instead of the space station, which might very well be the case. What a way to cast a pall over Lord Geiker's legacy of loyalty and courage—slaughtering his only child aboard a pirate ship.

"You are in no danger," the man said. Lying, obviously.

"She said this would be easy," growled the first man, and Ari almost cried out when she realized that he'd prowled much closer to her corner of the garden. She hadn't heard him. But now, through the leaf, she could see he was a large, rough-looking man with a prominent forehead and a stubbled jaw. He had enormous hands, and he wore a black uniform with a silver lily embossed on the synthsteel chest plate. He seemed the very essence of pirate-ness. He was probably very good with a gun and a sword and hurting people and killing them and—

"Well, it can't be hard," the woman replied patiently. "She's in here somewhere."

"She'd better be," the rough-looking man said. "All I know is, I won't be the one who tells the queen, 'Sorry, we couldn't find a'—"

He pushed Ari's leaf aside, and his eyes widened as he said, "—'slip of a girl'—" before Ari cracked him sharply over the head with the flat of the shovel. Then he yelled and staggered backward, covering his head with one hand, raising the other hand to ward off Ari's next blow.

"You...evil—" Ari cried, "murdering...horrible...you killed her, *you killed her!*" She raised her arms again, but the pirate had already recovered and seized Ari's shovel in a very firm grip. Ari immediately kicked him in the shin.

"What the hell is going on over there?" the second man's voice demanded, and he and the woman pirate burst into view to see Ari kicking and shoving at the first pirate.

"You killed her!" Ari repeated, nearly blinded by tears. "She's dead—you—"

The first man tossed the shovel away and then spun Ari around like a top and held her so that she was facing away from him while he pinned her arms behind her back. She couldn't hit or scratch him, and it was harder to kick him, too. All she could say, over and over, was, "You killed her, you killed her!"

"Well, I found her," he grunted.

"Looks like it," the woman, short and muscular, said.

"And you're cowards," Ari shouted at her. Her heels slipped and gave in the dirt, and only the pirate's arms held her upright as she struggled. "You only fight people who can't fight back—you don't dare face anybody strong—"

The woman's eyes widened. "Nobody told us she was out of her senses. My God, can't you shut her up?"

"May Mír forgive me," said the second man, and before Ari could say anything else, he shot her.

CHAPTER 19

When Ari opened her eyes, the first thing she saw was a splendidly potted and cared-for *Barmensis nobu* sitting on a small table across from her bed. Her enormous and extremely comfortable bed. Which was not the bed in her quarters.

Ari blinked. The last thing she remembered was a pirate had shot her. So, was she dead now? In some sort of pleasant afterlife? She didn't think so. Her head hurt too much. She raised a hand—her arm felt very heavy—and rubbed her forehead.

Then she sat up. She wasn't in her quarters. Not only was the bed bigger, the whole room was bigger, too. On the wall across from the bed hung a painting of the *Crown Lily,* magnificent against a background of stars. Ari turned to the left, and in the corner of the room by the door, she saw a painstakingly crafted model of an ancient ship—the kind that had once sailed the seas of Homeworld long before space travel became possible.

Both items were surprisingly old-fashioned; paintings and models that were made by hand and didn't shimmer and move like holographs did. They contrasted sharply with everything else in the chamber, which was all modern lines and the latest technological conveniences. The space was far more sleekly designed than anything in backwater Nahtal, even after the improvements Ari's father had made. Such a room spoke of fabulous wealth and luxury.

No gardens, though. She already longed for her trees.

Where *was* she?

Ari slid out of bed and got unsteadily to her feet. The rug was soft beneath her toes. She wandered out of the open bedroom door and beheld another, enormous room outside.

It wasn't so much a suite as it was one cavernous space arranged so that there was a different place for everything—a sitting-area, an office, even a statue in the middle of it all. It rose proudly in the middle of the room, about eight feet tall: no elegant marble carving, but rough-hewn from stone. Still, as unrefined as it was, Ari could tell it was meant to be a woman. But the central focus was the enormous, floor-to-ceiling window, through which Ari could see dozens of pirate ships and...and the control tower of the space station, facing her directly.

She was on a pirate ship. No. She was on *the* pirate ship. The *Crown Lily*. Ari gasped.

So, they'd shot her with a stun-gun, then, and dragged her to the flagship. She'd sort of anticipated something like that, but this didn't exactly look like a torture chamber. Ari knew that part of her fuzzy-headedness was the fault of the stun-gun, but she had a hunch that even without it, she'd have been confused.

She wandered across the room to the window and pressed her hand against the glass. It was so strange, seeing the station like this. Feeling so exposed by this enormous window, even though she knew that nobody outside would be able to see her. It was even more overwhelming than the great windows of the Observatory.

She wondered what was going on in the station itself. Were the pirates rounding up people? Were they killing them? Or was everybody still in lockdown, still waiting for doom to fall? Ari shuddered. Meanwhile, she was waiting for the very same thing here.

She heard the hissing of a door behind her. She jumped—she hadn't even realized there was a door, but there had to be one. She whirled around to see who was coming. Pirates, no doubt. Guards or torturers to take her to her doom.

Assistant glided through the door, clad in a long black gown, looking right at Ari with her beautiful blue eyes.

Ari stared at her. There was no sound in the room but her own heartbeat. Then her legs gave out, and she landed smack on her rear.

Assistant paused and looked down at her with raised eyebrows that said more than words ever could; the familiar bemused, beloved smile tugged at her lips.

A sound emerged from Ari's mouth that wanted to be a cry, but couldn't be, because she didn't have enough air in her lungs. And then, before she knew it, she'd jumped to her feet, flown to Assistant, and thrown her arms around her while gasping out, "You're alive! You're alive! Oh my gosh! You're alive!"

Assistant staggered backwards slightly as Ari slammed into her, making an "oof" noise. But she slid her arms around Ari's waist all the same, patting her back soothingly.

Only Ari couldn't be soothed. How could you soothe joy like this? "How, how," she sobbed, pressing her face hard against Assistant's throat, inhaling her familiar, wonderful scent, "how is this...how are you...I thought you were dead, they said you were dead—"

"Dead?" Assistant said, and the sound of her voice alone was enough to make Ari sob again. "No, I'm not dead."

"B-but the freighter." Ari pulled backward far enough so that she could see Assistant's face, which was a little blurry on account of all the tears in Ari's eyes. "They showed pictures—it was gutted—"

"There were ten survivors, as a matter of fact." Assistant brushed her thumb gently over Ari's wet cheek. She wore an enormous ring on her index finger, topped with a blood-red stone in an oval shape. "Although nine are now prisoners of the fleet. But alive, nevertheless."

"Prisoners?" Ari blinked. Assistant had been taken prisoner, too? Were they trapped here together? But...but that was okay. Being a prisoner with Assistant would be okay. Assistant was alive and everything in the universe was a thousand times better—Ari still couldn't believe it—it was asking too much, that more than a month of grief should be overcome in one minute—

"I have to sit down," she said.

"I think you'd better," Assistant agreed, and slid her arm around Ari's shoulders, helping her to a nearby cream-colored sofa, where they sat down together.

Ari sank into the surface of smooth, rich suede.

"Take deep breaths," Assistant instructed.

"Truh, truh, trying," Ari said, and indeed, she tried. After the third deep breath, she felt less like she was either going to pass out or start screaming.

There was a box of tissues on the end table; Assistant offered a tissue to Ari and looked away politely while Ari blew her nose. "Better?" she asked.

"I-I guess," Ari said. Then she added, "No," and held out her arms again, shaking like an oak leaf beneath the air recycler.

Assistant obligingly reached out, pulled Ari in, and held her so close Ari could feel her, smell her, hear her heartbeat.

"There now," Assistant said after a long moment, patting her back again. "This is far too much carrying-on for a woman who ambushed a member of the Honor Guard. You are lucky you weren't hurt," she added sharply. "They have far faster reflexes than that idiot guard who hit you. Thankfully they have even faster brains, and he didn't break your neck. What possessed you?"

"I don't know," Ari whispered. "I-I just got a little upset."

"A little upset," Assistant mused, and stroked Ari's cheek. "What you mean is you let your feelings get in the way of your common sense yet again. But why? There was no wayward slave to protect." She chuckled.

"It's not funny," Ari rasped, and Assistant's smile vanished. Maybe the raw pain in Ari's voice had gotten to her. "I thought they'd killed you. I wanted to hurt them, too. To k-kill them, even."

"Did you?" Now Assistant sounded troubled. But her expression was benign enough as she pushed Ari to arms' length. "Let me look at you." Apparently, she didn't like what she saw, and she scowled. "What's happened to you?"

"Pirates stunned me," Ari said. She must still be feeling the aftereffects. Ever since she'd seen Assistant, she'd had the faintest ringing in her ears. At least it hadn't been as painful as the shock rod.

"You look like you haven't eaten since I left," Assistant accused. "Nor slept."

"I sleep and eat," Ari said defensively. Well—when she remembered to eat a ration bar, or take her sedatives, or when Dr. Eylen or Rellin or Dr. Ishti reminded her. It was better than nothing.

"Skin and bones," Assistant said. "How did you even lift that shovel?" Her scowl was deepening.

With Assistant alive and well in front of her, it suddenly seemed foolish to say that grief had made Ari lose her appetite. "I'm sorry," she said instead, because no other response would come to her, even though a million things needed to be said.

"Well, we've had one 'gosh' and one apology already," Assistant said. "Things are almost back to normal." But she still sounded troubled as she rubbed one warm hand up and down Ari's back. "Did you come down with something?"

"Um…no…" Ari bowed her head and looked at her lap. Might as well admit it. "I missed you," she husked. "I thought you were dead."

"Hmm," Assistant said. She kept her hand on Ari's back. "If that's how it is, I'm glad I came when I did."

Ari blinked at her. *"You* came?"

Assistant looked surprisingly hesitant. "Yes. I came."

"But, where are we?" Ari whispered. She glanced around the room. "This place is huge!"

"These are my rooms," Assistant said. Then she amended, "Our rooms."

"Ours?" Ari stared at her. "What? We're—huh?" She pushed her hair out of her face with a trembling hand and looked into Assistant's piercing blue eyes.

Assistant was looking back at her with the expression she'd worn across Ari's kitchen table on that terrible day when she'd asked to be set free. Assessing Ari, looking right down into the bottom of her soul, and seeing everything Ari couldn't hide.

Assistant reached up and rubbed her thumb over Ari's bottom lip, and then her chin. "Ariana," she said gently, "who am I?"

Ari longed to say "What?" or "I don't understand." But she couldn't. Because she was suddenly too busy thinking about too many things all at once.

Like the fact that the pirate attacks had stopped right around the time Assistant was captured from that scouting rig. And that they'd started up again once her freighter had been attacked. And that Assistant had always been the cleverest, most authoritative person Ari had ever met, including her own father. And that, for a humble slave, Assistant had always seemed to know an awful lot about, about...

Ari felt the blood draining out of her face.

"Who am I?" Assist—no—*she* repeated.

"M-Mír," Ari croaked. "You're...you're Mír."

"Yes," Mír said, and let her hand fall from Ari's chin down into her own, black-robed lap.

Black ship, black armor, black gown... Ari's head spun. "Oh," she heard herself say. "Well," and she started to rise from the sofa. Not that she had anywhere to go, but her body was propelling her up and away from the truth.

Mír stopped her with a firm hand on her right elbow. "No," she said quietly. "You stay right here. We're going to talk."

"You don't like talking." Ari gripped the edge of the sofa with her left hand while she kept her eyes on Assistant's grip on her elbow. "I tried to get you to talk and you never would. And I talked too much—"

"Chirped, even," Mír said, as if she was trying to lighten the mood. Something inside Ari began to collapse at the familiar words, the affectionate tone.

"I've found I quite missed the chatter," Mír said. "But you are right— it's finally my turn to have my say." She loosened her grip on Ari's elbow and rubbed her bicep up and down. "You always wanted to know about me. Here I am."

"Yeah." Ari closed her eyes and rubbed her forehead. *Think like a scientist. First principles. Go back to the beginning.* "When you were captured...they thought, they said you were a slave on the rig."

"Yes. It's a funny thing, survival." Mír looked thoughtful. "How easily the urge for it overcomes pride. When I looked around and realized that my crew was dead, and that our scouter was about to be boarded..." She shrugged. "I had a slave on board. She had a spare dress. I dropped my gun and sword and decided it would be best to be someone else for a while."

"What happened to her?" Ari said inanely, in the face of all the other, more pressing questions she didn't want to ask.

"Didn't I mention that my crew was dead?" Mír said sharply. "I don't know why I was spared, Ariana." She chuckled ruefully. "Although they say nothing can kill me. Would it be tempting fate to wonder if that's true?"

"You...you...thirty-two soldiers from the station," Ari said. She hid her face in her hands, shaking harder than ever. "It was you. It was you—"

"Ariana—"

"It was you who killed those mercenaries, too, and, and you asked me if the story excited me—before you, before—" Ari wondered if she was about to throw up. She couldn't look up from her hands.

"I wondered if I'd regret telling you that someday," Mír said dryly.

"All those people," Ari gasped, "all those innocent people...you—"

"Innocent? Really? Who?" Suddenly Mír pulled Ari's hands away from her face, forcing her to look up. Her jaw was tightly set, and her gaze was relentless. "The mercenaries? Your father's soldiers—who made the choice to be soldiers, who accepted the dangers when they signed up for the job? Just as I did, and my own people did?"

Ari wrenched her hands free and scuttled back against the arm of the couch. "But there've been others!" she said. "Nobody's seen your face—everyone knows you leave no survivors—"

"I let no one go," Mír said. "That's true. Soldiers are killed; civilians are captured and enslaved. If they don't know anything and are wealthy enough, they're ransomed; if they resist, they are also killed. I don't pretend I'm a good person, Ariana, or a kind one, or a merciful one." She tilted her head to the side, her blue gaze still boring through Ari. "Except to you."

Ari froze. "Me?"

Mír rose gracefully and began to walk around the sofa, hands clasped behind her back—prowling, almost, much like she had the night after the banquet, when that man had said she'd needed whipping. Only now she didn't seem furious. Not exactly. Just sort of...tense.

"I appear to have developed an unaccountable weakness for you," she said. "Of course, you were kind to me. Did you find the note I left?"

That note, that impersonal note. "Yeah. I did." Ari swallowed. "You said I'd been nice and you wouldn't forget it."

"And so I haven't. How could I?" Mír chuckled again, gazing out the enormous window at the control tower. "I'll *never* forget the sight of you, waving your little coffee branch at that idiot sentry and telling him to apologize for being so rude to me. Oh, my."

Was...was Mír making fun of her? *Now?* "He wasn't an idiot if he caught you trying to sneak out," Ari snapped.

"True enough, I suppose," Mír acknowledged with a tilt of her head. "Should he have struck me?"

"No!" Ari said, before she could think better of it. Then she hunched her shoulders and repeated, "No."

"No?"

"You—" Ari grimaced. "You couldn't fight back. As far as he knew, you were just a slave. He didn't have any right to hit you." She swallowed hard. "That's not how people should behave to each other. You know what I think about that."

"Yes, I do." Mír regarded her for a long moment, as inscrutable as ever. Then she said, "I can't believe you gave me all your money."

"*Oh,*" Ari moaned, and hid her face in her hands again.

"It's come in handy." Mír laughed.

"I let you go." Ari choked. "I set you free."

"And I do appreciate it."

"You've been, you've been marauding again, and killing people, and it's my fault. I was the one who—"

"Don't flatter yourself," Mír said, though not unkindly. "I certainly would have escaped soon. Your father's death simply precipitated matters. I remain sorry for your loss, by the way."

Oh, *sure.* Mír was sad that her greatest enemy was dead. Ari didn't bother holding back a bitter laugh. "Yeah, I bet you do."

"I do," Mír said. "He was a formidable opponent, as I've told you before. I would have preferred to test my wits against his instead of winning by default, so to speak."

"He could have beaten you at Q'heri the first time, I'll tell you that!" Ari jumped up to her feet, unable to sit on the sofa for another second. She paced away from Mír and curled her hands into fists.

Stupid. She'd never felt so stupid in her entire life.

Mír looked wary as Ari moved away, but didn't try to stop her. "I often wonder if perhaps I could have escaped sooner than I did." For the first time, her voice sounded uncertain. Hesitant, even. "If I'd...tried a little harder."

"I'm sure you could have." Ari turned to look out the giant window again, at the space station that now seemed blurry. She wasn't crying, though, thank goodness—but then again, she wasn't sad, either. She didn't know *what* this feeling was, except that the urge to scream was back. "You can do anything. You always could."

She'd fooled Ari—or Ari had just been too blind to see the obvious. She'd even made Ari love her like it was easy, like it was nothing at all.

"You didn't have to," Ari said, finally telling Mír out loud what she'd thought to herself for weeks. "You didn't have to go to bed with me."

Then she turned and looked right at Mír as she said, "That was wrong of you to do." Because it was. In spite of everything, it seemed like the most awful thing Mír, the pirate queen, had ever done: seduced Ari, made Ari think she was cared for, and broken her heart. For no reason at all. As if she wasn't feeling bad enough, fury joined the pain in Ari's heart. What right did Mír have to play with her that way? "That's a *terrible* thing to do. I would have let you go anyway if you'd asked!"

"I know," Mír said.

"What?" Ari stared at her. Mír's face, as always, gave nothing away. "Then why—how could you?" Had she just done it for *fun?*

"I wondered that many times," Mír said, and looked away again, this time gazing thoughtfully at the statue in the center of the room. "I always knew that you would free me, Ariana, if you were able. I realized that very quickly." She tapped her lips with her be-ringed finger. "I knew that, if anything, making you attached to me would make it harder for you to release me. Not easier."

"I did, though," Ari said. "Because I..." She squeezed her eyes shut. "You said I don't know anything about love. But I bet I know a whole lot more about it than you ever have." She swallowed down a sob that was doing its best to work free. She wondered if her head was about to explode.

Mír walked to stand in front of Ari. "Do you love me?" she asked, as if it was the simplest question in the world.

No, Ari ought to say. *I don't. You're an evil person.* That was what she ought to say because that was how she ought to feel. Wasn't it how she'd been thinking of Mír for weeks? Mír, who had killed and lied...

Mír, who had held her close in the night, who had dawdled in her own escape, who had been her only friend.

"I don't know," Ari said, cursing herself when the truth slipped out. "You're not who I thought you were. And you—you said you didn't want me to love you."

"I never said that." Mír reached out and combed her fingers gently through Ari's hair, pushing it away from her temple. "I said many things, but never that."

Ari ought to move away, ought to at least move her head, but she couldn't manage it. She was having trouble breathing again.

"Let's get this out of the way first. I'm the same person I was in your quarters. The very same. I knew it was a bad idea to make you care for me. And I knew I was doing exactly that." Mír's fingers kept stroking Ari's hair. "I couldn't resist."

Ari trembled and looked away.

Mír's voice was dropping into the low, hypnotic purr that only meant one thing. "I believe I've mentioned on more than one occasion that I find you irresistible, in fact."

215

"Don't," Ari managed. "Not now." Because she felt dirty. She felt dirty that Mír, who'd done so many terrible things and who'd deceived her so thoroughly, could touch her and still make her skin hungry. Something had to be wrong with her.

"No?" Mír inquired, her fingertips dropping down to stroke Ari's cheek. Ari bit her lip. "No."

Mír's fingertips paused. Then she pulled her hand away and cleared her throat. "As you wish. I do have more to say."

"Okay," Ari managed, breathless with relief at her reprieve. Maybe she could get her head together a little if Mír didn't touch her, didn't stand so close.

"I had not planned to come here so quickly," Mír said. "I knew your father's legacy would endure a while longer. I knew your station would not welcome me as the others have."

"Oh, yeah," Ari said, latching on to the new topic at once. She needed to put off thinking about...about the other thing for just a little longer. "How did you get in so easily? I know my father left better safeguards than that!"

Mír hesitated. "Do you remember that stack of your father's documents? That you kept by the bed?"

This time Ari didn't speak. She just wailed as she covered her eyes yet again.

"It's not your fault," Mír said. "You didn't know that he'd left sensitive information on those chips. I'm sure he didn't mean to. But his carelessness worked in my favor."

"He wasn't careless!"

"People are many things when they're near death. Even the great ones." Mír sighed. "Did you even notice what I'd taken?"

"No," Ari said miserably. "I hadn't looked through them all before you left." She hadn't had time.

"I thought not," Mír said. Then she repeated, "It's not your fault. It's his, if it's anyone's."

"It's yours!" Ari cried out, looking up again. "You're the one who stole them!"

"Mine? Oh, no," Mír said, shaking her head. "I am not to be blamed for seizing a tactical advantage. Although..." She trailed off, before continuing in a slightly strained tone, "perhaps I am to be blamed for using it prematurely." She tapped her foot. "I always intended to come for Nahtal Station. I can't overstate how useful Exer's ore mines are going to be to my enterprise. That's why I was scouting there in the first place, though I certainly had no idea your father had such a close watch out." She pursed her lips. "As I said...formidable."

Ari remembered, suddenly, the way "Assistant" had stood before her father's body and given it a respectful salute. Not a gesture from a slave, but from one foe to another. Her face grew hot, and her eyes pricked with tears she would not shed. She swallowed hard.

Mír had never behaved like a slave was expected to. Not once, even when her independent attitude had gotten her into trouble. Ari had admired it, sometimes even been intimidated by it—*very sensible of you,* her inner voice whispered—but she'd never questioned it deeply enough. Mír had refused to speak of her past, but shouldn't Ari have been able to put two and two together?

She couldn't have expected that her beloved friend was a pirate queen, but she should have noticed that *something* was off, and then maybe this debacle wouldn't have happened. But she'd kept her eyes closed. Like someone who didn't want to see.

Stupid. Stupid. Stupid.

"Then there was that useful tidbit your colonel dropped in the mess about the forthcoming upgrades to the security system," Mír continued, "I didn't want to wait for those, naturally. And yet..." She glanced toward the window at the station. "It would have been wiser to delay a while longer before coming here. I know this."

"Then why did you do it?"

Mír just looked at her. And kept looking.

Ari stared back, and then swallowed very hard, feeling like she'd never be able to move again. "Me?"

"I haven't been sleeping well, either." Mír glanced out of the huge window again. This time her chuckle was rueful. "I always slept well when you were there. You wouldn't believe how often I've kicked myself for not bringing you with me when you asked." She shrugged. "Though that would have been unwise at the time. I didn't know what was going to happen. How safe I could keep you."

"Lord Koll said I was all you were asking him for," Ari said.

"So far," Mír said. "I will have more from him. But yes. You were the first thing I wanted."

The first thing. Not person. Thing.

"Am I your slave now?" Ari whispered as her anger—at Mír, at herself—vanished in a cold wave of dread.

Mír regarded her thoughtfully. "That would be a neat trick, wouldn't it?" she said. "Our roles reversed. Very tidy. I began as your slave; you end as mine."

"You were never my slave," Ari said. How many times had she said so, to Mír and everybody else? "You were my father's. I never thought of you that way, *ever*. I let you go—"

"Yes, I know, and yes, you did." Mír's gaze grew even sharper.

Ari shivered at the sight of it.

"What is a slave, I wonder?" Mír continued. "Certainly, I will never call you 'Slave.' I will never deprive you of your name. I will never force you to do anything—not even to be my lover, should you refuse. Will you, by the way?"

"I-I don't know," Ari stammered, wondering if she could refuse if Mír touched her again, and even if she should. It was probably a terrible idea to refuse pirate queens something they wanted. She remembered yet again the story of the mercenaries who had tried to deny Mír what she'd demanded—and how that had ended for them.

Mír never turned her gaze away. "Well, then," she said. "You'll keep your name. You'll keep your will. You'll have your own servants to attend you—you will have everything you ask for."

This couldn't be happening. "No, wait, I don't—"

"Except one thing," Mír said.

Ari froze.

"Don't ask me to let you go," Mír said. "Do you understand? Do not ask me." She tilted her head. "Is that what truly makes a slave? The inability to come and go as you please? I haven't decided."

Ari tried to speak. She couldn't. She had no idea what to say to that.

Mír's penetrating gaze was turning into something else—something even sharper and more intent, more predatory. "I really can't seem to do without you. Do you know what it was like? Realizing that?" She seemed angry, and Ari took an involuntary step backward. "Wanting you sexually—that I can certainly accept. If others could see you as I have seen you...everyone would want you. Everyone."

"No," Ari managed. "I mean, I really don't think so." She looked down at herself and realized for the first time that she had dirt from her garden on her nightgown and that her hair was probably a fright. "Um."

"No?" Mír murmured. A shiver ran up and down Ari's spine; the purring tone was back. "I disagree."

"I...I..."

"But it wasn't just that. No, that did not vex me at all," Mír continued. "It was *you*. With those stupid leaves in your hair, and not knowing how to talk to anyone at all, and those damn plants you love like your own children—I've never seen anyone like you. Not in my life. Not with the way I live." She suddenly looked bewildered as she said, "Are there many others like you? Even in some place far away from violence and fear—I can't imagine it. And yet." Her eyes suddenly gleamed. "You took so naturally to sex. You got yourself hit with a shock rod in my defense. And just how eager were you to brain my guardsman?"

"That's why you want me?" Ari didn't even know where to look. "Because I'm *weird?*" Because she was an exotic curiosity, an amusing plaything who could be discarded at a moment's notice? She had thought, once that Mír—that Assistant—had seen her as she really was, and had grown to care for that person she saw, at least a little. But she'd been wrong about so very many things.

"I want you," Mír said, "because you were going to plant my favorite flower—I trust now you know what that is—and you're smarter than you know, and you are brave. Reckless, in fact. And if you protected me from myself, then it's time I did the same for you. Doesn't that seem fair?"

Before Ari could splutter that this was the least fair thing she'd ever heard of, Mír took both of her hands in a strong grip. "I have to have you," Mír said, almost gently, as if she was breaking bad news to someone. "You have to be mine. You are mine."

"Have me—" Ari closed her eyes and shook her head. "No. That's not love. That's not..."

"I don't know if I'm capable of love as you define it," Mír said. "I don't think I love like that." She stepped in closer.

Ari, who kept her eyes resolutely shut, felt the heat of Mír's body against her own.

"It doesn't matter," Mír said. "I've tried to tell you this before—we don't need love. You're mine and I'm yours. That's the way it works in here."

"What does that even mean?" Ari said. "I don't get to leave the room?"

"Do you want to?" Mír sounded both amused and astonished. "You?"

"I could always leave before, if I wanted," Ari said, opening her eyes and looking straight at Mír. "That's different. You know it is."

"I do know it," Mír acknowledged. "Of course you may leave the room. You may go anywhere you like on the ship. As for beyond the ship...we'll work that out later." She glanced toward the space station. "It's certainly not possible right now."

"Someone at least has to take care of my garden." Ari bit her bottom lip. "Some other people have seen it now."

Mír raised her eyebrows. Her voice was lower, almost cool, when she asked, "They have? Who?"

"Well, not many people, but sometimes the nurses stopped by when—" Ari cut herself off.

"Nurses," Mír said, because she never missed anything. "I knew it. You have been sick. Were you hospitalized?"

"I don't want to talk about it!" Ari yanked her hands from Mír's grip. "I just want to make sure someone will take care of my plants!" She felt something hot and awful building up in her throat.

"I'll make sure of it." Mír sighed. Then she smiled, obviously trying to make Ari feel better. "We'll bring a few of your more portable specimens here to tide you over."

Ari took a deep breath and nodded, trying not to shake herself to death. *Plants. Think about plants.* Don't think about how she'd handed Nahtal Station, the final achievement of her father's life, over to his worst enemy. Don't think about who his worst enemy was. Don't think about how she'd ignored all the clues and how she'd been lied to. *Think about plants...*

"I can even stand to have that praying mantis around my quarters," Mír added. "What was his name again? Cridley?"

Ari clapped both hands over her mouth and finally burst into tears.

"All right," Mír said after a moment, "evidently I shouldn't have mentioned Cridley."

"Cranli," Ari moaned. "I killed him. I just woke up and I was in the dirt and I'd knocked a shelf on top of him—I'm a muh-murderer—"

"Ariana—"

"—and then I forgot to eat, and that's when I woke up in sickbay, and he was my favorite, and why did that happen, why did I do that, why—"

"Oh, my." Mír sighed again and stood, tugging Ari to her feet as well. She pulled Ari's hands away from her face. "Take a deep breath," she said, in the tone Ari automatically obeyed. The tone everybody automatically obeyed, apparently. "Exhale," Mír reminded her sharply, and Ari did. "Now. Again." Ari did it again. "Better?"

Ari nodded wordlessly, even though it wasn't better at all.

"You need to get some rest," Mír continued. "You appear to be a little overwhelmed. Understandable, I suppose."

Overwhelmed? That was putting it mildly. Ari couldn't possibly rest, not now, when she felt so worked-up.

But neither could she scream, stamp her feet, or do anything else she wanted to do. It wouldn't accomplish anything with Mír—and it would make Ari look as if she had indeed lost her wits, as the female pirate had said. Crying over Cranli had been bad enough.

Ari needed to cool down, and then she needed to think, and she needed time and space to do both of those things. It seemed like Mír was about to give her some.

Ari nodded again and swallowed hard. Tried to sound calm when she said, "Sure. Rest."

"And I must meet with your stationmaster, this so-called Lord Koll," Mír continued. She sneered. "If he thinks he'll be getting a 'My Lord' from me...well."

"He told me I didn't know anything about military tactics," Ari mumbled, and swayed a little. She was so tired. She wasn't thinking straight. *I need time.*

"I expect you could manage, if you cared to learn," Mír said, giving her a little smile. "I expect you have many surprises left for me yet. Come along." She took Ari by the arm and led her back to the big, luxurious bedroom. "I know we woke you in the middle of the night. Sleep now."

Ari stared blankly at the bed. Her bed, now? Or what?

Mír, reading her thoughts, pushed her hair off her forehead again and gave her that same resigned, almost-apologetic smile. "You'll sleep with me at night," she said. "Sex or no sex. Again, I'm afraid I absolutely insist on that point."

Ari glanced at the bed again, and remembered how good it had felt when Assistant's—Mír's—arms had wrapped around her every night, and wondered if it would feel quite so good now, after everything that had happened. She could only say, "Mm."

"I'll return as soon as I can," Mír said in a brisk tone. "You have free access to anything in our quarters, although I strongly suggest you don't try wandering around the ship just yet. There are clothes for you in the closet." She gestured toward a whole wall of paneled doors.

"Uh...okay." Ari sat down on the edge of the mattress because her legs were about to give out. Then she looked up again.

Mír was standing in front of her, looking down at her with the same expression she'd often worn as Assistant: puzzled, tender, and curious all at once. In spite of all the rest, it tugged at Ari's heart, but this was not the time for heart tugging.

Figure this out, Ari ordered yourself, *before you pass out,* and she managed to say, "Hey, before you go, maybe you could tell me, um, what you're doing. With taking over the space stations, and...and rebelling...and all." She blinked. "I mean, when I didn't know it was you, I thought... But now I don't know what to think."

"You haven't guessed? I'm surprised. We'll talk more about it later." Mír brushed out a wrinkle from her gown and swept toward the open door. Then she looked over her shoulder at Ari with a diabolical, little smile. "But don't you think 'Empress Mír' sounds rather...I don't know, natural?"

Ari's jaw dropped, but then Mír was gone. Stunned, Ari sat on the mattress, staring at the doorway until she heard the outer door of Mír's vast chamber open and shut.

Then she stared at the huge bed, in the huge bedroom, adjacent to the hugest room of all, and suddenly felt very tiny and alone. That probably never happened to Mír. This was probably the only place on the ship capable of containing her. Ari staggered to the wall and pressed the button to shut the bedroom door, to close off a little of that enormity. It helped. Some.

More than anything, she felt tired.

She had to think. She couldn't think. Now that the adrenaline was wearing off, she was about to fall over.

How long did she have? Surely meeting Koll wasn't the sort of thing you could knock out in thirty minutes, no matter how efficient Mír might be. There was an alarm clock by the side of the bed. Ari would allow herself half an hour of rest. No more.

Lacking any other sensible alternative, Ari crawled back into the enormous bed, pulled the covers over her, and fell asleep at once.

CHAPTER 20

When the alarm went off, Ari knew she'd been dreaming, but she couldn't remember what about. She didn't think it had been about doorways or stars or anything like that, though. She could have slept for hours more, but there was no time.

Just as if she was getting up for a midnight check on her plants, Ari dragged herself out of Mír's bed.

Still half-asleep, she got up and stumbled to the adjacent bathroom which, like everything else, was huge. The bathtub could comfortably hold five people. And to think Ari had believed that her own quarters must have been such a revelation for a slave used to serving on tiny pirate ships.

She used the toilet and showered. The hot, pounding spray felt wonderful, and when she was done she felt much more human. She wrapped herself in a towel and wandered back into the bedroom, looking around apprehensively in case Mír had returned during her shower. She hadn't. Ari relaxed.

More time. She needed more time to collect her thoughts, so she could sort apart the ones that were furious at both herself and Mír from the ones that hoped Mír was safe. How many times, since meeting a woman with dark hair and a silver forelock, had Ari wondered that someone could make you feel so many things at once?

Remembering what Mír had said about fresh clothes, Ari pressed the button to open the closet doors. Then, as they hummed and hissed open, she gasped. There were racks and rows, and behind them more racks and rows. Was that a hallway down the middle?

Ari blindly grabbed for a plain green dress. After scavenging through several drawers, she found some underthings and dressed herself with shaking hands. She and Mír were roughly the same height, but Mír was broader in the shoulders and hips, so the dress felt a little baggy.

Still, once she was clothed, Ari felt marginally more capable of facing that vast, empty room by herself, and headed through the door.

The *Crown Lily* remained in the same position, pointing ominously at Nahtal Station. Ari shivered and hugged herself although the room's temperature was reasonably warm. Not quite warm enough for her plants, though. Maybe that's why she felt cold. Just the difference of a few degrees from what she was used to made it seem chilly.

She thought about going back for an extra layer of clothing and shuddered at the idea of braving that closet again. Instead, she looked at the station's control tower and wondered what was going on over there. Had the pirates completely occupied it? Was Mír still "meeting with" Lord Koll? Had the station tried to put up any resistance? Was anyone hurt? What about Dr. Eylen, Dr. Ishti, Rellin, and the others who had been so kind to her? Surely pirates wouldn't hurt medical personnel?

They might just enslave them, was all. Ari closed her eyes.

Then she went to the statue. The female figure carried a shield and sword. Was it Mír herself? There wasn't much of a resemblance, but the effect was fierce enough that the statue could *represent* a pirate queen, even in the abstract.

Or you could subtract "pirate" and be left only with "queen." That was what the guard had called Mír in Ari's quarters. *I won't be the one who tells the queen we couldn't find a slip of a girl.*

If they saw Mír as their queen, they thought of Ari quite differently—just a slip of a girl. Apparently Mír had even told them that it would be "easy" to capture Ari. She'd expected her to come along with no resistance at all.

Assistant had often underestimated her, and Mír was apparently no wiser. Sure, Ari had no idea how she was supposed to resist anything in her current position, but she had to find her feet. Had to ground herself like the roots of a tree.

Ari took a deep breath and let the curl of anger inside her grow bright. She couldn't let it overwhelm her, but she could let it focus her, just like she had when she'd ordered the guard away after he'd hit her with the shock rod. If she didn't let it focus her, then the stars only knew what she'd do—let herself get sentimental, soft, forgive Mír for everything just because Ari was glad she was alive.

"I will never call you 'Slave,'" she said, repeating Mír's words under her breath. They rang hollow.

Mír had said something else. *I really can't seem to do without you.*

She'd spoken as if it was a regrettable truth. Ari supposed it was, for her. In fact, she'd said that love made you weak. Ari had thought that was ridiculous at the time, but it probably wasn't a good idea to get too attached to people when you were a pirate queen. Or to get used to thinking of people as people, instead of objects to be torn through on your way to a goal.

Only, Ari hadn't been so hot at doing without Mír, either, during the last month or so. She'd learned what rage was like, and had learned how to hate people, how to want to kill them. And before that, she'd learned about love and desire and joy and fear and grief and…she really hadn't been alive at all before her new "slave" had arrived in her quarters, had she? Ari couldn't forget how she'd felt at seeing Mír just a few…hours?…ago in this very room. Like the nightmare was over.

Now it seemed a new nightmare had started in its place.

"Don't ask me to let you go. Do you understand?"

Ari shuddered. No. She didn't understand. Oh, she understood the urge to keep someone you cared about near you. But she could never do it. She could never have kept Mír enslaved on the station, no matter how much she needed her company. How could Mír do the same to her?

Think, darn it. How *could* Mír do the same to her? And why couldn't Mír do without her? She'd said she couldn't, but she hadn't really explained further, other than saying that she liked having Ari in her arms at night and found her generally endearing. It was almost what you'd say about a beloved pet.

Mír wouldn't have brought her fleet out here just to pick up a pet, though.

Ari rubbed her temples. It had to be more than that, *Ari* had to mean more to Mír than that. Mír wanted something from her, and until Ari figured out what "something" was, she was stuck.

It had to be something that nobody else could offer Mír. Something she couldn't get from her fellow pirates, or from slaves, or even from power. Otherwise, coming back for Ari made no sense. If it wasn't that big a deal, Mír could easily have waited until her plans would have brought her out to Nahtal anyway.

Whatever Ari could offer Mír, then, was something Mír really, really wanted. Maybe it was even something she needed. And only Ari could give it.

Whatever it was, it was the sole card in Ari's hand. If only Rellin could see her now—this wasn't like any game of Catch he'd taught her.

Ari took a deep breath as she looked up at the rough stone face of the statue. It gazed impassively at Nahtal Station through the giant window. It was as cold, hard, and immovable as Mír must have been for decades.

Ari set her jaw. Rock was strong. But given enough time, vegetation could overtake it, cover it up, even take root in the crevices and cracks. Let Mír be the rock; Ari was content to remain a tree.

Her stomach growled. She was apparently a hungry tree. Weird, since her stomach should be in knots. But if she'd needed rest, then she also needed food—and maybe a healthy dose of caffeine wouldn't hurt, since she couldn't crawl back into bed and forget all her problems.

Mír hadn't said how to get food. There had to be a mess hall or canteen somewhere, but no way was Ari going to wander around on her own.

Ari remembered how Mír had tried to escape from Ari's quarters within minutes of arriving at them for the first time. She'd been caught and beaten. Ari wasn't stupid enough to expect better treatment on a pirate ship, no matter how safe Mír said she'd be.

Escape. Ari looked through the window again at Nahtal Station, overrun by pirates, and at the other ships in Mír's fleet on every side of the *Crown Lily.* There was nowhere to go. Not unless Ari downloaded a manual on how to fly a shuttle, stole one from the docking bay (wherever it was), and traversed hyperspace to the heart of the Empire.

Seemed unlikely.

Further inspection of the room revealed an intercom at the vast desk—which appeared to be carved from one large piece of mahogany. Another antique. No wonder Mír had been so taken with Ari's mother's Q'heri board. However, a wooden panel on top of the desk probably concealed a computer interface, and all the drawers had electronic locks.

Ari frowned at the intercom. It seemed more complex than the one in her quarters. There were certainly more buttons, probably because a pirate queen needed to contact people all over her ship at a moment's notice. Ari took a risk and pushed the largest button on the intercom, right in the middle of the interface with a big star on it.

"Hello?" she said as she held it down. *"Is anybody there?"*

She didn't have to wait long for a reply. Within moments, a woman's crisp voice replied, *"How may I serve you, Lady Ariana?"*

Ari rocked back on her heels. But it made sense that Mír's people would know who was in her quarters. *"Um, hi. I was just wondering if I could get some food. And coffee, too, maybe. I don't know who to—"*

"What would Your Ladyship like?"

"Well…what do you have?"

"Anything you like." It might have been Ari's imagination, but the woman's voice sounded a little dry. *"Up to and including Ufordian squid, should it please you."*

Ufordian squid hadn't pleased anyone Ari had ever met, so far as she knew. Hopefully it didn't please Mír, either. "Uh, I'm not picky, really. *Whatever the kitchens are making is fine. Something fast. Just no squid."*

"I'll send Her Majesty's favorite dish to Your Ladyship. We always have that prepared for the flasher—it will need but a few moments to cook."

Her Majesty? Ari could picture her father's disgusted expression. For her part, she already knew better than to underestimate the pirates' loyalty to their queen. *"That, er, sounds fine. Thanks."*

"It is our pleasure to serve Her Ladyship."

What did people on this ship know about her? About her history with Mír? *"Ah, great. Sorry, but who am I talking to?"*

"I am one of Her Majesty's personal assistants. We have been instructed to give you privacy until you requested otherwise. We are ready to appear in person at a moment's notice should you wish it."

"No!" It came out much more rudely than Ari had intended. Whoever she was, the woman seemed polite, and there was no point in antagonizing anyone unnecessarily. It could only be a good thing if the people around Mír thought well of Ari. *"I mean, no thank you. Just the food will be great."*

"As Your Ladyship desires. Is there anything else?"

"No. Not right now. Except, do you know when"—Ari couldn't manage "Her Majesty", she just couldn't—*"she'll be back?"*

"Her Majesty keeps her own time."

Of course she did. Ari managed not to sigh. *"Okay. That's all. Thanks."*

"We are at your disposal, Your Ladyship."

The light on the intercom blinked off.

Ari fidgeted. She'd prefer not to be stuffing her face when Mír returned. How long would she have to wait? The food had to be prepared, and the ship was huge, and who even knew where the kitchens were? If it was anything like Nahtal, it would probably be at least twenty minutes.

It was just over five. A stocky slave woman appeared with a covered tray in her hands. She seemed to be in her fifties and was well dressed, as those things went, in a crisp white tunic that had embroidered detailing on the hem. She bowed. "Your Ladyship."

No matter how well they were dressed, the pirates' slaves had no name but "Slave." Ari couldn't bring herself to say it. She reached out for the tray, even as she peeked over the slave's shoulder to see what lay beyond Mir's door. Just a corridor, ornately carpeted but framed by steel walls, that led to another door.

When Ari tried to take the tray, the slave seemed surprised, and even made to draw back. "I'm happy to set up the table for Your Ladyship."

"Oh...that's—" Ari paused and stopped herself from dismissing the slave completely. Could this be an opportunity to learn what was going on? She forced a friendly smile. "That's not necessary, but I'd love somebody to talk to. Come on in."

The slave woman froze, and Ari's heart fell. The woman dropped eye contact and said in a subdued voice, "That isn't my place, Your Ladyship."

"But—" *But Assistant talked to me all the time.* Yet again, Ari could have kicked herself for her stupidity. She should have known. "That's okay. I'll just take the food."

The slave hesitated again but then handed over the tray. It seemed like she couldn't help giving Ari a quick once-over, but she never met Ari's gaze. "Is there any other way I can serve Your Ladyship?"

"No. No thank you." Ari bit her lip. "Uh, have a nice day."

Now the woman looked kind of spooked. "As Your Ladyship wishes," she said, bowed again, and hurried away.

Ari balanced the tray on one arm as she pushed the button to close the door. Fantastic. Within hours of her arrival, people already thought Ari was as weird here as they did everywhere else. Ari would probably get a lot more respect on a pirate ship if she snapped her fingers and yelled at slaves than if she was polite to them.

The thought was so depressing that the tray seemed heavier in her hands as she took it to the low table in front of the sofa.

When she took the silver top off the tray, she found a linen napkin, fine silverware, and a china plate bearing a beautifully browned steak, next to a side of vegetables. A thermos of coffee sat on the edge of the tray.

Ari looked at it and shook her head. She hadn't passed a single moment on the *Crown Lily* that matched her long-held ideas of what pirate ships were like: dirty, disorganized, and crude. Mír had spoken so often of the discipline of her fleet, and apparently, she hadn't been lying. Her flagship seemed like a floating palace.

Fitting, for a pirate queen who wanted to be Empress. The memory struck Ari, and she nearly gasped. Mír had tossed it out so casually right before Ari had fallen asleep, and for a second, Ari wondered if it had only been a dream.

No, it was no dream. Not with the way Mír had been angling at power instead of just roving and pillaging as she'd done for decades. She really, honest to goodness wanted to take charge of the whole Empire, and the unlimited scale of that ambition took Ari's breath away.

She could think about that while she ate. Ari couldn't remember the last time she'd had steak. She cut into it, relieved to see that it wasn't red and oozing inside. She wouldn't have put it past either Assistant *or* Mír to eat raw meat.

She couldn't help thinking of "them" as two separate people. But Assistant was the woman who'd played Q'heri with such abandon that she'd used the riskiest possible maneuver to take it all. Ari had beaten her on points, but real life didn't have points. There were no technicalities that let you wriggle away from a crushing defeat. Mír was proving that in real life every day.

Ari managed to get down about half of the generous portion, even though the steak had been perfectly cooked. Mír ate like this every day? She must have felt starved with Ari, but she'd never said anything about it. Ari covered the tray, pushed it away, and sat back on the sofa with the thermos of coffee in her hands.

If only she knew enough about Mír, beyond the horror stories she'd heard and the behaviors she'd observed. What was going on inside that razor-sharp mind? It would be crazy to antagonize her or make her angry until Ari was surer of her own place in this new world.

Problem was, Ari was still plenty angry herself, and the more energy she got from her rest and her food, the worse it got. Fear would have been better—at least a little of it, enough to keep Ari from saying the wrong thing or overstepping in a way that would end in catastrophe.

She'd been cross with Mír before: angry when she'd hurt her wrists in a futile struggle, insulted when Mír had implied she was a hermit, downright furious when Mír had told her people were basically bad and laughed at her letter to Dr. Phylyxas. Ari hadn't bothered holding back her pique. Far less had been at stake on all those occasions, but Mír had never seemed annoyed by any of Ari's displays. She'd even seemed to respect them.

You can't count on that here. You can't count on anything. Ari worried her bottom lip.

The door hissed open. Ari looked around with a gasp as the door closed again behind Mír, who stood in the doorway for a moment and silently regarded Ari. She looked a little tired but unharmed.

About a third of Ari's brain was protesting, saying she needed more time to think. Another third was ready to get this over with, however it ended.

The final third, the worst and most treacherous part, went dizzy with relief at seeing Mír safe and sound. *Maybe love really does make you weak,* Ari thought, and then told herself to shut up, because thinking about either love or weakness wasn't going to help.

She cleared her throat, set down the coffee, and stood. "Um...hi."

"Hello." Mír began walking toward Ari, the black silk of her gown rustling as she moved. Ari remembered her from the holos—clad in black armor and helm, always from a distance. It'd looked natural on her, that was for sure. But so did the dress, and personally, Ari was glad Mír wasn't wearing any intimidating armor right now.

"Are you feeling better?" Mír asked.

Ari almost cringed as she remembered the way she'd carried on before falling asleep. She had to do better this round. "Yeah."

Mír glanced at the covered tray and nodded in approval. "I'm glad you've eaten something. Did you rest well?"

It was so solicitous, as if Ari was a guest to be made comfortable instead of...whatever she was. A prisoner? A companion? Both?

Might as well respond in kind. "Yes. Thank you."

Her tone of voice—polite, almost reserved—clearly caught Mír's attention. Her eyes narrowed a little, and even that was enough to make Ari's heart rate increase. Mír didn't seem angry, but she was already on alert.

Stay calm, be cool, test the waters... "How did the meeting go?"

"Fine." Mír glanced out the window at the space station. "I have what I need for now. We'll depart soon." Then she looked back at Ari, her eyebrows raised. "I wasn't terribly impressed by Lord Koll."

Ari couldn't hold back a snort. "Neither is anybody else." What would Mír say if she knew her opinion was backed by Nahtal's medical staff during their off hours?

She surprised herself by adding, "It was stupid of the Emperor to send him out here." Then she snapped her mouth shut. She hadn't meant to say that, she wasn't sure she'd even thought those words before, but the truth seemed so obvious now.

"On that we agree." Mír drew closer to Ari, but not as close as she had before, when their bodies had nearly pressed together. Now she left a couple feet of distance between them. "Your Empire is infected with incompetence and sloth. The infection is growing outward from the center." She spread her hands. "Here I am with the cure."

"You mean, you?"

"Exactly." Mír looked Ari up and down. "The dress is too big, but green suits you."

"Thank you," Ari said, but she was not to be deterred. "You really want to be Empress?"

"I *will* be Empress." Mír gave Ari a canny look. "Surprised?"

"Sort of. Maybe. I thought..." Ari ran a hand through her hair. "I would never have guessed it before I knew"—she paused—"I mean, before I met you. But now..."

"That was a telling hesitation, Ariana," said Mír, who had never let Ari get away with anything and obviously wasn't going to start now. "You don't feel you know me?"

"You told me I didn't!" Oops. Ari lowered her voice to sound less snappish. "When I said I..." *Loved you.* It hurt too much to say now.

"You didn't know me then." Mír raised her chin. "I think that's fair to say, don't you? But the big secret's out. You've got the final piece."

"I don't think so." Ari willed her heart rate to go down. "I should have figured it out before now. Not that you were—but I should have realized *something*. I feel so stupid." Unable to meet Mír's piercing blue eyes, she looked at the statue again.

"We've been over this." Mír sighed. "You're not stupid. Naïve and trusting, certainly."

Ari fisted her hands and walked away from Mír toward the statue. "It feels like the same thing right now." She looked up at the woman hewn from rock. "Is this you?"

"Yes and no." The cautious tone was back in Mír's voice. She was undoubtedly keeping her gaze trained on Ari. "I took her from a dig site on Helenor 5 perhaps...five years ago? Shortly after the reconstruction of the *Crown Lily*. She's supposed to be over two thousand years old, but I see myself in her."

"So do I." Ari looked the statue up and down again. "She's beautiful." It was true. Even roughly carved, the figure carried a great deal of dignity on her stone shoulders. "You 'took' her?"

She turned on her heel to see Mír watching her with a wry smile. "Yes, I did."

"Well, now that you've got all my money, maybe you can pay them back," Ari said bitterly.

After a pause, Mír said, "You're serious, aren't you?"

Ari hadn't realized it until then. She nodded.

Mír exhaled through her nose. "She wasn't for sale. She was about to be sent to some museum's warehouse, perhaps to be trotted out for a special exhibit now and again—but more likely never to see the light of day. Now she faces the stars. Which strikes you as more of a waste?" She crossed her arms. "Nothing is black and white. Not out here, or even back there." She gestured at Nahtal.

"You can't just take what you want." Here it came. Ari braced herself and tried to breathe evenly. "Not all the time."

Mir pursed her lips. "Tell that to the current Emperor while he lounges around all day on silk pillows. I know what it means to sacrifice."

"Sacrifice what? Why do you even want to be Empress?" Her father had said once that he wouldn't take on such a job for all the riches in the Empire.

"I don't want to be, I need to be," Mir said, and then looked a bit surprised—as if she, too, was saying things she hadn't meant to. "This has been in the works for a long time, Ariana. Accelerated, I admit, by the time I spent on the station."

Accelerated thanks to Ari's money, she meant. Not to mention the useful information Mir had picked up. Ari closed her eyes.

"What would you prefer?" Mir continued. "That my fleet keeps rampaging while the Empire grows weaker and the Kazir close in? You might be surprised by how little I wish to see that happen. Or would you rather that we give it all up entirely, and go enjoy sybaritic lives on some tropical world?"

That last one didn't seem so bad. There would probably be a lot of plants. "It sounds safer."

Mir rolled her eyes. "You let me worry about our safety. In the meantime, I don't suppose you've noticed that this little revolution has largely been accomplished without bloodshed?"

"Carellian turned on the Imperial forces," Ari reminded her. "They blew a ship into pieces!"

Mir clicked her tongue. "There were some growing pains."

"*Growing pains?*"

"Of course. This is a new enterprise. It wasn't on my orders—I have since made sure that no one makes such a move without my permission. Carellian now has a new commander." Mir lifted one shoulder in a half shrug. "I will grant you that I didn't write the Emperor a note of apology."

"Oh, for..." Ari glanced back at Nahtal. Had it always looked so dingy and small? Or was the *Crown Lily* already distorting her perceptions, shrinking everything else around her? "Are all the pirates leaving? Are you going to keep any ships here?"

"No," Mír said. "There is more work to be done back in our pocket of the Empire. I don't wish to overextend my forces by leaving some of them stranded out here by themselves. We got what we came for, and now we're leaving." Her eyes gleamed. "Although we'll be back."

"You said you wanted stuff besides me." Ari hesitated. "Like what?"

"Many things," Mír said, sounding careless—and then she reached out and hooked her arm around Ari's waist, pulling her in closer.

Ari squeaked, Mír smirked, and Ari's heart began to pound.

"Schematics of the mining shafts on Exer," Mír added. "Records of outputs and resources." She paused, smiled a little, and added, "And let's not forget about four hundred tons of ore. That'll fuel one third of the fleet for a full cycle. Not bad, is it?"

"Um..."

"And on a lesser note, those excellent star charts in the Observatory. They really were a revelation when I saw them for the first time. We have nothing to equal them in the fleet." She smiled softly. "I memorized as much as I could. I can't tell you how useful some of those precise co-ordinates have proven. But it'll be nice to have all of them at my fingertips."

She slid her hand up and down Ari's back. Ari grabbed at her shoulders and squeaked again as their bodies pressed fully together.

Mír said, "Speaking of what I have at my fingertips..."

Before Ari could say anything, Mír kissed her.

The kiss roused Ari, all right, but not in the way Mír undoubtedly intended. Mír's lips were so soft, so familiar, pressing against Ari's as if everything was as it had been before. And, as always, it felt so *right*— but Ari couldn't let herself be fooled that way again. She'd allowed herself to believe all along that what they'd been doing was right just because she'd wanted it so much.

She wanted it now, too. She hated herself for it, and she hated Mír, and she loved Mír, loved the way their bodies fit together and how Mír's embrace felt like coming home. It was all too much to contain, and with a groan, she turned her head away and pushed, stumbling back when Mír let her go.

Shaking, she met Mír's gaze, which had darkened considerably. Ari had to say something. But what could she say? What was most on her heart?

"You're angry," Mír said coldly. "Aren't you? Angry that I'm not who you thought I was. Angry at the life I lead and the blood I've got on my hands." She sneered, looking as contemptuous as she had on the day they'd met. "How dare you be angry at that? How dare you judge what I—"

"I'm angry you *left me!*"

Silence fell. Mír's sneer vanished. Her eyes widened.

Ari was shaking again. She'd found what was on her heart, all right. Okay, so...she couldn't blame Mír for lying about who she was on the space station. Mír would have been crazy to trust Ari with her real identity. And if she really was trying to change her ways, be something more than a pirate—a force for good, even—Ari should at least try to be open-minded. Hear her out, talk it through, and learn more.

This, though. *This.*

Mír had let Ari think she was dead. She'd let Ari think, for over a month, that she was dead, and that it had been Ari's fault for letting her go, and that Ari was alone in the universe, and...

"Couldn't you have told me?" Ari whispered.

Mír frowned. "Told you what?"

"That you were alive." Ari swallowed harshly. "Didn't you know I'd think you were dead? Didn't you know I'd hear about the freighter?"

"I assumed you would, but why—"

"What do you mean, why? You could have just sent me something saying you were still alive—not telling me who you really were or anything, but—"

"Impractical," Mír said firmly, holding up a hand. "Any transmissions from a pirate ship would instantly have been intercepted by your station. In fact, you would have gotten in a great deal of trouble if they thought you were communicating with pirates."

"I wouldn't have cared. I would rather have known." Ari would have traded every plant, every seed in her garden, every drop of blood in her own body for the knowledge that Assistant—Mír—had been alive and well. She curled her hands into fists.

"I cared," Mír said. "It would have been much more difficult to snatch you from some Imperial brig than the safety of your own quarters. You might consider that."

"Oh," Ari said, startled. "You—you would have done that?"

"No," Mír said, "because I would have cunningly avoided the possibility in the first place by not sending you a message."

"Oh," Ari repeated, wondering why this wasn't making her feel any better. Mír was alive. She had, in fact, come back. She'd had good reasons for not telling Ari the truth. So why did Ari still feel as if she was about to come apart at the seams?

After a pause, Mír spoke again. She sounded as if she was carefully spacing her words when she reminded Ari, "For what it's worth, I came for you as soon as I could. Sooner than I should have." She stepped forward.

"I...yeah." She tried to breathe more evenly. "You did."

"I admit, I hadn't guessed you'd be quite this upset," Mír said.

"What?" Ari wondered if her eyes would pop out of her head. Surely Mír hadn't really said— "Are you kidding? You didn't...how could you possibly—"

"Possibly think you would have starved yourself?" Mír asked coolly. "I knew you wouldn't be dancing down the corridors, but are you telling me I should have anticipated that?"

"I didn't do it on purpose! I wasn't thinking straight. I..." Ari grabbed herself in a tight embrace. "I don't remember much about it. It was just that you were dead, and so was my father, and I didn't, I didn't know what...I didn't know how..." Her voice cracked, and her throat grew thick at just the thought of how awful those days had been. "I just remember waking up in sickbay and they put a tube in my arm."

Mír said nothing, but she reached out and touched Ari's shoulder. This time, Ari couldn't move away. She couldn't look away from Mír's eyes, watching as realization dawned in their cool, blue depths.

What was she thinking? Perhaps that Ari was weak, pathetic, a quitter. Mír would never give up on anything, even if she did lose people she cared for. Ari managed, "Honestly, I wasn't trying to..." She couldn't finish. She waited for the judgment, for Mír's stern reproof of her weakness. Or, worse, for the mockery that would drive Ari to say something really, really imprudent.

To her surprise, Mír only told her, "Well, that's all over now. Everything's all right." Her voice was surprisingly light.

It had, in fact, been a little *too* light. She was trying to sound that way.

Ari kept looking into her eyes when she asked, "Is it?"

"Of course it is. We're together again, and we won't be parted." Mír cupped her shoulder and rubbed her thumb against Ari's skin. "Why shouldn't it be all right?"

Ari stood for a moment in silence, struggling with herself. Then she took her courage in both hands. She was going to need all of it, considering that she was about to defy the most dangerous person in the known universe.

"It's not all right," she said.

"What?"

Ari closed her eyes and braced herself. Here went nothing. She was either going to take the emperor or lose the game, and what would happen then? Nothing good, that was for certain.

But she had to say it anyway.

She whispered, "Will you really not let me go?"

Mír snatched her fingertips from Ari's arm. Ari tensed all over, unable to help the frigid wash of fear. Mír wouldn't hurt her physically.

But Ari had learned that there were ways to break people that had nothing to do with their bodies, and Mír probably knew them all.

Mír clamped her hands around both of Ari's arms. But her voice was even and calm when she said, "No. I told you not to ask."

"I know." She opened her eyes again to see that Mír had gone paler. "But you really won't?"

Mír's grip was almost painful now as she stepped in close enough for them to be pressed together, almost nose to nose. This close, Ari could tell her heart was racing in her chest, nearly as fast as Ari's own. Ari didn't try to shake her off or protest.

"Don't be ridiculous, Ariana." In the space of a few seconds, her voice had gone from even as glass to rough as the rocks. "I said—don't make me repeat myself."

"I don't want to be your slave," Ari said, hating the way her knees shook, unable to stop them. *Be like the trees. Take root. Be stronger than stone.* "You've *been* a slave. You know what it's like. Any freedom you had came from me—that's not how it should be. Why do you want that for me?"

"Stop," Mír said. "I told you that you don't have to—you are not a slave."

"So, what am I? A prisoner? I know you said—"

"Why are you talking like this?" Mír demanded, and for the first time since they'd met, Ari heard a crack in her voice.

Try to keep this calm, Ari's inner voice begged her. *Try to figure out what she's thinking.* "I just don't understand—"

"There is nothing to understand." Now Mír's voice was much too flat to be truly tranquil. Her grip, for only a moment, shook on Ari's arm. "For God's sake, you almost starved to death without me."

Ari really wished she could deny it. There was one important fact she had to point out, though. "I didn't," she said. "I would have lived. It would have been awful, but I would have done it. I would have kept going."

"I'm very glad to hear that," Mír said tightly. "Keep going here."

"I will," Ari said. "I mean, I don't want to leave you, but..." What did she want? "I just want..." She had no idea. She didn't understand anything about life anymore, if she ever had.

Mir snarled and let go. Ari's heart stopped, and not just from fear. Here she was, bargaining for her freedom—or for something she couldn't name—and the thought of being parted from Mir seemed worse than death all over again.

Maybe Ari really was as crazy as people sometimes said, but how many times could one person endure being left behind or cast aside? All she wanted was the right to make the decision herself—for once.

Mir turned away. Ari heard her taking a deep breath. Oh, no. She'd never seen Mir so visibly try to control herself. What was she repressing the urge to do?

Before Ari could come up with a thousand unpleasant possibilities, Mir rounded on her again. Ari couldn't stop a little gasp, but she managed not to curl in on herself protectively. Mir's icy blue eyes were all fire now. They'd looked like that on the night of Ari's love confession, too—when Ari had reminded Mir that she wasn't with the pirates anymore. She'd been trying to reassure her. Talk about another situation she'd misread completely.

"I know what you want. You want to believe people are decent," Mir said. "Isn't that right? Isn't that what you said to me once?"

"Yes." Ari licked her lips. "At least, that's part—"

"I'm not," Mir said. "I am not like you. I do not want to be like you. The most I can do is to protect you from other people like me. And there are a lot of people like me." She stalked forward again and leaned in until her nose touched Ari's cheek. Ari could feel her breath, could nearly feel the edge of her teeth against her skin. "Listen to me. *I will give you everything you want.*" She took hold of Ari's arms again. "Things you didn't even know you wanted."

"You're hurting my arms," Ari said, trembling despite herself. Fear? Desire? She couldn't sort it out. "What do you think you're going to give me, exactly?"

"The Empire!" Mír snarled and let go of her once more. Maybe because her hands were shaking again. She never stopped looking into Ari's eyes, though. "What are you pining for? Your little room full of plants? By the time I'm through, you'll have that thieving Senior Royal Botanist licking your shoes for forgiveness. By the time I'm through, I'll have built an empire that your father would have been proud to serve and defend—"

Ari, who had been frantically trying to think of ways to calm down a pirate queen, couldn't help herself. "He was proud! He—"

"Rightfully proud," Mír spat. "Are you incapable of thinking on so large a scale? Or do you think I'm incapable of doing this?"

"No," Ari said at once. "I already told you, I know you can do anything. I—" She shook her head, rubbed her arms. "But how am I supposed to help you? I mean, what good am I about any of that? I just do stuff with plants!"

"You might realize you've opened my eyes on the uses of plants," Mír said, sounding slightly calmer now that Ari had given her something else to focus on. "Crops. Fuel. You were the one working on a hardier pea, weren't you? Saying that you wanted it to be of use to someone?" She sighed. "You'll be of use to me. In that, and other ways."

Ari stared at her. "I'll be *useful?*" That certainly didn't sound like any love poem she'd ever read.

"You once told me you wanted to be." This time, Mír took hold of Ari's hands instead of her arms. Her grip wasn't painful this time, but it was decidedly firm. "You will be. I need you with me. I need you here."

Ari had something that nobody else could give Mír. She'd already known that. She'd been thinking of it as a card to play, or a piece to move across the board—but really, it was something simpler and far more important.

"Tell me what you need from me." Her voice shook. "Tell me what's so important that you want to—" Not "imprison," that wasn't right. "Keep me."

The words made her eyes sting, made a hot lump grow in her throat when she hadn't expected it. To be kept, to be wanted, by someone she loved, someone extraordinary...for the first time, to be wanted...

Before Mír could reply, that slipped out of Ari, too. "Everybody always goes. I don't get a say in it." Her mother, her father, Mír, teachers and slaves she'd lost over the years, Ari always left behind to start over with her plants. "I just want the choice, I want it to be me, for once, who gets to pick."

Mír's uncomprehending expression made the hot lump grow bigger, and Ari didn't know how to make it go away. "How can I make you understand?" she gasped. She didn't try to tug her hands away from Mír's. She needed that contact, the reminder that someone was with her to tether her to the ground. "What do you need from me?"

Mír's throat worked. Her lips had gone white.

"I need you to choose me," she rasped.

Ari lost her breath as if all the oxygen had been sucked out of the room. Mír's words felt like an explosion inside her, heat racing through her in something too intense to be called joy, or relief, or pain, or anything at all. That was exactly what she'd needed to hear, the only answer that could come close to filling the hole inside her that she'd kept covered with leaves for ten years. *"Oh."*

If Mír realized the incalculable gift she'd given Ari, she didn't show it. Instead, she snatched her hands away and spat, "Does that satisfy you? Is that little ego of yours pacified now? Hearing that from me." Her eyes burned.

Ari surfaced from her daze just in time to realize how Mír had sacrificed her pride, and how that could go very sour, very quickly. She could only think to tell the truth: "Nobody's ever said that to me before."

The anger that had been creeping through Mír's frame, drawing up her shoulders and calling blood into her pale cheeks, seemed to drain away at once. She inhaled, let it out a little shakily, and said, "I know."

She slid her arms around Ari's waist again, bending to kiss her forehead, her cheeks, and finally her mouth. She repeated, "I know."

Ari sighed, unable to help it. The energy she'd been carrying since Mír's arrival was still curling inside her, demanding release. *No, not yet,* she begged her wayward heart. *I just need—I have to know—*

"Don't ask me to do what I can't do," Mír muttered against Ari's lips. "I can't do everything. Believe it or not."

"What would I do here?" Ari said when Mír turned away just enough to kiss her cheek again. She couldn't stop herself from putting her hands on Mír's shoulders. "What would I be to you?" A warm body in bed? An amusement, kept separate from the rest of Mír's life, as isolated as she'd always been?

Mír kissed her throat and whispered into her ear, "You would be at my side."

Ari went still. Her breath stopped. Her fingertips dug so hard into Mír's shoulders that it had to hurt, but Mír made no protest.

"Kiss me," she managed. "Right now, right n—"

Mír gasped, then slanted her mouth over Ari's and kissed her again. It wasn't like it had ever been before—this was another explosion, an end to lies, a new beginning, and Ari wasn't sure yet who she'd be when it was over, but it would be someone *more* than she'd been. That was a lot to ask of a kiss, but the second one was the same, and by the third, it no longer mattered where they were.

Good thing, too, because they ended up on the floor. Mír made a noise that was half laugh and half moan as she lay between Ari's spread legs, kissed her again, and tore at the buttons of her dress.

"Without this." She bit and sucked at the skin she uncovered, from Ari's throat down to her breasts. "Without this for a month." She took Ari's left nipple in her mouth with a moan, and Ari grabbed her head while her body came all the way back to life.

She bent over and rubbed her nose in Mír's soft black hair, gasping for air. She had enough brain cells left for one question. "Wh-why," she said, "why wouldn't you ever let me touch you?"

"You can," Mír panted, yanking Ari's dress down around her waist and sucking hard at her throat, like she'd always loved doing. "You can, but first let me—I have to—" She set to kissing and touching Ari like she had on their last night together, going crazy with it, not stopping until Ari's new dress was practically in shreds and Ari was a breathless, sobbing puddle beneath her.

Ari should have known she was a pirate queen. No—even that wasn't right, she should wonder if Mír wasn't a creature out of ancient lore, a powerful spirit that descended onto mortals and whisked them away into another world. She should never have believed, not even for a second, that Mír was an ordinary person like Ari, content with life's daily offerings. Nothing seemed to be enough for her. In her kisses, Ari tasted a boundless hunger, and her caresses left no spot of Ari's body unclaimed.

It all felt so natural. As natural as petals unfurling from buds in the spring. Ari found herself returning all Mír's kisses with her own hunger, sliding her hands into Mír's black hair and whispering *more, more* against her lips until they were wrapped around each other on the floor, so tightly they might as well have been one person.

For the first time, Ari ran her hands up and down Mír's back to hold her close, but she still couldn't get close enough.

Mír apparently agreed. "The bedroom," she gasped as she licked a drop of sweat from between Ari's breasts. "Our bed. I'm going to—" She paused and then reared up on her elbows, looming over Ari. Her face was flushed, her eyes wild as she said, "Get ready, Ariana, because I am going to *fuck* you."

Once, Ari had found that word obscene, too dirty for what the act meant to her. Tonight, it made her moan because oh, yeah, she needed exactly that. Again and again. "Yes!"

"Yes," Mír agreed, staggering up and managing not to trip on her own gown, still intact. She took Ari's outstretched hands and tugged her to her feet, wrapping her arms around her again. The remains of Ari's dress fell and pooled around her feet. Her bare body felt so good pressed against Mír's that for a moment, she wondered if they wouldn't go right back down on the floor.

By some unseen mercy, they didn't. Mír tugged Ari back toward the bedroom. Ari still ached with unsatisfied need, wondered if she'd ever stop aching, especially when they had to stop in the doorway so Mír could push her up against the wall for more kisses.

"Please, please," she moaned against Mír's mouth.

"My God. Put your legs around me," Mír gasped, cupping Ari's bottom firmly. For once in her life, Ari spared no thought to her own clumsiness and threw her arms around Mír's shoulders before hopping up and wrapping her legs around Mír's waist. Mír was as strong as she had ever been and didn't so much as grunt with effort. She kissed Ari again and walked them backward toward the enormous bed, her soft breasts pressed beneath Ari's, her heart hammering against Ari's own chest.

And then she lay Ari on her back in the middle of the enormous bed and removed her underwear, not bothering to make it slow or seductive this time, just yanking it over Ari's hips and tossing it away so she could drive her fingers in and out of Ari while Ari writhed underneath her and Mír said "*yes, yes, yes*". It was dark, almost as dark as it had always been in Ari's room, and so there was nothing to focus on, nothing to cling to but what Mír was doing and the way she felt against Ari's body.

"Tell me how it feels," she panted. "Ariana. Tell me—"

Ari couldn't tell her anything of the kind. She could only manage to say, high-pitched and breathless, "Harder!"

Mír gasped, complied, whispered, "Take it," as Ari rose to meet her. "Yes—please—"

"Do you have any idea," Mír moaned into her ear, her fingers going faster and faster, "how many times I came while doing this to you? And never told you?" When Ari cried out, she breathed, "Oh, yes. Oh, yes, darling, yes I did." She curled her fingers, and Ari keened. "So pay attention now—" And she went stiff against Ari, giving a soft, shuddering little cry. Her fingers kept moving, but lost the rhythm; the cry turned into a groan.

Realizing what was happening, what Mír was doing, Ari curled her body around that hand and let go with a cry of her own. She pulsed and ached with release, a white-hot burst of pleasure that started deep in her core and filled her whole body. Like she'd walked into the heart of a star after all.

"Yes," Mír said again, her voice a hiss of triumph. "Yes. Made for this. Made for me." She kissed Ari's chest, panting gently as Ari finished. "Mine."

"Oh," Ari said, shaking everywhere. She felt like she'd lost all her bones sometime in the last few seconds. "Oh."

Mír's fingertips touched Ari's lips. Ari groaned as she tasted herself, and she licked the remains of her arousal away. Impossibly, it flared inside her once more. She fumbled for the dress's clasp on Mír's left shoulder, only to be denied by Mír's touch stopping her in place.

"But it's my turn!" she gasped. Whined, really. Her own tone made her wince.

Mír gave a brief, slightly breathless huff of laughter. "I'm well aware. But haven't I shown you there's something to be said for patience?"

"Yeah, whole weeks of it. You—you are going to let me, right? Soon? I mean, tonight?"

"Insatiable," Mír muttered, and kissed Ari in the darkness. "Believe me. You'll get your turn, once I catch my breath."

Good thing she couldn't see Ari's frown. Mír might have come, but she hardly seemed exhausted, and they'd gone for longer before. That wasn't really why she wanted to wait. So, what was the reason? There weren't any secrets left between them, were there?

But no still meant no, and it wasn't "no" forever. All Ari could say was, "Okay." She felt a little better when Mír put her arms around her and pulled her in close. It didn't exactly cool the heat inside her, and from the way Mír's breath caught, they were both feeling it.

Patience. Wait and see. Ari reached up again until her knuckles brushed the Mír's cheek. She stroked them against the skin there, reveling even in this tiny intimacy. "You're so soft here."

"I'm not soft in many places," Mír said dryly.

"No kidding." Ari's hand slid down to touch Mír's firm bicep. "When your guards came...I wished I was stronger. That I knew how to fight."

"You should learn how to defend yourself," Mír agreed. "Not that I intend you should be in a moment's danger, but everyone should know the basics."

Ari had been speaking in the abstract, but Mír had translated it into practical action—something in a future, a near one, that involved them both. She seemed to be taking it for granted that they would continue on together, but why was her body tensing up against Ari's own, when she should be relaxed and "catching her breath"?

"Would you turn on the light?" Ari asked.

Mír made a noise of assent and rolled away. Ari's naked form felt suddenly chilled. The room was cooler than she'd thought. Then she heard the click of the bedside lamp coming on, and the room filled with soft light.

Ari hoped she wasn't being too obvious about looking at Mír, inspecting her flushed cheeks and mussed hair. The silver forelock somehow seemed even more appealing as it dangled over her eye until she brushed it away impatiently. For all her level-headed words, she was agitated. Ari could subtly try to figure out—

"So?" Mír said. "What do you see?"

Darn it.

Ari took a deep breath and tried to center herself. *Be the tree rooted into the ground.* If they weren't going to have sex, then it was time to see if Mír really meant what she'd said. "You said you'd give me everything I wanted. The Empire."

"And so I will." Mír sat up and took hold of Ari's hand. She squeezed it and kept looking into Ari's eyes. "Give me a year, and you'll sit at my side in the Imperial throne room. Well"—she rolled her eyes—"until you get a headache. But you know what I mean."

"Oh," Ari said. Mír's grip kept her right hand warm, but her left hand was starting to feel clammy. "That's, uh...I can see why you'd want to, but I was thinking we could start smaller."

"I already said we can bring in your plants—"

"I don't just mean plants. I mean people." At Mír's obvious look of surprise, Ari continued, "The nurses and doctors who took care of me.

They were very kind. They became my...well, they almost became my friends." There hadn't been enough time to establish a real, deep bond with Rellin, Dr. Eylen, or Dr. Ishti. But if there had been, Ari thought something meaningful might have grown from it, even if it couldn't compare to what she felt when she was with Mír. "When you come back to Nahtal—if they're still there, and there's a fight—"

Mír's eyes widened in understanding. She nodded. "I'll give orders that they not be harmed." She stroked Ari's hair. "Hell, I'll honor them. After all, they did me a great service. I am thankful."

"Me too." Ari closed her eyes and savored the feeling of Mír's hand in her hair. Depending on how she reacted to Ari's next request, it might not happen again for a while. "And there's just one more person."

Mír must have picked up on the hesitant note in Ari's voice, because her hand paused. She asked cautiously, "Who?"

"That guard who hit me with the shock rod," Ari said.

Mír pulled her hand out of Ari's hair. Ari kept her eyes shut as Mír said, "I know you well enough to think you're not about to demand his execution."

"Kind of the opposite," Ari agreed. She took a deep breath and opened her eyes. "I know he was horrible. I hate him, too." She hadn't realized it until she said it out loud. "But I don't want someone to be murdered or tortured because of me. I know that's why you'd do it. I remember that look on your face."

It wasn't hard to remember, considering that Mír's current expression was similar to it.

"He struck you," Mír said, voice soft with barely controlled anger. "He hurt you."

"I lived. It was an accident. Are you mad because he almost hit you, too?"

Mír pursed her lips. "I was trying to get into that control center, you know. No, I am not angry because some fool stumbled into doing his job. But then he struck my—" She hesitated, and though Ari held her breath, she finished with, "It sends a terrible message if I forgive him for that. I would lose the respect of my crew, and then I'd lose everything else."

"Nobody else knows what happened," Ari reminded her. "I don't think he'll be eager to start spreading the news now." Shoot, at the first opportunity he got, he'd probably flee to another system and change his name. Then an awful thought occurred to her. "Um...unless you already..."

Mír ground her jaw and shook her head. "He is in custody on the station. I intended to have him brought to the *Crown Lily*'s brig before we departed."

Ari gulped. "Does anybody know why?"

"Not unless he's blabbed." Mír sighed. "I'll make you a deal." When Ari bit her lip and nodded for her to continue, she said, "If he has remained silent on what happened, I'll send him to the mines, no explanation necessary. If he has not, then I will have him killed swiftly, with no pain or suffering. He cannot—" She held up a hand when Ari made to protest. "He cannot get away with it, Ariana. You've bargained for the best mercy he could ever hope for."

A quick, clean death was mercy in the world of pirates. Ari hung her head and nodded again.

"Ariana," Mír said quietly, "I don't compromise for just anyone. Not on matters like this."

That had to be true. And it was what Ari really wanted: not for Mír to give what it pleased her to give, like palaces and servants, but to show that she could give even when it was hard, even when it went against her own inclinations.

If she was going to demand that of Ari, then she had to be willing to do it, too. Pirate queen or not.

"However," Mír said, "there's still one thing that needs to be made very clear."

Ari fought not to sigh. Had the idea of compromise been too good to be true? "What?"

"You tell me."

"Huh?"

Mír offered no further clarification. She just kept looking at Ari as if, for once, she wanted Ari to read her thoughts, access the deepest recesses of her mind. That didn't seem easy. Besides, what was there to clarify? What did she need Ari to make absolutely—

Oh.

Ari closed her eyes and clasped her hands in her lap, hard enough that they wouldn't shake. She didn't have to keep her eyes open to see the shape of her future, unexpected, full of shadows and light like the sun coming through a forest canopy.

"I'm choosing you," she said. "And—and I love you." She opened her eyes again. The expression on Mír's face took her breath away, a starving woman hovering over a banquet table. She recovered enough to stammer, "You can't tell me I don't. You don't have any right to say tha—"

Mír reached out, pulled her in close, and kissed her. Hard.

And then, to Ari's surprise, she rolled over on her back, bringing Ari to lie atop her. A soft, breathless "oh" escaped Ari before she could stop herself.

Mír took Ari's hand and guided it upwards until Ari's knuckles were brushing Mír's cheek, and then her throat. Ari gasped, and felt her body flood with heat yet again as she realized what was happening.

"Well. Speaking of giving you what you want." The faint tremble in her voice belied her cool tone. She amended, "What we both want."

"Why wouldn't you let me before?" Ari whispered, her eyes fluttering shut as she slid her hand down the side of Mír's throat.

Mír shivered, reached up, and unhooked the straps of her own gown.

Ari heard the ping of the clasps releasing, and the slither of silk falling loose, unveiling the skin beneath to the waist. Her face caught fire. She couldn't help staring at Mír's pale breasts, bared to her for the first time, tipped with pink nipples and larger than Ari's own. Her head swam with all the possibilities. Ari was about to have everything she'd dreamed of—all those kisses and touches she'd longed to bestow. That was something else worth more than palaces or thrones.

"You were more right than you knew." Mír's voice recalled Ari to the present, made her jerk her head upward to meet Mír's blue eyes. "I never feared you, but I was hardly in charge of my situation. In bed, I could make you react—I could watch you lose yourself in pleasure."

Ari thought about it for a second. "You could watch me lose control."

"Believe me, it was sublime. But—" Mír set her jaw. "I couldn't allow myself to—"

"You think I could have made you do the same?" That didn't seem possible. Ari would have had no idea what she was doing. She'd thought, in fact, that she'd have to rely on Mír for guidance. Surely, she couldn't have made anybody, much less a woman like Mír, lose control in bed.

"I'm sure of it," Mír said hoarsely. She touched Ari's cheek. "You're a scientist," she said. "Show me what you've learned by observation."

Ari should be smooth, subtle, and take her time. But that idea was insubstantial and unimportant as she bent down and kissed Mír's left breast, feeling the nipple harden beneath her tongue with a dizzy sense of wonder.

"Oh," Mír cried out, and arched up.

Ari had already figured out that she wanted to do this a whole lot more. She moved her tongue again, and Mír actually whimpered; she began to suck, trying to be gentle, and Mír moaned and grabbed Ari's hair.

Wow. Oh, *wow.* "Is this," Ari panted against her, "I mean, do you…"

"Oh," Mír rasped, and shuddered. "You're…a quick study—"

"I've been thinking about it a long time," Ari said, suddenly shy. She brushed her lips again over Mír's soft skin. She let her hand wander down lower, over Mír's ribs and abdomen—and paused when her fingertips encountered a thin, smooth line.

A scar. She paused.

"That's not the only one," Mír said. "You'll see them all soon enough." She did not sound embarrassed or ashamed; quite the contrary. "I wish I could say I got them all doing something heroic."

252

"I wish you could say you won't get any more." Ari's fingers trembling as she touched the scar again.

"I assure you, I do my best to avoid it," Mír said. Then she reached up and dug her fingers into the hair near the back of Ari's neck. It hurt a little.

"Stay with me," she said. "Stay."

Ari shivered, bent down, pressed her forehead against Mír's. "Yes," she whispered. "I said I would. Do you need me to say it again?" She would say it as many times as Mír needed to hear it—needed to hear that Ari chose to stay with her, chose not to leave because she loved and was loved.

She hadn't quite realized how tense Mír had been until she relaxed beneath Ari. "That's enough." A pause. "For now."

They stayed like that, breathing together, for a long, silent moment. Then Mír shifted impatiently. "So," she said, "were you planning to call it a night?"

"Oh!" Ari said, and blushed. "No, not yet." Definitely not yet. She bent and kissed Mír's throat again, very gently, until Mír trembled, too. "You...you have to tell me what to do," Ari added.

Mír sat up, and with a *shuff* of silk, tossed her dress cleanly off the bed. Then she pulled Ari close, and Ari's mind went completely blank as she was pressed up against another person's naked body for the first time in her life. Their breasts rubbed together. She gasped.

"Why don't I just show you," Mír whispered, and kissed her again.

When Ari came up for air, she managed, "Oh, yes," and sat up so she could see her lover. As Mír must have known they would, her eyes automatically tracked to the scars: a raised, white slice beneath her ribs, a longer one on her right thigh. Ari bit her lip.

Without a word, Mír rolled over onto her stomach, presenting Ari with her naked back. Ari gasped again, but with the farthest thing from delight. Mír's back was crisscrossed with scars in an unmistakable pattern.

"You were whipped." Tears came to Ari's eyes. That must have felt even worse than a shock rod, which left no lasting marks.

"I was." Mír looked at Ari over her shoulder. "And worse."

Ari didn't even want to think about it. She blinked back her tears, pressed her lips together, and looked back at Mír, who eventually sighed. "How else would I know how much a fleet needed reform if I hadn't suffered its excesses? We have to live in the world before we can change it, Ariana."

"True," Ari said slowly. It sounded trite, but she was in bed with someone who was in a position to change the world—worlds, plural. If everything went like Mír planned, then so many things could be different—over time, so many things could be changed.

Even slavery. If Ari could get Mír's ear on that, remind her how degrading and dehumanizing it was, talk about finding a better way...

Best to start small. Whatever happened next had to begin with them being together, becoming fully themselves before they could change anything else. For now, Ari stuck with a simple truth: "You're amazing." She trailed her fingertips over the network of scars. "I'm so sorry."

"Don't be." Mír rolled over again, her cheeks a little pink as she presented Ari with a far more appealing view. Ari gave herself a few moments to ogle those beautiful breasts again, because now she didn't have to pretend she didn't want to, before her gaze traveled down the rest of Mír's body. Now that she'd seen the scars, she was more able to focus on the belly with a smattering of freckles just above the navel, the hips, and the patch of fine, dark hair between two muscular legs.

"Beautiful," she breathed.

Mír obviously wasn't inclined to throw off compliments like Ari often did. She seemed quite pleased as she said, "Thank you."

Ari grinned, took a deep breath, and passed her fingertips over Mír's belly, just brushing against the black thatch of hair. Her five senses were working overtime; she listened to Mír's breathing grow rougher as Ari continued to caress her. She watched the flush rise in Mír's cheeks. She smelled the warm scent of their bodies together, she tasted their kisses in her mouth. She touched Mír's body, and that was the best of all.

No wonder Mír had become addicted to touching her, she thought dizzily as she bent to place a soft kiss on one strong shoulder. It was so powerful. When you touched someone like this, her body changed for you. Ari's hands could make Mír's skin flush or prickle with goosebumps. Her mouth could make Mír gasp and sigh. And all of it together could make Mír slick between her magnificent thighs. In fact, Mír was in no shape to give instructions, so Ari just did whatever she wanted, and it seemed to be going great so far.

Maybe, Ari thought as she nuzzled beneath Mír's right ear, they could alter the whole conquest schedule and spend the next year or so doing nothing but this.

She kissed Mír, kissed and kissed her, until Mír finally made an impatient sound and took hold of Ari's hand, guiding it between their bodies, between her legs. "In," she growled. "Now, Ariana, inside me."

"Yes," Ari gasped, and placed two fingertips against Mír's soaked entrance. She hardly had to use any pressure at all before she was sliding in, sliding home. The wet heat around her fingers made the edges of her vision go gray for a moment. She hadn't been prepared for that at all—how could it make her ache as much as if Mír was doing it to her? It was so tight and hot, with slick surfaces Ari already wanted to spend eons exploring.

"Is this good?" She kissed Mír's panting mouth.

"Oh—yes—" Mír arched back, her pale throat covered by a flush. She quivered around Ari's fingers, and Ari recognized the signs from last time. She was close. She was going to come on Ari's hand.

"Do it," Ari moaned, beyond either the ability or the desire to control her words. "Oh yes, do it, let me see."

But Mír didn't. She opened her eyes with a gasp, pushed at Ari's wrist until Ari withdrew her fingers in dismay, and wrapped her legs around Ari's waist. Her heat pressed against Ari's body, her wet flesh rubbed against Ari's own, and the contact made Ari grab at the sheets with newly sticky fingers.

"No, please! What do you want?" Ari gasped. "Don't make me stop. Tell me what you want. I'll do it."

Mír groaned and rubbed her nose in the sweaty hair stuck to Ari's temple. "You will?"

"Yes!" *Calm down*, Ari told herself helplessly, *this is for her.* "I will, I will."

"If I ask you to touch me?"

"Oh—yes—" Ari could imagine Mír's heat around her fingers again, clenching in ecstasy.

"Or to please me with your mouth?"

Ari's eyes fell shut and she hid her face against Mír's neck. She'd thought about that, too, doing for Mír what Mír had so often done for her. Learning as she went how to bring such pleasure. Just the thought made her even wetter. "Y-yeah—"

"Or what about my mouth?" Mír kept her legs around Ari as she began to smooth her hands up and down Ari's sweaty back. Ari was shaking all over now, fighting not to grind down and get the pressure she needed so badly. "Imagine sitting on my face, feeling my tongue against you..."

"Um—" *It's for her, it's for her, oh no—* "Wait a second. I'm...I'm..."

Mír cupped Ari's buttocks and began to rock against her more urgently. "Feel me licking you all over while I finger myself, taking us both over the edge."

Too close. Ari was too close. She wasn't going to be able to stop, and this was her turn! No way was Mír taking control now, right when they were almost...

"Do you still want to tie me up?" she whispered in Mír's ear.

Mír's words died in a gasp, which gave Ari just enough time to slide a hand between them and push one finger inside her. And although Ari wasn't the most experienced lover in the universe, it worked. Mír cried out and trembled in climax, her voice broken with pleasure, and it was all because of Ari's hands and mouth.

That was more than Ari needed, and she tumbled over the edge after Mír with a groan that seemed to come all the way up from her toes.

She barely managed not to collapse on top of her, too. They lay together in the gigantic bed, winded and damp with sweat.

After a few moments, Mír managed, "What are you thinking?"

"Hmm." Ari paused in the middle of licking her fingers. "That you taste good."

Mír's eyes widened. "Good God, Lady Ariana. You'll be the scandal of the Empire."

Ari couldn't help a smile as she pushed her face against Mír's throat. All eyes were on the fabled pirate queen; who would pay any mind to the love-struck botanist in her shadow? Ari would settle for being scandalous in private. "I doubt it," she said.

"So do I." Mír kissed her cheek. "Especially if we both die of thirst before you get the chance."

Mír's words called Ari's attention to her parched mouth. She smacked her lips and swallowed, feeling the effort it took. "Gosh. Yeah. Can we fix that?"

"It's fixable. What do you want?"

Everything I already have, Ari didn't tell her. The only thing she could think to say out loud was, "Not grog."

Mír's eyes lit up, and it was her turn to laugh. "Certainly not tonight. I can think of better drinks for celebrating."

"If you get me too tipsy, I bet I'll start reciting poetry," Ari warned, already feeling merry and foolish.

Mír's shudder might not have been totally theatrical. "Stars preserve us all. I'd rather talk about gardening."

"I can do that, too."

"You can do all kinds of things." Mír cupped Ari's cheek. Her gaze softened. "And you always surprise me."

"No telling what I'll say next," Ari agreed, and then recalled something—the most recent time Mír had admitted to being surprised by Ari. She sat up too as her eyes widened. "Oh gosh! I just remembered. Hummingbirds *love* lilies. Well, certain varietals, anyway. Those are your favorite flower, right? Obviously, it's not a top priority, or even close, but maybe when things are a little bit quieter I can look into getting—you know what? I'll make a list. Especially if we're bringing some of my plants over from Nahtal. And then—"

The warm press of Mír's lips on her forehead stopped her, and seconds later, the curve of those lips into a smile made Ari melt all over again.

"Still chirping, huh?" she offered.

"Always," Mír whispered, and kissed her again.

EPILOGUE

Ambassador Bors relaxed back in his seat with a feeling of wary approval. The negotiations had been a success, and the Empress had not been as entirely unreasonable as her predecessor. Which was good—neither was she as vulnerable. Had she wished to pursue war instead of peace, the Kazir would have had a more difficult time of it than Bors liked to think.

"A drink?" the Empress asked, and when Bors inclined his head, she gestured at a servant. She kept no slaves at her court—one of her many eccentricities. The man who filled Bors's goblet was paid to do so. Kazir intelligence had even picked up word that an initiative, still in its infancy, was underway to abolish slavery throughout the Empire. At the beginning of Mír's reign, that would have been unthinkable—it would have destabilized her regime before she'd even begun—but now she was turning preference into policy.

Bors couldn't understand it himself, but he supposed it was none of his business.

"To the peace," the Empress said, and they raised their glasses. There would be many more toasts at the banquet tonight, given by officials in varying degrees of intoxicated pomposity, but Bors doubted any of them would be as heartfelt as this one shared by two exhausted, triumphant people. It was not unpleasant to drink with this Empress. Nor, if he were to be honest, was it unpleasant to look at her. She was a superb example of her species, even if she was past her prime. Well, in all fairness, so was Bors. He wondered if she thought he had aged well, too. He believed he had; his scales were as supple and iridescent as they had been in his youth, and he hoped she appreciated them, as he appreciated her own beauty.

"Are you anticipating the banquet?" she asked, with something like laughter in her eyes.

"I'm anticipating sleeping well afterwards," Bors said, and the Empress smiled. She had a disconcerting smile—there was something about it that made him profoundly uncomfortable, even when it seemed genuinely meant.

At that moment, the door chimed, and the servant hurried out. He returned in a moment, bowing respectfully. "Your Majesty," he said, "Lady Ariana wonders if you have a free moment."

The Empress scowled and rubbed at her forehead. "I knew she'd forget I was in a meeting.".

"Our business is concluded until tonight, Your Majesty," Bors said, deciding to make a gracious exit. "Do not let me detain you further."

"No, stay," she said, and waved her hand. "Send her in," she said to the servant, and then added to Bors, "I would like you to meet my consort."

"Oh," Bors said, settling back into his chair with renewed interest. Rumors circulated within and beyond Mír's empire about the Imperial Consort—Lady Ariana, the little gardener who'd kept the all-powerful Empress enthralled for almost a decade now. Some said she was mad, or simple, or childlike; others said she was kind, and decent, and refreshingly guileless. Nobody, however, said that she was a natural choice for an imperial consort.

Within the moment, Bors saw why. A young woman hurried into the room without seeming to notice him. Her hair was disheveled, and she had...was that mud all over the hem of her skirt?

"Hey," Lady Ariana said breathlessly, and bent down to kiss the Empress on the cheek. For her part, the Empress looked resigned, but not angry. Perhaps even a little amused. "Are you busy?" She glanced over and saw Bors. "Oh!" She straightened up and brushed her skirt down, appearing self-conscious. "Oh, gosh—you told me about this meeting, didn't you? I'm sorry. Is this the Kazir ambassador?" Before the Empress could reply, Lady Ariana extended her hand to Bors with a big smile. She had dirt underneath her fingernails. "Hi. I'm Ari."

"Ambassador Bors," the Empress said dryly, "permit me to introduce you to Her Excellency, the Imperial Consort and Senior Royal Botanist." Her eyes danced with laughter. This was obviously not the first time she had made such an introduction.

Gingerly, Bors took Lady Ariana's hand. "A pleasure, Your Excellency," he said, trying to keep the incredulity out of his voice. He'd heard that the surest way to start a war was to insult Lady Ariana in front of the Empress, and he refused to think that the last six months of negotiations had been for nothing.

"Oh, thanks," Lady Ariana said, and turned back to the Empress without further ado, her eyes shining. "The fuel cells work! *Mustopher illis* synthesizes so much faster. I just sent it off to the lab. We should know by tomorrow!"

"Wonderful." The Empress patted Lady Ariana on the hip. "I suppose this means you'll be making a non-appearance at the banquet?"

"Oh gosh, I forgot," Lady Ariana said, looking acutely distressed. "I'm going to be so—Do you want me to come?"

"If you could be there for the first round of toasts before your headache develops," the Empress said, "I'd appreciate it."

"First round of toasts. Okay. Eighth hour, right?"

"Seventh."

"Oh. Seventh. Right. Got it." Lady Ariana's brow furrowed in concentration as she obviously tried to commit this to memory.

"Don't forget this time," the Empress said.

"I won't. I'm so sorry about last time. It's just that I have so much to do before I go to the conference next week." Lady Ariana winced. "I'll make sure somebody reminds me by sixth hour."

"See that you do," the Empress said, and sent a meaningful look to the servant by the door. He clearly understood that he would be the one to remind Lady Ariana or suffer the royal displeasure, and nodded.

"I will. I'll see you at the banquet!" Lady Ariana said, and bent down to peck the Empress on the lips. The Empress patted her hip again, and Ariana flew out the door, just barely remembering to give Bors a nod as she left. He stared after her, feeling rather as if he'd just staggered out of a brief, bewildering whirlwind.

When he turned around, the Empress was watching him with hooded eyes.

"Thank you for introducing me," Bors said, unaccountably nervous. "I... What is this conference Her Excellency is attending?"

"Some botany thing," the Empress said, volunteering no further information as to place or time.

Bors was not surprised. He had heard that the Imperial Consort did not travel a great deal, though whether from her own inclination or the Empress's protectiveness, he did not know. He did know that his apparent curiosity about Lady Ariana had brought out something fierce in the Empress's eyes, and he abruptly remembered that, less than a decade ago, this refined and elegant monarch had been the most bloodthirsty pirate in the known galaxy.

"She's pregnant," the Empress added.

Bors, long practiced in diplomacy, needed less than a second to collect his wits and say, "My sincerest congratulations."

"Thank you." The Empress tapped her fingertips on her desk. "She is nearly three months along. But you can't really see it yet."

Indeed, you couldn't. Human reproduction was still something of a mystery to Bors. "The birth of the heir will be great cause for celebration," he said delicately, already planning to alert his masters to this bit of news as soon as he returned to his suite. Everyone had wondered what would happen to Mír's empire after her death. Apparently, she'd decided on a plan.

"It will," the Empress said, confirming his suspicions with the merest lift of her eyebrows. "It's time for the news to get out. You might as well hear it from the source." She gave him a little smile. She was not exactly the image of impending, radiant motherhood, but for a moment, her gaze had softened again. "We do what we must."

"Er...yes," Bors said, and cleared his throat. "I have six offspring myself. They're blessings." And would have their own clutches soon enough.

The Empress smiled blandly, her boredom obvious. However much she would care for her own brood, Bors could not envision a time when she would enjoy making idle talk about children. "I'm sure they are."

She rose to her feet, and he scrambled to do the same. "Don't let me detain you further, Ambassador. Please enjoy your rest before our little gathering tonight."

"Indeed, I will, Your Majesty." Bors bowed. "And you as well."

"I'd better," the Empress said with a sigh. "It will be a late evening. And I promised Ariana I'd look at these fuel cells once she got them working. I wager you anything that I'll spend tomorrow morning on my knees in the dirt."

Bors tried his very best to imagine this. And failed. Instead, he nodded and smiled as respectfully as he could without laughing, and then bowed as he took his leave.

An odd pair, he thought to himself as he returned to his quarters. An odd pair; an odd marriage; an odd arrangement altogether, really, even to the producing of the heir. But it appeared to be working. Everything about the Empire appeared to be working. Certainly, Bors hoped his people never had to contend with Mir's power.

Although if they did, and if they lost, perhaps she wouldn't be as monstrous as she'd been painted. She'd been all gentleness with Lady Ariana. She was not, Bors thought, a woman without pity. Without mercy. Surely?

Well...perhaps. But really, Bors thought as his door closed behind him, he would prefer not to find out for himself.

###

ABOUT ROSLYN SINCLAIR

Roslyn Sinclair is a writer and teacher currently living in Georgia. Though a Southern girl, she's found writing inspiration everywhere from Kansas City to Beijing. First thing in the morning, before she goes off to prep lesson plans, you can find her writing her books in longhand at her kitchen table. When she's not writing or teaching, she's probably reading, taking long walks, or going for a drive on the twisty mountain roads near her home.

OTHER BOOKS FROM YLVA PUBLISHING

www.ylva-publishing.com

Primal Touch

(revised edition)

Amber Jacobs

ISBN: 978-3-95533-858-9
Length: 255 pages (99,000 words)

Rumors of a rare, white tiger have lured wildlife photographer Ashley Richards deep into the Indian jungle. There, she crosses paths with a ruthless poacher and Leandra, a mysterious, feral woman, who seems at one with the fierce felines she protects. In this charged, exotic, lesbian romance, Ashley faces danger, a deadly vendetta, and the clash of two worlds, which changes everything she knows.

Second Nature

(second edition)
(The Shape-Shifter Series – Book 1)

Jae

ISBN: 978-3-95533-030-9
Length: 496 pages (146,000 words)

Novelist Jorie Price doesn't believe in the existence of shape-shifting creatures or true love. She leads a solitary life, and the paranormal romances she writes are pure fiction for her. Griffin Westmore knows better—at least about one of these two things. She doesn't believe in love either, but she's one of the not-so-fictional shape-shifters.

Rock and a Hard Place

Andrea Bramhall

ISBN: 978-3-95533-902-9

Length: 289 pages (100,000 words)

Jayden Harris is an expert climber filled with demons after surviving an avalanche. When she and marketing executive Rhian Phillips are forced to work together for a reality show, she expected it to be hard. They both expected things to get rocky—they are facing snow, ice, and a daunting mountain range, after all. But neither of them ever expected the hardest thing would be resisting each other.

The Brutal Truth

Lee Winter

ISBN: 978-3-95533-898-5

Length: 339 pages (108,000 words)

Aussie crime reporter Maddie Grey is out of her depth in New York and secretly drawn to her twice-married, powerful media mogul boss, Elena Bartell, who eats failing newspapers for breakfast. As work takes them to Australia, Maddie is goaded into a brief bet—that they will say only the truth to each other. It backfires catastrophically. A lesbian romance about the lies we tell ourselves.

COMING FROM YLVA PUBLISHING

www.ylva-publishing.com

Survival Instincts

May Dawney

Civilization ended long before Lynn Tanner was born. Wild animals roam the streets, but mankind is still the biggest threat to a woman alone in the ruins of a world reclaimed by nature. Lynn survives by sleeping with one eye open at all times and trusting no one but her dog.

When she is forced to go on a dangerous journey through the concrete jungle of New York City, Lynn does all she can to scheme her way to safety. Her guard, Dani Wilson, won't be played that easily, however. As their lives become entwined, Lynn finds herself developing feelings for Dani and is forced to find the answer to the question that scares her most: is staying alone really the best way to survive?

Fast-paced and full of adventure, *Survival Instincts* introduces a post-war dystopian world where the only person you can rely on is yourself...unless you fall in love.

The Lily and the Crown
© 2017 by Roslyn Sinclair

ISBN: 978-3-95533-942-5

Also available as e-book.

Published by Ylva Publishing, legal entity of Ylva Verlag, e.Kfr.

Ylva Verlag, e.Kfr.
Owner: Astrid Ohletz
Am Kirschgarten 2
65830 Kriftel
Germany

www.ylva-publishing.com

First edition: 2017

Credits
Edited by Lee Winter and Amanda Jean
Proofread by Paulette Callen
Print Cover by Adam Lloyd
Print Layout by eB Format

Printed in Great Britain
by Amazon

60509836R00163